Time-Crossed Wedding

Guardians of the Stones
Time Travel, Book 2

Jane DeGray

Leavesly Park Publishing

To my mother and father who allowed me to believe I could accomplish whatever I decided to do.

To my daughters Meredith and Amanda, and my son James, for providing inspiration and background for modern day Ashley and Robert.

To my husband who will celebrate with me a milestone wedding anniversary on the date of Time-Crossed Wedding's publication.

I love you all!

Contents

Prologue

1363 England

Restless, the enormous black stallion swished his tail in impatience and stomped an impressive hoof against the rocky ridge upon which his master held him. Damien Lundene, Baron of Bedford, might have blended as a shadow into the landscape dressed as he was from head to toe in dark clothing. A cape extended over the back of his horse and tussled with the wind along its edges to show an occasional glimpse of a white shirt underneath. The jaunty red feather in his cap set him apart from his surroundings. His attention was focused on the tiny cottage tucked into the valley below that belonged to Olde Gylda of Hampshire. He did not understand what he saw there.

He was here only because of the bizarre tale his blacksmith had told him. The man had shown up for work still drunk and sporting scrapes and bruises from an evening of debauchery. When questioned, the man told him of falling afoul of a lovely blonde woman he had followed to an inn. Much to his surprise, Bedford realized his smithy had described Lady Ashley Duvall, his former betrothed. She was an obsession he had yet to quit. Why was she not at Hertford Castle? Fearing for her safety, Bedford had promptly dropped everything to track her small party to Olde Gylda's cottage.

Pulling a spyglass from his saddlebag, he squinted into the device and blanched at what he saw. Robert Spycer, the Earl of Hertford's heir and Bedford's nemesis, stood out among the people below. He identified Robert's sister, Elena, standing between Olde Gylda and Cedric, the Hertford soothsayer. All were gathered around Lady Ashley in front of the old witch's house.

He was certain his friend Hertford had not given his children permission to visit Olde Gylda. The earl himself had banned the crone from his castle for practicing the Dark Arts, so why were the young people here and in the company of a witch and a wizard? Bedford shuddered and tried to shake off a premonition something evil was afoot.

The delectable Lady Ashley still occupied his foremost thoughts despite her wanting nothing to do with him. He would protect her at all cost if need arose. Even betrothed to another, she still drew him to her. He did not understand his own fixation, but like a bear to honey, he knew he would be stung, yet he pursued her anyway.

Needing to make sense of what he watched below, Bedford scanned the familiar faces. All were poised at the entrance to the cottage, ready for . . . *what?*

He absently scratched the silver-haired side of his head as he pondered the question. Then Lady Ashley ran to Lady Elena and hugged her tightly. He grimaced, thinking they looked upset. What were they discussing that was so unsettling? Surely he was not at fault, was he? Both women had rejected his offer of marriage. Hertford had not blamed him for that, so why would they? He sighed unhappily.

Still contemplating that notion, a sudden gust of wind whipped his hat off his head. He deftly snatched it before it soared over the ridge, but not before the red feather was sucked out of its nest in the cap. Startled, he watched the feather be inhaled by a larger twister that swirled, whirled, and then enfolded Lady Ashley in its winds. In a flash, the whirlwind was gone . . . *and so was Lady Ashley.*

He was stunned. For a moment he could not breathe as if his lungs had been snatched along with his feather. Gasping, he shook his head and tried to locate his wits. Expecting pandemonium below, he searched the faces of the remaining four and was shocked by their responses. Their distress was apparent, yet they seemed to accept Ashley's disappearance. They hugged each other before entering the cottage in a somber single file.

The last to go inside, Robert hesitated in the doorway, turning around to peer at the spot where Ashley had vanished. A moment later, he strode to the exact place she had stood and leaned down to dig out of the ground what appeared to be a paving stone.

The deep sound of Robert's voice reverberated in the now empty valley, as he intoned something Bedford could not quite make out, three times in quick succession.

How very odd.

The thought had only to form in his head when the mysterious twister was back, engulfing Robert in its winds. This time when its fury subsided, Robert was nowhere to be found. *He was gone.* Like Lady Ashley, the man had disappeared.

God's blood! Where did they go? What dreadful thing was this?

Cold shimmied down his spine as remnants of the whirlwind riffled and crackled through the dry grasses jutting out from the rock beneath him. His stallion sensed his unease. Threatening to bolt, he danced sideways, forcing Bedford to rein him in even tighter.

'Twas rumored Olde Gylda performed serious black magic, but no one had ever suspected her of making people disappear into thin air. This was outrageous. What should he do? What could he do?

Dismayed, he decided to investigate the cottage when no one else was around, thus avoiding Olde Gylda and her dark magic. He made a silent vow to find the stone Robert had held and get to the bottom of the mystery.

People do not simply disappear.

Lady Ashley had to be somewhere. Perhaps if he found and rescued her, she would return to him as his rightful betrothed and become his wife. The thought pleased him. Still, he had to contend with Lord Robert, did he not?

With much to think about, Bedford heaved a sigh, spun his stallion around, and gave the big black his head. In seconds, they were engulfed by the swirling mists that settled in around them.

Chapter 1

Present Day--Salisbury Plains

Time. It would never be the same for her again. She used to think she understood all about time. You know . . . past, present, future? It used to make sense. But not anymore. Who could imagine slipping from present to past and then back again? Perhaps one day she would go to the future and back, too. The witch, Olde Gylda of Hampshire, said she could.

A cold shiver arrowed from her core to her fingertips, like ice cracking on a frozen pond. Immediately, large, warm, deeply tanned hands surrounded her waist and pulled her tighter into the heat of the very male, broad-shouldered body behind her.

"You are cold, are you not?"

Ashley Duvall nodded and tenderly placed her fingers over his, still a bit shy to think of all he had just sacrificed to be with her. If he were not holding her this moment, she would think Robert Spycer from 1363 England was but a dream brought on by loneliness, desire, and a fierce imagination. Fortunately, he was as real as the thumb calmly drawing circles on the back of her hand.

"It'll be warmer if we sit. You can be my windbreak," she teased, pulling Robert down into a sitting position on the ground and bracing her back against his chest.

"Here, I shall make a nest for you, my wee little dove." He complied by stretching his legs out to encase Ashley's long limbs and rested his head lightly on the top of hers. Her shivers from a combination of cold and nerves subsided as Robert held her in his arms.

From this vantage point they could clearly see the winding dirt road while they watched for her Uncle Zeek. She hoped to see his banged-up silver SUV rather than the shiny black one Abasi drove. How would she handle it if he showed up before Zeek? She couldn't hide Robert or the way he was dressed.

She was pretty sure Abasi had suspected her of time travel even before it had happened to her. That's why he had followed her to her archeology work site and intimidated her as much as he was able. She shuddered.

"Are you not yet warm?" Robert rubbed her arms up and down to chafe them.

"I'm working on it," she replied, wishing she could be rid of that worrisome man even while she searched the darkness for signs of him.

Olde Gylda told her Abasi's goal was to catch time travelers and make them ferry antiquities to him for his business. As the largest antiquity dealer in London, he had his nose in every facet of that industry. In return, he would protect them from exposure to the rest of the world. How generous, Ashley thought. Like he would want others to know and horn in on his goldmine!

Thus far, he had not caught one of Gylda's time travelers, but he had witnessed Ashley's departure from this very spot. Was he hiding somewhere nearby ready to jump out and capture them? Robert was so much bigger than Abasi she didn't worry about him physically accosting them, but the man was crafty and sly. Who knew what he might have in mind should he catch them. She sincerely hoped Uncle Zeek made it here before they had to find out.

Meanwhile, the best part of the evening was their panoramic view of the stars above the Salisbury plains. As the sky grew darker, thousands of pinpoints in the canopy began to glow. The worst part was now it would be almost impossible to tell one make or model from another because the car would be invisible except for the headlights.

"What are you thinking, love? I can feel your spirit darting about."

Ashley laughed and shook her head not wanting Robert to know she was worrying over Abasi. "I know, Robert. Everything Olde Gylda told us keeps rolling around in my mind. I still can't wrap my head around the fact that I'm a Guardian of the Stones. At least I'm not a witch like Gylda, although that might have been interesting."

"If 'tis magical powers you want, methinks you have plenty now." She heard the smile in his voice as his breath blew softly across her hair. "I ne'er thought I would fall in love with a woman who moved through time with the help of stones."

"Listen to us. We sound insane!"

"Mayhap we are."

Ashley chortled at the truth of the statement, but then her brow furrowed and her expression turned somber. "I had to come back to my time period for my family, Robert, even if I'm forced to deal with Abasi. With my father still missing, I can't simply disappear like he did. My mother and brother would have to suffer all over again." She paused and smoothed back a strand of hair that persisted in poking her in the eye. "Are you sorry you followed me?"

"*No!*" He squeezed her tightly and nuzzled his lips against her neck for a time before he continued, "I understand your feelings. I, too, would not wish to make my family grieve if 'twere in my power to prevent it."

"They don't know you're here, do they?"

"Olde Gylda will know, and Elena will figure it out."

For a moment neither spoke as thoughts turned inward. He pulled her hand to his lips and kissed her fingers. "And we shall return, so they need not worry. They will know I have come to protect you. So fear not, my sweet, Abasi will ne'er hurt you while I am near." Ashley turned her face up to his and thanked him with a long kiss.

Night sounds played around them, echoing as the air thickened with moisture. Robert examined his surroundings, his eyes taking in the empty spaces. "This could be the land around Castle Hertford."

"Yeah, well, that will change pretty fast once we get on the road with my uncle. You've seen the photos on my phone, but in person, it will be stunning."

"Aye. I shall try my best to fit in."

"I don't think that's an option, Robert. You'll stand out wherever you go."

"Why?" Robert's body tensed.

"You may be able to hide the fact you are from medieval England, sweetheart, but you are still tall, well-built, and handsome. That did not change."

"So you think me handsome, do you?"

"*Uh-huh.* You know you are."

"Is that so? You think me vain?" Robert tickled her ribs and Ashley giggled like a little kid until he quelled her with a fervent kiss. She was thrilled to be here in the arms of the man she loved and not stuck in time somewhere. Life was far better now that Robert had chosen to use the Guardian stone to follow her. That was true love.

Ashley had dreaded the time she would spend apart from Robert. Now he was here in her world, safely wrapped around her like a human coat. Dressed as he was in his black leather, he looked like an escapee from a World Wrestling Federation bout. She wouldn't tease him right now. It might make him worry about what was in store for him in her world. He would find out soon enough on his own. At the moment, she was determined not to look back, but to go forward and make this visit work. The trip home had promised to be a solitary one for her to make, but Robert had changed all that.

For the first few minutes after his arrival, they had been lost in each other's arms like their lives depended on maximizing bodily contact. But now as night closed in, the enormity of their situation was closing in as well. For Ashley, being dumped into life in the fourteenth century had been shocking, but history and movies had given her some idea of what to expect.

For Robert it would be much harder even though he had

seen Ashley's pictures and video on her smart phone. He had little knowledge of the rest of her world and even less of what had transpired between his time and hers. He said he had come to her world to protect her from Abasi, but he had no idea what he was up against. Her guy had confidence he was up to the challenge, though, and that had to count for something.

As the first light of a new moon popped overhead, the wind began to riffle through the grass. It scooted bits of dancing debris awkwardly across its surface like skateboarders attempting tricks in the dark. A fluffy red feather incongruously kick-flipped over their ankles and Robert reached out and snagged it before it could go further. He presented it to Ashley with a flourish as if it were a fine floral bouquet.

"What's this?" Ashley blinked and looked hard at the bright red plume in Robert's hand. A hazy memory nudged her, but then evaporated when Robert took advantage of her momentary lapse to tickle her nose with the downy end of the feather.

She grabbed the offending fluff out of his hand just as she sneezed multiple times. Once recovered, she burst out laughing at the absurdity of it all.

"*Geez,* where does a plume come from in the middle of an archeological site on the Salisbury plains?"

"*Hmmm,* only it knows where it's been." Robert took the feather from her and wielded it like a wand, cutting figure eights in the air. "Shall we ask it? Mayhap 'tis *magic.*" His voice repressed a snort as he finished his incantation by tickling her ear with the fuzzy tip.

Perhaps it was his warrior side warning him, but he stopped his teasing and turned to look toward the road as if something in the dark called to him. His sharp eyes narrowed as he searched into the distance. Ashley tracked where he pointed and spotted car lights snaking their way to them in the dark.

"Please let that be Uncle Zeek."

With her eyes pinned on the car lights, she was unaware of Robert now watching a sharper light from above shooting straight down in front of them.

A falling star.

Robert sucked in a breath and gently guided Ashley's head so she could see it streak through the sky. Words were failing him. Not long ago he had made a wish on another star to find his true love, and now, sitting cuddled against him was his Ashley. He knew exactly what wish to make upon this star.

Chapter 2

Excited, Ashley jumped to her feet and pulled Robert up behind her as her Uncle Zeek's beat-up, silver Jeep Wrangler came solidly into view. A peek back at Robert found him with narrowed eyes warily eyeing the SUV as it rolled to a stop, bathing them in a dusky headlamp glow.

Zeek lurched out of the vehicle seconds later and scooped Ashley up in his arms, hugging her tightly, all the while cursing her for disappearing without a trace.

A giggling Ashley gave her uncle a final hard hug. "Enough, Uncle Zeek. *Enough.* I didn't mean to leave the work site, ya know."

∞∞∞

Zeek Duvall swung her around and unceremoniously dropped her on her feet. "You little minx. I know these hairs are turning gray, but I'd like to keep what's left of 'em. Have you any idea how crazy upset everyone has been since you disappeared? Especially your mother!" Was he excited, angry, relieved, or all three? He didn't know.

Ashley smiled up into his face, and his thoughts turned to her dad. He knew he could never take Rick's place, but he was thankful he could be here for his brother's kids in times like this. As if she had read his mind, she reached up to give him a peck on the cheek. "Well, I'm back now, Uncle Zeek, so quit tugging on your hair like that and maybe I'll let you keep it."

Zeek grinned at his niece's pert response and only then became aware of the hulking body pacing behind her at the edge of the circle of light.

What had Julie said when she called to tell him of her daughter's reappearance at the work site? Something about needing an extra ticket home? *Who is this?*

As Zeek picked up on the man's presence, Ashley turned and grabbed the guy's wrist pulling him out of the shadows and into view in the harsh light of the headlamps. Zeek sucked in a startled gasp and instinctively took a step back. Ashley flinched at her uncle's reaction, shaking her head at him with what he recognized was a silent scolding to behave himself. He'd try, but this guy had his hand on a knife sheathed on his hip, and he didn't look happy.

The headlights were lighting his unsmiling countenance with an under-glow that made the sharp contours of his face and his square jaw appear ghoulish and threatening. His rugged frame towered over Zeek who had always thought himself a tall man. For some reason he could not make himself say a word. Instead, he was impolitely staring at the ancient clothes the guy wore. With effort, he tore his eyes from the man and rolled them to Ashley with a raised eyebrow. It was past time for an introduction and an explanation.

Ashley gulped for air and wrapped Robert's arm around her waist, tucking herself securely under his elbow. "So, Uncle Zeek, I'm sure you want to hear where I've been and who this might be, right?" She laughed, the sound high-pitched and shaky.

Zeek struggled to keep from gawking at the massive man his niece had pulled around her like armor as he sought and held her eyes. He noted her nervousness, but no fear lurked in those familiar eyes at all. Pride, determination, perhaps, and . . . *love?* A quick glance back at the huge man now protectively holding her, and it was obvious to him a strong connection existed between the two. Had Ashley fallen in love with this guy?

In the next few minutes, his mind took giant leaps and bounds as it hopscotched through history. By the time Ashley finished her tale he was shaken. He was supposed to believe the guy was from medieval England? Could that be? Yet everything about the man fit that description. Speechless, Zeek nodded his head and hoped his racing wits would soon catch up sufficiently for his mouth to work again.

Introduced as the son of an earl, Robert Spycer appeared to be an intelligent man of stature in his own time. He displayed the manners and grace of an aristocrat and the body of a warrior. Caught off guard, Zeek was surprised when Robert bowed to him before declaring his love for Ashley.

"Lady Ashley, as she is known to my family, will return to Hertford Castle with me once she bids her family goodbye." His chin was up, perhaps expecting an argument, but what was there to say? At this point the two lovebirds were smiling at each other with all the love their pure, young hearts could muster.

Am I a fool or are they?

Did they have any concept of what this *visit* meant to people like him who studied history and civilizations for a living? His mind may doubt the veracity of their story, but his eyes did not. His knowledge of artifacts had told him the clothing and armor gracing Robert's body were truly from the fourteenth century. Dozens of questions formed in his mind demanding to be asked as his professorial mode kicked in. Where to begin?

Ashley made the decision for him a second later when a shiver rippled through her in the cooling night air. She snapped to and organized for them what he was incapable of doing at the moment.

Stepping out of the crook of the big guy's arm she jerked open the back door of the SUV. It groaned loudly, making Robert hesitate, frown, and peer at the door as if it were a living thing.

"Uncle Zeek, how far are we from your place? We need to get out of here before Abasi finds us."

"Abasi?" This couldn't be good. He leaned against the

driver's side door, caught his niece's eyes, and braced himself to hear what she had to say.

"Yeah, he was here when the wind took me away. I don't think he saw the stone, though."

"What! He saw you leave?"

"Yup. I know. I was pretty upset at the time, but I'm sure he didn't follow me. At least we never saw him anywhere on Robert's side."

"My God!"

"Do you remember the old lady I danced with as a little kid in Hyde Park the Christmas we visited you in London?"

Zeek nodded, fearing her next words.

"That's Olde Gylda of Hampshire and she knows who Abasi is. She's the one Mr. Munroe described as the old lady in black clothes from another century. She's a witch and a Guardian of the Stones." Ashley shivered again. "*Geez*, let's go! I'll explain in the car. Do you have my things from camp? I'm freezing and my jacket should be with the rest of my stuff."

With her free hand she guided her reluctant partner through the opening and pushed him the rest of the way in. He begrudgingly folded up his frame enough to get in and sit down. Ashley nudged him until he moved over, and then she slipped in and snuggled up to him.

"Thanks for picking us up, Uncle Zeek. I am in dire need of a bath and a change of clothes. Plus, we'll need to find something for Robert to wear that won't attract so much attention." She slammed the door shut leaving a stunned Zeek with no option but to get in and drive them to his flat.

Chapter 3

Please don't let me get caught. I need my job.

Zeek was sweating profusely even though the evening was clear and brisk, the sun having gone down an hour ago. He threw open the heavy glass door to Al Mustafa, setting off the door chime jingle, and was greeted by pungent food odors. Breathing deeply, he tried to avoid an overwhelming sense of claustrophobia. Still, the stifling scents of strong spices, vinegary pickled vegetables, and over-ripened fruits swamped him anyway. His stomach flipped over, and he summoned all his resources to focus on his mission here. This little grocery store on London's Edgware Road supposedly had a door to the rear of the shop that would put him out in the back alley.

His friend, Joe Westman, who used to work in the Humanities Department, had helped him find someone to secure a passport for Robert on short notice. Neither man discussed the legality of the request, but he was pretty sure Joe knew he needed one where few questions were asked. Zeek had filled out the paperwork needed for the passport, complete with fake stats, and given it to Joe along with a picture of Robert. He was to meet this "someone" here tonight to pick up the finished product.

The store was set to close in five minutes. The hang-faced shopkeeper lifted his eyes from the magazine propped in front of him without moving his head. He acknowledged his customer with a raised eyebrow and a less than covert glance at the clock on the far wall. Zeek nodded and felt a trickle of sweat roll off his forehead and slide unimpeded down his face. Hastily, he swiped at it with the back of his hand before it dripped off his chin. He swallowed convulsively. Should he just walk on through and out the back door to the alley? Would this guy stop him? Stalling for time, he scratched his head and pretended to examine the contents of a barrel of dried fava beans.

Startled by a tap on his shoulder, Zeek almost dumped the entire bean barrel as he twisted himself around to confront the intruder. He found himself staring into the unsympathetic dark eyes of Abasi himself.

No-o-o-o!

The "someone" Joe had arranged to do the job was *Abasi? Damn, damn, damn.* How would he get out of this? The man knew way too much. Zeek pinched his eyes closed for a moment, took a shaky breath and battled to force his heart out of his throat. Abasi gave Zeek's arm a jerk and motioned with his head for Zeek to follow him. Known as The Boss because he ruled the world of antiquities dealing in London, Zeek had no other option and fell in behind him.

Should he be worried that the saggy-eyed clerk purposely looked the other way to avoid seeing them head out the back door into the alley? If this business went all wrong he was sure the guy would never admit to having seen him. What was he getting himself into? His blood rushed through his veins as if he were running a marathon.

He tried to calm himself by breathing deeply and focusing on what he knew of Abasi. The man with slicked-back hair, perhaps in his late forties, operated in the often shady world of antiquities. Only a couple of weeks ago, a departmental donor of solid standing had requested Zeek verify the authenticity of an ancient alabaster vase he wished to purchase. Not wanting to risk offending a valuable resource, Zeek had been forced to leave his students in the field and go to London to oblige. Unfortunately, the brilliant but unscrupulous Abasi had turned out to be the dealer in that transaction. With a gap-toothed grin and hooded eyes, he was a man Zeek did not want to cross.

"S-s-so, Professor, we meet again so s-s-soon." Abasi raised an eyebrow and all but dared Zeek to meet his basilisk stare.

Zeek shuddered and could only nod a response, remembering how Abasi had handed him a business card at the end of the meeting and told him if he ever needed a *favor*, to call on him. Somehow Zeek was pretty sure The Boss meant an *illegal* favor. He had shrugged off the offer with a rather curt goodbye and beat it out of the office never once thinking he would actually call on the man for help. And he had *not* called on the man. How was he to know Joe would contact Abasi for this?

"Tell me, how is little Miss Ashley Duvall from Texas? *Humph?*"

The man would cut right to the point, wouldn't he? What should he say? Ashley had accompanied Zeek to London for that consultation. While she waited for him, Abasi had introduced himself to her in a threatening fashion and then followed her to her dig site to further harrass her. As misfortune would have it, Abasi was getting out of his car when the stone and the wind swept her away. How would Zeek explain that event? Should he tell the man she was back in London? How should he identify Robert? Hiding anything from Abasi was next to impossible from what he knew of the man.

But what alternative did he have now? It was too late for him to go home and avoid the guy. Besides, he needed a faked passport and he needed it yesterday. Who else could he find to do the job Abasi apparently had already finished?

Finding his voice, he choked out, "She's f-fine. Can we g-get on with this?"

Abasi grinned at him like the pro he was. He wouldn't be caught. Zeek felt that smile puncture any shred of confidence he still possessed. He could see himself under arrest and explaining to the police why he needed a passport for a twenty-three-year-old guy from 1363 England. *Yeah, that's right, officer, fourteenth century England.*

"Such a charming child. I look forward to s-s-seeing her again."

Was that a threat?

"At another work site, perhaps?"

Uh-huh, definitely a threat.

How could he protect her? It would be tough because just like her father, Ashley had a mind of her own. She had informed Zeek she was going back in time with this guy Robert as soon as she said goodbye to her family back in the States. No discussion about that bombshell. She was adamant she had to go *home* to the States to say her good-byes. Her mother, brother and friends couldn't come here. Nope, that would be too easy. So here he was at the mercy of Abasi. End of story.

Busying himself with digging through the satchel he carried, Abasi seemed to know the extra time weighed on Zeek. A single security lamp on a pole beamed down through the moist night air, capturing the pair in the private world of its circle of light. The darkness beyond them was alive with sound. Dogs barked an aria to each other in the distance, and cats further down the alley engaged in a screech-off. A rat took off near his feet, its smelly trashcan dinner interrupted by their untimely entrance.

He would like to have fled in a similar fashion. He pictured himself, a ginormous rat, running hell-bent down the street with the police hot on his heels. The incongruous image made him nearly crack a smile. Nearly.

"Here is what you requested, Profes-s-sor. I hope you like it," Abasi rumbled in a low, conspiratorial voice, air hissing through his teeth even more than ususal. Zeek *hated* being in league with the guy, but thrust out a hand and took the offered document.

Examining it with care under the stark light, Zeek was impressed by the very professional job. This passport would be impossible to tell from a real one.

"Looks good, Abasi. What do I owe you?" *Please let me pay you and be gone.*

"Ahhh, *nothing,* Profes-s-sor. It is a gift."

Zeek looked hard at the man and knew without a doubt what he was saying. Abasi wanted Zeek to owe *him* a favor. *Ugh.* He could imagine what this man would want him to do that would compromise his every principle.

"I would prefer to pay you." Zeek pressed his lips together in distaste.

A warning flared in the depths of his unblinking eyes as Abasi smiled slowly at Zeek, the gaps between his teeth revealing themselves one at a time. "I am sure you would, Professor, but I *insis-s-st!*" Those reptilian eyes roamed up and down Zeek for a moment, before he cocked his head and asked, "Who is the young man in the picture?"

"Just a kid who isn't a U.S. citizen who wants to marry my niece in the States next week."

"Ah, so our lovely Ashley is engaged?" Zeek nodded. "Then she has returned from her . . . trip?"

Zeek swallowed hard. Why didn't he know when to shut up? What was he supposed to say to that?

"Yeah, they don't have time to wait through the proper channels. Hey, it takes six weeks or more to get a passport. This makes it all easier." Realizing it sounded like they *had* to get married, he patted his abdomen and raised his eyebrows to complete the ruse.

Abasi didn't look impressed. Nor did he appear to buy Zeek's story. *My God, just get me out of here.*

The dealer narrowed his eyes at Zeek, taking his time to look him over, head to toe. "You are sure this-s-s has nothing to do with the antiquity now missing from the British Museum? Yes-s-s?"

"Of course not!" Zeek snapped, and then caught himself. *"Whoa.* What's missing?" An alarm blared in his head. Surely there could be no connection.

"I see," Abasi hissed, glaring at Zeek, his skepticism apparent. "Your office has been notified of this-s-s, no?"

"No, no, I don't think so, but then I haven't been in the office. Is it in the media yet?" Abasi had not told him any specifics, and he didn't want to appear to question the man about anything. He would find out soon enough if it were important to the university. Though no link to Robert came to mind, unease niggled his insides.

"The media does not know yet ... but s-s-soon."

How did this guy know everything going on with any antiquity? He grimaced at being sucked into Abasi's world. Zeek muttered his understanding, hoping Abasi couldn't hear his heart trying to bust out of his chest. Why was he certain The Boss had learned his secrets, even though he couldn't fathom how?

Abasi's heavy-lidded eyes cruised up and down Zeek one last time, digesting his response and finding it acidic, judging from the pained expression on his face. Nonetheless, he released Zeek from further scrutiny, said goodnight, and stepped outside the sphere of light where he melted into the black depths of the alley.

Zeek froze, not sure how to escape. The light from under the shop door blinked off, making the decision for him. Zeek hung for a moment in the comforting glow of the security light. Then he cursed into the darkness and like a cockroach scuttled his way out of the alley, Robert's needed passport tucked securely inside his jacket.

Chapter 4

Ashley's eyes roamed lovingly over Robert's studious form as he bent to work over Uncle Zeek's laptop, engrossed in reading Wikipedia's "History of the World." He had been wide-eyed when she showed him how it was possible to find anything he wanted to know on the computer. Hooked, he had mastered the track pad within minutes. Typing had been another story. He struggled with the modern spelling of words and his fingers were too big for the keyboard. Watching him hunched over with his brow furrowed, hunting and pecking for the right letters, had her stifling giggles. *He is just so cute.* Yet, this quest was all for her, so she couldn't keep the warm tingling in her body from bursting into flames every time she looked at him.

The power of Robert's intellect impressed Ashley as he digested the knowledge now at his fingertips. So smart and quick, Robert was sucking up information at a rate Ashley feared she might not be able to keep up with. She had settled on Wikipedia as a means to focus his searches and fill in the intervening centuries for him. When something caught his interest he clicked on a link and found more pictures and descriptions of events. He had barely breathed for hours as he tore through the decades of the past in a fury to learn all he could.

She had encouraged him to skip searching for specifics on his own family. She didn't want to know any details about the lives they were soon to live when they returned to Hertford Castle. After thinking about it, Robert agreed. He had been riveted, however, by the story of the English succession of kings and was struggling to understand why Richard II had chosen to alienate the aristocracy.

She smiled. How incongruous it was for her medieval man to now be clothed in Diesel jeans and t-shirt with Dr. Marten boots on his feet. He had even consented to a haircut that made him look like Thor with clean hair--a little shaggy, but enticingly curled around his neck and ears. They had dressed Robert in Zeek's ill-fitting clothes only long enough to make a short visit to Selfridges on Oxford Street. He was now set up with a small wardrobe that would serve his purposes on either side of the Atlantic.

Ashley nabbed an item or two for herself along the way since all her clothing had not made it back from the work site. Clean, clothed, coiffed and combed, Ashley and Robert were feeling much better and looking very twenty-first century.

On their outing, Robert's eyes had bugged out at everything around him. Everywhere he went something new snared his attention. Paved streets, electric lights, cars, buses, swarms of people scurrying to and from the underground rail. Ashley knew he was equal parts enthralled and repelled by it all, but he had put on a game face and followed her without hesitation.

A yawn broke Ashley's reverie, and she tried to quell a squeak to avoid interrupting Robert. She slipped out of her chair next to him, stepped to the window, and stretched her limbs as she stared out over the street. Her back popped and complained, venting the nervous energy responsible for keeping her muscles constricted. Night had fallen and Uncle Zeek had yet to appear with the passport from his source for Robert. With it they would be on their way to Texas.

As if on cue, a worried-looking Zeek strode through the door. Relieved, Ashley opened her mouth to say a cheery hello and ask about his mission, but the scowl on his face stopped her cold. Something was wrong. Without breaking stride her uncle made his way to the laptop Robert hulked over at the kitchen table and plopped into the chair next to him. With no warning, Zeek grabbed the computer out from under Robert and jerked it to sit in front of himself.

"Sorry," Zeek muttered to a surprised and wary Robert who looked his question to Ashley. Her uncle never behaved like this.

"What's happened, Uncle Zeek?"

"That's exactly what I want to find out," he growled. "Have either of you run across a headline about an antiquity disappearing from the British Museum?"

"Why would that be a prob-...? Oh. *Oh-h-h...*"

Ashley interrupted herself as she began to understand the significance of what her uncle said. After all, Robert was sort of an antiquity himself. "How could that be due to anything we've done?"

"I don't know, Ashley, but I wish I did. My contact turned out to be Abasi."

"No! Abasi was there? He's the man you were supposed to meet?" Zeek nodded. "My God, that man is everywhere!" Horror filled her as she realized Abasi now had all of Robert's faked information.

Zeek continued, acknowledging her concern, "He asked me point-blank if getting the passport for Robert had anything to do with the missing antiquity, so *he's* making a connection." Zeek shot her a hard look. "He saw you disappear from an archeological work site and now an antiquity has disappeared. Seems a stretch until you throw in my asking him for a forged passport."

"Know you what is missing?" Robert eyed Ashley with raised brows. He seemed to understand her mind was already chasing rabbits.

"No. And I didn't want to be too interested or too uninformed in front of him. The man makes my skin crawl. His people are probably watching this house right now to be sure I was straight with him." The color drained from Zeek's face.

Peeking out the window, Ashley half expected to see Abasi looking in. "Did you have to tell him much about Robert to obtain the passport?"

"Some. I let him think you and Robert had to marry. Kind

of like you were in a hurry to get hitched so the baby would be born in the States."

"You what?" Ashley blurted, blushing a rosy pink. She glanced in embarrassment at Robert only to find him grinning rather smugly at her.

"You got a better reason?" Zeek flicked through news topics in his browser at a rapid clip. He stopped, took a deep breath, and apologized to his niece. "Sorry. I didn't think he'd ask. It was the only excuse I thought of on the spot to explain the rush to get our guy to the States. Besides, I don't believe telling him the truth was an option, huh?"

"I-I guess not." Ashley rolled her eyes at Robert who grinned and pulled her onto his lap.

"How can we find out if there is any link to Robert without Abasi knowing?"

"We'll just have to watch the media to see if the story breaks. Meanwhile, I'll check it out with my colleagues."

"Can we still leave tomorrow as planned?" Ashley cringed, dreading a negative response.

Zeek slid back his chair and turned to face the pair eyeing him speculatively. *"Hmmm,* maybe it would be better to go through security and customs before any of this gets out and officials have time to organize a search."

Ashley sighed in relief, her shoulders dropping to reveal the depth of her worry.

"Or, maybe you'll just be walking into the flames. Damn it, I don't know."

Chapter 5

"I can't believe the line is so long." Ashley stood on her tiptoes to spot the security agent's podium through the press of people ahead of them.

From his vantage point a full head taller than most, Robert nodded agreement as he surveyed the dizzying array of travelers crammed into queues in the crowded airport terminal. The day promised to be a very trying one for him. Ashley had patiently explained all that flying across the ocean would entail, so he understood what would happen. Still, the endless lines of passengers shoved up and bumping against one another had him on edge. How was he to protect Ashley in a crowd of humanity like this one?

"Stay close to me," he muttered. Ashley only blinked at him and appeared unconcerned.

He had been told he could take none of his weapons with him and that had him glowering. Before they walked out of Zeek's flat Ashley had taken a hard look at him and told him the knife tucked in his boot had to stay at Zeek's. His jaw had dropped in amazement. How had she known he had slipped a knife into his boot?

Ashley confessed she had guessed he might have a weapon on him but came undone when he stripped himself of three knives. He had hidden one in each boot and hooked a small dagger under his belt. Zeek was apoplectic over that. Robert had feared for the man's health since he turned more purple than red.

Ashley had reminded him once again on the way that if

he had any weapons on him they would be detained and his passport scrutinized. That would likely get them both thrown in jail. All his weapons had to be left behind, she said, because the machines at the airport would detect anything dangerous on him. How, short of magic, could that be? In the end he had to trust Ashley to see him through.

"Don't worry, Robert. We're halfway there. We have our boarding passes and our luggage checked with the skycap. All we have to do now is get through security with our hand baggage and then we can relax until our plane is ready to board."

"We shall fly across the big water to the place you call the States," Robert repeated like a mantra, making her smile at him.

"The line is moving along faster than I thought it would."

"It is?" Robert sighed impatiently. He had never waited in a line in his life and this was killing him. With no way to separate the aristocrats from the commoners, everyone was mashed in line all together. A frazzled, young mother behind him kept rolling her giant baby cart over his ankles every time the line moved forward, but she never seemed to realize it.

Looking out over the sea of heads he knew not where to direct his attention. Summer in London prompted females of all ages to strip down to what Ashley called tank tops and shorts. Was he not compromising them every time he looked at them? Were they not embarrassed to be displaying so much skin?

The most peculiar part to him was women were often dressed the same as men. How confounding. One woman wore a long skirt, but her bodice covered her breasts and nothing else. He did not understand. Ashley was happy to wear these strange fashions, and she did blend in with everyone else. He accepted that until he realized other men were ogling her long, shapely legs and her plump breasts, too. Seemingly unaware of this, Ashley clearly did not mind. He would prefer she dress as she had at Hertford Castle and share her assets in private with only him.

He gazed wistfully at the beautiful woman leaning against him and bent to nuzzle her ear. His hands had not left

Ashley for more than a few seconds at a time since their arrival. Now she looked up at him and grinned her understanding. Her eyes told him she was uneasy too, so he stroked her hand to reassure her. They would get through this together.

Feeling other eyes on him, Robert spotted a uniformed guard across the room watching their every move. Zeek had given him strict instructions not to engage anyone unless spoken to first, so he focused his attention down at Ashley and smiled stiffly at her. She winced at his unnatural smile, but had no chance to comment because they were called as next in line to go to an open passport station.

Ashley sucked in a deep breath and stepped up to the podium ahead of Robert. This was the moment she'd been dreading. Would they find a problem with Robert's passport? Would they ask questions he was unprepared to answer? Her heart pounded such a loud drum solo in her ear she wasn't sure she would be able to hear when the agent spoke to her.

Ashley thrust her passport to the woman who opened it with an efficient flip to the appropriate page. Looking bored, she studied Ashley, one eyebrow hitched up, and compared her person to the photo. Suppressing a yawn, she asked, "Your occupation?"

"Student." Ashley smiled. The frowzy agent looked unimpressed.

Stuffed in a dark blue uniform a size too small, the frizzy-haired woman might have been thirty or fifty. It was impossible to tell. She completed her routine by shoving Ashley's passport under a device that checked for authenticity. Not remembering this gadget from her previous flight, Ashley panicked inside. What if Robert's passport couldn't pass this kind of screening?

Without glancing up, the agent stamped Ashley's passport, thwacked it back in her hand and like a bleating sheep bellowed, *"Next."* Ashley scampered aside and paused to wait for Robert. He stepped forward and with only a slight hesitation placed his passport on the desk in front of the agent. The woman must have felt the light change as Robert's sizable frame filled the space in front of her. As she rolled her weary eyes up to meet his, her mouth dropped open, and she sat up straight and tall. Her dull brown eyes widened in awe at the magnificent male specimen standing in front of her.

Quick to catch on, Robert planted a heart-stopping smile squarely on the agent. Ashley hid her amusement as the woman melted under his thousand-kilowatt gaze. Flustered by her own response, the woman stammered as if she couldn't remember her own name, let alone what she was supposed to ask him. Full of sympathy, Robert directed his dazzling smile into her eyes without breaking eye contact. The poor, befuddled woman just stamped his passport and motioned him to go. She never did say a single word to him. Ashley tugged his arm and motioned him to collect his passport and move on before anyone intervened.

∞∞∞

"That went better than expected," Robert whispered as they took their places in the security screening line.

"You devil! You might as well have used a stun gun on her."

"I only smiled at her," Robert smirked.

"Just be glad you got a female agent susceptible to your charms." As Ashley scanned the line ahead, she dropped her teasing tone. "Something tells me one of the male agents, like that one up there, won't be quite as easy to get by." With a tip of her head, Ashley indicated a stone-faced guard in front of them whose eyes were glued to Robert.

"Ah, that one," Robert breathed in her ear. "His eyes followed me earlier." The man now stood at the screening station directly in front of them.

"Here's where you have to take off your belt and hoodie."

Preoccupied with the insolent way the man kept staring at him, Robert's heart clutched in anger. He took off his belt and plunked it in the plastic bin. Though the man's scrutiny frayed his last ounce of patience, Robert tried not to engage him. Every instinct told him to tell this underling who he was and make him snap to or face the consequences. In his world as the heir to an earl, no one ever dared look at him like this man was.

"Are you okay?" Ashley turned her back to the agent as she shoved her bin through. "Your face is red and you're gritting your teeth."

He caught his breath, nodded understanding, and exhaled deeply before stripping off his hoodie. He laid it loosely across his belt, already in the bin, and sent them on their way through the machine that magically could see into each item.

Trailing Ashley as she headed for the human scanning machine, Robert watched her trip through without difficulty. She turned and gave him an encouraging smile. He dogged her footsteps, pausing to raise his arms above his head just as Ashley had demonstrated. Buzzers blared the moment he stepped into position. His heart stopped.

The stone-faced guard jumped on Robert in a heartbeat, asking him to step out of the scanner and move to a separate area where they would search him. Robert's eyes sought Ashley's and read sheer panic in them. He surreptitiously shook his head at her to let her know he had no weapons on him, but it didn't seem to register with her.

To Robert's relief, a much friendlier person waited at this checkpoint wielding a wand like a magician over the person ahead of him. Already agitated, Robert's attitude bordered on surly until the woman smiled at him. He sneaked a glance at Ashley who winked at him, and he knew what he had to do.

The woman grinned big as he approached her, snapping her gum noisily to a tune only she could hear. Ashley had told him about gum. He had never understood the point of chewing something he was not to swallow.

She wafted her wand over Robert's left hand. "I think that pinky ring is the problem, sir. How 'bout you take that off and put it in this little bin, and we'll see if that's the issue."

Robert's eyebrows shot up at the agent's command, and he momentarily thought about arguing, but the woman still smiled at him and seemed to mean no harm.

"Sorry, Robert. I forgot about jewelry sometimes being a problem," Ashley said as she moved to stand by him. She had collected the items from her bin and re-dressed.

The signet ring refused to come off easily, making him wince as he twisted it from his finger. It was a large, solid gold ring with the Hertford crest embedded in the crown. He knew not the last time the ring had been removed from his hand since he stamped correspondence without taking it off. Hiding his concern at letting it leave his possession, he dropped it into the little basket and allowed the woman to use her magic stick to scan his body again.

She's enjoying this way too much, Robert thought, watching the woman wave her wand over his man parts with an even bigger grin. The gum came precariously close to falling out of her mouth with each smack. Turning his attention to Ashley, he wanted to confirm he had rid himself of all his weapons. He had. He was stubborn, but not foolish.

"Indeed. It must have been the ring since you're clear otherwise."

The agent held out the small bin for Robert to take, but Mr. Stoneface interceded, grabbing the bin before Robert could lay a hand on it. The grin faded into a frown on the woman's face. She swung her head around and glared at her partner, her face a question mark as to why he was being so rude.

The pudgy man, perhaps in his late thirties, stared straight into Robert's face with an unmistakable glint in his eye. "Where you two headed?"

The forced machismo the guard radiated made Robert angry. The man had even punctuated his question with an upward bob of his head. *Hmph.* Those double chins begged to be punched. Before he had time to answer, Ashley grabbed his fist and turned to face the man. "We're goin' to Texas to visit ma' fam'ly," she drawled.

The guard produced another one of those upward head bobs that bobbled a bit and said nothing for a moment as his head swiveled between the two. Robert squeezed Ashley's hand to warn her he might burst. He would not tolerate being baited in such an obvious way much longer. Ashley kept a firm grip on his fingers or he would have grabbed his ring and moved on. She implored him with her eyes to be patient and wait.

Ashley turned her attention to the guard. "Yeah, this is my boyfriend's first flight, and even though he prob'ly won't admit it, he's scared spitless."

Robert's head jerked around, incredulous over Ashley's betrayal, and almost missed the demonic ear-to-ear grin that split old stone-face's visage like a hot knife through butter. Should he stomach this insult? Ashley stood beside him grinning at the guard. Heat whooshed over him. What was he to do?

"Ah, so ye don't like flying, eh?" The overbearing, balding guard with the careful comb-over latched onto the idea of Robert being afraid to fly. "And overseas, at that." He snickered as he thumped Robert on the shoulder. "Don't worry, laddie, they usually make it without dumpin' ye in the ocean."

Robert opened his mouth to defend his manhood, as well as his honor, when Ashley poked him hard in the back. The goal was to get *through* security not fight it. Reluctantly, he swallowed his retort and tried to laugh at himself, but it sounded more like a strangled groan. He jammed his hoodie over his head hoping to hide his anger. His desire to use his belt as a whip on the man overwhelmed him, so he focused on Ashley.

He did try.

Giggling coquettishly, Ashley twanged an "Ah hope so," but the man relished Robert's vexation and kept grinning at him like a devil. Robert's jugular throbbed with pent-up fury by the time Ashley pointed to a clock on the wall near the exit. "Oh, Robert, we'd better git to our gate."

She reached out for the little bin the guard still held with a question in her eyes. The man finally rolled his head in her direction and with a smirking, upward nod plucked the ring out of the bin. He bounced it in his hand for a moment. "Heavy," he declared, surprise registering on his face.

He looked it over closely for a moment before dropping it into her hand. She passed it to Robert who shoved it on and wheeled to go. Not quite finished with him the man thunked him on the back with a "Have a nice flight." Robert stiffened and his nose flared, but he would not give this person the satisfaction of turning around.

He was appalled when Ashley, leading the way, smiled her thanks over her shoulder and actually gave the man a wink as if she were in league with his joke. Robert never wanted to see that man's nasty smirk again. Why was she being so friendly to him? He wanted to ask, but then they rounded the corner and were into the terminal.

"We made it," Ashley quietly crowed up at Robert as they strode the concourse to their gate. "We're in."

Robert returned her giddy comment with a steely look intended to arrow straight to her heart. Was she so unaware of his feelings that she was happy about that encounter with the guard?

"I know not if I can do this, Ashley. 'Tis not in my ken to grovel to men like that who wield their small power like a saber. Were I at home he would ne'er have challenged me because of my rank, and if he had dared, I would have skewered him without a thought."

"Oh, I'm so sorry," Ashley crooned in his ear. "You know I meant none of that. I only wanted to get us through security. I could see what kind of guy he was, so I just played to him. Baby, you have to know I didn't mean it."

"*Baby! Ba-by?* Are ye calling me a *baby?*" He was so indignant forming words was nearly impossible.

"Whoa, soldier!" Ashley caught his arm and stopped to sternly face him. "*Baby* happens to be a term of endearment used by lovers to indicate their loved one is precious to them. There's no wee babe in the picture, I can assure you."

That took the wind out of his sails. After staring blankly at her for a beat, he sullenly pitched forward again to take the lead, although he had no idea where to go.

A few steps later, Ashley skittered up to his side, slipped her arm under his and rested her head against his chest. He sighed loudly, letting go the worst of his anger.

No one ever said this would be easy.

Chapter 6

'Tis harder than I thought it would be.

His head pressed against the side of the plane, Robert watched in despair as the infinite blackness whizzed by his small window. Only muted lights above the passengers and along the aisle kept the interior of the airliner from matching the pitch-black outside.

Drained emotionally from the trauma of takeoff two hours ago, Robert and his mood were blacker than the newly fallen night sky.

Some protector I am.

He might as well have been a small child the way Ashley had held his hand and talked him through boarding and take-off. Still, he did not understand how something as gigantic and heavy as this plane stayed in the air. Only Ashley's untroubled purr in his ear had kept him seated and sane through it all.

Happy with his life at Hertford, Robert was comfortable with his family there and firmly in control of his life. Now he sat at the mercy of people he could not see and knew not. This world was so . . . *large,* and Ashley clearly belonged in it. 'Twas disturbing to find he was only a pinpoint of light in the vast universe of stars when he had always thought he was the sun or the moon. How emasculating. He carried no weapons, he dressed oddly, people spoke with strange accents, his rank went unrecognized, and no one cared.

Mayhap I should not have followed Ashley.

Mayhap I should have trusted her to return to me on her own without my help.

Mayhap...

No!

I wanted the adventure almost as much as I want Ashley.

Had he not been bored with the sameness of his days until Lady Ashley Duvall turned up in his world? Life was never dull with her around.

Robert dropped his gaze fondly to Ashley's beautiful, relaxed face snuggled into his side. Her long, honey-blonde hair wrapped around her like a blanket. Unconcerned, she slept soundly, a soft snore seeping out between her luscious, parted lips. He wanted to capture that sweet sound with his mouth over hers, but did not want to wake her. She had not slept much before the flight and neither had he.

No, I am right to follow her.

If not, he would be at Hertford Castle worried sick about where she dwelt and if she would return to him. 'Twas much better to be here with her tucked in beside him. She was his and she was all that mattered.

Robert decided he would relinquish control to Ashley for now. He would not let her know how unworthy he felt in her modern world. When they returned to his territory as intended, he would once again be in charge. For now, he would fit in with her world to the best of his ability as she had in his. He would learn whatever he needed to learn to keep afloat to make her proud of him. He would protect her from the man called Abasi. This visit would be over soon...*I can endure this.*

Feeling calmer, Robert closed his eyes and tuned in to the steady hum of the plane he no longer feared would fall from the sky. Mayhap if he shut his troubles out, sleep might come.

∞∞∞

Ashley's eyes flew open in a panic only to find the subject of her fright calmly reclaiming the aisle seat next to her. She surmised the tiny Asian lady was just returning from the plane's restroom.

Robert's arm draped protectively over her shoulders in a possessive hold that made her grin. Her warrior took care of her even in his sleep. Robert grimaced as if troubled and restlessly pulled her closer.

This time travel stuff was tough on him. He was so out of his element here, and yet he worked so hard at keeping a stiff upper lip just for her. The warrior in him didn't want her to know how worried he was about absolutely everything.

Hang in there, sweetheart. I've got your back.

She patted his hand and Robert woke up just as the flight attendant handed them their meal trays. He eyed the teeny, plastic-wrapped tray through squinty eyes and quirked an eyebrow at her.

"I know. They're small."

His annoyed double take made her laugh when it ended in a snort. Scandalized by the miniature dish of food he held in the palm of his huge hand, he rolled his eyes at her, and they both chuckled over the incongruity.

Now having fun, he daintily pulled back the cover on his entree so as not to squish it and after peeking in, fluttered his eyelashes at her. "Small?" he said, pressing his lips into a straight line in his best Lady Margaret manner.

Ashley snorted at that, the memory of the lady still too fresh for comfort. She answered as haughtily as the woman herself, "'Tis true, those nibbles would not feed a falcon, let alone the son of an earl."

Her response launched fifteen minutes of Robert playing irreverently with their food. His impression of a merlin pecking jerkily at the plate for each bite made her giggle until her stomach ached. Their seatmate looked more than ready to press the call button to send for a flight attendant to shut them up. It was time to straighten up.

He'll survive. He can still laugh.

∞∞∞

Julie Duvall stared one more time at the stainless steel clock above the microwave and realized it was exactly four minutes since she had last looked. Sitting in a bar chair at her kitchen counter sipping coffee, she shoved a wayward chunk of blonde hair out of her face. A ragged sigh of aggravation ripped through her.

Exasperated by her own impatience, she plunked down her cup a bit too hard on the granite surface. The sound echoed in the small, empty kitchen as if it mocked the loss of its once-noisy family. Sometimes it unnerved her to be home by herself with the kids gone. It was still too soon to pick up Josh from his overnight at Parker's house before leaving to meet Ashley coming in on the early flight from London.

She thought for the hundredth time today how impossible life would be without her children. Rick's departure had about done her in for good. With no kids as a reason to get out of bed each day, she would be finished for sure.

"Rick, honey, where are you when I need you?" If only he would answer.

Always in some part of her being she had known she wouldn't be able to keep Rick forever. Not with his time walking abilities. Still, she missed him with every fiber of her being. Julie scrunched her eyebrows together to ward off the pain before shaking away the hurt like a dog shedding water. Their children would be enough to keep her going.

Julie drummed her polished nails on the counter top while she focused on sorting her options. If she left the house now, she and Josh would need to kill time somewhere else before going to pick up Ashley, which would be even more uncomfortable. Josh possessed flea-sized patience, so the thought of having to listen to him whine about her wasting his time was more than she could tolerate at the moment. She'd simply suck it up and wait longer here--in the quiet, empty house.

A twinge rippled through her chest, making Julie realize she should quit drinking caffeinated coffee if she wished to fare the wait better. She hopped up and stepped to the sink, slinging her hot drink down the drain and flushing it clear with what should have been cold water but was almost as hot as her coffee. After all, August in Houston meant the pipes in the attic heated to boiling all by themselves. She was too fidgety to stand there and run water for a drink until it cooled. Her mug rinsed, she spun around to the refrigerator and filled it with crushed ice and water.

Her nerves had been balled-up and screaming for too long. When Zeek first called to tell her Ashley had vanished from his archeological dig, she was distraught. She had wanted to plead to the heavens for everyone in the world to search for her precious daughter.

All the hurt of her husband's disappearance had swamped her once again. Rick had walked away from work almost two years ago and no one had seen him since. As planned, he had left on a time travel, as he had many times in the past, but this time he had not come home. Aside from his parents, she and Zeek were the only two family members who knew of Rick's adventures.

They all feared the worst: he had been killed while away in another time period, and they would never find out what had happened to him. Now, despite Ashley's safe return this time, she had to fear the same thing would happen once more. Why did her daughter have to be a Guardian of the Stones like her father? Could she stand that kind of stress again?

She gulped down the freezing cold water, marveling at how her hand shook as it traveled to and from her mouth as if she were a palsied crone. Was it the caffeine or horror at the thought she might one day lose another family member to time travel? She wiped her mouth with the back of her free hand and then rubbed her chest, hoping the tremors there would die a quick death.

Fortunately, Zeek had reminded her it was highly unlikely harm could have befallen Ashley at the work site. Always careful of what he said regarding his brother's travels over the phone or in writing, Zeek told her Ashley had "gone visiting." That was their code for time travel. Thus, to explain her absence, they had agreed to inform her classmates that Ashley had been called away by her mom for a family emergency.

The other students seemed to accept her departure without question, according to Zeek. He reported a few of the guys were genuinely sorry to see her go. He had waggishly noted, however, that a few of the girls looked happy about the loss of Ashley from their group.

Now that sounded like her Ashley, Julie grinned. Her daughter was a determined kid who generally found a way to get what she wanted in spite of what others might deem her due. Boys had been drawn to her classic American-girl, blonde looks and vibrant personality since her toddler years. This was the kid who came home from school as a first grader with rings and small gifts from boys who wanted to claim her attention.

That was only the beginning. The older she got, boys began to be attracted to her *force of nature* persona. Ashley had never understood what their attraction to her was all about. She thought herself pretty average in all things. Perhaps that was because her girlfriends were happy to keep the power of Ashley tamped down as much as possible. Otherwise, how else could they compete with her?

Julie had waited long hours over several days for her cell phone to ring before flying to England to look for Ashley herself. It had been a frustratingly futile trip and Zeek had urged her to return to the States, likely because she was driving him nuts. She had been home what seemed like minutes when the long-awaited call from Ashley arrived. Julie's hands trembled so much she had been forced to set the phone on speaker and place it on the dining room table. Twice Ashley's voice had faded away and twice she'd had heart failure imagining Ashley had disappeared again. Once her travel home had been arranged, she and Josh had danced around the kitchen with pure excitement over Ashley's safe return.

Josh did not yet know about time travel and Julie knew she would have to tell him soon. The relief that she and Zeek had made the right call in not seeking help to locate Ashley threatened to overwhelm her emotions. If she had been wrong and Ashley's body had turned up after having suffered some kind of abduction, she could not have lived with herself.

Delighted to have Ashley coming home, Julie wondered what to expect from the extra person her daughter was bringing with her. She didn't even know if this person was male or female. Knowing Ashley, she had managed to pick up a guy someplace who was smitten with her. That would not be surprising. Wherever she went, Ashley left a trail of infatuated young men in her wake, all the while certain they were only good friends. Honestly, some of them would probably die for her.

Julie shook her head wryly, thinking of her cherished child and how oblivious she was to her own charms, when an unwelcome thought struck her. Surely this person wasn't a fellow time traveler? *Ouch.* Would they be skipping all over time together? Would she have to worry and fret like this always? Oh, why couldn't her family ever be normal like everyone else's? Her questions would be answered . . . *if that blasted second hand would ever move.*

Chapter 7

Zeek hated himself for doing this. He felt like a freaking gigolo manipulating his friend this way. Dr. Monica Wilson, a professor in Zeek's department, had taken it into her head Zeek was interested in her. He wasn't. A tiny, bird-like woman in her mid-thirties, she had a slight lisp, a sharp mind and a cutting wit. He liked talking to her because of her interesting and engaging personality, but no spark of physical attraction to her existed at all. In fact, she perpetually had the sour breath of a woman who fretted too much and ate too little. She subtly chased him at every turn, and he just as slyly thwarted her at every turn. Some days, keeping her at bay was a full-time job.

But today he needed information from her. Monica had worked for the British Museum for a dozen years or so before embarking on her university career. Consequently, she had many friends and colleagues still at the museum with whom she kept in contact.

Monica was sure to know what antiquity Abasi had been talking about, if indeed, there was one. Zeek had scoured the papers and news media for any clue as to what the dealer referenced, but found nothing. Now he hoped to weasel the info from the woman without having to sell his soul, or more specifically, his body.

Zeek waited for Monica in the break room, tapping his toe and slurping his morning coffee. He was trying not to wolf down all the pastries someone had generously placed on the worktable when the sound of her high-heels clicked crisply down the hallway. Every muscle in his body tensed as he braced for her to whisk imperiously around the door in her usual morning haste. A woman on a mission wherever she went, her morning ritual always unfolded the same way. She required one cup of tea to be waiting, already steeped in a pot courtesy of her assistant. It must be served in an English china teacup and saucer with one lump of sugar and a splash of milk, stirred three times with a silver spoon. It was uncanny to watch her complete the same moves precisely the same way each and every morning.

Zeek plastered a cheery smile on his face. "Hello, Miss Monica! How are you this fine summer day?"

Instantly, he wished he could take the words back as he obviously had come on too strong. Monica's eyes narrowed, wary of his good cheer.

"Really, Duvall, are you sure you are quite all right?" Her words clipped out in her aristocratically British way, each word like a dart thrown at his head.

"Sorry, Ma'am, you can tell I am very happy to be away from my charges for a while. You know it's seriously nerve-racking to keep twenty-some, twenty-somethings out of trouble on a work site. They try my patience sometimes more than I care to admit, so conversing with another adult over the age of thirty is nice." *Geez,* he was still laying it on too thick.

Monica cocked an eyebrow at him and studied his expression, her green eyes flaring, still unconvinced this was the same Duvall who so steadily kept her at arm's length.

"I see." Having accepted this explanation for his momentary exuberance, she deftly completed the third swipe of her tea with her silver spoon.

Mercy, now what should he say to her? He dug around in his brain for some way to transition into his question without drawing further undue attention to himself. Never great at small talk, he would cheerfully scarf the rest of the sweets to have an excuse to say nothing else.

"This summer no one has uncovered much of anything beyond a seventeenth century horseshoe. All frightfully dull and uneventful with nothing of significance to report." Surely she would take her cue and reveal something significant. He ripped into another treat.

"I see." He flinched as she eyed what was left of the sweets he was sucking down at an alarming rate.

Damn the woman. Did she always have to make things so difficult? He searched for a napkin and wiped the jelly off his chin. "I thought I'd give this class some respite from the heat with a weekend in London. Perhaps a visit to the British Museum? Would that appeal to them, do you think?" How much more would it take to get her to spill what she knew without asking?

"The British Museum is always an excellent destination, Duvall. You could not go wrong there. I helped mount the current exhibit in the Reading Room."

Zeek sighed and took a big gulp of his coffee, nearly scalding himself.

"But a bit of a flap occurred there this last week of which perhaps you should be aware."

At last.

This would be what he wanted.

Monica tucked an auburn curl behind her ear and gave him a shrewdly assessing glare. "This is not for public consumption, you understand, but everyone at the museum is most upset over the disappearance of an antiquity."

Zeek frowned and tried to look taken aback by this news, but not too taken aback. God, his acting skills sucked. *"Hmm, I haven't heard of anything like that. How could something disappear out of the British Museum? That place is guarded more tightly than the crown jewels."*

Monica looked at him warily, sensing something out of sorts with him, but continued her narrative anyway. "Well, that is just the problem. The item vanished from its display case without any trace of anyone in its vicinity according to the security cameras. No sirens went off, no alarms rang, nothing. In fact, no one is entirely sure when the article disappeared."

"You can't be serious." Would that nudge her enough to

keep talking?

"Truly. Housekeeping reported it when a sharp-eyed cleaning lady polished the case and found its spot empty. They are trained to note such occurrences if signage is not in place confirming the removal of the artifact."

"Hmm, yes." He stopped for a moment in an attempt to look thoughtful. "So, what is missing?" There, he had asked it outright. He held his breath awaiting her answer. *Please let this have nothing to do with Robert. Please.*

"Oddly enough, it is a 14th century signet ring of the house of Hertford." Monica succumbed at last to the lure of the pastries in an effort to snag one before he finished them off.

Horns blared in Zeek's head. It was as bad as he feared. Thankfully, Monica appeared oblivious to his alarm as she munched on her plump strawberry tart.

"A sig-net r-ring."

Still, not connecting with his stunned response, Monica balanced her treat on the saucer and picked daintily at it.

"Just so."

Grasping for the shreds left of his wits, Zeek sought to confirm his worst suspicions. "So, what you are saying is this ring vanished out of a case without it setting off any security and with no one shown on the video tape?" He paused for effect. "How can that be?"

"That is it in a nutshell, Duvall. It is why the media reports nothing at this time. No one knows what to report as to how it disappeared or even when." She finished her sticky pastry, frowning in dismay at the red jelly covering her spread fingers. "Tis a myst'ry!" She looked up and smiled, solving her messy dilemma by sensuously licking the sweet stuff off her fingertips, undoubtedly for his benefit.

Zeek blanched. He wasn't sure if it was news of the ring or the jelly sucking that turned his stomach. He *was* sure if he didn't leave fast those numerous tarts he had gorged on would present themselves a second time. Without a word falling from his pasty-faced lips, he stumbled over his chair in his hurry to exit the room.

Monica stared after her colleague wondering what demon possessed him, before she dismissed his strange antics from her mind with a single shake of her head.

She finished licking her fingers, topped off her tea, and whipped out the door ready to manage her world down the hall, fortified if not satisfied.

Chapter 8

Julie put the car in park and sent a fifth text to Josh telling him she was sitting in Parker's driveway, waiting for him. He had ignored the first text she sent when she left the house, and the three sent while sitting at stoplights. Was he being stubborn or had he not heard those messages *bing* in? It was early and she wanted to avoid waking the family. He and Parker would probably be in the game room at the back of the house. Maybe if she walked around to the patio she could knock on the glass and get his attention.

Peering in through the sliding glass door a couple minutes later, she felt like a peeping tom, but there was Josh, stretched out on the couch still asleep. His phone sat inches from his head. She shouldn't be surprised. The kid had slept through his alarm every day of the last school year, so why would he wake for a few texts now?

She gave the sliding glass door a gentle push to see if it was locked. It slid open silently on its track. Good. She could shake him out and be gone without waking the whole house. Stepping past Parker who was sound asleep sprawled in a recliner with a controller still in his hand, she searched the room for Josh's backpack.

The TV still displayed a Call of Duty home screen, waiting for the next players to begin a new skirmish. The game room bore the remains of its own private war. Wrappers, empty snack bags, pizza crusts, and soft drink cans littered the place like the miniature remains of a battle-weary city. Had they been up all night playing video games? No wonder the room was trashed.

She spotted his pack at the end of the sofa and picked it up. *Good God, it weighs a ton.* Tip-toeing behind the couch she hefted the pack up and propped it on the back of the couch. Reaching over, she gave her son a shake on the shoulder. She must have startled him because he sat straight up and gasped for air with the whites of his eyes showing. Was he going to be sick? Instead, he let out a belch loud enough to wake the dead and grinned at her.

Relieved it wasn't worse, she shook her head and shushed the mess that claimed to be her son even though Parker had not so much as stirred. Josh gave his eyes a vigorous rub with both fists that left dark rings under his road-mapped eyes when he finished. With his sandy blond hair matted to his head he could have passed for thirty rather than half that. The bedraggled thing smelled of sweat, garlic, and teenage boy. She let his pack drop into his lap with a thud and pointed him toward the bathroom with whispered instructions to brush his teeth and comb his hair. He needed to meet her at the car in five minutes or they would be late picking up his sister.

Josh scrunched his face and opened his mouth with the start of a whine, but thought better of it. With a weighty sigh, he rolled off the sofa and struggled to his feet, slinging up his heavy pack with one hand. He headed to the bathroom unaware of the havoc he had wrought with his bag as it swept across the garbage-strewn coffee table on its way to his shoulder. Empty soda cans bounced on the carpet but made no discernable noise. Wrappers flew through the air like paper jets. Julie squatted to pick them up and put them back on the table.

Parker snorted in his sleep and turned over, still oblivious to the intrusion of a mom. Normally, she would make Josh stay and help clean up, but they would have to wake Parker to do so. If Josh was any indication of the amount of sleep the pair had gotten, his friend needed the sleep more than a clean room.

Julie took a deep breath and tried to quiet her nerves. She knew she'd been a wreck over Ashley's disappearance, and it hadn't been easy on Josh. He missed Ashley, too, and although he had never said it aloud, it was clear he had worried over her absence. She'd been short on patience with him, even knowing he didn't mean to push her buttons. He just did. After all, he was male and fifteen.

∞∞∞

No longer early, Julie and Josh walked into Houston's George Bush Intercontinental Airport minutes before Ashley's flight landed. The stop at Parker's house had burned the extra time in getting Josh out the door and into the car. She missed Rick's sure hand at times like these in dealing with their son, because, honestly, she'd like to wring the kid's neck. He said he was hurrying, and she wanted to believe him, but he had moved at the speed of molasses. Her patience had been seriously challenged. Judging from the fact he had said nothing in the car the whole time she railed at him, he knew he'd pushed her too far.

Julie sighed and some of her frustration slipped away now they were safely in the baggage area for international flights. She gave Josh's shoulder a squeeze and realized somewhere along the way he had begun to be presentable. Even his red eyes had whitened and the bags under them had receded, leaving him looking once again like a teenager.

Sensing the storm had passed, and he was now forgiven, Josh gave her one of his sure-fire, disarming grins in hopes the sun might come out again. She couldn't resist gifting him with a dismissive headshake, accompanied by a wry smile, in return for his efforts. Somehow she never stayed mad at him for long and he knew it.

Julie directed her attention to the mass of people trooping in through double doors from customs and scanned for Ashley's blonde head. Josh, a lanky foot taller, bumped himself up on his toes to get a better look.

"Do you see her, Josh?" Julie frowned up at him.

"Nah, not yet. I hope she doesn't take forever getting through customs like she did the last time."

Julie groaned, remembering how Ashley's penchant for shopping had custom's officials sorting through every item in her suitcase. She had harbored no contraband so there had been no problem for her. The rest of the family, however, had been left to cool their heels during a lengthy stay in the waiting area.

"What do you know about this person with Ashley? Is it a girl?" Josh asked, his eyes roving over the crowd.

"Nothing." Julie checked her watch again as if that would make all this waiting business move faster.

"What if she's hot and has a wicked accent!"

"She might be bringing a girl home, but my bet, knowing Ashley," she paused and rolled her eyes over to Josh, "is that he's male and good-looking."

"Hm-hmm, good thing I don't bet against you, Mom, 'cuz I think I see her with a guy . . . no wait . . . make that a *man* . . . "
Josh's voice roller-coastered up an octave. *"A very big man."*

Julie's eyes shot to Josh in time to witness his eyes widen in shock and his jaw drop. A nameless panic flooded Julie as she traced Josh's eyes to her daughter's face before landing on *the man* beside her. Josh was right. This was no high school boy or college guy. This was a man--and a stunningly handsome one at that.

Julie made note of this tall, gorgeous guy with an arm wrapped protectively around her daughter's shoulders. He eye-balled the press of people from above them, his head swiveling like a surveillance camera watching for trouble. Unbidden, the two glanced at one another and the look they shared sent a cold chill down Julie's back. *They are in love.* Signs on their foreheads proclaiming it to all the world would not have been more obvious.

Who is this?

Before she had time to ponder her own question further, Ashley spotted them and took off at a run. She pulled the man by his wrist behind her, nearly shoving people out of the way in her haste to reach them.

"Mom!" A mix of emotions fleetingly dashed across Ashley's face as she pulled her mother into a bear hug. In that brief moment Julie saw excitement, love, and joy, but what caught her attention most was one of worry underneath the others.

What is going on here?

Did Ashley think she and Josh wouldn't like this man? Did it have to do with her disappearance?

Time-travel?

Her heart thumping, Julie couldn't wait to get home to hear Ashley's story, but first she braced herself to meet *the man*.

Moving on to Josh, Ashley grabbed her brother's arm and squeezed it. *"Geez,* Josh, what are you eating? You've grown half a foot while I've been gone."

Josh grinned down affectionately at his sister as he hugged her. "It's only three inches this month, Ash."

"Only three?" With her usual sarcasm intact, Ashley punched him in the arm. "My, my. Maybe you need growth hormones." Ashley stood before them grinning her delight.

Julie shifted her attention to the towering Adonis waiting patiently behind her daughter. It was time for introductions.

"Mom, Josh, this is Robert Spycer from . . .," Ashley hesitated, ". . . Hertford, England." She looked perplexed for a moment. "I'll fill you in later on all the details."

Robert dutifully took a step forward and began what could only have been a bow. Ashley stepped directly in front of him before he was halfway down, forcing him to grab her shoulders to steady them both. Robert looked chagrined and smiled apologetically at Ashley, their foreheads touching.

Julie's heart stopped, but her mind was a centrifugal force, spinning itself to spit out the answer she feared most: *Ashley loves a man from a different time.* He had been making a formal bow to her, chivalrous, but just not done by anyone in this day and age.

She sucked in a breath, having held it in angst, and

sneaked a glance at Josh. He stood there gaping at this man called Robert with his mouth open and a glazed expression of adoration in his eyes. Granted, all fifteen-year-old boys stood with their mouths gaping open, but Josh's face indicated an instant admiration for the hunk of masculinity he faced.

Julie turned her head and met Robert's warm, hazel eyes and much of her fear drained from her like sand through her fingers. These were not the eyes of a dangerous man, but a man filled with confidence, honor, and intelligence. Her gaze swooped down his body, noting the broad shoulders and narrow hips before settling on his right hand. She took a deep breath before thrusting out her own hand for a welcoming handshake.

Still smiling at Julie, Robert took her hand gently in both of his and moved to bring it to his lips. Ashley nudged him in warning, and he awkwardly shook it instead.

By now Josh openly giggled at Ashley's less-than-subtle cues and Ashley, having at first glared at him, abruptly burst out laughing, too. The moment of tension eased into smiles all around. Robert lifted an eyebrow and looked a bit confused, Julie thought, but his smile was genuine. He was clearly a nice guy.

"Okay, we've got a lot of explaining to do," Ashley conceded with an embarrassed giggle. "You're both going to love this guy as much as I do. Well, maybe not that much." A blush rushed up her face. "But it's all good, so let's *go-o-oh.*"

Josh snickered as his sister spun him around, heading him towards the parking garage with a hand in the center of his back. She grinned impishly over her shoulder at Robert who winked at her and followed in their wake.

Julie brought up the rear. Excited yet fearful, she wondered how all this would play out. *Rick, why are you never here when I need you?*

∞∞∞∞

Ashley insisted Robert ride "shotgun" beside her mother on the way home. The term baffled him, but he understood her purpose when explained. He marveled at what he could see of modern life in Houston from the seat next to Julie. The freeways, however, made him tense, and he cringed as cars whizzed around them. Over and under their car sped as they drove through what Ashley called spaghetti junctions and figure eights on the drive home.

"Does my driving make you uncomfortable, Robert?"

"No, my la-" *That is wrong.* "No, ma'am." He took a deep breath. "Where I come from we have no roads like this." That was an understatement but essentially true.

"Over there, Robert, is the Houston skyline." Ashley pointed to structures that towered over the landscape in the distance.

"Castles?" These buildings dwarfed those in London. What were they? Josh snorted and Julie gave him a long sideways stare. Had he said something wrong?

"That's so . . . poetic." Ashley warned him with her eyes to cease talking, so he did.

"Yeah, these may look like the castle in the old Oz movie from here, but the green hazing effect is probably just pollution."

What was that?

"Houston doesn't have polluted air like that anymore, Josh," Julie said." Don't listen to his blather, Robert. Industries that polluted the air now must change their ways."

That still did not explain it to him, but he sensed he could let it go as a little brother mouthing nonsense. He understood that.

Robert found himself working hard to appear relaxed in what Ashley called a captain's chair when he was anything but at ease. The chair might be comfortable, but the speed of travel disturbed him. Once again, not being in control was bothersome, even unnerving. Meanwhile, he had never seen such sights before. He imagined his eyes popping out while he bit down on his cheeks to keep from saying something Ashley would not like.

She intended to tell her mother and brother their situation once they got to her house, so he tried his best to act calm. He must be failing at the job because Ashley talked nonstop trying to cover for him. Telling them everything about nothing important, she barely took a breath while doing so.

God's blood, he missed home! Was that blood he tasted? His tongue swirled over the tender spot where he had bitten into his cheek. He had to get control of himself before they got to Ashley's place.

Chapter 9

She knew *he* was in the restaurant the minute she walked into McDonald's. Years of casually searching for him everywhere she went had honed her senses to detect his presence. That skill told her he was in the building as easily as if he had smelled like a skunk and had neon lights blaring flashing arrows at his head.

Ryan Sanders is in the house.

Her eyes floated over the customers seated in the booths and landed on the eyes of the guy she sought. Due to her much-embellished tale of skimpy plane food, they were stopping for a late breakfast before going home.

Ashley never dreamed she would find Ryan here.

A year ahead of her in school, she had idolized him since her days as a preschooler at the local Montessori. She recalled vivid memories of him chasing her around the huge outdoor playground while she squealed with glee. Her mom wanted to put a stop to it after he grabbed her by the back of her shirt one day and it ripped up the back. The endearing part was he never quite figured out what to do with her once he caught her. She would giggle and twist a foot in the dirt until his hand loosened, and then she would pull away and launch another chase. That game never got old.

Over their elementary and middle school years they shared a solid connection. During that time Ryan never missed an opportunity to notice her. Once when she fell off the monkey bars in third grade, Ryan was the one to rush up to help her to her feet. He even insisted on walking her to the nurse to get her bloody knees patched up.

By junior high, Ryan was a hunky blue-eyed blond who chose her for every slow song at every school dance. She had been the envy of her friends, much to her delight. But in high school as the varsity football quarterback, Ryan had decided to go his own way. He dated anyone and everyone but Ashley. She remembered tracking his dating throughout his high school years, jealous of every girl. How disappointing to have that longtime friendship drop away like the last "love-me-not" petal pulled off a daisy. She had not laid eyes on him since his graduation a year ago. A couple months later he had moved on to the University of Texas.

As sensitive to her moods as always, Robert responded with concern to the slight tightening of her hand in his. He had no trouble spotting the source of her anxiety, arrowing in on Ryan sitting with some friends across the room. She could feel Robert's tension rachet as he sized up the new guy and judged him a possible physical threat. It was Ryan, however, that pushed the issue further by looking at her in an intimate way that she found cringe-worthy.

Robert raised an eyebrow in surprise at this. She had never told him of an interest in anyone else, and he was not sure what to make of it. Ryan, the beast, would not look at Robert and had eyes only for her. Robert's response was to drop her hand and pull her under his arm in a protective move, as if she might suddenly be snatched away.

Sucking in a breath and somewhat shaken, Ashley met Robert's questioning look. She blinked long and hard as if trying to decide what to do before focusing on her mother and Josh. "Just order us a couple of #7 breakfast sandwiches, an orange juice for me and a coffee for Robert. Thanks." He was going to love coffee.

She paused and blew out her breath. "I need to introduce Robert to the guys over there." She jerked her head in Ryan's direction, making her mom nod in sympathy and Josh grin impishly at her. They were aware of her history with Ryan, and Josh was enjoying her discomfort as only a younger brother could. Ashley shot him a withering glare that fazed him not at all. Reluctantly, she turned Robert toward the crew seated in the corner booth and headed their way.

When Ryan Sanders' eyes locked on hers, it was designed to rankle Robert. Ryan's voice purred like he wanted to reach out and stroke her as he greeted her. "He-e-e-ey, Ashcat! Long time, no see-e-e-e." Standing up slowly to reveal a sculpted body under his tight black t-shirt and khaki shorts, Ryan threw his muscled arms out wide and stepped to her. That left her no choice but to step away from Robert and hug Ryan.

Pulling her too close, Ryan held her too long, and managed to shape her entire backside with his hands as they slid down to land on her hips. Robert would be livid. Ryan tipped her back without releasing her at the waist to gaze into her face. "Wow, Ash, you look fantastic! Where have you been keepin' yourself?" He set her down and took a step back, letting his eyes roam over her and taking time to appreciate each curve. "I've been tryin' to see you since I got home from school."

No, no, no-o-o-o. This could not be happening now. She had waited for Ryan Sanders to pay attention to her for the last five years and nothing. *Nothing.* Now with Robert at her side, he does this?

Ashley glanced uneasily over her shoulder at Robert to gauge his mood. His eyes narrowed on Ryan, but he said nothing. She ignored Ryan's questions and slid back under Robert's arm, taking a deep breath before she launched into the needed introductions.

"Robert, these are some of my *child*hood friends." She let her eyes slide over each of the guys still in the booth as she rattled off their names. "I want you to meet Brandon Blair, Justin Smith, Alex Rodriguez and Ryan Sanders." Ashley smiled up at Robert from under her lashes. He offered her a weak smile in return.

"Guys, this is my f---." She had started to say "fiancé," but realized she hadn't broken this news to her family who were standing only a few feet away. Stuttering for a moment, she substituted, ". . . f-friend from England, R-Robert Spycer."

Robert looked down at her, obviously betrayed at being called a friend rather than her betrothed, but she could only plead with her eyes for him to understand.

Ryan was quick to note her hesitation, as well as Robert's response. "F-friend, huh? Well, good to meet y'all, R-Robert from England." Smirking at Ashley, Ryan jutted out his hand to shake Robert's.

The glint in Robert's eyes told her he would sooner throw Ryan into the nearest wall than shake hands with him. Ashley pleaded silently with a smile not to go there. He was not happy, but at least he understood she wanted this introduction to be bloodless and over.

As he stepped in to grasp Ryan's hand, Ashley was delighted to find Robert was half-a-head taller and the brawnier of the two. She watched him squeeze Ryan's hand until the smirk left his face in favor of a grimace. Then Robert nodded his greeting to the other three guys who were intently watching the faces of the two men battle for supremacy over Ashley's attentions.

To break a moment of awkward silence, Ashley told her friends about her summer as part of her Uncle Zeek's archeological dig near Stonehenge. She indicated she had met Robert there. Only a small stretch, she thought. They were suitably impressed with her travels and eyed Robert speculatively as they asked a few questions about her work. She noted that while Ryan was quite a physical specimen, Robert was even more impressive. Judging from their expressions, she was pleased this was something those still seated, as well as Ryan, did not miss.

When Ashley finished asking about their year away at college, since all were at least a year older, it was time to make their escape. "Well, nice seeing y'all. My beast of a little brother is about to dive into our food, so we need to go back before he does just that."

"Great to see ya, Ashcat!" Ryan winked and smiled his

goodbye through very straight, white teeth. "We'll have to get together sometime real soon." He was still grinning when he turned and nodded toward Robert, but his eyes lost their warmth as they encountered Robert's.

Ashley pulled Robert away before he punched his fist through those sparkling teeth. Really, Ryan didn't know whom he was taunting. "Sure thing," she tossed over her shoulder, squeezing Robert's hand to let him know she didn't mean it. He winked an eye as he tipped his head toward her to let her know he got the message.

Happy to have the encounter over, she led the way to join her mother and Josh at their table on the opposite side of the restaurant. Shoving food into his mouth with both hands, Josh's head popped up as they slid into their seats. He grinned ever-so-innocently at them through the hash browns stuck to his teeth.

"So, how's Ryan, *Ashca-a-t?*"

Ashley winced at the pet name Ryan had given her years ago, thinking of how special she had felt whenever he used it. Now she winced every time she heard it because she knew it made Robert see red.

"Ah, come on, *A-a-shcat!* Answer the question for me, *Ashca-a-t!*"

By now Josh was batting his eyes, pretending to purr, which made him spew hash browns out the corners of his mouth. He was laughing so hard at his own joke that even Robert, as ticked off as he was, couldn't keep his lips from beginning to twitch in amusement. She shook her head in disgust and flashed her eyes at Robert, begging for his sympathy, before she finally bit her lip to keep from cracking a smile.

Brothers! You just gotta love 'em.

∞∞∞

They rolled into Ashley's subdivision a short time later.

Her mom reported over breakfast that Houston had experienced record rains the week before. Everything surrounding the house was a luscious, jungle green. Thick, green plants crowded other thick, green plants, each battling for supremacy, with touches of color from flowering bushes and tiny trees. All was lush and vibrant.

"What are those tall tree trunks with the spiky tops? They offer little shade, do they not?"

Josh thought that was funny and Ashley explained what little she knew about palm trees. As they got closer to her house she ceased her nervous babble and intently sucked in her surroundings like a prisoner given a last meal. She wanted to remember everything once back at Hertford Castle.

Her mom had now taken up the task of keeping a monologue going, but when she turned the corner to their street she stopped mid-sentence. "Ashley, is that *Jasmine* in front of our house?"

Ashley peeked over her mom's shoulder in time to spy her best friend, Jasmine Brown, peering down the street at their car. As always, Jazz had her cell phone glued to her ear. Before Ashley could confirm, Jasmine started bouncing up and down and waving with all her might.

Ashley and her mom laughed in unison, Julie shaking her head affectionately. *"Yuh-huh,* that's Jazz all right. Who else would be that uninhibited in the middle of the sidewalk?"

Jazz ripped open the door the moment their car turned into the driveway and shrilled her welcome home. Jumping out, Ashley pulled Jazz into a bear hug and the two girls danced around with well-matched enthusiasm.

"Oh-ma-god, oh-ma-god, oh-ma-god! It's *so-o-o-o* good to see you, Ash. I've missed you *so-o-o-o* much. You just don't know how boring everything has been around here without you."

"Ah, Jazz, I can't believe you're here. We've only been on the ground an hour. How'd you know I was home?"

"Ash-l-e-e-y, you *have* been gone for a while, haven't ya? The guys tweeted it from McDonald's, silly girl. Everybody prob'ly knows by now." Jazz grabbed Ashley's arm and twisted her around to stand beside her. "Let's get a selfie, so I can tweet 'em back." Ashley had no time to catch her breath, before she found herself looking into Jazz's phone camera still grinning like a kid at Christmas.

Jazz snapped the picture and busied herself tapping buttons on her phone before Ashley had fully recovered her balance.

∞∞∞

Who is this crazy person?

Thankful to step out of this machine called a car, Robert stood next to Ashley and smiled at her friend. When Jazz looked up she froze, struck dumb. Her hands in mid-punch, Jazz's face held a blank expression and her jaw flapped repeatedly until finally words formed for her again. "Oh. My. God."

This Jasmine person was a whirlwind. She was long and skinny with very short, black hair and creamy, dark skin. He had noticed people with skin colors in various shades from light to dark in London and on the way here, but he had not been this close before. She was beautiful. Staring back at him were dark, flashing eyes full of life and an ear-to-ear grin that displayed pearly-white teeth. She wore a brightly colored top and short pants that exposed more skin than they covered. He found himself looking her up and down despite the fact he should be embarrassed for her and avert his eyes. Noting Ashley did not seem to be put out by Jazz's state of undress, he guessed it must be normal here. He did not mind looking, if it did not bother Ashley.

Robert recognized a moment too late Ashley had introduced him, and he should respond. In the midst of bobbing his head to bow, he remembered he was not supposed to do that, so he looked the girl in the eye and smiled. "A pleasure to meet you, Jasmine." He sneaked a peek at Ashley who winked her approval

68

at him. That made him happy.

Jazz's sparkling eyes got bigger with her smile spreading even further across her face. "Girl, you are so-o-o-o busted. No wonder you didn't text me all summer. I believe you were occ-u-pied." Jazz's eyes danced between Ashley and Robert, her thumbs tucked neatly into the belt loops of her cut-offs. "I guess I don't have to ask you if you've had a great time."

Robert put his arm around Ashley and pulled her back against him, which made Ashley turn a deep pink and giggle.

"Hm-hmm, thought so," Jazz ribbed them, good-naturedly. "Well, you two will just have to go to the beach with the gang tomorrow and tell me all about it." She looked pointedly at Ashley. "I want all the details, ma'am." Grinning at Robert, she added, "I'll pick ya up around two. See ya then." She wheeled and headed to her car leaving Ashley to hurriedly check with her mom for permission. Julie's smile told him it must not be a problem.

"Thanks, Jazz. We'll be ready." Jazz appeared not to hear Ashley since she was already absorbed with punching at her phone again. She climbed into her bright red machine and departed with a screech moments later, waving her goodbye out the window.

"This trip might all work out perfectly, Robert. I can say good-bye to all my friends at once, and they can meet you." As they followed her mom and Josh toward the house, Ashley whispered, "We have to make them understand everything tonight."

"We shall do our best." He kissed her cheek and silently prayed all would go well, so they could go back to Hertford as planned. He was ready to go home now, but he reminded himself he was on Ashley's time, not his own. He would be as friendly to her friends and family as he could be. That was important to Ashley. He would do it for her.

Chapter 10

Robert enjoyed Ashley's tour of her home. He was surprised to find it so very small compared with Hertford Castle, but he told her he liked all the things stuffed into it. To him every room over-flowed with a wealth of furniture, pictures, plants, rugs, pillows, etc. So many *things.* He had glanced into Ashley's closet only to be amazed by the number of clothing items she possessed. They agreed his sister Elena would pass out with excitement over that much clothing. When he questioned how anyone wore it all, she had to admit, he had a point.

Josh's room held greater appeal for Robert with its multitude of sports and video equipment. All the technology intrigued him. He had enjoyed Zeek's laptop and seeing more devices excited him.

The beds stacked on top of one another were a different story. He consented to sleep in Josh's room on the bottom bed because she insisted, but the knowledge Josh would be sleeping in the bunk above worried him. She thought that was pretty cute.

Ashley left Robert with her brother expounding on his video games, so she and her mom would have a moment or two alone. She had a lot of explaining to do, and now was as good a time as any to start.

Julie joined her daughter in the living room with two tall glasses of iced-tea in hand. As they sat side by side on the couch to sip and catch up, Ashley noted her mom's painting above the couch and smiled to herself. *It does look like Alice and Meggie.* What might the two sisters at Hertford be arguing about now?

Ashley sighed. Where to begin?

As usual, her mom couldn't wait and beat her to the punch, cutting right to the chase.

"So, what time period is Robert from?"

Ashley's mouth dropped open and for a moment all she did was stare at her mom.

"How did you know?"

"Sweetheart, not too many men have bowed when introduced to me, and I don't think anyone has ever tried to kiss my hand."

A nervous giggle escaped Ashley, and she took a sip of her tea to calm herself. "Yeah, you would notice that, wouldn't you?"

"Yeah," her mother replied. "You know how I am."

"Mom, Dad was a Guardian of the Stones, wasn't he? Is that why he traveled so much?"

Julie nodded, her eyes filling with bright tears.

"Did Dad time walk and not return? Is that what happened to him and why he vanished?"

A lifetime of memories sprinted through her mother's face as she struggled to find her voice. "Yes," she breathed. "I wondered if you had put all that together, sweetie."

Now tears flooded Ashley's eyes and robbed her tongue of words. Julie reached out and pulled her in for a hug and a kiss on her cheek. The two sat in silence for a moment, each wrestling with her own thoughts.

"He came to me in a dream, Mom."

"Your dad?" Julie pulled back and searched Ashley's eyes. "Really?"

"Really. I think Dad is still alive, Mom. I think he's stuck wherever he went and can't make it home yet."

Julie grabbed Ashley's hands and clasped them in her own. "What m-makes you say that?"

"Well, he told me in the dream he wasn't lost. He said he had to stay there for a while." Julie's brows lifted and her breath caught. "He said we shouldn't worry and it was too complicated for him to explain it to me right then."

Hope flickered to life in her mom's face. Ashley prayed she was not wrong, and her dad lived, because the last thing she wanted to do was give her mother false hope. The loss of her dad had been crushing for her whole family, but especially for her mom.

Carefully, Julie licked her lips and asked quietly, as if a loud sound might scare away the answer she wanted to hear, "You're sure about this? One Guardian to another?"

Ashley's face split into a grin. "Yeah, Mom, Guardian to Guardian. She gave her mom's hand a gentle squeeze.

Julie sucked in a breath and burst out laughing a moment later. "Yes, yes, *ye-e-e-es!* This is the sign I hoped for. Some kind of message that your dad's alive." She thrust her hands above her head in supplication to the heavens and cried, *"Whoo-hoo!* Thank you, Rick, thank you. I always believed if you weren't dead you would find some way to let me know."

Tears streamed down her face, "I love you, honey." She wiped them away with one hand, tossed her head back and added to the universe, "Don't worry, baby, we'll find you." She caught Ashley's eye, still not able to keep from laughing and crying at the same time. "I don't know how we're going to do that, but I have to believe with your help, we can... can't we?"

Her mother avoided meeting her daughter's eyes, fearing the reply would be negative. A wave of sympathy flowed over Ashley, making her silently vow to keep her mother's happy bubble intact for as long as possible. They would have to figure it out together. Tears of love flowed for both mother and daughter allowing neither to speak, so Ashley nodded, and her mom smiled.

Having heard his mother's shriek, Josh came whooshing into the room with Robert on his heels. "Everything all right in here?" He studied his mother's face and his sister's. "You're both crying, but you're smiling?" He shook his head and glared at them.

"Women!" Disgust mixed with confusion played across his

young face. "Why? Why are you two boohooing? What's happened?"

Robert took up the space beside Ashley, dropping an anxious hand on her shoulder while frowning the same question to her.

Julie spoke first, still smiling, "Sit down, Josh . . . Robert. We have to talk."

Robert found the easy chair closest to Ashley and sat down, his soft, hazel eyes searching her face for signs of trouble. Josh threw himself into the overstuffed chair across from his mother and plunked his bare feet down on the oak coffee table that separated them. Julie scowled, giving him her patented irritated-mom look to move his dirty feet off the table. Just like old times, Ashley watched Josh purposely ignore their mom until she warned him again, "J-o-o-sh . . . " The lady was not above embarrassing him in front of Robert if he didn't cooperate.

Josh grinned big to let her know he was messing with her before he complied. Julie rolled her eyes at him, but a telltale smile ticked up the corner of one side of her mouth. Josh had a knack for making anyone smile. He worked that talent anytime their mom's mood prevented her from telling them what bothered her.

"Well, it seems we have a lot to talk about," Julie began by securing three sets of eyes on hers. "I don't think we can afford to keep any more secrets from each other and there is much to share."

Josh squirmed in his chair and Julie's eyes shifted to Josh's with a mother's tenderness. "And you, Josh, have been kept in the dark for too long."

Josh twisted one side of his mouth up to meet the nearest eyebrow in disbelief. "What are you talking about, Mom? Am I adopted or something?" He looked around at the others expecting a smile, and instead found three faces staring sympathetically at him. *"What?* Are you saying I *am* adopted?"

"No, idiot-bro!" He cringed when she called him that, but

he deserved it after his *Ashcat* tease. "She means that I discovered the family secret by accident, and now you need to be told before something similar happens to you."

"Oh, is that all." Josh plopped his feet unceremoniously back on the coffee table. "So we got bodies buried in the basement or somethin'?" He glanced around at all three. "Care to be a little less cryptic ... anyone?"

"Ooh, *cryptic.* Good vocabulary word, Joshie," Now Ashley grinned ear-to-ear. It was so much fun to rankle her brother.

"Stop it, you two. To think I have missed having you both at home," Julie chided. "And get your feet off the coffee table, young man." She sighed in exasperation and turned to speak to Robert. "Sorry! Do you have siblings that tease each other like these two?"

"I do ... Mrs. Duvall." Ashley confirmed his choice of address as the right one with a quick wink.

"Robert's little brother Elric and his sister Elena were my best friends before I met Robert. Elric is seventeen and Elena is fifteen. You'd love 'em both, Josh."

Not to be sidetracked Josh's curiosity burned in his face, "So what don't I know?"

"For starters, Josh, your sister doesn't believe your dad is dead." Stricken by this information, Josh jerked his head from his mom to Ashley for confirmation.

"*Yup!* He came to me in a dream to tell me he is stuck in time and can't get home."

Josh deflated like a balloon. "A dream? You believe a *dream?*"

"It's a bit more than that, Josh." Ashley sat forward and locked eyes with her brother. "What do you know about time travel?"

"Okay, you guys do know what cryptic *means,* right? Vague, veiled . . .?" He squirmed, uncomfortable in his chair. "Where is this going? Why are we talking about fantasy stuff?" Josh complained, turning to their mother in hopes she would intervene.

She did.

"Because it isn't fantasy."

Two beats fell while Josh examined his mother's face. He shook his head. "Now you've lost me. Can one of you start at the beginning?"

"Sure, honey." Julie acknowledged the encouraging look Ashley sent her with a nod. "Your dad and I met at the university when I was a sophomore and he was a senior. Your Uncle Zeek, by the way, was a freshman that year. From the moment I spotted your dad it was love at first sight." Her eyes teared as her face melted into the memories. "He was so wonderful and exactly what I was looking for."

"Did you meet him in class?" Ashley asked.

"Ah, that was sort of the funny part." Julie's eyes twinkled. "I was dating a varsity football player pursued by the pros. He was injured on a play late in one game when your dad, a trainer for the team, helped him off the field." Julie smirked at her kids. "I needn't tell you which guy was the bigger deal. It was Texas, after all. Anyway, I shot to my boyfriend's side in a flash since I was already on the field as part of the cheer squad and-"

"You were a cheerleader?" Josh's voice cracked in amazement, making Ashley snort. "Dang, Ma, what else have you not told me?" He took a deep breath. "Oh, yeah, all this. Go on."

"Well, I won't keep you in suspense. My boyfriend acted like a total jerk before it was all over. He was hurt and all, but still. Your dad was so handsome, mature, and professional in his handling of the situation I couldn't dump this other guy fast enough. After that, I had to turn on the charm to encourage Rick to ask me out, but then we were pretty much joined at the hip thereafter."

Robert's brow puckered over that last bit and Ashley whispered, "She means they were together all the time after that." The corner of Robert's mouth twitched as he nodded his understanding.

"So what, then?" Josh's impatience surfaced again.

"We dated for a while without incident, but then Rick just

dropped out of sight for over a couple of weeks three separate times. Each time he left without any warning, his whereabouts unknown. When he got back he wouldn't say where he'd been, either. He made one lame excuse after another." Julie shuddered. "It made me feel so insecure. I didn't know if he was seeing someone else, or if he was engaged in some illegal activity like drug smuggling, or with the Mafia, or whatever. I imagined all kinds of things."

"So, where did he go?"

Julie ignored Josh and continued with her story. "It became a real source of contention between us. Finally, I told him if he didn't tell me where he was going and when I could expect him back, we were done." She shook her head at her kids. "I couldn't live like that always wondering what was going on. Unhappy about that, he sat me down and told me I wouldn't believe him if he told me. I said, 'Try me!' and so he told me."

"M-o-o-o-m! Just spit it out!"

She did.

"He told me he was a Guardian of the Stones and a time walker." She sent Josh a silent, "So there!"

Josh's face was blank for a moment. "So what, he's one of the X-Men? Seriously, Mom, what did he say?"

Ashley was enjoying her brother's fluster, but decided she had better rescue her mother. "She's telling you the truth, meathead. I know because I've time walked, too." Her air of superiority made Josh grind his teeth.

"Oh, yeah? How stupid do you think I am?"

"You're not stupid, Josh, but it is true. Robert is from another time a few *centuries* ago, so he can vouch for what I'm saying."

"So it's true!" Julie gasped and studied Robert until her face flushed.

"Come on, Ash, this is ridiculous. I'm supposed to believe Robert is from another time? What, like some lord from *Game of Thrones* or something?" He cackled at his own witticism and checked to see if everyone else appreciated it.

Robert smiled and directed his response to Ashley. "We played that video game in Josh's room. Most fascinating." She nodded agreement, and he turned to focus his attention on Josh. "'Tis a bit different, though. My father is the lord, the Earl of Hertford, and I am his heir. We live at Castle Hertford, which resembles something of Winterfell in your game."

Josh could not shut his jaw and glared at each of them, not sure if any of them were to be believed. A moment later, his suspicion cleared and a lopsided grin emerged. He turned his attention to Robert and cocked his head. "Wait . . . is that why you said the warrior in the video used the mace wrong?"

Robert nodded, "Yes."

Julie had recovered enough to gingerly ask, "Robert, what time period do you come from?"

He glanced at Ashley and then answered the question. "The year in my time is 1363, Mrs. Duvall."

"So long ago? *Oh, my!*" Julie's hands flew to her face in astonishment. "I'm not so sure I want to know all this. God help me if I lose Ashley to 1363." She thought for a minute before she pulled her hands from her face. "Or, are you here because you have chosen to live in Ashley's time?" She kept her hands still in her lap while she listened intently for the answer she hoped to hear.

"You're all *serious*, aren't you?"

Their three heads bobbed up and down as Josh whipped his head from one to another in sheer shock. Everyone was quiet while the truth was digested. Soon the silence was too much for him. "You said Dad was a Guardian of the Stones. What's that?"

"The family secret, Josh. Our dad is a Guardian, and I found out I'm one, too. That's the family secret you need to know about."

The next few minutes were the longest ones in the poor kid's life. Josh's head was undoubtedly spinning as he tried to comprehend the story of Ashley's unintended visit to a time over 650 years ago. All courtesy of an inscription on a stone. He couldn't wrap his head around it when she explained Guardians of the Stones could travel from one time period to another in order to help mankind grow. Ashley told him of a witch, *yes, a witch*, who had told her she was to help women gain some human rights and not be so subjugated. She told Josh and her mom about Elena and about the marriage of Elric and Charissa.

Josh's eyes popped out when he realized the two were only seventeen and fifteen. Ashley was happy Josh thought that was crazy, too. But when she told them about the plan to marry her off to a baron over twice her age without her consent, Josh's confusion cleared. He looked at her with new respect as he began to understand she had stood up to a powerful man without having the right to do so in that world.

Their mom seemed to be taking it all in with an eerie calm that had Ashley shaking her head in amazement. Julie picked up the story from Ashley and described what she knew of her husband's travels through time. Their dad would tell her he would be gone for a while, but never for how long or to what locale. He would wait to tell her the specifics after he got home. He told her he didn't want her to worry by expecting him within a certain time frame he might not be able to uphold. Plus, he didn't want her to sit around and wonder about any specific location in time. All the partial unknowns were much worse than the complete unknown in his opinion. Their mother had not liked any of it, but accepted when she wed him that he would travel without her.

"Kids, your dad worked as an independent mechanical engineer, so he was free to time walk for swatches of time without anyone noticing he was gone. He told me the most amazing stories of his experiences visiting different time periods. He wanted to share them with you himself one day. I'm so sorry he never had the chance before he disappeared." Julie's voice trembled over the last words as she sucked in a steadying breath. "Ashley, if you are truly a Guardian of the Stones like your father, I'll have no choice but to accept it, just like I did with your dad. But, sweetie, I'm not sure I can handle all this again."

"I know, Mom. I know." Ashley understood all too well

what she meant. "What role did he play as a Guardian? What did he try to do for mankind?"

For a moment it looked as if Julie wouldn't answer as she stared into space, but then the question registered with her. "It seemed to evolve over time, honey." The pain caused by his disappearance showed in her face. She fiddled with the wedding ring she still wore, twisting it around and around her finger. "It started out he would help people with simple engineering since that was part of what he had trained to do in college. But eventually, he added basic medical care since it was always so lacking everywhere he went. As an athletic trainer he wanted to learn more, so he studied in his free time to become an EMT. That gave him a few other ways to help people." A wistful smile flitted across her face. "He loved returning home having made a difference. He was forever amazed at what a little sanitation engineering and a little first aid could do to help conditions wherever he went. Those were his calling cards."

Ashley thought of the lack of plumbing around the garderobe along with the filthy moat at Hertford Castle and knew why her dad had needed to do what he did. She sneaked a peek at Robert, wondering if he had made the same connection and found him lost in thought.

"Damn. Er, dang!" Josh corrected himself as his mother raised a brow. "I actually have an X-Men dad and now I know a real lord of a castle." Everything was starting to register with him, and Ashley was not surprised he found it all pretty mind-blowingly awesome. In fact, now he stared at Robert with eyes wide with wonder and excitement. "Hey, Robert, could you teach me how to fight like a warrior with a mace . . . or . . . or maybe a longbow?"

Robert almost contained his grin at Josh's exuberance, but his lips quirked at the corners giving him away. "Of course, Josh. You remind me of my brother." A shadow crossed his face at the thought of Elric. Ashley knew Robert wondered, as she did, if they would ever make it back to Hertford Castle again.

Ashley felt her mother's eyes on her and turned to find her

mom studying her.

"What?" An unspoken question held court on her mom's face.

"You haven't explained how Robert arrived with you."

As if strings were attached, Ashley found herself pulled to the arm of Robert's chair. Her arm snaked around Robert's shoulder and his around her waist.

She grinned at him, his soft hazel eyes holding her spellbound. "That part was unplanned."

Ashley tore her gaze from Robert's eyes and found those of her mom and little brother. "With Dad still missing, I couldn't just disappear, too. I knew what that would do to you." Julie winced and Josh stilled. "You see, Robert and I are betrothed . . . that's engaged, Josh, and I intend to marry Robert and live with him at Hertford Castle."

Julie let out the breath she had been holding with a slow hiss. She dropped her face into her hands once again, but spoke not a word. Ashley was sorry she had to confirm her mother's worst fears. Stifling a sob, her mom was having trouble catching her breath.

"You're getting married? For real?" Josh's eyes darted from Ashley to Robert and back again, as if he couldn't quite envision his sister marrying anyone, let alone someone like Robert. "So's Robert a Guardian, too? Am I a Guardian?"

"Good questions, little bro. Robert is not a Guardian and I don't know if you are or not."

"How'd you get here, Robert, if you aren't a Guardian?" Josh struggled to make the puzzle pieces fit.

"I heard Olde Gylda tell Ashley the stones would reveal themselves to a Guardian for use when needed, but they could be used by anyone if found by chance. That is why the stones hide themselves after a Guardian uses them to prevent that kind of accident." Robert gazed up at Ashley to find her smiling at him. "I cannot describe the pain of watching Ashley call upon the stone and then disappear. I believed I might never see her again." Ashley reached down and gave Robert a gentle kiss on his forehead. "I waited for everyone else to go inside and then dug up the stone I had watched slide into the earth. I repeated the inscription over it three times and followed her."

Josh bounced in his chair, letting Robert's words sink in. "Whoa, so if Robert can follow Ashley here, I can follow you guys there. Right, Ash? Even if I'm not a Guardian." The mere thought excited him to the max. "Mom, can I go back with them? It'd only be for a while. Then I'd come back home. *Please? Please?*"

∞∞∞∞

Julie had listened to Robert's story and was beside herself with worry, pain, excitement, and awe, each rocketing through her at the same time. She was afraid to give herself over to the hope travel between time periods might work both ways. *Oh, please let it be so.* Maybe Rick could come back and Ashley wouldn't go to Robert's world forever as she feared at first. Maybe she could go *with* Josh to visit. With that thought, it was as if the darkness lifted and whole new worlds spread before her like choice chocolates in a box. She could do this. She could.

"Wow," Julie cried, her head whirling. "What a lot to take in." Her gaze sharpened on Robert. "I had thought you were a Guardian, too. I had no idea anyone calling upon a stone could use it. Rick never told me that. At least he never asked me to go with him on his travels."

"That would be so cool, man." Josh was in alt.

Julie grimaced at her son who was still enthralled with the thought of traveling back in time. "Slow down, buddy. We don't have enough information to be certain it is even possible. Ashley and Robert may not be able to go back." Josh looked crestfallen, but agreed his mom had a point. "It would be a blessed relief, however, if we could all travel at will back and forth." She smiled sideways at her daughter, her eyes misting, "I don't think I could survive if all my family disappeared on me."

"I know that, Mom. Otherwise, I wouldn't be here. My

destiny lies with Robert in his world. At least that's what Olde Gylda prophesied and I believe her."

Julie rose to her feet, her eyes never leaving Ashley's, and found her way to her daughter through the tears blurring her vision. She slipped an arm around each of them. "You are so very young Ashley, but I am aware you and Robert are up to this challenge and love each other. If not, you wouldn't be time-crossing worlds to be with one another."

She lightly dropped a kiss on the top of each head and sighed heavily. "Who am I to tell you that you can or cannot be together?" Fighting to gain control of her emotions, Julie stood and offered a hand to each which Robert and Ashley took without hesitation. "I can only give you my blessing and pray I will see you again once you leave here."

In an instant Ashley was in her mother's arms sobbing right along with her mom. Watching them, Robert understood why Ashley had insisted on traveling back to clear things with her mother. Torn between two worlds himself, he was not impervious to the pain each woman felt.

If there was this much hurt involved, were they doing the right thing? His heart skipped a beat as he considered life without Ashley ... before it thudded again more sure than ever. Ashley was his. They belonged together.

They would do whatever they had to do to stay together.

Chapter 11

The night air was heavy with sound, tiny tree frogs competing for the melody with cicadas tuned up and already singing. Robert and Ashley found refuge in the A-frame swing tucked into a secluded corner of the backyard. Ashley had forgotten how thick the air could be after dark in Houston, wrapping around her like a dip in the pool. It might easily be 98 degrees at midnight in this climate. Very tropical, yet home. She settled comfortably into Robert's side, his arm cushioning her head as he stroked her hair.

"Is it always this . . . moist at night?" Ashley laughed out loud at that. Was he reading her thoughts?

"Absolutely! It's strange, isn't it? Since it rarely freezes here everything keeps growing and growing with no time off for cold weather." She flicked off a mosquito and added with a shudder of disgust, "Even the bugs. You know, insects, as in mosquitoes."

"Something tells me you are not a fan of these bugs anywhere."

"*Uh* . . . you'd be right. They bug me." Noting Robert's confusion over her use of the expression, she explained the idiom. "They irritate or annoy me." He nodded, "You mean they find you delicious, too.

"Yeah, 'fraid so. Remind me to introduce you to roaches and fire ants sometime," she grimaced. "After that, no doubt you'll be right there agreeing with me."

"Dost thou know what buggeth me?" Robert teased, his eyes narrowing to hoods as they landed on Ashley's. Having seen that look before, Ashley's whole body shivered despite the warm temperature.

"Do tell," she managed to eke out, her anticipation flaring.

"Not enough alone time with--." The last word was lost as his mouth closed over hers in a smoldering kiss, at last in complete accord with one another.

Dinner had been wonderful with high-spirited catching up and tales of their adventures shared. Still, they all knew their time together would be limited, which placed a tension on the whole evening that was palpable. It was like trying to outrun the inevitable. Escaping to the backyard was a relief and a release.

Her mom and brother seemed to accept Robert as part of the family without difficulty, and Robert appeared more than happy to be with them. Ashley marveled at how Robert won her mother over while they dined. Were his shy smiles wistful because he remembered his own mother, now long gone? Josh was pumped about every aspect of life at Hertford Castle. The bonds formed tonight would have to be strong enough to withstand all the absences to follow.

Ashley pulled back from their kiss, gasping for air, and reached for Robert's face, a hand on either side of his head. "Robert, do you have any idea how much I love---"

But Robert was in no mood for words. Breaking her hold, he pulled Ashley securely onto his lap and wrapped his arms around her like double steel bands. A sigh broke through their kiss as Ashley relaxed into him. She wanted to be nowhere else but here in Robert's arms. Maybe. Just. Forever.

Robert's hand slid under Ashley's loose summer top and a smile almost broke his kiss as he appreciated one nice feature of current clothing styles. She knew easy access to a lover's under things excited him because she wore no under things beneath her top. When his hand shaped her curves underneath the halter-top, she decided Robert needed no extra help to adjust to her modern wear.

In her opinion, Robert needed to wear fewer clothes in

this heat, too, so she grabbed the hem of his tee and pulled up with all her might. Robert got her message and relinquished his find long enough to lose his shirt. Greedily, Ashley ran her hands over his beautiful body and found herself straddling Robert which then presented her bottom for an inviting squeeze that left both of them panting.

Discovering Ashley's shorts were not fitted at the waist, Robert ran a hand right inside and smoothed over her bare bottom. Locked in a battle of tongues with one hand grasping her bottom and the other a breast, Robert was one happy man.

That is until the back door popped open and Josh bolted out hollering, "Hey, you guys, had enough of mosquito heaven for one night?"

With the slam of the backdoor, both sat up and began putting themselves to rights. They searched madly for the t-shirt Ashley had ditched over her shoulder. She found it and tossed it to Robert who shoved his arms through it inside out and backwards judging from the tag displayed under his chin.

"Anybody wanna play *Game of Thrones, or Fortnite?* I've got *Scourge of War: Gettysburg in 3D* that Grandpa sent for my birthday . . . Hey, where *are* you guys?"

Hearing him tramp along the crushed granite walkway, they plopped fully clothed back into the swing side-by-side at the same moment Josh rounded the corner and spotted them. Something must have registered in Josh's mind as he stopped and stared at them in the moonlight. Perhaps it was the tousled hair or the too-bright smiles pasted on their faces. Or, perhaps it finally occurred to him they were, in fact, actual lovers, a too-much-information-thought for Josh. They felt his embarrassment in the dark at finding them as clearly as if they had seen him blush in daylight.

One would have thought Josh had been caught doing something embarrassing, rather than the other way around. Robert gave Ashley a sideways grin of apology. "'Twould be interesting, Josh. I shall be in to join you soon."

Josh could not leave fast enough. In fact, the backdoor

slammed before Robert had finished his sentence.

His hasty exit prompted Ashley and Robert to burst out laughing as they found each other for one last steamy kiss. Robert reared back some time later long enough to ask the question bothering him, "What is "Gettysburg in 3D?"

Ashley answered with a firm swat up the side of his head, followed by a scorching kiss.

Josh could wait.

Chapter 12

Ashley awoke to the sun streaming into her room around 8 a.m. because she had forgotten to close her blinds again. Ah well, some things never change. Sound sleep, an impossibility due to jet lag and an emotionally charged evening, had escaped her even though she was bone tired. Squinting into the morning brightness, she rolled over, stuffed an extra pillow under her head and wondered if Robert still slept.

Around 4 a.m. she had been awakened by *thunks* that sounded like intruders breaking into the house. Scared, she had found a baseball bat in the hall closet and gone to investigate. As it turned out, Robert was showing Josh how to take out an enemy without a weapon during a break from the game monitors. *Males. Wrestling.* Although tempted, she had not swung the bat at them. Good thing! Maybe they were just little boys at heart, but the fact they had bonded, pleased her. She would let Robert sleep a little longer if need be.

Jazz would be coming at two to pick them up for the beach, so that left a good deal of time this morning for a tour of town, perhaps. She looked forward to showing Robert around, but she also needed to maximize every precious moment of her time here at home.

Her eyes roamed over the familiar contents of her room, of her life here in this world. Stuffed with her collection of angel knick-knacks, classic rock posters, frilly pink pillows, dried prom flowers, and tons of clothes, it held her former life. Strange how she had not missed this room much while at Hertford.

Expendable.

All of it was expendable. The only thing she really would miss would be her mom and her brother . . . and perhaps Jazz. The rest was just stuff. Stuff had never made her happy.

She squirmed in her bed as she thought of what did make her happy.

Robert.

Even if life would be more different than she ever thought possible, she knew she would gladly trade her life here for the one with Robert at Hertford Castle.

She would, however, enjoy the shower while she had one. Ashley slid out of bed and headed to the bathroom.

∞∞∞

"No-o-o, not so fast, Robert." Ashley's squeal turned into a giggle.

"God's blood," Robert cursed, popping his foot off the accelerator. The car slowed so fast they were thrust forward in a head-snapping whiplash before screeching to a stop, another jerk happening once his foot stomped on the brake.

They stilled for a moment. Then Robert did a slow take, turning to Ashley with a heart-stopping, mind-blowing grin that could not decide if it was thrilled or horrified. That made her cackle in glee all over again. He laughed with her until they howled so hard they had trouble sitting up.

Starting off after breakfast to take a drive around Ashley's old stomping grounds, she caught Robert watching her every move as she handled the SUV. It was obvious he wanted her spot behind the wheel. That would be fun.

As she circled the parking lot at the high school, Ashley finished describing her final four under-whelming years of school, but Robert had ceased to listen. His eyes were on the steering wheel. With the parking lot deserted, she realized he would be able to try his hand at driving without encountering anyone else. Only a couple of cars sat in the student parking lot with about a mile of empty pavement glaring up at them in heat waves off the morning sun.

Ashley proceeded to painstakingly explain the operation of a vehicle to Robert. She demonstrated starting, stopping and turning for him, emphasizing the similarities between the foot feet and a horse's mouth. Light, gentle pressure was much better than hard pressure.

He missed that part.

When Robert dropped his booted foot on the accelerator, the SUV took off like a cannonball shot across the pavement. Ashley shrilled for him to stop, and so he did, nearly hurtling them through the window.

"Perhaps my horse needs a kinder foot."

"You think?" Ashley wiped tears of laughter from her eyes.

"I did not realize how powerful this is. Your machine is so big and heavy I thought it would be harder to make it move than it is."

"Ah, no wonder you drive with such a heavy foot. Hey, at last someone with a heavier foot than mine! Don't tell my mom."

"Might I try again?" Robert held his breath waiting for her answer, itching for a second try at controlling the beast.

"Sure. Just press gently, gently this time, okay?"

"Yes, my lady." Seconds later, they both snorted as Robert inched across the parking lot in not-so-subtle lurches. Determined not to give up, Robert soon got the hang of it, and giggles aside, he wheeled them around the school like a pro. After the tenth smooth swing around the parking lot, Ashley declared Robert's driving lessons a success.

"Home, James. Mom will be expecting us for lunch."

Robert's heart stuttered like his earlier driving and he shot a glance at Ashley, careful to avoid her eyes. "Who is James?"

For a moment Ashley frowned at him, puzzled by his

question, then her face lightened into a smile. "Oh . . . got it. That's an expression, Robert. *James* used that way refers to the driver of a chauffeured vehicle." She chewed her lip as she tried to explain another troublesome idiom. "Sort of like the name for the driver of a wagon or carriage?" Her voice trailed up along with her eyebrows as she did her best to describe its meaning.

"Ah, I am happy 'tis not another man I need worry about."

"You mean like Ryan Sanders?"

Robert paused before nodding, as if embarrassed to admit it.

Surprised, Ashley's brows shot up and her eyes widened. "You don't ever have to worry about any competition from another man, Robert." She reached over and grabbed his arm to make him look her in the eye. "Remember that."

Robert gifted her with his heart-stopping smile before heading out of the parking lot to Ashley's house, only a few blocks away. He appeared satisfied for the moment, but Ashley worried that his insecurity in her world still niggled deep inside him.

∞∞∞∞

Ashley knew from the moment they hit the beach something weird was going on. Way too many people were here. Many she didn't recognize. Yet, her old crew rushed to surround her with open arms. It was awesome to see them, but she sensed something was still wrong. Stiffness and a reserve clothed everyone they met like a starched t-shirt or itchy shorts.

Tension filled the air. She and Robert had quarreled about dress for the beach after lunch and feelings were still tender. He had come unglued when she bopped out of the bedroom in her bikini carrying only a t-shirt. He wanted no one else to see her so unclothed and no amount of explaining would make him change his mind. She finally borrowed a cover-up from her mom and felt like an idiot wearing it. Even when Jazz teased her about it in the car, she chose not to feed the fight with Robert.

As they walked from the parking area to the beach, Robert caught her eye at the first barely clad beach-goers and his expression turned a tad sheepish, she thought. Was he sorry for the argument? He had agreed to wear the board shorts and t-shirt they had picked up from Walmart for him, but he still thought himself under-dressed. Now he was forced to admit Ashley was right about what her friends would wear. Duly chagrined, his nose scrunched up as he mouthed the word "Sorry!" She winked back, and they smiled at each other, relieved to have made up.

Still, some weird vibe hung over the crowd. Was it due to Robert's presence? Did his size intimidate them . . . or his looks? She hugged and chatted with her longtime friends Maddie and Jess and then searched the crowd for Robert. She found him swarmed by a half dozen bikini-clad girls she did not know. He must not be that intimidating after all, if they were begging him to join their beach volleyball team.

He didn't know how to play volleyball, so he did not take his eyes off Ashley, hoping she would intervene. Was that what upset him, or was it the scantily clad females hanging all over him? *Bless him.* The poor guy was simultaneously excited by the modern styles and horrified by their impropriety. Still, it was these females-from-wherever with their hands all over his person that really ticked her off.

Okay, enough! Get your hands off my guy.

Moving to rescue Robert she spotted *him*, a man-shark skimming through an innocent school of girl-fish. Ryan Sanders rose from the sea in their midst as if Poseidon himself, and tread a beeline toward her. He left a wake of spurned females behind him, his eyes holding hers, so she dare not look away.

He was beautiful. Tall, tanned, his impressive pecs glistening in the sun. No question but what he commanded an audience, and he certainly held one here. To everyone in view he was dumping the girls he'd been playing with in the water *for her*.

What was going on? Why was Ryan here . . . and with her crowd? Then the obvious hit her. Her appearance did not surprise him one bit.

He had been waiting.

For her.

Was the atmosphere so stilted because Lord Ryan was running the show once again? He had been gone for a year at college, yet he still controlled the underclassmen like a master puppeteer. *Amazing.* She pulled her eyes from Ryan's long enough to find Robert who was missing not a moment of Ryan's progress toward her.

The sun beat down with white light on the beach, and a fishy smell wafted in with the breeze. The combination of sea, sand and sun made her woozy, like seeing a desert mirage. He couldn't be real. Could he? She wobbled, dazzled and confused.

Suddenly, Jazz was beside her apologizing and with an explanation for everything.

"Ryan made us bring you to this beach, Ashley. You know how he is when he decides he wants something."

"Are you saying you knew about this?" The heat of betrayal colored her face.

"Not exactly. Remember I tweeted you were back yesterday and it kinda went viral around town from there."

"What? No one ever cared where I went before. Why now?"

Jazz snorted at the truth of Ashley's words. "Because now Ryan wants *you.*"

"Me?" Ashley's eyes burned so hot Jazz squinted into them as if seeing sunspots and took an awkward step back. "You've got to be kidding me. He hasn't so much as sent a smile my way for years. What would he want with me now?"

"Don't know," Jazz glowered. "Ask him."

Ryan descended upon them a second later, stopping a step too close for comfort inside Ashley's personal space. With sympathy, Jazz reached up and squeezed her shoulder before escaping to talk to Maddie, leaving Ashley to fend for herself with Ryan.

"Hey, Ashcat."

"Hey," Ashley watched water sluice off Ryan's hair and drip from his chin.

He gave her a twisted smile, turned around, leaned down and shook his head like a dog to shed the water. He stood extra tall and posed. "Better?"

Ashley laughed at his silliness. "Not really. It's your hair."

"What's wrong with my hair?" Ryan smirked.

"Have you been trying to pull it out or have little sea creatures played havoc on your head?" She gestured for him to get the picture. "You have tufts."

"Why don't you smooth it down for me, then." He bent over and invited her to touch him.

"Uh, I think I'll pass." An unintended growl of disapproval came out her mouth. She stepped out of Ryan's way and sneaked a glance at Robert to see if he was watching.

He was.

"Ooh, gr-ow-rrr!" Ryan grinned and pretended to claw the air. "I like."

"I don't," Ashley snapped. "What's going on? I don't have time for this game." She peeked again at Robert, but Ryan followed her gaze and caught her this time.

"What's the matter, Ash-kitty? Can't make a move without the *boyfriend* over there? Are you afraid he might be mad if you talked to another guy?" He flexed his muscles while he popped his knuckles, like he'd love to fight Robert for her.

"You don't understand what you're saying, Ryan." Ashley sent her best reassuring smile to Robert. He did not look happy, and she had no doubt he would defend what he believed to be his, if challenged. This scene could turn dangerous in a hurry. She rummaged through her head for a way to lighten the situation. Her eyes flipped back to Robert only to find he'd been dragged into the volleyball game, not a happy camper, and a solution popped into her brain.

"Come on, Ryan, let's go play some volleyball," She took off on a run toward Robert. "You'll never beat me," she all but purred, trying to take the sting out of the taunt.

The two sides had already formed evenly when Ashley attached herself to Robert's side, so Ryan had no choice but to join the opposition. He scowled angrily upon arriving a few steps behind Ashley, his feet kicking up sand in silent protest. Playing a game was clearly not Ryan's plan.

The girls on the other team made pouty lips at Ashley and grumbled as she took her place beside Robert. They got over it and smiled a moment later, though, when Ryan joined their side.

Who were these beach babes? As they fired off greetings to Ryan, she got her answer. Of course, they were Ryan Sanders devotees--just followers of the *Ryanator. Ugh.* They actually called him that. How had she ever found this egomaniac attractive?

Sensing there might be a show, a crowd congregated on both sides of the sand court. Robert looked worried as Ashley caught his eye.

"Thou knowest I have ne'er seen a volleyball before. What must I do?"

"You'll be fine, Robert," she soothed. "Just watch what everyone else does and do the same. The object is to hit the ball back to the other team, but keep it inside the court in the field of play." Now he looked even more troubled. "You'll catch on quickly. Just stay by me and I'll cover for you until you get the hang of it." He nodded, but his lips formed a straight line and his body tensed.

Ashley saw Robert give Ryan a stare that would have cowed a seasoned warrior in his world. Ryan glared back with disgust written all over his face. He would not be an easy opponent.

The teams lined up into the requisite two rows and Ashley's team served. In the back row, Robert stood directly behind Ashley. Her years of competitive volleyball came hurtling back along with the ball, and she found herself all over the court, covering for those less able to play. Over the next few minutes it became apparent that only one other girl on her side seemed to have a clue. Everyone else just wanted to be fabulous in a bikini on the beach while pretending to play hard. It was not much of a match.

Ashley spiked a return and her team cheered, causing a brief pause in the action. Robert, a bit calmer now, returned the ball a time or two, but sweat poured off him despite being on the beach with the cooler breeze.

His opponents shed their t-shirts, so he did, too, a collective sigh sounding as he revealed his well-muscled chest. All eyes trailed his massive frame, watching him wipe the sweat from his forehead with the tee before tossing it to the side. After watching spectator heads go back and forth between Ryan and Robert, it occurred to Ashley they were comparing the two men.

Hands down, Robert won.

He was taller, broader and more thickly muscled. Robert smelled the change in the air, too, and made sure to puff out his chest a little more. Ryan, not at all pleased to have the competition and not used to being bested by anyone at anything, simply sulked.

As the game progressed, Ashley thought Ryan aimed his shots at Robert, and vice versa. Neither would be happy until the other got smacked by the ball. A solid athlete, Robert mastered the spike by his second attempt and smashed the ball in front of Ryan's face. Ryan dodged the shot, but missed the return as a result, making the rag-tag game tied at twenty with a win riding on the next point.

Ashley turned around to find the big-busted blonde named Erica, easily the worst player on the team, rotated into the server's spot. Earlier in the game she had missed getting the ball over the net twice. The girl made missing the ball a performance art form, so it would take a miracle for her to put the ball in play. Ashley gave a shrug to Robert who covered the front line. They'd just have to see if Erica managed to serve the ball over the net.

Alex and Brandon, who had appeared on the sidelines midway through the game, cheered for Ryan with gusto. Perhaps that was not a bad thing since everyone else sided with Robert's team, sensing an underdog in the match.

In the moment before the final serve, Ashley noted the gulls screaming overhead, the surf crashing, and the sun sinking right into the line of vision for her team. Would they all be blinded and miss the ball? She sighed and braced herself for disaster.

Unbelievably, Erica made the serve of her life and got the ball over the net. Ryan returned it with a fierce slam in front of Robert. Digging for the ball, Robert caught it with the tips of his fingers before it hit the sand, and sent it straight up into the air. Ashley flew in over the top of Robert, blindly punching the ball as it made its way back down. She landed in a heap on top of him, unsure if the ball had gone over the net.

Neither breathed as they waited for the ball to touch sand on the other side. Then the air erupted into shrieks. At first, she thought her team had won, but as she and Robert untangled themselves, she discovered it was the other team who celebrated. Her exuberance deflated, she crashed to the ground where she stayed until Robert pulled her to her feet.

But then a funny thing happened. Ryan's team was enjoying their win, but everyone who witnessed the game from the sidelines was yammering about the play she and Robert had made. As it turned out, her shot had missed its mark by a mere inch, and she and Robert had looked awesomely athletic on the play. More people chattered at Robert, amazed he had never played the game before, than celebrated with Ryan. *Hmm,* point for the win to Robert, Ashley chortled to herself.

The hot and sweaty players raced for the water and all the tension of the game faded away. Ashley rode out into the waves on Robert's shoulders. He even let her take off her cover-up and the day took on a friendlier cast. Except for Ryan, who was still . . . perturbed. Poor Ryan. He was not used to losing, Ashley thought, and definitely not something he wanted. Why he wanted her now at this late date, she couldn't fathom. Was he just someone who always wanted what he couldn't have?

Exhausted from thinking about anything to do with him, she turned to playfully splash Robert in the face to make him chase her. Who didn't love getting caught?

∞∞∞∞

The sun dropped swiftly, sliding into the surf with darkness mere moments away. Sunburned and tired, Ashley and Robert wanted to go home, but not a reinvigorated Jazz. Brandon had decided to play in the water with her after the volleyball game, and Jazz was having too much fun with him. Ashley cursed herself for not remembering Jazz was never the most dependable transportation.

Stepping away from everyone, Ashley called her mom to apologize for not heading home sooner. Ryan appeared at her side with a couple of hot dogs and bags of chips in hand. As she thanked her understanding mom and said goodbye, she found herself led by the elbow away from the bonfire to a blanket spread underneath a small beach cabana.

Not happy to be intercepted, she searched for Robert. Ryan shook his head. "He's busy for a while. I need to talk to you, Ashcat. Here, eat." He thrust a hot dog and a bag of chips into her hands. Indeed, she spied Robert sitting beside the bonfire, and he did seem busy, but she was not at all sure she liked what she saw. Erica was regaling him with tales of something. Ashley could see through the firelight he dutifully listened even though his eyes were unable to avoid landing on the bouncing bundles in front of him. How did she make her ample chest shimmy like that?

Reluctantly, she sat down under the faded canvas cabana, facing Robert where she could keep an eye on him. As she munched on the hotdog, she realized she was hungrier than she thought. Best to get this meeting with Ryan over and done with. Maybe he could tell her what today had been about. She had never seen him so disgruntled.

He sat down next to her and deposited his food on a towel between them. In a vain attempt to focus all her attention on him, he reached for both her hands and held them securely in his. He sighed and stared at her for a moment. Ashley's eyebrows rose in question, and she stopped mid-munch on the verge of asking him if he were okay. Finally, he spoke in soft, wistful tones.

"I'm afraid what I have to tell you may be too late, Ash." He had her full attention now. She cocked her head to the side and studied his face. His obvious concern alarmed her despite the fact nothing seriously wrong came to mind.

Ryan gave her a one-sided, rueful smile and blurted, "I've been in love with you since sixth grade."

Ashley giggled in relief. *"Geez,* Ryan, you had me worried there for a second. I thought something might really be wrong."

He grimaced. "You don't understand, Ashcat. What I am trying to say is I have loved only you for the last eight years."

Ashley pulled her hands away and didn't try to hide her disbelief. "You have a mighty funny way of showing it. I don't think you have said ten words to me in at least four years, Ryan Sanders. Do you honestly expect me to believe that proves how much you love me?"

"You deserve an explanation, but I don't think you're gonna like it much."

"Probably not, but let's hear it anyway." Curious, she wanted to find out what he meant. She popped a chip into her mouth and crunched loudly, not caring if she was obnoxious.

Ryan ran both hands through his hair, covered his eyes for a moment and then shook his head to clear his thoughts. "It started when I was a love-sick puppy in sixth grade. You were all I ever talked about at home. At first my parents thought it was cute when I declared I would marry you some day. As I got older and still seemed obsessed, my mother started to worry. She distracted me over our junior high years by making sure my involvement in sports left me little time to think about you. It didn't work out so good. My fascination with you continued."

Ryan tried to take her hands again. Ashley carefully avoided the move by grabbing his hot dog and taking a big bite, something she used to do when they were kids. It made Ryan grin.

"You were beautiful even then, Ashcat, and you got more beautiful every year. As I looked around, other guys like Brandon and Justin thought so, too. I was bitterly jealous when you talked to them and furious when they talked about you. I couldn't stand the thought of anyone else kissing you or holding you and that's all guys think about 24/7. So, in my mind, you have always belonged to me. I knew I'd marry you some day, and I didn't want anyone else touching you in the meantime." Ryan's face took on an angry, possessive look that made Ashley gulp down the hot dog and sit still, listening closely.

"My mom believed I was nuts and sat me down for a talk before you entered 9th grade. She made me believe if I dated you through high school our relationship would burn out before we graduated and you'd marry someone else. I couldn't have that. She pointed out most high school sweethearts never marry, but go on to college to find their spouses. She persuaded me to leave you entirely alone in high school and save the serious dating for college if I truly wanted to marry you. What can I say? I agreed, but not happily, 'cuz I didn't want you fallin' in love with anyone else. And that brings me to the part you're not gonna like."

"You lost me. Whatever are you talking about, Ryan?"

"Please don't hate me, Ash. I did this 'cuz I wanted you for myself, not 'cuz I wanted to hurt you in any way."

"What? What did you do that was so terrible?"

Ryan swallowed and looked her straight in the eye.

"I fixed it so none of the guys at school would date you."

Stunned, a beat fell before Ashley could respond.

"You *what?*" Ashley's mind raced to understand the implications of his words.

Ryan looked white in the faint moonlight. He attempted to explain himself. "You see, if I couldn't date you, no one else could either. I used my influence over the guys on the football team. They, in turn, used theirs over everyone else to make sure no one you might be interested in would go out with you."

For a moment, Ashley's mind was too ravaged to form words as his revelation sunk in.

"Y-you mean my going nearly dateless in four years of high school was *your* doing?"

"*Uh* . . . yeah," he nodded, squinting as if he expected her to slap him at any moment. "We let a few nerdy guys date you so you wouldn't suspect anything. I was pretty sure you wouldn't fall in love with any of them, so they weren't a big threat."

The hot mess that had been her high school years became chillingly clear. *Ryan had controlled her life for the last four years.*

Then an even uglier thought possessed her. "Did Jazz know about this?"

"Ashley, baby, everybody was in on it. They thought it was romantic."

"Did they think it was romantic you dated anyone and everyone you wanted to date while you kept me dateless?" Ashley spit out the words like she was firing bullets at his heart.

Ryan's breath caught, and he held it for a moment before letting it whoosh out all at once. "I am sorry, Ashley. I made a mess of things, I know, but I didn't do it to hurt you."

"Well, you *did,* Ryan."

Ashley shook her head slowly as the whole picture of betrayal sharpened. "How could you, Ryan? How could you put everyone up to this?" Hurt spread through her body like a poison. "I can't believe even my best friends were in on it. How do you think that makes me feel?"

Tears began to slide down her cheeks. Tears of fury? Of scorn? Or, perhaps relief she wasn't the pariah she thought she'd been? Feelings warred in her mind, threatening to take her down, until fury won out. "I thought it was *me,* you idiot. I thought I was someone no one would ever like, let alone *love.* You made me feel ugly and worthless . . . a real nobody."

"I didn't mean for that to happen, Ash." Ryan grimaced. "I thought I'd created a harmless plan to put you on hold until I was ready to settle down for real. Besides, just look at you.

You're gorgeous. You're smart. You're a blast to be with and you're good at everything. I didn't believe you could possibly think otherwise."

Indignation stole her voice.

Ryan took her silence for acquiescence. "I can see now it was wrong. But you gotta understand, I *could* do it and I *wanted* to do it 'cuz you belong with me. You're mine and you always have been." He picked up her clenched fists and held them, leaning in to kiss her cheek. "Now that you have graduated, we can be together. We can marry some day."

Ashley came to life and jerked her hands free from his. "You got one thing right, Ryan. *It is too late.*" She found her feet and was stepping away when Ryan grabbed her ankle and felled her, catching her in his lap and holding her arms down straight-jacket style.

"Ashley, don't go," he whispered frantically in her ear. "I know you're mad now, but think about it. You know I love you. I always have and I know you love me, too. Jazz always tells me I'm the only guy you ever talk about."

So, Jazz, too? That was the last straw. Maybe she wouldn't miss her best friend when she went back with Robert after all.

Ashley still seethed, but her words returned. In fact, so many words flooded into her brain at once she had difficulty ordering them.

"Let. Me. Go," she commanded, marshaling all her efforts into those three little words. "You are missing one very important piece of information. No, make that three pieces of information. One, I do not love you. Two, I'm engaged to marry Robert, and, three, *I do love him.* It's over, Ryan. You lost!"

Ashley struggled to stand, but Ryan wouldn't release her. He tried to soothe her with a rush of calming words, unwilling to believe it was over. "It's okay, Ashcat. It'll be okay, you'll s-"

A giant shadow loomed over the cabana and Ashley was snatched from Ryan's grasp before he uttered another syllable. Robert now held her like he feared she might break, breathing his question to her in a grim tone, "Did he hurt you?" As her eyes met his she saw he was itching to put a fist in Ryan's pretty face.

"Yes. No. Not anymore. He has no power to hurt me ever again," Ashley's voice carried enough for Ryan to hear. Robert's nose flared as he sought to keep his emotions in check. "He is not worth your energy, Robert. Let it go."

"You are mine to protect, Ashley. I cannot let anyone hurt you, especially not *him*." He stopped and set Ashley on her feet behind him, and then turned back to face his foe.

Ryan had squared off against Robert, ready to fight him for Ashley like some age-old ritual, when someone screamed loud and long at the water's edge. Angry words followed, ripping apart the calm of the night. Once the scene of friends and lovers enjoying an evening bonfire at the water's edge, the quiet beach erupted into chaos.

Brandon raced toward the cabana shouting for Ryan. As he neared and spotted his quarry, his words became clear. "It's Alex! They've got Alex!"

Spoiling for a fight anyway, Ryan took off running to meet his friend, demanding the details as they headed for the action on the beach.

"Alex was with some girl," Brandon huffed out. "I don't know her name. She didn't tell him anything about a boyfriend, but there is one, 'cuz he's here with his crew. If we don't help Alex, he's gonna get creamed."

Ryan wasn't completely surprised. Alex thought himself a ladies' man and had probably put the moves on this girl without thinking about the fact she might be attached to someone else already. Typical Alex move.

Seconds later he pushed his way into the circle that had formed around Alex and the boyfriend. Ryan's intimidating presence made things go from bad to worse in a heartbeat. The boyfriend, a swarthy, smallish guy, with the wiry build of a street tough, wore nothing but jeans rolled up at the ankle. As if one foe was not bad enough, a glance at the guy's three friends holding down a side of the circle, told Ryan all were thugs. Members of a gang of some sort out to prove themselves, all three were shirtless and barefoot. Well, he thought, he was primed and ready for a fight. This one would be as good as any. Besides, his friends out-numbered this guy's by at least two to one.

The moment the boyfriend laid eyes on Ryan, he pulled a knife and the game changed. Ryan heard gasps and a shriek behind him along with whispers of "He's got a knife!" shimmer through the crowd like liquid fire.

Ryan's heart lurched at the sight of the gleaming steel blade just before his adrenaline kicked in. Apparently this was not to be a friendly fistfight, but a deadly skirmish. Why did he think the girl set them up for a knife fight? His emotions were still roiling over Ashley, and he felt reckless, but he didn't want to be maimed or die. He racked his brain for a way to defuse the ugly situation unfolding in front of him. He was betting the three friends had knives as well . . . or maybe worse.

A girl behind him called 9-1-1. Even if police found them in the dark, it would be at least ten minutes before officers arrived. By then it might be too late.

"Hey, now," he heard himself say in a voice that sounded much steadier than he felt, "no need to get violent here. Alex didn't know she had a boyfriend, okay?" Puny little Alex's fearful black eyes looked like pools about to spill over. "No harm done so why not take your girlfriend and go?"

The boyfriend peeked at his girlfriend who silently egged him on, obviously thrilled to have guys fighting over her. "I don't think so." He crouched into a knife-fighting stance, this time aimed at Ryan.

Well, at least Alex, Mr. I'm-a-Lover-not-a-Fighter, was not the focus any longer, and he watched his friend slink into the crowd. Ryan busily assessed his next move and wished he had worn shoes instead of flip-flops so he could kick the knife from the guy's hand. The blade looked about six inches long, with a wicked jagged edge. It would cause lots of damage if it connected with him.

Sensing movement behind him, Ryan saw the boyfriend's eyes flare with fear for a moment. Just then a low voice rumbled in his ear. "Take this." Robert shoved a solid piece of driftwood about three feet long in front of him. Ryan snatched it and relief swamped him. At least he held some kind of weapon. Tearing his eyes from the boyfriend for a moment, he glanced behind him. Robert had quietly armed himself and a number of others with similar pieces of wood, undoubtedly stolen from beside the bonfire. The game changed once again.

"Look out!" Robert yelled.

Taking advantage of Ryan's momentary inattention, the boyfriend lunged. He would have cut Ryan if Robert hadn't shoved him out of the way and caught the blow with his own driftwood staff.

As if someone had blown a whistle for the brawl to begin, it instantly turned into a free-for-all. Those with driftwood weapons swung them like bats against the sideline thugs who wasted no time pulling their own knives and jumping into the fray. *Thunks* sounded as wood connected with bodies. Still, it took at least two bats on a thug to convince them to head on down the beach, despite the fact they were out-numbered.

Having regained his footing, Ryan chased after the thugs, while Robert skillfully knocked the knife out of the boyfriend's hand with a well-timed blow. Since Robert towered over him, it was enough to send the guy running after his friends. Thinking the fight was mostly over, Robert stepped back and caught his breath.

Then it happened.

Bang! A gunshot cracked, echoing in the night air over the water.

Everyone froze.

Their foe had found a different weapon that would change the game yet again.

Robert knew that sound from playing video games with Josh. Hearing someone crying softly behind him, he hoped it was not Ashley. He called her name and flinched in surprise when she appeared at his side. They searched through the blackness ahead of them trying to see if anyone had been shot.

Ryan emerged out of the dark at a dead run with his friends in close pursuit, just as sirens blared in the distance. "Clear the beach! Go!" He shooed people as he hollered. "They're coming back with more guys and more guns. *Get. Out!*"

Pandemonium ensued for the next few moments amidst cries of "Is anyone hurt?" "Where's my bag?" "I can't find my car keys!" and *"Run! I can hear them coming!"*

The beach cleared in what seemed an instant as if no one had ever been there, leaving a lonely bonfire to burn itself out.

"Come on, Robert, we've gotta get outta' here before the cops arrive. We can't be detained over this." They sprinted toward the parking lot.

Ryan was right behind them as they neared the cars. Robert pulled up and turned to him, asking with a look if he needed to stay. Ryan took in Ashley's frantic demeanor and hollered, "Get her outta here! I can wait for the cops in my car. 'Sides, I owe ya one."

Robert nodded and let Ashley haul him away.

"Jazz!" Ashley screamed over his shoulder, still angry with her best friend, "Get your sorry butt over here now!"

"What is your problem, girl. I'm right here," Jazz answered at Ashley's side. Taking off at a dead run, she shrieked, "Last one to the car drives. I'm too scared to hold the wheel."

Nothing was ever simple with Jazz.

Chapter 13

Halfway home fear was still pumping through Ashley's veins. By default, Robert was driving and doing a pretty fair job of it all things considered. He was the only one of the three cool-headed enough to take the wheel, despite the fact he was a true novice and had no license. Ashley was in front spitting out directions while Jazz, a basket-case in the back seat, kept her eyes glued to the road behind them, sure they would be followed.

"Just get me home, just get me home," Jazz moaned, making all kinds of deals with the universe for safe passage to her door.

Ashley's thoughts bounced from Robert to Ryan to the fight and back again. Too much had happened for her weary brain to keep up with. She was as frazzled as Jazz, but didn't want Robert to see how traumatized she was.

A warrior to the core, Robert seemed to be in complete control behind the wheel, his foot having found the right pressure on the accelerator. Fortunately, traffic was light on the freeway and Ashley coached Robert to stay only slightly above the speed limit and keep to the slower lane on the right. They didn't want to be stopped for speeding after all that had happened.

Robert reached up and adjusted the rear-view mirror. "Jazz," he asked in a calm voice, "are we being followed?" He had noted car lights coming up fast behind them.

Startled, Jazz answered in the affirmative by emitting a sound like a trapped animal, low and terrified. Ashley clenched her jaw and in an unsteady voice said, "Can you speed up, Robert?"

For the next five minutes no one so much as breathed, or so it seemed. Robert gave in to his heavy foot and held the car steady as they evaded the black sedan coming up on them. They could never quite see through the tinted windows to get a solid look at the occupants. Whoever was in that car wanted to catch them. That much was mighty clear. It couldn't be good.

Twice Ashley thought they would be over-taken, but then Robert would strategically move around traffic to box them out. Apparently military training of whatever era paid off. Riding in the far right lane with an SUV ahead of them, a truck to their left and a pickup behind them, they had protection for the moment. They hoped to keep the screen in place until they got off the freeway. Then without warning, the truck bolted to the far left lane. The black car immediately found them, and within seconds took the truck's place, effectively locking them in.

"Speed up! Speed up!" Half hysterical, Jazz's hands splayed across the glass as if that might be enough to hold them off.

Ashley swore under her breath and clutched the arm-rests hoping somehow that would keep them all safe if she squeezed hard enough. Robert's jaw was clenched in frustration. They were trapped with no place to go except off the highway through the grass and into the ditch. At the speed they now kept they would likely wreck.

The full-size sedan held the space beside them, occasion-ally swerving threateningly in their direction like a big bully teasing a little kid. Then the tinted window rolled down, and they let out a collective gasp, fully expecting the guys from the beach to be aiming a gun at them. "Ash-leeeeey! Jaaaazzzzz!"

Justin poked his head out and whooped a hello, his adren-aline still obviously pumping from the fight at the beach. Bran-don was driving what must have been his dad's car because it certainly was not his usual. Alex, whose attentions to the wrong girl were the root of all the trouble, waved an apologetic hand at them from the back seat. Clearly, he was not quite into the revelry of his friends.

Shocked, Robert took his foot off the accelerator for a

moment and it was just enough for Brandon's vehicle to surge erratically ahead of them and into their lane. Then the black beast shot off the freeway onto an exit ramp and sped out of sight.

Stunned by the antics of their erstwhile friends, Ashley and Jazz said nothing. Robert muttered something Ashley couldn't understand as he shook his head. She had never experienced anything like that before and the blood rushing through her ears had yet to quit humming. It was minutes before any of them spoke, their minds still replaying the close call that never happened.

Ashley pointed to the next exit that was quickly upon them and Robert soon brought the car to a jerky stop at the light once off the freeway. Pausing for a moment, they all took a much-needed deep breath. The light changed to green and Ashley told Robert to turn left under the highway. They wasted no time getting to Ashley's house, where a traumatized Jazz had to take the wheel of her car. Her need to go home was so great, she almost took off before Robert and Ashley had reclaimed their beach bags from the back of her car.

Shaken, Ashley stumbled in the driveway, her feet not wanting to move as directed. Robert grabbed their beach gear in one hand and guided her toward the house with his free hand squarely in the middle of her back. Home at last and unscathed. It had been a rough night.

Heading for the side door, Ashley stopped dead in her tracks, forcing Robert to swing around nearly face to face with her.

"What is it?" Robert read the concern on her face.

"I don't know who that car belongs to," Ashley replied through gritted teeth. A compact black car sat before them, tucked back in the driveway as if in hiding. Who was here? Could it be related to the fight at the beach? Or Robert's fake passport? Were they discovered? Should they go in?

Still debating what to do, the porch light flipped on and Julie opened the front door. "About time you two got home. We have a visitor."

Before either of them had a chance to respond, Uncle Zeek stepped out on the porch behind Julie. "Come inside. We've got some things we need to talk about." Zeek motioned to Julie to go ahead of him, and they ducked back into the house.

No hello. No nuthin', Ashley thought. This can't be good because Uncle Zeek hadn't planned to follow them back to the States. In fact, he should still be with his students on the dig. As they dumped their sandy bags on the porch, Ashley stoically looked at Robert and took a deep breath, letting it hiss out slowly. She had to suck up enough courage to find out what awful thing had happened to bring her uncle home. Robert wrapped his arms around her and held her for a moment before ending the embrace with a kiss on her forehead. Then hand-in-hand they headed inside to hear what else had gone wrong on this very long day.

∞∞∞

Zeek looked terrible. Haggard. Every crease in his face had deepened, especially around his bloodshot eyes. His beard showed several days of growth and his clothes were rumpled. Smack dab in the center of his shirt was the yellowed splotch of a food-spill. He paced in the living room, alternately tugging at his hair with one hand and smoothing his brow with the other. He was a mess.

Ashley had never seen her uncle look so bedraggled. Frankly, it scared her to the bone. Before she could ask why he was here, he took charge. "Sit down, kids. This is complicated, so listen closely. We may be out of time, and we've got decisions to make."

Robert and Ashley sat on the sofa side-by-side, holding hands, and gave him their undivided attention. Wide-eyed, Josh was sitting in one of the side chairs opposite them, equally alarmed. Ashley could tell her mom was trying hard to keep from panicking, but it was not working.

Standing beside the sofa, Zeek said nothing for a moment as he stared at their clasped hands and started nodding. "Just as I suspected." He stepped in front of Ashley and Robert and picked up their joined hands. Pulling Ashley's away, he dropped it as if it were husk drawn from an ear of corn. Then he displayed Robert's hand for all to see.

"This is the problem. Right here on Robert's hand. I should have thought of it, but who had any idea this particular item would find its way to a display case in the British Museum?"

"Uncle Zeek, what are you saying?" Ashley didn't like his tone of voice, and she particularly didn't like how he was treating Robert.

"It's the *ring,* Ashley. The ring on his hand." Zeek was beside himself with worry. "That signet ring cannot exist in two places at once. Since Robert is the original owner, when he appeared in this time period wearing it, the relic at the British Museum *disappeared.*" He finished with a magician's flourish to emphasize the fact that the ring had vanished into thin air.

"Why would anyone make that connection, Zeek?" Julie's voice wavered, proving she was not as calm as she pretended. "Who would be able to tie that disappearance to Robert? Who knows who he is besides us?"

Zeek, Ashley and Robert all started to talk at the same time, so Ashley and Robert yielded the floor to Zeek, whose face was ashen.

"I believe there is someone else."

"Abasi?" The color drained from Ashley's face as she thought of the implications.

"Yes-s-s! Abasi," Zeek confirmed, imitating the man's hiss. "I thought he suspected a connection between the passport I asked him to fake and the missing antiquity at the museum. Now I'm sure he believes there is one."

"Who is that guy, Uncle Zeek? Why would he want to cause us problems?" Josh's face scrunched in puzzlement over how a missing ring could be such a big deal.

Uncle Zeek sighed and took out his distraction on his hair, tugging on it like he wished to pull it out, strand by strand. "Let's just say, Josh, this guy is a dangerous one. Did you ever watch the old Indiana Jones movies?" Josh nodded. "Do you remember how everyone fought over ancient relics and how ruthless they were?" Josh's eyebrows edged up as his eyes widened. "Well, this guy's for real and is known for being cold-blooded and operating on the other side of the law. That's how he ended up making Robert's passport. He's filthy rich having made a fortune off selling antiquities. Legally, or otherwise."

Zeek continued to pace as he voiced his fear of the dealer. "I think Abasi arrived at the conclusion time travel exists long ago, and now he's sure I know something about it I'm not telling. This is a business opportunity for him. If he can connect with a time traveler and blackmail him by threatening to expose him, he'd have a steady supply of antiquities to sell, wouldn't he?" Zeek paused and let the truth of his words sink in for Julie and Josh. "I have no doubt when my request for a counterfeit passport coincided with the disappearance of the relic at the British Museum, Abasi put two and two together. I wouldn't be surprised if he's tailing me."

He turned his attention to Julie. "That's why I'm here. I couldn't phone, text or email you because I'm almost positive he's tapped into lines wherever I am. We don't want any kind of written or auditory reference to the family occupation, do we? I had no choice but to come here and deliver the news in person."

Ashley squeezed Robert's hand. "There is more to the story than that, Uncle Zeek."

Zeek stopped harassing his hair long enough to roll his eyes from Julie to his niece. "What is it?"

With Robert's occasional input, Ashley explained how they had encountered some difficulty boarding the flight to the States. She described how Robert had been forced to take off his ring by security people because it set off buzzers. Unfortunately, a couple of them had taken a solid look at the ring.

Zeek listened to the last part of their tale with his hands scrunching his face. He took them all in with a sweeping upward glance, before announcing, "We're screwed."

"How can you say that, Zeek?" Julie bit her lip, her concern now apparent.

"Easy. Abasi has contacts everywhere. I'm betting half the agents at Heathrow are on his payroll, and the other half are bribed as needed. By now he's made the connection between Robert and this damned ring."

"How can we be sure of that?" Ashley's mind was already busily sorting through escape scenarios.

"We can't," Zeek retorted. "That's the rub. We have to assume he does know, and return Robert to his own time as fast as possible."

"And me. I'm going with him, remember?" Zeek studied his niece's face and said nothing.

Julie clenched her fists as she glared at Zeek. "We've got to protect these kids, so what do we do now? Will it be fight or flight?"

"That's a good question." Zeek shrugged and started to pace again. "I'm not sure they can go through customs now without being detected. After all, Abasi is the one responsible for Robert's faked passport."

Josh piped up, "If he ditches the ring and gets a different passport, would that work?"

"Maybe. But where are we going to get another counterfeit passport? Last time I checked, Walmart doesn't carry them," Zeek sneered and then looked contrite. "I'm sorry. I don't mean to be so angry, I just don't know what to do or where to find another Abasi."

"I've got Rick's passport in the office, Zeek. Could it be altered if we find someone who does that sort of thing?" Julie's voice was edged with determination.

"Hey, Houston gets a steady stream of illegals crossing the border from Mexico," Ashley said. "Surely there is someone around here who could make a passport for each of us under different names. We just need to locate 'em, right?"

"Wow, I never thought I'd hear my family seriously tossing out illegal options." Josh laughed at them, breaking the tension for a moment as they realized how they sounded. Even Zeek's lips curled into something resembling a smile. It was out of character for the Duvall family to subvert the law, but Julie was the real stickler for honesty in all things. With her family in jeopardy, however, her mother bear was emerging. They could all depend upon her to do whatever was necessary to keep them safe.

"That's a good idea, Ashley," Julie said, returning to the problem at hand. "I volunteered as an assistant at a small school that teaches English as a Second Language a few weeks ago. Perhaps someone there would be able to help me find the right person to help us."

"Well, I guess it's as good a place as any to start until we can find something better." Zeek turned to give Ashley his full attention. "And you, my dear niece, need to be on the look-out for an escape stone. You're a Guardian. Aren't they supposed to find you if you're in trouble?"

"Yeah, that's what Olde Gylda said. If there is a way to call for it, no one has told me what it is, though." She sighed and stared off into space, her mind searching for that better way.

"Sweetheart? Have you said all your good-byes here?" Ashley held her mother's gaze until both had tears pooling. This was all moving too fast for comfort. She had hoped for more time with her family than this.

"I think so, Mom. I had wanted to go to Brenham to see Grandma and Grandpa Duvall before we leave, but I don't know if that's even possible now." She looked at Zeek who just threw up his hands in defeat. Shrugging, he plunked himself into one of the overstuffed chairs where he proceeded to chew what was left of his fingernails.

"*Uhm,* if we *can* go, I would like for us to marry in the chapel at the Vintage Rose Bazaar like you and Dad did. It's only a few miles outside of Brenham so it would be easy for Grandma and Grandpa to be there."

"You want to be married there?" A smile pushed Julie's cheek upward just enough to force a tear over the edge. It silently rolled down her face where she caught it by her mouth with a swipe of her hand, her eyes never leaving Ashley's.

"That would be okay, wouldn't it, Robert?"

Robert's hazel eyes met Ashley's and the questions in his made her sit up straight and face him. "What is it?" Alarm rushed through her.

"Do you still want to marry?" Robert whispered in her ear.

"What? Why would you even ask that?" All eyes in the room landed on them at once.

"You have never told me what you and Ryan talked about. It seemed very serious to me."

"You're right, it was." Ashley's head bobbed up and down. "You saved me from that jerk before all hell broke loose. Remember?"

Julie sat forward in her chair, "Ashley, I think you'd better tell us what happened to you at the beach, *huh?"* Ashley could *feel* her mother's concern.

"It wasn't just the beach, Mom. As horrible as it was there, the drive back wasn't much better. Robert doesn't even know all of it because I didn't have a chance to tell him on the way home."

Ashley lost no time explaining her tête-à-tête with Ryan Sanders. Robert was seething by the end of it and wishing aloud for one more swing at Ryan's pearly-whites. Ashley reminded him that Ryan had turned out to be more friend than foe during the ensuing fight, but it didn't calm him much.

Julie was incredulous, sitting with her mouth hanging open in an unintentional imitation of Josh, who was more than impressed with Ryan's audacity. Zeek, looking worried, was up and pacing again.

"Could these guys who fought you be connected to Abasi?" Zeek grilled, tugging at his disheveled hair again. Poor man was intent upon pulling it out of his head, Ashley thought.

"I think not," Robert answered after a moment. "They appeared to be more interested in a fight with everyone on the beach than with either one of us."

"He's right, Uncle Zeek. I think maybe they were thugs or gang members. They were not so happy with Robert 'cuz he took out the girl's boyfriend and his knife without any difficulty. I don't think they were used to losing." She gave a shudder at the memory and snuggled in under Robert's arm.

"My God," Julie's voice trembled with a mixture of fear and rage. *"My God.* You both could have been killed."

"Ain't it the truth. And here I told Robert all about how civilized we are in this country, and within 24 hours of being home, he's in a fight with knives and guns."

"I believe we are safer at Hertford Castle, Mrs. Duvall. We have an army to protect us there."

"An actual army?" Josh bounced up and down again. "I gotta go see this place, Ma." Julie's eyes narrowed on her son, silencing him for the moment, at least.

"So, Mom, Uncle Zeek? Can we get married at the chapel with Grandma and Grandpa there?" Ashley asked again.

"There is a three-day wait between getting the license and the ceremony in Texas," Julie cautioned. "Do we have enough time?"

Uncle Zeek guffawed, startling everyone. "Where they're going they don't need the state's permission."

"Oh!" Julie and Ashley said at the same time.

"Let my dad marry them," Zeek suggested. "He's a deacon in the church. He may even have a mail-order license. It doesn't matter if it's legal here, so do it the way you want." He stopped pacing and faced them all. "While you're busy with that, I'll try to figure out what to do with the passport fiasco."

Ashley was on her feet hugging her uncle. "Thank you. I'm sorry this has caused you so much grief, Uncle Zeek." She pulled back and looked him in the eye. "By the way, who did you leave at the dig site to cover for you?"

"That's a whole 'nuther story, my dear." He rolled his eyes down to Ashley, punctuated by a little snort. "Do you remember when you first arrived in London being introduced to Dr. Wilson?"

"Oh yes, the little lady with the stiff upper lip?" Ashley did a fair impersonation of the lady's accent and deportment.

"That would be the one. She's the contact who told me about the ring disappearing from the British Museum, and the only one who would fill in for me on such short notice. I never like being in her debt because there's no telling what she'll ask to even the score, but I'll deal." He wiped the corners of his mouth with one hand. "Speaking of Monica, I need to borrow a computer for a while to see how she's doing. Do you mind, Julie?"

"Of course not! I think we are forever in your service for coming all this way to help us sort out our mess." She shook her head side to side. "I don't know how we're going to handle all of this, but I'm sure glad you're here to help."

Zeek gave his sister-in-law a brusque nod. They may not have voiced it, but Ashley knew that was a reference to Zeek filling in for her dad. The two headed down the hall to the office, discussing plans along the way.

Josh grinned at his sister. "You never used to be this entertaining, Ash, or I would have missed you more."

"Thanks a lot, Joshie." She ruffled his hair and then turned her attention to Robert. Suddenly Josh realized he was the third wheel again and flushed. He jumped up and took off for his room. "Ya get tired of Ashcat, Robert, we'll play that Gettysburg game again." He didn't wait for a response and loped into his room leaving Robert and Ashley alone for the first time all day.

"Are you all right, *Ashcat*?" Robert mocked his former rival, all the while dropping soft kisses on her forehead, her eyelids and the tip of her nose.

How she loved this man. He would be hers, maybe as soon as tomorrow. Ashley breathed a huge sigh of relief. She was with her family, and they were safe for the moment. Uncle Zeek was here to help them. Best of all, she and Robert were going to be married and her grandparents would be there to witness it.

As she imagined what it would be like, her brain got fuzzy from the heat of Robert's kisses. He made her melt faster than ice in a Coke on a hot Houston day.

Yes, it could all be worse.

And then they heard Uncle Zeek swearing loudly from her dad's office.

Now what?

Chapter 14

Dr. Monica Wilson settled down for the night on a narrow, uncomfortable cot, a wooden slat poking a sharp edge into the center of her back. Why did she agree to do things like this for Duvall? He never bothered to be nice to her.

Even blanketed in silvery moonlight, the cramped quarters, serving as both bedroom and camp archive for the archeology dig, were a disaster. A typical male mess, she thought. Nothing put away with care, but rather dropped in the first available spot. Who knew what all was here? She would begin organizing it tomorrow once the students were afield.

The GPS on the Jeep Wrangler Duvall had loaned her had almost been accurate, *almost* being the key word. After wandering side roads for quite some time, she finally located the camp. By then dinner was over and activity winding down for the night. Roger Simpson, Duvall's teaching assistant, had taken one look at her and suggested they make plans to meet in the morning. Tired, hungry, and needing time to get oriented, that suited her just fine.

So, here she stood, out of sorts, in the middle of the night in the middle of Duvall's mess. Caught in a weak moment, she had agreed to cover for him when no good reason to refuse him had presented itself. Besides, he had begged. He said he had a family emergency, but she noticed he never explained what the trouble entailed. Still, Duvall begging her for anything was a new thing. What to make of that?

As if it all were not confusing enough, upon leaving the university today, she had bumped into that dreadful Boss character about whom her colleagues joked. The man called himself Abasi and hung around the university way too much. Did anyone even know his last name? He made her blood run cold, gaping at her like he could see her naked. Instead of being sexually titillating, he made her skin crawl. This time, however, she believed Duvall was his real target. When she told him Professor Duvall had gone to the States due to a family emergency, Abasi's hooded eyes had taken on the flat look of a snake. She wished she'd kept that information to herself.

It had taken her fifteen minutes to lose the man because he followed her to the parking lot, questioning her the entire way about Duvall's plans. He wanted to know all about the young man Duvall's niece was to marry in the States and even hinted that the girl might be pregnant. Why would he think she had that kind of information or would share it with him?

Besides, what the man really wanted her to appreciate was his assistance in obtaining a passport for the fiancé on short notice. That part bothered her since she knew of no official government office to which Abasi would be connected. So, that meant it was likely *illegal* help Duvall had received from him. She found that troubling, indeed, because the Duvall of her acquaintance was an honorable man who would not knowingly break a law. Something was definitely amiss.

All in all, her quick mind scoured through the day's events and fitted puzzle pieces together where possible. What exactly did she know? Well, Zeek Duvall must be in some kind of trouble requiring illegal assistance. An antiquity of any sort garnered Abasi's interest. And, somewhere in all that the missing artifact from the British Museum played a relevant part, as did Duvall's niece and her fiancé.

Curious and curiouser.

Hmm, she would spend some time figuring out the connection in the morning. Tomorrow would be soon enough to deal with it because her mind was too weary tonight to seek answers. She twisted, poked and prodded the miserable excuse for bedding on the cot until she was semi-comfortable and let sleep take her.

∞∞∞

Bzzzt, bzzzt.

Monica reached behind her for the cell phone she kept on her bedside table, only to find herself hitting the ground. Actual ground. Awake, with a sharp pain in her side, she reached down and pulled her shoes out from under her. The infernal cot had tipped her out like unwanted baggage.

Bzzzt, bzzzt.

She grabbed for her phone on the camp stand at the head of the cot and struggled to focus her bleary eyes on the message displayed on the screen.

It was a text from Suzanna, her office mate at the university. *"Thought you should know, 2nd signet ring missing from BM. This one with letter B. Same era. Picture to follow."*

Oh, my, Monica thought, dragging herself to her feet. This is getting interesting. Was Duvall involved? Abasi? They had to be. Why else all the questions? She must let Duvall know before Abasi found him. What was that saying? *Forewarned is forearmed?*

She would need to be careful in communicating with Duvall if that despicable person had her friend in his sights. If the man could secure a counterfeit passport for Duvall, there was no telling what nefarious skills or connections he possessed. Or what he might do to get what he wanted. She shuddered at the thought.

Perhaps if she texted Duvall to check the school faculty site for an update regarding the class she covered for him, it would not raise suspicion. There, it would be easy to privately fill him in on Abasi and the latest missing artifact. By using the closed university server it should at least delay Abasi's attempts to discover what Duvall might know. Of course, Abasi may have access to that, too. She would not put it past him.

∞∞∞

Zeek swooped into the family room swearing a blue streak with Julie and Josh hard on his heels before Robert and Ashley finished detaching from one another. Ashley took one look at Zeek and wondered if he might die of apoplexy. She didn't know for certain what that meant, but it was what people always said when someone's eyes bugged out of their head. Zeek qualified on that score.

"Robert! Who do you know who wears a signet ring with a 'B' on it?"

Robert paused, looked at Ashley, and then both said in unison, "Bedford!"

"Who is that?" Zeek demanded.

"He is a baron whose lands adjoin ours," Robert said. "Why do you ask?"

"Huuuhhhh," Ashley squeaked, sucking in air, "You can't mean Bedford is in this time period, too."

"No other explanation fits what Monica told me," Zeek retorted. "This is fast becoming a disaster."

"Gah. That means he is on the loose with no one there to help him," Ashley cried. "I may not like the man, but I can't say I'd wish this on him." Robert nodded in agreement.

"Think you he is alone and roaming the same area where you found us?"

"Yeah, I do, Robert. If your ring disappeared out of the British Museum when you landed in this time period, perhaps the same has happened for this man Bedford. Monica, Dr. Wilson, that is, promised to follow up with a photo when her colleague sends it to her. You would recognize the ring if you saw it?"

"Yes," Robert answered, squeezing Ashley's hand to comfort her.

"My God," Julie fretted, "you say this poor man is wandering around with no one to help him at all? What will happen to him?"

"My guess is that Abasi will happen to him, if he hasn't been found yet," Zeek groaned. "If Abasi is on top of this like I suspect he is, he's looking for this guy at or near our dig site."

"It sounds exactly like something Bedford would get himself into. The man has a knack for sticking his nose in where it shouldn't be." Ashley was alarmed at the thought of a captured Bedford. What would he reveal that he should not? While she may not like the man, he would be the proverbial sitting duck for someone as cunning as The Boss. That she did not wish upon him.

"I have no way to stop Abasi and his men. I'm afraid I've sent Monica into a very bad situation." Zeek rubbed his hands up and down his face as if doing so would wipe away his misery. "How do I explain any of this to her so it doesn't implicate Ashley and Robert or the rest of our family? I flew here to tell you in person, and I should fly back to do the same for her."

"There isn't much time to do anything here, is there?" Julie placed a hand on her brother-in-law's shoulder and made him look at her. "Perhaps you should go back. I can work on the passport issue."

"You may be right. We can do nothing else tonight in any event. I need sleep. By morning Monica should have forwarded the picture she told me about, and we'll know for sure if our suspicions are correct." He cocked his head to gather his thoughts for a moment. "Why would this baron choose to follow you two? Were you friends?"

Ashley shivered. "The baron is about your age, Uncle Zeek, but he decided he would marry me."

"Oh, Ashley, this is not the one you were betrothed to before Robert, is it?" Julie's frown deepened as she remembered Ashley's earlier account of her time at Hertford Castle.

"One and the same. The guy was obsessed with me and didn't want to give me up, especially not to Robert. I bet the jerk followed us to Olde Gylda's place."

"Think you he saw us use the stone and dug it up to follow us?"

"I don't know, but how else would he wind up in this time period? Besides, if you could follow me then he could, too, right? If he watched where the stone hid itself, he would have no problem locating it to dig it up. He's tenacious enough to have done just that."

"Hmm, if true, then he got more than he bargained for, did he not?" That comment prompted Robert and Ashley to grin at each other.

"You were buh-bee-betrothed to a *baron*?" Josh scratched his head in confusion, as if the notion of his sister engaged to anyone else but Robert was impossible.

"Yeah, Josh, and I would be married to him if not for Robert. Women are without rights of their own and are powerless to do anything but what men tell them to do."

"See! Another reason I need to go there. Instead of women controlling me," he grinned at Ashley and his mom, "I would control them."

"Goodnight, *Josh,*" Ashley and Julie replied in sync. They looked at each other and burst out laughing. Leave it to Josh to hear only the part he liked.

What a long night.

Chapter 15

Monica waved goodbye to the last of the students departing for their assigned work sites and took a tentative sip of her tea. *Blech,* the brisk, early morning air had cooled it too fast. Roger was driving a group to a new site and would not return until late morning for their planned meeting. His task was to get the students started at their new dig, while hers was to strike some organization into Duvall's disheveled quarters. She required an efficient space in which to work.

Not having slept well after the late night text from Suzanna, she had the dull thrum of a headache pounding in her temples. It kept her slow and thick rather than her usual crisp self. Agitated, she dumped out the remains of her tea and pivoted on her heel, depositing the dirty cup in the camp mess hall tent. On the way back to her quarters, she decided to work off her sluggishness.

She delved into her job with a lack of enthusiasm she found shocking. Sorting out messes and organizing things was her forte. A half hour later, she was still struggling to discover the madness in Duvall's method of organization.

A banging sound coming from the direction of the mess tent was almost a welcome interruption. Dropping a file box on the nearest stack, she stilled where she stood and cupped her ears to better listen for the sound to repeat itself.

Ha, something banged again. She suspected an animal of raiding the empty mess tent for goodies. Having lived in camps many times, she knew critters would always help themselves to unattended food. The little beasties made big messes, too. She scanned her tent for the broom she had put down minutes before and spied it leaning against her bedside table. Thus, armed to the best of her ability, she sneaked out of the tent and aimed for the mess hall like a mythic Diana on the hunt.

Approaching the mess tent, she saw the flaps at the entrance flapping in the riffling breeze that whisked its way in gusts through the center of the camp.

A shiver rippled up her spine having nothing to do with the cool morning air. Were not those same flaps tied back when she deposited her cup only a short time ago? She thought of no wild critter able to untie them, which left a human critter as the only possible culprit. The thought made her confidence waver. She was alone here with no one around for miles.

Perhaps a wayward tourist from Stonehenge or a curious farmer had wandered in. Neither would be too terrifying. But what if it was a criminal, bent on stealing from the students while they worked away from the camp?

Should she confront this unknown intruder or slip into Duvall's car and leave?

Noises coming from inside the tent increased while she debated what to do. The frantic nature of them seemed to ratchet up by the second, as if this interloper were in some kind of distress. The lack of stealth made her mind jump to another explanation.

What if it were a student in trouble? She had not counted bodies as they left for their dig sites. Perhaps one of them had stayed behind and was experiencing some kind of medical emergency. As the professor in charge of the camp, the students were her responsibility, so making a run for it might not be the smartest thing.

She made up her mind to do her duty.

Monica raised her chin and white-knuckled her javelin-hold on the broom. Taking a deep breath she summoned her British spunk to enter the tent to find out who or what lurked there.

She stopped dead in her tracks the moment she spotted

her quarry. Ten lifetimes would never have prepared her for what appeared before her eyes. Stunned, she always supposed it to be an impossibility, but the answer to the hopes and prayers of her entire career stood in front of her.

Blood rushed through her body at an alarming rate and any fuzziness from earlier was long gone. A corner of her brain tried to warn her she should feel threatened, yet she did not back away.

There, rummaging through the camp food bins, stood a powerfully built man, dressed all in black, in unmistakably medieval garb. A casual observer would have thought him an escapee from a period festival, but Monica knew otherwise. Her years of research and professional training told her that the man's leather pants, his hand-crafted shoes, his leather jerkin pieced together with leather cords were the real thing.

Puzzle pieces of the last few days dropped into place. Duvall's crazy behavior, the disappearances of two signet rings from the British Museum, Abasi's intense interest. It all made sense now. A time traveler was standing in front of her.

What to do?

The man made the decision for her. Intent upon digging through the food bins, he had been too busy to hear her at first. Now he sensed her presence and wheeled to face her, his eyes wide.

Fear dominated his demeanor. Surprised by Monica, he looked ready to run rather than fight. His eyes were dark with a feral glaze to them as he searched for another escape route from the tent and found none.

She let the broom drop to the floor while she threw up her hands, palms out, to show she would do him no harm. He relaxed a degree as his hands unclenched. An impressive man, he would have no problem overpowering her, yet he appeared not to want to confront her. Frozen in place, he stared steadily into her eyes.

Monica drank him in with delight. Morning sun now streamed through the flaps as a stiff breeze whipped them back, allowing her to get a better look at the man of her dreams. The reality amazed her.

From where she stood she judged he was taller by a head or more. She let her eyes embrace the breadth of his shoulders and his trim hips. The light glistened off the silver temples of his dark hair, which hung about his face and over his collar.

She smiled.

This was a man, not a boy. His aristocratic forehead ended in bushy brows over black, black eyes, and his nose had a classic shape set over a strong chin. What a remarkably handsome man, she thought, as a quiver of excitement surged through her. Although his aura was dark and dangerous, she did not feel threatened. Instead, she felt drawn to him in a way she had never experienced before. The very air seemed to hum between them.

The man's eyebrow tipped up on one side and a smile flickered about his lips. Monica's smile tripled in size and the two stood there staring in happy silence at one another as if time stood still just for them.

Monica's mind focused at last long enough to assess his need, and her tongue eked out a single word.

"Hungry?" she asked, pantomiming the task of eating.

The man responded with a slow nod, never breaking his soul-searching gaze. His sweet smile told her he liked what he saw. As Monica stepped toward him, taking care not to ruin the moment, the unmistakable sound of a car crunched into the parking area next to their camp.

She frowned. It was way too soon for Roger to be back, so who could this be? A glance at the man told her he was ready to blow past her to escape the confines of the tent. She held up her hand and commanded, "Stay. I shall send them away. Hide." She pointed to a space off to the side of the tent where crates of food supplies were stacked above and below a camp table. Not waiting for him to argue, Monica strode out into the bright sunlight, prepared to greet the latest intruder.

A car door slammed and Monica held her breath wondering who would appear. She must get rid of the unwanted guest before her man found another way out of the tent. He was magnificent, and she would not risk losing him because of an intruder. Sucking in a fortifying breath, she calmed her nerves with a quick exhale. She waited for the driver to come around the corner of the student sleep tent and into view.

Monica's stomach dropped to her boot tops in the span of a heartbeat. Only sheer will kept her from shrieking *no-o-o-o-o* at the top of her lungs.

Rounding the corner was none other than Abasi.

Not now. Had she not already suffered her fill of him? Not just pushy, the man was way too nosy. She thought she had answered all his questions yesterday, and yet here he was . . . again.

Abasi wore slick black, pinstriped suit pants with a matching vest over an open-necked, silky white shirt. The white threads of his suit complemented the white strands in his hair. She hid her smile as she noted his trademark shiny-black dress shoes were already coated in the chalky white dust so typical of the Stonehenge area. All in all, he was clad from head to toe in unsuitable attire for an archeology campsite. So, what was the wretched man doing here?

Monica held her ground, tilted her head to the side and quirked an eyebrow trying to adopt an imperious attitude. Not an easy thing for one as small as she. She did not speak aloud to him, but waited with an intentional wave of irritation speaking for her.

Abasi pretended nothing was amiss and approached her with a simple, but cunning smile, his false, subservient airs firmly afloat. The man was incorrigible.

"Dr. Wilson! Good day to you." He gave her a small bow before stopping in front of her, too close for comfort, in a show of dominance designed to make her take a step back.

Monica refused to budge, well aware of his desire to make her squirm. She acknowledged him with a quick bob of her head and glared into his eyes.

Those half-lidded eyes roamed about the campgrounds, taking in the various tents and equipment. Privately, she rejoiced when the man took a solid step back as he did so. Good. Perhaps he sensed her push back. She was done being nice to him, and bullying her would only heighten her anger.

Even though Monica's heart raced double-time and her knees threatened to buckle, she knew she looked unruffled on the outside. Being a diminutive woman she had perfected her controlled, unflappable persona years ago, and it had worked for her many times throughout her successful career. She continued to look Abasi in the eye, forcing him to speak first.

"Madam, your tale of covering for Dr. Duvall on such short notice intrigued me, so I thought I would drive out to see how you fared."

Monica only tipped her head to the opposite side, lifted both eyebrows in apparent disbelief, and waited for the interloper to explain himself.

Abasi, bemused by her persistent silence, sailed on, unabashed. "How interesting you are, Dr. Wilson. Are you in need of any assis-s-stance today?" Abasi's eyes glimmered with unspoken meaning behind the simple question.

Monica shook her head as she dismissed his question as not worthy of a response. "Why are you really here, Abasi?"

This time his smile was genuine, revealing the gap between his front teeth. "My dear lady, as you know, it is my be-e-s'ness to know what treasures from ancient worlds are being uncovered in digs such as these. Might I inquire as to the succes-s-s of this venture?"

"You may not. It is my business to supervise these students for the university, and as their professor, I must ask you to leave. This camp is closed to visitors." She sniffed, "Especially to you."

Abasi's face crumpled in mock horror. "You wound me, Dr. Wilson. I mean you no harm. You know I am only here to see if you need assis-s-stance with anyone who might be traveling through . . . " Abasi paused, lifting a brow as he completed the thought, " . . . here."

Had he said the word *time* or had she mentally filled in his pause with the word? He was baiting her, was he not? Had she blinked? Flinched? She held herself steady before shaking her head in disgust. Adopting her most commanding air, she drew herself up to her full height. "Abasi, I have much work to do to get this camp moving, and I do not have time to spar with you for your amusement." Monica gave him her best squinty-eyed glare and without flinching ordered, "Leave here at once."

She wheeled and walked briskly toward her tent, dismissing him as if he had been a private in the army to her general. Pulling the flap back with a flourish, she disappeared into the tent.

Panic-stricken, Monica listened from inside as Abasi took his time walking around the camp. She hated behaving like a scared little bunny burrowing in a hole. Her heart all but stopped multiple times from the suspense as she listened to flaps being pulled back, knowing Abasi peeked into tents as he passed them. She held her breath with every flutter of rustling canvas, expecting her medieval gentleman to be discovered at any moment.

Minutes later, having finished his tour of the camp, Abasi pondered his next move. The lady professor had delivered a masterful performance. He was not sure if she was telling the truth or if she was, indeed, hiding something.

Nothing out of the ordinary indicated an unusual find, human or otherwise. The place sat quiet and empty of all but the good professor.

The recent disappearance of the signet rings, however, had his mind working overtime. He had almost caught a time walker several years ago, missing the old woman by a hair as she vanished into a whirlwind. Then there was Duvall's niece to consider. He had watched the same thing happen to her not long ago. Something was afoot. The bizarre way these rings disappeared without a trace from their cases indicated to his mind time walkers were afoot again. How else could rings disappear from the well-guarded British Museum, he reasoned?

This time the facts connected these two professors to the

rings. He was sure he was on the right trail. Determined to find evidence, he would make contact before any government entity did. His mouth watered as he thought of how a time walker would make him a rich man. Not only would his future be secure, but also that of his entire family, and his was a very large family. It would happen. One of the two would tell him what he needed to know. He smiled. It was only a matter of time . . . and, perhaps, a little persuasion here and there.

He simply had to figure out how to apply the right pressure at the right time. The too-nervous Zeek Duvall had a great deal more to tell than he pretended. Of that he was certain. Why the ever-honest Duvall would turn up wanting help with a counterfeit passport was the real question he must answer. The professor had been outwardly pleasant to him during their last encounter, but Abasi could tell how repugnant his very presence was to the man. With that in mind, he could not imagine why Duvall had deemed it necessary to step outside the law for his niece's fiancé. That story did not ring true. The professor was far too skittish. He would assign some of his men to watch over this camp to see if anything turned up. Meanwhile, he would track Duvall's movements in the States to see if it uncovered anything of interest there. If something big were afoot in either place, his men would undoubtedly find out about it and let him know.

Shifting to thoughts of the prickly little professor and her strong-arm tactics, Abasi's black eyes danced in amusement. He did so love a sharp opponent. It made his work so much more enjoyable. Shooting one last glance in the direction of the admirable Dr. Wilson's tent, he made his way back to his car.

Listening from inside her tent for Abasi's movements, Monica stood statue still, hoping to calm her raging nerves. She was horrified that awful man had followed her to the camp and terrified he might have seen something of the lovely man hiding in the mess tent. Dealing with Abasi was like fighting quicksand. The more you battled, the deeper you sank.

Would that dreadful man be back? Could she fend him off

alone and protect her time traveler?

Did she have a choice?

And where was Duvall? That fellow had some explaining to do.

The moment Abasi's car crunched the gravel drive, she was out her door and running for the mess tent, praying her medieval man was still there.

Chapter 16

Damien Lundeen held his breath waiting for calm to descend upon the camp before he deemed it safe to move about. The past few days had been a nightmare, and he wished with all his heart he had not followed Lady Ashley Duvall. What a fool he had been. All he wanted was to go home and resume his life as the Baron of Bedford. He would think twice before pursuing another woman so recklessly.

Nothing was as it should be in this strange land. Confused, he had walked for days after the whirlwind set him down, unable to find game to kill with a simple knife. Reduced to foraging for berries or any foliage that did not make him sick, he was starving. Now, standing in the encampment he had found the night before when the smell of food had lured him in, he risked everything just to eat.

But what a peculiar place! People had no horses but instead rode in the most amazing carts that moved all by themselves. The noises those carts made both frightened and fascinated him. Men and women inhabited the camp, shockingly dressed alike, and they talked to flat rocks they held in their hands. Music played, but there were no instruments to be found. All in all, it was a puzzle too difficult to solve. How could a whirlwind move him so far from his home? It made no sense, yet here he stood.

He had waited all night in hopes the camp would empty out in the morning. It had. Alone at last in the camp, he had hurried into the tent that housed the food, determined to relieve his hunger. Then the oddest thing had happened. A person caught him in his search for food, and he thought himself finished for sure. To his surprise, it had turned out to be a woman in the garb of a man--one with a beautiful face and an even more beautiful smile. His heart recognized hers, and he knew for certain she would help him.

Then noise coming from beside the camp startled them. One of those loud wagons again. This time a man arrived with a deep, silky voice he had trouble understanding. 'Twas obvious, however, his new friend did not like this man by the tone of her responses to him. Bedford had been prepared to rush to her defense if she had needed protection, since he was sure he could overpower the unwanted visitor without difficulty. But then he heard his lady tell the man to leave with commanding force and clarity. That made him stop and just watch through a small hole in the fabric of the tent to see what this person would do next. The man proceeded to inspect the camp, so Bedford concluded he should not be found and hid behind the table as the lady had indicated he should.

Now, in the quiet, Bedford was unsure if he should go to the lady or if he should wait for her to come to him. Anxious for her to return, he thought about her so hard he almost forgot the rumble in his belly.

As if he had ordered it, the flaps of the tent snapped back and the woman appeared before him, a charming smile upon her lips. He grinned and held out a hand to her, palm up, in an invitation for her to take it.

She did so without hesitation.

That made him happy, and he held her small hand in both of his while he gazed into her eyes. Tiny and feminine despite her odd dress, she had shiny, dark red hair pulled pack in a serviceable knot that should have made her look severe. Instead, the sparkle in her blue eyes countered that, making her demeanor warm and welcoming.

As a gentleman, he thought he should take the lead, so he bowed, still holding her hand. "I am Damien Lundeen, Baron of Bedford. What name are you called, my lady?"

Bedford felt the woman shiver, yet as he looked up from his bow into her eyes, 'twas not fear that shown in their depths, but excitement. Her light blue eyes melded into his dark ones and suddenly years of loneliness peeled away from his heart.

The lady gaped at him as a frisson of delight passed between them. Recovering, she spoke in a soft voice. "I am Dr. Monica Wilson, the professor in charge of this camp."

Bedford's eyebrow shot up. A woman? In charge? Where were the men who should be here to guard her? This lovely lady had no protection visible anywhere in the camp. No weapons of any kind except for a very charming smile. His instinct was to claim and protect her. Contrary to his having been spurned by both Lady Ashley and Lady Elena, this smiling woman appeared to be as enamored with him as he with her. A thousand questions perched on his lips needing answers. Before he found words to ask, his lady took matters into her own hands and looked up at him with a shy smile. "You are hungry, are you not? Perhaps you would like to break your fast with me?"

The hunger raging in his stomach decided all else must wait. He returned her smile with one of his own and nodded his acceptance to her. A feeling of calm nudged out the unease that had been his constant companion for days. The sweet smile she sent in response was as familiar as if he had always known her. For a moment, he imagined himself in his own world with her at his side, and hope filled his soul. He was the Baron of Bedford, after all, and here was a woman who seemed to recognize his stature and desire him. Perhaps the world could yet be righted. Meanwhile, he would enjoy watching this attractive woman as she made his meal. There would be time later to learn all the particulars regarding his whereabouts.

∞∞∞

Monica's lifetime of professional training had not prepared her for this personal moment. After unsuccessfully pursuing several other attractive, intelligent men over the years, she had recently tried without success to capture the attentions of Zeek Duvall. Discouraged by her failures, she always wondered why she could never form an intimate relationship with any of them. Now, in an instant, this man had stolen her heart, and she knew she had stolen his. *Incredible.*

Tearing her gaze from his eyes, Monica glanced down at the hands still holding hers and stilled. Her eyes widened in awe. There, for all the world to see on the little finger of his left hand, was a large, gold signet ring with the letter "B" clearly showing. Exactly the ring Suzanna had described.

Wonder filled her eyes as she met his once again. He *was* from another time. All her suppositions were right. Her face alight with joy, she set about the task of finding food with a smile adorning her lips and a simple melody becoming a symphony in her heart.

Chapter 17

The next morning the entire family looked sleep-deprived, Ashley noted. By dawn everyone but Josh was up. Even he had only one eye open and a wicked case of bed head when he toddled into the kitchen an hour later.

Uncle Zeek was on his cell phone with an airline, trying to talk his way into a last minute seat on the first flight out of Houston to London. From the sound of things, that was not going well.

Her mom was doing her best to help everyone find something to eat for breakfast. In between times she made plans for a wedding to take place in a few hours. Judging from her frequent sighs, she was trying not to stress out. That was not going so well either.

Robert grinned whenever his eyes found Ashley's. He seemed the least stressed of the lot, and Ashley found his grin the most encouraging thing about the day. She wanted their wedding day to be joyous more than anything else. Yet the stress rolling off her mom and Uncle Zeek steamed into the air like dew burned off in the morning sun. Ashley felt bad she was the cause of all this unrest, but what could she do about any of it now?

"Ma, the milk's gone." Josh glared at everyone and silently accused each of them. "Who drank all the milk?" Robert's face crumpled with guilt and Julie sent her son a withering look.

"Eat your cereal dry or find something else, young man. As you have failed to notice, we are all working at the job of getting on the road this morning." She placed a warning hand on his shoulder and said plainly in his ear, "Today isn't about you, so your job is to be as helpful as possible. As soon as you've eaten, water the patio plants and then find something clean to wear for your sister's wedding. School appropriate should be fine since this won't be a fancy affair."

Josh grimaced and slithered out from under her hand. "All right, Mom. Just sayin' we got no milk. No big deal." He sat back in his chair and squinted at his mother busily loading the dishwasher. "Have you called Grandma and Grandpa yet? Do they know about all this?"

Ashley handed her mom two dirty cereal bowls and turned to him. "We called them before you got up, sleepy head." She couldn't resist ruffling his full head of unruly hair. "They said they'll meet us around noon at the Vintage Rose Bazaar. And you need to talk to Robert. He has something to ask you." She handed him a breakfast bar she plucked out of a nearby cupboard. Josh grabbed it, reached past her for a second one, and then sauntered off into the living room to find Robert, already having wolfed down the first bar.

Julie tossed plates into the dishwasher like frisbees, preoccupied with all that needed doing. Ashley had to grab her arm to snag her attention.

"Mom, Robert is going to ask Josh to stand up for him as his best man, and I was wondering if you would stand up for me?" Her mother's face was so blank Ashley launched into an explanation of why she couldn't ask Jazz when her mother's face blossomed into a smile. She pulled Ashley in close for a hard hug, tears threatening to run down her face.

"Of course I will, sweetheart. I would be delighted to stand up for you."

"It may not be the normal thing, since you're the Mother of the Bride, but I can't ask anyone else. In all honesty, I don't want to."

Ashley dried the tears from her mother's eyes with the tips of her fingers and gave her an extra hug before they released each other.

"Well, today might not be the wedding day of your dreams, but we are excited for you. Everything will work out."

"Hey, Robert and I just want to be married. This will be fine for us. I'm only sorry Robert's family isn't here to join us. Then the day would be perfect."

"No, sweetie, it would only be perfect if your dad were here, too."

"Yeah," Ashley replied, her voice catching in her throat, "you're right, Mom." She reached out and tucked a strand of her mom's hair behind her ear. "But maybe we'll find him soon, and we can celebrate all over again."

"Wouldn't that be wonderful," Julie sighed. "Well, no one is getting married anywhere if we don't leave this house soon. Let's find you something to wear. What about the white sun--"

"--Mom, Mom, Mo-o-o-m!" Josh burst into the room and skidded to a stop in front of her. "I'm gonna be a best man! Robert asked me to be his best man."

"How wonderful, honey. You'll do him proud, I'm sure. How about we find something for you, too, *hmm?*" She took off down the hall to the bedrooms, spitting out possible selections in rapid-fire order.

Josh and Ashley looked blankly at each other for a moment and then shook their heads and followed. There was no stopping their mother when she was on a roll.

∞∞∞

Two hours later they said goodbye to Uncle Zeek, who left for the airport still not having secured a seat on an early flight. He found one for much later in the day, but he hoped to pick up an earlier seat as a stand-by. Knowing Zeek, he would finagle a way to board that plane. The poor man was still frazzled, and Ashley said a silent prayer for him as he walked out the door. He had promised to do everything in his power to contain the Abasi threat from the London side. Now, Robert and Ashley had to find a way to get back across the ocean on their journey home to Hertford Castle.

An hour later, they had settled in for the drive to Brenham. Ashley sat in the front seat this time, helping her mother navigate the mid-morning traffic. Robert and Josh sat in back where Josh busied himself playing a video game on his phone, while Robert absorbed all the sights of Houston.

As they headed northwest out of town, the weekday traffic thinned a bit and attention turned to the wedding only a few hours away. The Vintage Rose Bazaar had been contacted, and as luck would have it, the little red chapel where Julie and Rick had held their ceremony was available. They would have no decorations and no flowers other than those on the grounds, but that would be plenty. The place was lovely with a magic of its own.

All had found appropriate summer attire for the wedding. From the back of her closet, Ashley's mom had produced a long, white sundress with little purple flowers banding a deep ruffled hem. Even though the dress no longer fit, Julie had kept it as a sentimental favorite. To Ashley's surprise, it was perfect and fit her to a tee. Robert had to make do with a crisp, white dress shirt once belonging to her dad, and the black twill pants they had purchased for him in London. Ashley thought him a gorgeous man in anything. Julie wore a lilac peasant top over a white, ankle-length skirt to coordinate nicely with Ashley's sundress. Josh matched Robert with a similar white dress shirt and black pants. They would win no style awards, but their dress suited the occasion pretty well.

Ashley kept Robert entranced as he watched her weave a section of her hair into a wreath around the crown of her head, leaving the rest to flow freely. Elena and Anna had taught her how to do that kind of braid at Hertford Castle. Her nod to Robert's family was to style her hair as if they were marrying at Hertford.

Having packed some small bags with a change of clothes

for after the ceremony, they hoped to have a relaxing dinner with the grandparents in Brenham. Ashley wanted Robert to sample barbecue at their favorite place before returning late in the day to Houston.

Under the bags in the back of the SUV was a stack of paving stones Julie had told Josh to load, despite his many complaints. Grandpa Duvall had said he needed them for a new pond he was building in Brenham. The unused pavers had been stored in an old shed behind Julie's house. Never one to buy something if he could get it for free, he had asked Julie to bring them along. It never occurred to Grandpa that this might not be the best time to deliver the stones. He would be able to match them with more from the emporium, and since they were all going there, it worked for everyone in his mind. Zeek had rolled his eyes upon hearing the request and told Julie to forget it. Her father-in-law would fret over them until they were in his possession, so for Julie it was easiest to haul them now and be done with it.

Josh grumbled about the task because he was dressed to leave for the wedding when Julie set him to work. Naturally, he dirtied a shirtsleeve. Julie fussed at him as she spot cleaned it on his body until he was altogether put out by the time they hopped into the car ready to leave.

Ashley perked up at the mention of stones and wanted to see them. What if they contained a Guardian stone? Josh said they were all blank and just plain heavy. He insisted there was nothing of interest there, so she let it go.

The drive through the Texas countryside was uneventful. Robert enjoyed seeing the pristine, rolling hills and told Ashley he liked the open spaces better than the crowded city sights. Her little brother whined about being hungry and Robert admitted he could eat, too, so they stopped for a sandwich at the deli in Chappell Hill. They finished off the meal with a tasty dish of Bluebell ice cream. Taken with the ice-cold treat, Robert wolfed down his and Ashley's, too. That made her smile.

Shortly before noon they pulled into the Vintage Rose Bazaar parking lot and spilled out of the car. Robert stood in utter amazement at all the plants before him. Josh had scooted off to find the restroom and Julie had been sidetracked by a row of beautiful pink roses next to the tree sporting brightly colored bottles. A warm breeze rustled through the gardens as Ashley led Robert to the little red church where they would be married. They admired the multitude of flowers surrounding the building like a colorful cloud as they walked around it peeking through the windows every few feet for a look inside. Robert tickled her on the neck with a rose and made her giggle. She loved this place. From the whimsical features spread throughout the nursery to the cats guarding the grounds like mystical spirits, something a little otherworldly called to her here.

Always shopping, Julie spotted a stone by a bench near the stream with an inscription that read *Love Blooms Here.* She and Ashley decided it would be the perfect accent for the stones in the back of her car. Not only would the new stone mark the occasion of Ashley and Robert's wedding, but it also would make a great birthday gift for Grandpa Duvall. Julie snatched up the stone and walked across the Bazaar grounds to the sales shed to make the purchase. She had to pick up the key to the church at the same place, so she set off on her mission, stopping to sniff roses along the way.

Josh dragged Robert off to run the rose maze with him, leaving Ashley happy to have some time to herself to contemplate the biggest moment of her life thus far. She was actually getting married . . . *to Robert.* A lot had happened to her since graduating from high school only a couple of months ago. She felt so much older and wiser now than then. How could that be? Yet, she knew it to be true. She loved Robert with all her heart, and he loved her. Marrying him was the right thing to do, and she was very excited her wedding was happening here where her grandparents would be present, too.

Thinking of them made her wonder where they were because the appointed gathering time was noon. Her grandparents were rarely late, and on this special day, she thought they would be here by now.

Ashley glanced toward the road as she heard a car approaching, sure this one would be them, but the car shot by. She was about to go in search of Robert and Josh when her cell phone set up a racket. She dug it out of her purse to read the caller ID. Jazz's face buzzed on the screen. She couldn't tell Jazz her location or what she was doing, so she stopped the call and put it back in her purse. Seconds later the phone sang again, and she dutifully dug it out. Jazz was calling . . . again. Exasperated, she figured at this rate Jazz would keep it up until she answered, so she might as well take the call.

"Hello, Jazz. What's up?" Ashley said, the irritation in her tone unmistakable. She was still a tad miffed with the girl.

"Hey, it's me, not Jazz," the baritone voice on the other end responded.

Ryan Sanders.

Really? Whatever did he want now?

She had a finger poised over the disconnect button, but something in Ryan's voice stopped her from punching it. "Don't hang up, Ashcat. I know you don't wanna talk to me, but I need to tell ya a couple things."

She hesitated for a moment. "Okay, Ryan, but be quick about it." The urgency in his voice did not go unnoticed. A car door slammed in the parking lot, and she wheeled around expecting her grandparents to be there. Instead, she saw her mom walking away from her SUV having locked the car door with a *blip.* Disappointed it was not her grandparents, Ashley motioned for her mom to come listen. She twirled the church key on her finger as she approached. Mildly frustrated, Ashley shook her head at her mother's questioning expression and put the phone on speaker, so she could hear what Ryan had to say, too.

"Yeah, okay, thanks, Ash." Was Ryan flustered? "Me and Jazz are at McDonald's and I borrowed her phone 'cuz I didn't think you'd talk to me otherwise."

"You would be right, Ryan. So . . . what is so important you have to borrow someone else's phone?"

"Well, first, I have to apologize to you for the way I behaved yesterday. I acted like a real ass and I'm sorry." He paused and admitted, "'Sides, everybody told me afterwards I was a jerk. *Uhm,* I didn't realize you were so . . . so committed to your . . . your . . ."

"*Fiancé?*" Ashley filled in, her impatience apparent.

"Yeah, him!" Ryan ignored her obvious frustration. "I'm sorry I did all that to you, but you gotta realize I didn't mean to hurt you."

"Yeah, we went through all this yesterday." Ashley rolled her eyes at her mom to commiserate. "What else do you have to tell me?"

"Yeah, *uhm,* I don't know how to say this, but are you or your . . . *fiancé* in trouble with the law or somethin'?"

Ashley spun around and started searching for Robert, her adrenaline kicking in. The hesitation in Ryan's voice as he asked the question told her he was not trying to aggravate her.

"What are you saying, Ryan? Why would you even ask that?" She tried hard to keep the fear out of her voice. Josh and Robert jogged toward her and she started flagging them for all she was worth. Her mother was staring at her phone with a raised eyebrow as if she expected a beast to jump right out of the phone and bite them.

"I dunno, Ashcat. Maybe it's nothin', but I went to your house this mornin' to apologize to you in person and to be sure you got home safely. While I was standin' at the door waitin' for you to answer, this big, black Range Rover pulled up in front of your house. At first I thought about running, thinking it might be those dudes from the beach. Then these other dudes got out of the SUV lookin' like FBI or somethin'."

"*What?*" Ashley did not like the sound of this at all.

"They wore black suits and had black reflective sunglasses on so I couldn't see their eyes. I started to leave, thinkin' they didn't look very friendly, but they blocked my path and wouldn't let me walk around 'em. Then they started askin' all kinds of questions 'bout you and the dude you were with."

"What's going on?" Josh asked in a loud whisper. His eyes sparkled and were full of curiosity as he and Robert hurried toward them. Josh apparently thought all this hugger-mugger stuff was exciting.

Julie shushed him with a cuff in the air since he was not close enough to really *whup* him up the side of the head. She settled for pulling the two off to one side as they reached her to quickly explain what was going on. Robert's face reddened when he recognized the voice on the phone, but Ashley held up a hand so he would understand she had it under control. He waited impatiently beside her, his hands tensed at his sides.

"What did you tell them, Ryan?" The attention of everyone was now riveted on the cell phone in Ashley's hand.

"What *could* I tell 'em? I said you weren't home 'cuz you didn't answer the door, and I was clueless where you were, or I wouldn't have been standin' there."

"Why did you think Robert was involved with them?"

"That's easy, Ash." His voice betrayed his grin. "They had *accents* like his," Ryan said, doing a poor impersonation of Robert. He let that soak in for a moment and when Ashley didn't reply, asked, "What's goin' on anyway? Those guys didn't look very nice."

Not wanting Ryan to know anything more than necessary, Ashley decided to cover their tracks with one more lie. *"Hmm,* my Uncle Zeek said he recommended Robert and me for jobs at the British Consulate in Houston. They must have been checking us out."

"Maybe. But then Jazz drove up and when she got out, they all started questioning her."

"Oh, no, not Jazz, too," Ashley muttered.

"Yeah, Jazz, too. They asked if you had relatives anywhere in the area and Jazz told them you had grandparents in Brenham. I stepped on her foot to shut her up, but that didn't help much, Ash. She'd already said too much. They wanted an address for your grandparents, so I jumped in and told 'em they'd have to ask you for that."

"Did they want anything else, Ryan?"

"Uh, no, not exactly." He quit talking for a moment. "Jazz had her phone in her hand like usual so they just snatched it from her, right in front of us. They looked through her phone until they found your information."

"They what?" Horror spilled through Ashley making her knees give out. She would have sunk to the ground if Robert hadn't stepped in and grabbed her around the waist to hold her up.

"Yeah! I couldn't believe they would do that. But that's not the worst part." Ryan took a deep breath for effect. "They found Jazz's 'Find a Friend' app, and they could see for themselves you were on Highway 290. She was lucky they tossed her phone back to her before they left."

Ashley was so upset she couldn't speak. Robert finally took the phone and asked the question that needed to be answered. "This is Robert. When did you talk with them, Ryan?"

"Hey, Robert? Didn't know you were there, dude. *Uhm,* it was 'bout an hour ago, huh Jazz?" Ryan and Jazz conferred in the background. "Yeah, somethin' like that."

No one spoke for a moment while everyone's mind whirred with this news. They all knew it had to be Abasi's men and that would mean nothing but trouble headed their way.

"You still there, Ash?" The phone connection crackled like it might break up, and Ashley exhaled the breath she had been holding, steadying herself. "Oh, and one more thing. Jazz said she saw another black SUV parked around the corner matching the one at your house. That one was sitting there waiting before she turned onto your street. She noticed 'cuz they looked really hard at her like they might know her." There was a muffled pause before Ryan got back on. "Jazz wants to talk to you."

"Ashley? Are you okay? I mean, who are those guys?" In typical Jazz form she didn't slow down for an answer, but rushed into the next thought. "I'm so sorry I've been such a mess. And Ryan and I never meant for anything bad to happen to you, ya' know. My bad, sweetie. I thought I was helping you with

Ryan, not hurting you. Can you forgive me?"

Petty grievances like this were far from Ashley's mind at this point. Instead, her brain was racing ahead trying to get a fix on where Abasi's men could be. It was definitely not on Jazz. Some part of her mind responded automatically, "Jazz, honey, it's okay. Everything's okay. We appreciate your calling to tell us about these visitors, and, I'm so sorry those men got aggressive with you. I'm sure it doesn't mean anything bad. We'll talk soon about all of it," she lied again. "Right now I gotta go. Thanks again, and tell Ryan goodbye, too." Ashley didn't wait for an answer but clicked off the call and stood motionless for a moment. It had yet to fully register that this might be the last time in her life she talked to Jazz.

Abruptly, everyone started yammering at once, until Julie put her fingers to her lips and let out a shrill whistle, silencing everyone.

Robert took charge before another word was said. Ashley knew he was forming battle strategy in his head. "How long before they get here?"

Julie answered, checking with Ashley for confirmation, "Drive time is about an hour and a half from our house if you don't stop."

"Do you think they know we're here at the Bazaar rather than in Brenham?" Josh asked.

Julie and Ashley shook their heads in concern. "I'm sure by now they will have located the house in town." Ashley checked the time on her phone. "Let's hope Grandma and Grandpa have already headed here."

Her mom grimaced, clearly worrying about a confrontation between her in-laws and Abasi's men. How would they explain all this to the grandparents? More importantly, what would they have to do now to escape those awful men? Should they wait for the grandparents here or find a place to hide? If they chose to hide, just where would that be?

As Ashley and Robert debated the next move, her mom turned her face to the sky. "Rick, why can't you be here to help me make a decision? I need you, sweetheart." She shook her head as if it might help to shake off the trouble, and turned back to reality and Ashley. "Well, what do we do now?"

Josh had been watching the road while everyone else debated. "A car popped over the hill back there. I can't tell what kind of vehicle it is yet, but we should be able to see it in a second or two."

All heads turned to look and everyone waited breathlessly for the car to breach the top of the hill. Hoping to see her grandparents' old, maroon sedan, the suspense made Ashley's stomach dropkick off her toes and send waves of nausea up her throat. She swallowed hard.

A huge black SUV made its appearance, cresting the hill like a battleship destroyer with the light shimmering off its highly polished surface. They watched it in horror, the air sucked out of all of them. Then a second SUV topped the hill and tailed the first one. *It was an Abasi armada.*

All anyone could think of was getting as far away from those vehicles as possible. No one said a word as they all took off simultaneously, running at top speed for their car. They clamored in and Julie flipped the car in reverse, speeding back out onto the road and heading in the opposite direction.

Out on the blacktopped road, the SUVs were about three-quarters of a mile behind them and gaining in a hurry.

Damn.

Obviously they had been spotted.

"Hey! That's Grandma and Grandpa's car coming over the hill behind 'em," Josh hollered to his mom from the back seat.

"Thank God! At least we know where they are. They should be safe for now." In a nervous burst of energy she jammed the gas pedal to the floor and sent them shooting down the road at a terrifying pace. Fighting panic, Ashley searched her memory for a place where they could hide. Wasn't there a bed and breakfast on the left if they turned at the first corner?

A T-intersection presented itself an instant later and Ashley screeched, "Left, turn left, Mom!"

Julie slammed on the brakes to make the corner at the same moment Josh emitted a sound she had never heard him make before.

"Eee-ahh-maaaa!"

Robert clapped a hand on his back. "Easy, Josh, 'Twill be all right." He spoke calmly, "They are now right behind us. We need to find a place where other people are. They cannot harm or abduct us so readily if others are present and watching."

Ashley wasn't so sure Uncle Zeek would agree with that assessment, but there was no time to argue. Surely, the presence of other people would at least slow them down, wouldn't it?

"There it is, Mom! That's the bed and breakfast. Pull in there. There!" Ashley waggled a finger at a tidy two-story house with cute little cottages behind it about a quarter of a mile ahead on the left. Now if they could only make it into the drive before Abasi's men reached them.

The two black monster SUVs needed only seconds to catch up with them once they rounded the corner. Ashley's heart pounded each beat in her head as they approached. Wooziness swept over her. She was either going to throw up or pass out. Air. She needed air. Gasping for breath didn't help. Is this what it feels like to be scared to death?

"No! No! No-o-o-o-o-o!" Josh shrieked from the back seat. Alarmed, Ashley forgot about herself and wheeled in her seat in time to see one of the SUVs passing their car. The passengers were ID'd as the men Ryan had told them about. Her mom would never make the left turn at her current speed. When the SUV stayed beside them, it became clear the men purposely blocked the drive to prevent them from turning in.

Double damn.

"Faster, Mom, faster! Don't let them pass," Josh begged, as Julie blew past the drive. She floored the car in a vain hope they could stay in front of the two SUVs.

Ashley panicked as the first Abasi vehicle ducked easily in line ahead of their car, sandwiching them in. Taking the ditch didn't seem like a good plan as the pitch was very steep on both sides. At this speed they would flip the car. Her addled mind could think of no other options.

Julie groaned as the powerful Range Rover in front of her forced her to slow down. "What should I do now?" The big SUV had forced her to a near stop. "Anybody got any ideas?"

Ashley put her head in her hands, feeling it was all over but the proverbial shouting. What would Abasi's men make them do? Uncle Zeek seemed to think they should avoid them at all costs. Yet here her family sat, waiting to be squeezed like a wrecked car in an auto crusher.

Just then Robert's voice rumbled in alarm, *"Ashley?"* Josh chimed in a second later. "It's *glowing!* Look at that, Robert. Is it radioactive? Don't touch it!"

"Don't touch what?" Ashley moaned, still sick over their imminent capture. The SUV would have them stopped in a matter of seconds.

"A stone back here seems to be on fire, Ashley. It has writing on it." Robert sounded shocked by what he was seeing.

Ashley had flung herself halfway over the seat before he had finished his sentence. Sure enough, the stone on top had writing on it.

"That's just the garden stone we bought for Grandpa's birthday," Julie said, the fight draining from her as she slumped in her seat. Their car cruised ever closer to a stop.

"Sorry, but it's not!" Ashley whooped, her excitement exploding. "I don't think the one you bought, Mom, says, *"Dihangfa Mewn Amser."*

"What?" Julie nearly hit the SUV ahead while looking into her rear view mirror to see what they were talking about. The car jerked crazily as a result.

"Woo-hoo!" Ashley howled, fearlessly snatching the stone in question from atop the others in the back of the car. Josh and Robert both growled their disapproval at Ashley's brazen move, but she ignored them completely. "Get ready, everyone! We're going on a little trip." Ashley settled herself firmly in Robert's lap, his arms holding her securely around her waist. With not

a moment to spare, Ashley held the glowing stone and clearly enunciated,

"*Dihangfa Mewn Amser.*

Dihangfa Mewn Amser.

Dihangfa Mewn Amser."

By the time she finished her incantation, a whirlwind visibly swirled about the car. Everyone stared at it with wide eyes, except for Ashley who gloated over her success until suddenly she panicked. *What if she was the only one transported?* She would leave Robert and her family in danger. As if in answer to her question the car lifted itself from the ground just high enough to be engulfed by the wind that encircled it. Miraculously, the whole car started spinning like a top.

Julie screamed. For once in his life Josh said nothing, his mouth hanging open as his head swiveled in an effort to see everything at once. With grim determination, Robert held Ashley tighter while she closed her eyes again, but this time she smiled. *They were making an escape in time.* She knew not where they would wind up, but it had to be better than in the hands of Abasi's men.

A thought struck her. This stone's inscription ended in the same word as her first one. *Twll yn Amser,* she had learned from the wizard Cedric, was Welsh for a *Hole in Time.* What did *Dihangfa* mean? Escape, maybe? Would she need to know? Before she could form any more thoughts, her mind became too heavy, and she dropped her head to her chest with a sigh.

Chapter 18

Alas, it was already dinnertime. Shadows stretched in the fading daylight over London. Sunshine nestled through the trees, sending low rays of light shimmering across the landscape as if touched by a fairy's wand. Returning from a romp in St. James Park a short distance from the family home, Abasi bounced his two-year-old nephew Fahrid on his shoulders. The lively lad needed to give his mother a break as she prepared the family's evening meal, and Abasi never minded the time he spent with the boy. Theirs was an extended family with many mouths to feed. The happiness in the child's eyes at nothing more than a trip to the park with him, made all his heavy responsibilities worthwhile.

As they rounded the corner with home in sight, Abasi's phone started buzzing insistently in his pocket. For a moment he was tempted to just let it buzz not wanting the idyllic moment to be interrupted. But then, he realized, it could be his men calling from America. Would they have news of his time travelers?

Without breaking his stride, he reached for his phone, confirmed it was his man in America, and held it to his ear hoping to be rewarded with good news.

"They're gone." No hello, no explanation. Unfortunate news dropped like a bomb. And then nothing.

Abasi felt the warm satisfaction of the last hour melt away quicker than his smile. All he could muster was, "What happened?"

The response was a long pause. He could hear the man's

indecision in the silence. Muffled sounds indicated others were trying to tell him what to say before he cleared his throat and said simply, "Sir, their car disappeared in a whirlwind." The man audibly braced himself for his employer's burst of fury at thinking them lying incompetents for having lost their prey . . . but it never came.

Abasi said not another word. With his free hand, he swiped the off button to disconnect the call with his thumb and shoved the phone back into his pocket. Tiny though he was, Fahrid sensed the change. The sweet child grabbed his uncle's head with both hands and grinned down into his face, trying to make him smile like before.

His nephew would enjoy no more smiles from his uncle today. Abasi slid the small body off his shoulders and with a gentle swat to the boy's rear sent him off to see if dinner was ready.

He sunk listlessly onto the top step of his porch entryway, not able to face the family just yet. The time walkers should have been in his custody by now. He would need a few minutes before he could accept they had eluded him again.

He buried his face in his hands and sought to control himself. Bills needed to be paid, but now must wait. Nephews and nieces had college debts mounting, yet he would manage. He always did. Eventually, he would catch a time walker, he assured himself for the thousandth time. Then his family's security would be ensured well into the future. He would prevail.

Abasi brusquely rubbed his face for a moment, trying to rid himself of the disappointment settling itself like a fog around his person. He forced himself to find his legs and head into the house as the sun set behind him, the bright rays of evening sun having dissipated into dismal darkness.

∞∞∞

Ashley woke up wondering if a bomb had exploded in her

153

brain. She vaguely remembered her head banging the ceiling of the car and bouncing twice before coming to rest on Robert's shoulder.

Ouch, she thought. Afraid to open her eyes for fear of what she might see, she peeked out from the corner of her right eye.

Josh was sprawled across the seat, his left foot lopped at an odd angle over the captain's chair in front of him. He was completely still.

Too still for Josh.

Ashley sat up quickly, almost taking Robert's chin with her. *Crunch.* He growled an unintelligible response, but let her go. In full panic, she reached across to shake her brother, *"Josh! Josh! Wake up, Josh!"* He did not respond and now she was beside herself. She slid closer, carefully putting one hand under his head, before smacking his cheeks with the other. "Wake up, Josh! Robert, he's not waking up. What should I do?"

Robert, still rubbing his own jaw, slanted her a wary glance. "Mayhap you should give him time to come round before you beat him to death."

"What?" Ashley glared her exasperation over her shoulder. "I'm not *beating* him, I'm trying to *wake him up!*" She turned back and put her face in her brother's just as he groaned and his eyelids sputtered open.

Josh took one look at Ashley's face inches from his and would have jumped out of the car if the door had not impeded his progress.

"Geez, Ashley. What are you doing?" he spat, clinging to the door handle with eyes like saucers.

"Clearly trying to kiss you, Josh. What else would I be doing?" She thumped him soundly across the chest with a wicked backhand.

"I see your sisterly devotion is back, my dear," Robert's lips twitched as he tried not to smile. "She will never admit, Josh, how relieved she is you are not hurt."

Alone in the front seat, Julie surfaced just in time to

witness her children's fond expression of love for one another. "Enough, you two."

Still shaking her head at her brother who was rubbing his reddened cheeks, Ashley turned her attention to her mother. "Are you okay, Mom?"

Julie twisted her shoulders to ease the tension and was rewarded with an impressive crack, audible to all in the back seat. "I'm better now. I've never been chased like that before." Exhilarated, she looked out the window for the first time and her expression changed. "Oh, my God, does anyone know where we are? None of this is familiar."

Four sets of eyes scanned the surroundings.

"Wow." Ashley let her eyes rove over the hills that surrounded them. The silence lasted for only a moment.

"My GPS is *dead.*" Josh's nose stayed glued to his non-functioning cell phone app until the ramifications of that hit him. "Does that mean we've really gone back in time?" Excitement danced in his eyes like it did when he got a new video game.

"All the trees are gone," Robert noted, surveying the landscape. "Let me take a walk around." Ashley grabbed his wrist before he could get out of the car and gain his feet. "Ashley?" His eyes landed in confusion on her hand holding his wrist. "Before you all leave the safety of the car, do you not think I should check round a bit?"

"Not so quick, mister." Ashley smiled up at him confidently, not wanting to be dealt with like a weakling woman. "I'm the time walker here, remember?"

"It may not be safe." Worry formed on Robert's handsome face.

"Then maybe we should all go," Julie answered, matter-of-factly. "If we stick together, we should be fine. I, for one, am not willing to separate even for a few minutes."

"Mom's right, Robert. There is safety in numbers."

He muttered something about not fighting needless battles, while he pulled Ashley from the car. Josh and Julie got out as well. They all searched their surroundings for anything familiar.

"I've heard of *in the middle of nowhere* before, but this is *really* out in the middle of nowhere." Josh shook his head in wonder after a moment of assessing the scene. "There ain't nuthin' here."

No one could argue that. The landscape was the same in all directions. Rolling hills covered in knee-deep grasses sported prairie flowers that dotted the sea of green like multi-colored polka dots on a summer dress. The only thing to interrupt the wafting grassland was a ribbon of dirt road. Winding its way around the hills, it stretched for miles in either direction of the car. This was a fearsomely lonesome spot.

Robert squatted to examine the trail ahead of the car. "This road has been traveled mostly by horses," he said, pointing to the hoof marks imprinted in the soil. "However, these marks are those of a wagon." Sure enough, they could make out a narrow, solid line snaking its way along the ragged, dusty roadway.

"So, no cars for sure," Julie agreed, "but we still can't pin down *where* we are or the *year,* can we?"

"We are obviously in a prairie, but the entire Midwest was a prairie at one time, wasn't it?" Ashley reasoned. "There is a road here, rustic as it is, so people must be around somewhere, right?"

"So what do we do?" Josh tapped his toes impatiently as his eyes floated over the open spaces.

"Well," Ashley continued, thinking aloud, "with no place to hide our car around here, I suggest we drive it further down the road. We might find some signs of civilization or at least some place to leave it that is out of sight."

"I think that's a good idea." Julie eyed her summer sandals and cringed. "Who knows how long the walk might be?"

"Ugh, I hadn't thought about that." Josh tried to shake the coating of dirt off his dress shoes by stomping, but succeeded only in sending up a plume of dust into the air. "Let's go, then." He clambered back into the back seat before anyone could say otherwise and slammed the door behind him.

"I see you smiling, Robert," Ashley teased. "You would be just fine walking in your shiny black shoes, I know." Robert didn't try to hide his amusement as they climbed back in the SUV.

After driving for miles with no sign of a town, they were all quiet, wondering if perhaps they had gone in the wrong direction. As they discussed which way to go, Ashley convinced the others their car had fallen from the sky onto the road in a specific direction for a reason. She believed they should honor that. With the sun dropping a notch in the sky on their left, they only knew they were headed north. Otherwise, it just seemed to be empty road stretching out to the horizon.

Glancing down at her dashboard, a frown puckered Julie's face. "You know, we need to find a place soon to leave this car because we don't have much gas left. I don't believe we're going to want to push it."

Josh groaned.

As if the fates had heard her speak, they rounded the crest of a hill and discovered the land dropped off on their left into a gorge. A stream that cut its way along the bottom of the hill came into view. As their eyes followed the water into the sun, a few trees bunched together to form a shady-looking glen.

"We shall not find a better spot than this."

"*Gee,* Mom, are you magic or somethin'? That's perfect."

"It is, isn't it?" Relief flooded Julie's face. "But how do we get there from here?"

"It's rocky along the far side of the creek, Ma. We should be able to drive along the edge without too much trouble."

"I'll check the depth of the water before we cross it." Ashley opened her door and stepped out. "We don't want to be stranded." She shut the car door with a bump of her hip and surveyed the area.

"Nay, I shall do that. You look too lovely and your gown will get wet." Ashley rolled her eyes, but gave Robert a smile as he got out of the car and joined her without further comment. They crunched their way down to the water's edge. The bottom was visible in several places where the water was shallow. A horse drawn carriage or wagon could easily roll over it, but a car would be swamped. Following the creek side for about twenty feet, they spied the safest place to cross where the ground was somewhat higher. Robert motioned for Julie to follow. They cleared her path of fallen tree limbs and rolled away the rocks that blocked her way. When she reached the water's edge, the creek appeared to be only a few inches deep. "You're going to have to go fast, Mom, if we want the tail pipe not to fill with water." Ashley and Robert jumped into the car.

Julie chuckled, "Today I can say I'm acquainted with fast." She added, "I'm glad you remember your $500 lesson, Ashley."

"I do, Mom," Ashley blushed and turned to Robert to explain. "She's talking about the money I made her spend to dry out this car. I stalled it going through high water in an intersection during a heavy rain last year." Josh snickered. "Shut up, Josh. It was an expensive lesson." She raised an eyebrow at her brother, but he did not miss the flicker of a smile on her lips.

"Everybody ready?" Julie asked. They all took a deep breath and held on. "Here goes nothing!" She slammed the car in gear and revved the motor. The small SUV responded with a lurch and jolted over the muddy creek. They were almost to safety on the other side with the vehicle halfway out of the water when the right rear tire stuck on something.

Spinning ineffectually, it created a spray of water that shot off the back of the wheel well. Robert bailed out of the car, managing to get to dry land and inspected the situation. Josh, riding shotgun, followed suit. Taking his shoes and socks off, Robert rolled up his pant legs before splashing into the water. He made short work of pulling the rock out from under the wheel, clearing the path to the shore.

They needed to get the car out of the water before it sank into the mud. Robert opened the front car door and positioned Josh to push from there, while he took up a similar position next to Julie.

"Go slow and steady," he instructed Julie, who did her best

to do as he asked.

Thankfully, it was a small SUV. The car rolled forward and made its way up the bank as if it were pleased to be out of the water, too. Robert and Josh were mud spattered, but the car was now in the clear and ready to be hidden in the trees in front of them.

∞∞∞

What to take with them? They all located their personal baggage and tried to figure out what they would need in order to condense it into one bag. Their changes of clothing for after the wedding were inappropriate now. Julie dumped out her bag and sorted through the items, choosing to keep her wallet, hairbrush, contact solution and a few other personal items.

Ashley did the same, combining hers with her mom's. She made sure her trusty iPhone was in the mix again. She was thankful she had invested in a solar charger because now she was pretty sure she would need it. The guys had only a toothbrush, hairbrush and cologne, the last rather oddly at Josh's insistence, to add to the main bag.

Footwear was another problem. Julie and Ashley had a choice of the dressy summer sandals on their feet or flip-flops. *Ouch.* Robert had packed his beach sandals and Josh a pair of athletic shoes. None were any better for a trip back in time than what they had on their feet. They decided to keep their dressier shoes on and leave all the extras in the car. Besides, their casual footwear was largely made of man-made materials that might be hard to explain.

While covering the silver car with loose branches to hide it, Ashley spotted a small box in the back seat she had not seen before. "Whose box is this?" She removed a branch to open the back door and retrieved the item. Julie hesitated a moment before answering, "I was saving that for you, honey."

"What is it?" Ashley's curiosity was piqued.

"You might as well go on and open it," Julie sighed. "I'm not sure now when you'll get to use it."

Ashley flipped opened the box and found a charming little nosegay of red roses inside. Of course, her bridal bouquet. She had been so excited about getting married she had not given bridal flowers a single thought. Her eyes filled with tears as her mom's words echoed in her ears: *I'm not sure now when you'll get to use it.*

Julie pulled the bouquet from the box and displayed it for Ashley, her excitement at having created it for her daughter showing in her eyes. "It's built on the same form I used on mine. It's my *something old* for you. It also counts as borrowed, because I want it back, and the flowers are new as is the blue ribbon tying it up. Every bride should have the *something old, something new, something borrowed and something blue* for good luck, don't you think?"

Touched by her mom's thoughtfulness, Ashley tried to keep her composure. After listening attentively to Julie's explanation, Robert turned Ashley around and gathered her into his arms where she dissolved into sobs like a fizzy tablet hitting water.

"I just want to be m-married."

"I know, sweeting, I know." Dropping soft kisses across her forehead and down the side of her face, Robert did his best to comfort her. "We shall be married soon enough and have a long life together. Olde Gylda said so, did she not?"

Ashley sucked in a shaky breath and tried to collect herself. "You're right, Robert. I'm just so . . . *disappointed* it's not today." She rested her head against his solid chest, still miserable, but trying her best not to show it. Robert bent down and whispered for her ears only, "You cannot be half as disappointed as I."

He shifted his weight against her and might as well have set her afire with a torch for all the heat that blazed up through her core. How she burned for this man. And how she wished they were alone. The desire in his lovely hazel eyes was full of the promise of wonderful things to come. But they were not married yet, and they were definitely not alone. Reluctantly, Robert set her away from him with a big sigh.

Her mother's sly grin told Ashley she was aware of their not-so-secretive longing for one another. *Oh, well. It was the truth, after all.* Red-faced, she watched her mom place the bouquet back in the box and return it to the floor of the back seat.

"Maybe they will dry nicely if we just leave them alone for now." Julie slammed the door and placed a branch strategically over it before giving Ashley's shoulders a sympathetic squeeze. Not having quite recovered herself from Robert's touch, Ashley noted his wicked smile. The man wasn't helping. He knew all to well what he did to her. Robert reached for her hand once again and pulled her to him, so he could kiss her cheek.

Ever impatient, Josh rolled his eyes at this additional display of affection. He was more than ready to hit the road. Shoving his sleeves up past his elbows, he unbuttoned his shirt another notch, and charged off down the road. "Let's go people! The day's moving on, and we're not getting any younger."

"Says the youngest one," Julie laughed. Josh didn't bother to answer and dashed ahead.

Ashley was pleased when Robert tugged her hand to his chest, kissed it, and then tucked it up under his arm as if for safe-keeping. He slung Julie's bag over his other shoulder and with Julie trailing behind, they set off to ... someplace.

Ashley hoped it would be friendly.

∞∞∞

The sun was hotter than Ashley thought possible after only a few minutes. Her shoes had worn a blister on her left heel, as well as her right little toe, so neither foot was faring well. She leaned harder on Robert with every step. Her mom had lagged even further behind them and was noticeably limping. Josh was so far in front at times he couldn't be seen over the swish of the prairie grass along the winding trail. The air was fresh but marked by the pungent smell of wild grass. Ashley couldn't help but wish she had Meggie and Alice's cart and the two of them to wheel her along like she'd had in her first time walk.

The one thing she was super sorry they didn't have with them was water. Where was her plastic bottle of water when she needed it? Old Edmund, of Ashdown had been so shocked at seeing it. Her smile wilted as she wished she had taken a drink at the stream when she'd had the chance. She had no need then. Surely this road led someplace civilized soon.

Trudging on for what seemed like an eternity, but was probably less than an hour, Robert cried, "Salvation, Ashley! There are trees up ahead." He squeezed her arm to shake her out of her plodding pace. "I do not believe trees would be there without water, so perhaps we can rest and have a drink."

It took Ashley a few beats to shed her tired state of mind sufficiently to understand what he'd said. *"Hallelujah!"* Sighing, she sent a look of thanks to the heavens. "My feet aren't going to make it much further at this rate."

They were almost to the trees when Josh turned back on a dead run. Ashley's heart platform-dived to somewhere around her blistered toe. What now?

"Someone's coming! Someone's coming!" Trying to keep his voice down as he warned them, Josh swooped into line beside his mom. "Heads up!" Their strange little band made its way into the trees, all four excited to have found a person at last, but apprehensive nonetheless.

A moment later, a rider headed out of the woods. He was not alone. A cow was being dragged along behind what turned out to be a young man on an old horse.

"Blazes, Romeo! You are one cuss-ed critter. I have half a mind to knock your bollocks off, boy." About Josh's age, he gave a sharp tug on his rope that the bull ignored without difficulty. "Must you chase after every long-legged heifer in Kansas?" The

boy had not spotted them yet, deep as he was into his tirade directed behind him at the bull.

Kansas, Ashley thought. At least they knew they were in Kansas.

Ashley scanned his appearance trying to determine the time period. The boy's shirt, open at the neck, looked like it was made of muslin, vanilla in color. His pants were an earthy-brown, bulky weave tucked into a pair of well-worn soft leather boots. He pulled off his cap, and sopped the sweat from his forehead and the back of his neck with a grungy looking scarf that he returned to his back pocket. Instead of putting his cap back on his head, he looked like he was about to throw it at the contrary creature. Ashley got a good look at the hat in a sudden burst of light through the trees. If she was not mistaken, it had the markings of a military hat of some kind. *Hmm,* it couldn't be, could it?

Before she had time to mouth the question to the others, Josh rasped, "He's got a Union cap in his hand." *Yup.* Ashley recognized the insignia above the brim of the dark blue hat, even though she had never played a Civil War video game in her life.

Still cranked around in the other direction and berating his bull, the boy was almost upon them before he sensed their presence. He spun around to face them.

Suddenly, the rifle, formerly hooked in the saddle behind him, was aimed at them.

Click.

They froze at the sound of the rifle, locked and loaded. Were they going to be shot like defenseless ducks lined up in a carnival game? The world wavered for a moment and seemed to slow down. Ashley trembled as if she were trapped in a slow-motion western where the horrific, bloody fight scene would be shown in excruciating detail. Her eyes rolled back in her head, and she teetered between fainting and not. Really, she would prefer to pass out if the only other option was seeing a loved one's brains blown out.

"What in tar-nation! Ohhhh, glory be!"

Slowly, it sunk in that no one carried a weapon, so there was no threat. The boy's eyes got bigger when he noticed two were ladies. He white-knuckled his reins and stared with squinty eyes at them from his perch upon his horse. The beast had seen better days, judging from the sway of its dappled gray back, but it obediently ceased its impatient stamping and held its ground.

"Whew-ee! I thought you was *Bushwhackers* fer sure, and my heart nearly stopped," the boy confessed, dropping his rifle to the saddle and fanning himself with his cap.

Ashley could see Robert had been assessing how best to protect them. She squeezed his arm, and he let out the breath he had been holding. Happily this encounter had not come to blows. His eyes focused on the long gun the boy held, intensely curious about it. She realized he had probably never seen one except in Josh's video games. She shuddered at just how close they had come to being shot.

Still stunned by having a rifle pointed at them, they had managed to say nothing at all to the young man. Swinging his cap around in an elaborate bow from atop his horse, the boy dove into his apology with fervor.

"Fair ladies," he smiled benevolently at Julie and Ashley, "and honorable gentlemen," he nodded to Josh and Robert, "my name is William Speer, but everybody calls me Billy. I do apologize most sincerely for aimin' to shoot you." His eyes narrowed and his frown deepened. "You must know if you are from 'round these parts that Bushwhackers have been threatenin' Lawrence for weeks now and all us Jayhawkers are pretty jumpy. What with the war and all," he drawled.

The young man flushed a deep red and sheepishly eyed Ashley and Julie. "Please do not take offense for my unseemly language just now. I did, indeed, think I was out here all alone with Romeo or I would not have spoke so rude." He nodded as he finished his apology, wiped his forehead with the back of his hand, and plunked his cap on his head.

∞∞∞

Relief flowing through her at having escaped with her life, Julie recovered enough to break out her widest smile for him, which Ashley echoed. The boy eased his grip on his rifle. Josh and Robert were still busy taking note of the rifle and his appearance and whispering to each other. The boy was somewhat disconcerted by this, but chose to ignore them. Between bashful looks darted at each lady, he explained himself. "Romeo here thinks every heifer needs a visit from him any time day or night. He is a devious devil, like smoke in the wind. I am most often the one chosen to chase him down. He gits harder to bring in ever' time he makes an escape." Julie was convinced that the lopsided grin he delivered along with the apology was designed to thoroughly captivate them. It did. "So, please, y'all," he sneaked a furtive look at Robert and Josh, "forgive my unwittin' words."

"There is nothing to forgive, young man," Julie grinned back. "We are just very happy to see you."

The boy smiled, all sunshine at her forgiveness, but then puzzlement clouded his face. "If you do not mind my askin', what are you doin' out here without a carriage or a coach or horses?" He abruptly recognized the impertinence of his question when a deep blush flushed over the tan of his face.

"A better question," Robert began, "might be how are you planning to capture Romeo again? He has taken advantage of your distraction and is trotting back into the woods."

Suddenly, every swear word the boy had likely ever known flowed like a river from his lips. Nothing impeded the stream of words--no tender ears of any lady, his father's probable dismay, nor anyone else for that matter. Dragging the rope tied around his neck behind him like an errant dog, the bull was happy to find itself free again. The lad took off as fast as his old steed could trot, giving chase to the wily critter who jogged away at a good clip.

For a moment, Josh and Robert looked at Ashley and Julie with a question lighting their eyes. Julie smiled indulgently at them. "Yes, go help him. He's our best chance to get to civilization, and we don't want to be after nightfall getting there."

Civil War civilization, Julie thought, as in Lawrence, Kansas, if she had heard the boy right. What did she know about Bushwhackers, Jayhawkers, and Lawrence, Kansas? She rubbed that thought around in her brain like a thumb on a worry stone. Robert and Josh took off after the boy, Josh crowing in delight.

She turned and her heart filled with tenderness as she spied Ashley roosting on a fallen tree, still dressed as a bride. She knew her daughter would love to have run with the boys if it weren't for her gown and the blisters she was now examining on both feet. Who would have guessed this morning their wedding day would turn out like this?

Lawrence, Kansas. It still niggled in the back of her mind. She would have to wait for whatever it was she knew about the town to float up. She was getting nothing now.

Julie's attention was soon diverted from thoughts of Lawrence by a giggle erupting from Ashley. As she looked up, Julie saw Josh running for all he was worth towards a downed tree with the bull on a beeline right behind him. It was a scene from a cartoon. She was aghast and amused all at the same time. Josh dived over the tree and ducked down with the skill of a rodeo clown dropping into a barrel. Sure enough, the bull jumped over the tree and kept on going. Josh reached out and snatched the trailing rope and let out a whoop of success. The bull reached the end of his tether and sent Josh flying headlong into the soft earth. A dead branch on the downed tree hooked the rope and kept Josh from being dragged behind the critter. For the moment the bull was back on a leash.

The boy swooped in on his horse and snagged the rope from the branch before the bull decided to change directions and charge them again. Without hesitation Robert moved in on foot and expertly grabbed the bull by the halter, bringing him to a halt.

Julie ran to Josh and was relieved to find him laughing at himself as he rolled over and sat up, spitting out dirt, but fortunately, no teeth.

"That was *awesome!* I can't wait to tell Parker I was chased by a mad bull. He's never gonna believe I actually *caught* him." Julie pulled him to his feet, brushed the dust off him and helped him right his clothes, all the while scolding him for taking crazy chances. Josh's eyes twinkled with mischief. "Sorry I scared the life out of you, Mom." He paused. "Heck, I scared the life out of *me!*"

Romeo appeared to respond to Robert who hummed soft, sweet words into the ear of the big animal. Either the beast was worn out or Robert had the magic touch, because now quite docile, the bull nudged his pocket like a horse awaiting a treat. Robert laughed at the incorrigible critter and scratched under the varmint's chin.

Julie thought the bull was a big fellow, but not a mean one, and not unlike those she remembered from the family farm growing up. Robert sighed and she wondered if he was homesick. All this time jumping had to be especially hard on him. There was nothing she could do for now but concentrate on getting her children to safety one small step at a time.

First, they had to get to town before dark.

Chapter 19

As it turned out, Lawrence, Kansas, was much closer than any of them had imagined. Julie and Ashley, not to mention their feet, were happy to be astride Billy's horse, Rusty, with Robert leading them along. Josh walked most of the distance backwards, tagging alongside Billy and pestering him with questions as they made for town. Billy prodded Romeo to lead the way but kept him on a short leash.

One moment they traipsed along a green, grassy field, and the next they popped over a small rise to find a little town nestled into a valley. A wooded gorge sliced the town in half before climbing up to a peak on the west side of town. Ashley thought it might be . . . well . . . *new.* As if Billy had read her mind, he announced with pride, "Lawrence grows ever' day as folks come to settle here." He pointed to the east to a pretty, white frame house on a tidy little farm on the outskirts of town. "Over to yonder is our place. It won't take long to git there and then you all can rest up."

Sensing that home was near, Romeo called out a long moo that was answered by several others moos moments later. Billy loosed his hold on the rope and Romeo darted off at a trot. This bull obviously ran the show, and it made them all laugh.

As their odd little band trooped up to the house, Ashley spotted an older man preparing to load a wooden table onto a big, rough-hewn farm cart. Two young men, obviously older than Billy, assisted him.

"*Hall-oo,*" Billy called, "I've brought some folks home to meet you, Pa." He turned back to Julie. "Let me get this critter back in his pen first and then I'll introduce you." He scurried ahead to do just that with Romeo snorting and calling out to the rest of his herd, for once going where he should.

Billy's father stopped upon hearing his son holler and brushed off his hands before walking toward them. The two young men, dressed in similar fashion with cloth caps set at a jaunty angle over their eyes, put the table down and followed their father. Mr. Speer looked somewhat out of place on the farm. Wearing brown tweed pants with a white collared shirt and string bow tie beneath a matching brown vest, he appeared to be a professional man. A studious air hung about him, perhaps due to the pair of wire-rimmed glasses perched precariously on the end of his nose. An untamed shock of dark hair rose from his brow as if he had pulled at it while thinking. He reached out to Julie with a quick smile and a great deal of warmth twinkling in his intelligent brown eyes. "Welcome! I see you've met Billy and our resident rogue Romeo. I hope neither has caused you any difficulties." Although he said nothing directly, he had not missed their strange dress and lack of conveyance.

Robert lifted Julie and Ashley down from the old red beast as if they weighed nothing. Julie put her hand out to formally greet Mr. Speer with such perfect grace and poise, that Ashley's brows shot up to her hairline. Her mother couldn't be that unscathed by all that had happened, could she?

Just then, Billy burst back onto the scene and took great delight in introducing his new friends to his father. He embellished the story of Romeo's antics like a budding raconteur until they all were laughing nearly to tears. What a gift, Ashley thought.

They learned Mr. Speer was the editor of the town's newspaper, *The Lawrence Republican*. He told them he had left work early in order to head home to haul some items for a community-wide picnic in the city's South Park. "You all are just in time to join us. Mrs. Johnson asked that my sons and I bring this big old table to serve as the ladies' pie table. Well, since she promised to reward us with a delicious slice of her famous apple pie, we could not refuse."

He turned to call to the two young men behind him, "Rob, John!" He proceeded to make the introductions with Rob stepping up first and slipping off his cap as he shook hands. Ashley found him, the younger of the two, to be a sandy-haired, soulful fellow with a soft voice and an easy smile. Rob's pleasant face featured light brown eyes that seemed golden in the late afternoon sun. She liked him right away. When she turned to his brother, she gazed up into cerulean blue eyes and her heart all but stopped.

Young John Speer's face split into a lazy, lop-sided smile. Those blue eyes flashed, and his silky black hair fell into a curl over his forehead as he doffed his cap and grinned down at her.

It was Elvis Presley, down to the sneer on his perfectly pouty lips.

Well, she knew it couldn't be, but this guy could pass for the young Elvis of the old Hollywood movies. Ashley heard her mother's gasp behind her and knew she had come to the same conclusion.

Recovering to the best of her ability, Ashley stammered out a hello, not unlike a thirteen-year-old girl at her first dance. Robert eyed her suspiciously. He was owed an explanation, or he would think she had lost her mind. Meanwhile, young John, knowing all too well his effect on women, just assumed she was taken with his swarthy good looks. He did his best to charm her, causing Robert to glower his disapproval.

Josh cocked his head as he studied the two brothers. Her little brother found something familiar about John, too, because he shook his head as if he were trying to shake off his confusion. He caught her watching him and glared at her.

Grrrr.

Ashley frowned at Josh, but he let her know the sound hadn't come from him. Josh's eyes shot up to seek his soon-to-be brother-in-law's, letting her know it had come from Robert. He whispered in Robert's ear loud enough for Ashley to hear, "Did you just *growl?"*

Did he do that? Robert's face betrayed him as guilty as charged. He adjusted his stance and stretched out his clenched fists before flashing a smile at Josh that bared more teeth than a smile. He calmed down some when Ashley sought his eyes and held them, beaming her love reassuringly to him.

Her poor man was suffering. This should have been their wedding day, after all. Surely, he didn't think she was flirting with this guy, did he? Of course, he would not know the guy was the spitting image of a long dead, iconic movie star. If they ever had a moment alone together again, she would tell him. She nudged her mom who was still staring at John with a smitten expression on her face. Goodness, if she looked that silly, no wonder Robert was put out.

Julie snapped to and disconnected from young John long enough to let Mr. Speer know of their need for lodging. Her mother impressed her as she made up a story on the spot about being from Texas and on the way to a wedding not far from Lawrence when their carriage slipped into a ravine crossing the stream. As Julie told it, their horse had gone lame and all of their baggage had been left at the scene of the accident. How convenient, she thought, inwardly giving her mother a pat on the back for creativity.

"Ah, I see," he replied, with understanding. "My wife left for Topeka yesterday morning with our little ones to attend her sister's lying in. With her absent it would not be proper for me to house all of you here." Julie's face fell, but Mr. Speer continued graciously, "However, your men folk can bunk here with me. You ladies can find a room at Emily Hoyt's boarding house across town. She's a widow lady who runs a fine establishment, and I think you will be well cared for there."

Julie's face must have broadcast her concern, or Mr. Speer just guessed that having no money bothered her. "Mrs. Hoyt owes me for advertising in my paper, so do not worry about the cost of your stay. I will simply deduct it from her account and all will be well." He pulled out a small card from his chest pocket, fished out a pencil stub from another, and scribbled a short note to Emily before handing it to Julie. "Just give her this and tell her we will settle up in a few days."

Julie's sigh of relief was audible, making Mr. Speer work to hide a grin. Then her mother looked down at her outfit and her face reddened.

Ashley picked up on her mother's cue. "Mr. Speer, we were not expecting to be gone for longer than the day, and we have no suitable clothes with us to go to a picnic with you. Perhaps we should stay here until you get back."

"Nonsense, my dear," Mr. Speer admonished. "We are a large family with plenty of clothes to suit your needs. You are more than welcome to borrow whatever you require until your own clothes can be reclaimed." He gave Julie an earnest nod. "My sister is back east visiting family and left a trunk of her clothes here as she is between homes awaiting the return of her husband from the war. I am certain Susanna's trunk contains garments that will fit you ladies. As for your men, we have clothes in many sizes." He gazed proudly at his three sons as proof. "We can readily accommodate them."

Once again, Julie sighed her relief as Ashley gifted Mr. Speer with a huge smile. "You are too kind, sir."

When Ashley turned to Robert she saw his brows had dipped even lower over his eyes. *Yup,* he was unhappy and frustrated, but what could she do? Scowl at the man who was helping them find places to stay and clothes to wear? It might not be what they had planned, but they all needed to make the best of it.

Wait, was it the smirk on John's face that bothered him? Yeah, that seemed likely since Robert's eyes were on the guy. She was not sure whether to be amused or mad when Robert swore a *God's blood* under his breath.

Mr. Speer, seemingly oblivious to Robert's dark mood, directed John to help the newcomers find appropriate clothing while he and Rob delivered the table to the park. John was supposed to accompany the ladies in the gig to Mrs. Hoyt's place to settle in and then go back to pick up Josh, Robert and Billy. Mr. Speer and Rob would put the latest edition of the paper to bed on time and then meet up at the picnic. With plans in place, Mr. Speer said his farewells and departed for town, leaving John and Billy to outfit their new friends.

A short time later, Julie and Ashley emerged from the tidy white house dressed neatly in trim gowns that made them fit in nicely with the denizens of 1863 Lawrence. At least the newspapers in the parlor had given them the month and year, along with plenty of advertisements for current ladies' clothing.

Julie, carrying a peach-colored shawl, had found a simple white blouse and a serviceable gray skirt she could roll up at the waist to shorten it some. Ashley was pleased to find a delightful blue muslin gown with a wide ruffle skirting the hem. It featured a dark blue ribbon tied at the waist that made her middle appear so small she imagined Robert could circle her waist with his fingertips. Julie had redone her hair into a braided bun to match the style of the era. Ashley chose to leave hers swinging in long golden ringlets around her face.

The makeover did not go so well for Robert.

∞∞∞

Fate is a cruel master sometimes. Robert might as well have been held hostage in the coat Handsome John had given him on loan. Itchy and two sizes too small, he was afraid to move much, or he would split open a seam. The shirt was somewhat better, so at the first opportunity he would lose the jacket. His pants were almost long enough. Almost. He had insisted on wearing his own shoes even if they attracted undue attention. Robert had the distinct impression John intentionally provided boots and garments he knew would be too small. Oh, the man was pleasant enough, but Robert noted the smirk that lurked underneath those thick lips. Still, beggars could not be choosers, according to Josh. That was easy for him to say. Josh was roughly the same size as Billy and had slipped into Billy's clothes like a second skin.

Robert wasted no time in letting John know that Ashley was his betrothed, yet it appeared to have no impact on the man whatsoever. If anything, he took it as a challenge, explaining how Lawrence was isolated and new so there were few eligible young ladies to pursue. Was he planning to pursue Ashley? Robert's fingers flexed involuntarily as they hung at his sides. He was feeling the odd man out at the moment, and he was growing unhappier about it by the second.

He and Josh had gleaned some useful information while they changed, however. John regaled them with tales of the picnics held in Lawrence, and they gathered this one was a belated Fourth of July celebration. The city had been on alert for a rumored raid by Bushwhackers for well over six weeks. Thus far the raid had not happened, and the city was tired of waiting and in need of some entertainment to ease the tension. Everyone in town would be attending tonight's festivities for delicious food and dancing. Old man Collamore, the mayor, had even promised fireworks. According to John, it would be a rousing fun time.

Robert could hardly wait.

Sigh.

∞∞∞

Ashley and her mother met John next to the gig that Rob had waiting for them in the farmyard. She wondered why Robert was not there to say goodbye. Where was he? John helped Julie up onto the single bench seat. Turning back, he surprised Ashley by lifting her up with both hands about her waist and dropping her onto the seat before she could protest. He hopped up on the gig, and scooted in snuggly beside her, ready to drive to Mrs. Hoyt's house.

Mr. Speer wanted John to return for Robert and the boys

to take them to the picnic, so she couldn't ask John to wait any longer for Robert. Ashley glanced at the smirking man beside her and realized he had helped her mother up first so Ashley would have to sit in the middle next to him. Without warning, John clicked the horses to trot off before either Julie or Ashley was quite settled. Julie let out a fearful screech and grabbed for the side bar. Ashley lost her balance and rocked back, only to be steadied by John's arm. Somehow he had managed to snake his arm around her waist to hold her tightly to him. Ashley, unhappy with the abrupt start, indicated with her eyes that his conspicuous hold on her waist needed to end. John batted his long lashes at her and innocently asked, "Wha-at?" Julie and Ashley both dropped their jaws at his audacity. Rolling their eyes at one another, they both recognized an incorrigible flirt when they met one.

"You can drop the arm, John. I think I have my balance now," Ashley grinned. "Thanks for your concern."

"But I cannot let you lovely ladies take a spill from this gig." His startlingly blue eyes sparkled with good humor, but he did not loosen his grip on her waist one iota. "I want to claim a dance with each of you before the evening is out, so I must protect you from any injuries."

Ashley giggled at his mock-serious answer. "Pouring it on a little thick, aren't you?"

"Why I do not know what you mean, Miss Ashley," John scoffed, which was difficult to do with an ever-present smirk. "I just want to dance tonight with the belle of the ball and I cannot reckon which of you two charmin' ladies that will be."

Julie groaned and that set all three to laughing and shaking their heads over John's obvious banter. Ashley decided she liked this Elvis guy. He didn't take himself too seriously despite his handsome face, and he seemed to have a wicked sense of humor. As they made their way across town to Emily's, John proved to be an entertaining companion with a lively commentary about Lawrence.

Ashley noted that every street they passed was named for

a state in the union. John told them the abolitionists who built the city hailed from every part of the country so it was a logical thing to do. The north/south streets were named after states, and the east/west streets were numbered. Ashley made a mental note that when they left the Speer house they turned onto 9th street. A few blocks later they turned onto Massachusetts St., which was the business district and home to his father's newspaper. They turned again, this time onto 10th street and passed Vermont, Kentucky, Tennessee, Ohio and Louisiana Streets before finally turning onto Indiana. When they pulled up in front of Emily's house, Julie and Ashley were surprised to see a solid-looking red brick structure with a comfortable wrap around front porch. It looked well kept on the outside. After promising to attend the picnic, they said farewell and started up the walk to Emily's house. John insisted on following, clearly not wanting to leave yet. Once they entered and looked around, they knew the house could not be more than a few years old at most. It was beautiful.

Mrs. Hoyt, a stern widow with a teenaged son, ran a tight ship. She wore a crisp white apron over a trim black dress and had not a hint of a smile for them when she answered the door. Furthermore, she did not bat an eye at being told Mr. Speer would settle with her next week on the rent. If these people were friends of the Speer family, it was good enough for her. She sent a reluctant John on his way home with a dismissive wave of her hand.

Ashley and her mother were marched to their room above the front porch, facing Indiana Street. There Mrs. Hoyt left them with snowy white towels and sharply given instructions about when she would be leaving for the city picnic. If they were late getting to her wagon, they would be walking. She was in charge of supplying many of the main dishes for the food tables and would not keep people waiting.

They got the message.

As soon as the door shut, Ashley collapsed on the bed and her mother sank into the chair by the window, still holding the towels. It had been a long day and it was tempting to miss that ride to the picnic in favor of a long sleep. Ashley sighed. She couldn't do that to Robert. He would be upset if she didn't come and worry about her. With no way to contact him, she had no choice but to suck it up and go. Besides, he must not have been happy with her for some reason when she left the Speer place, or he would have been around to say goodbye.

He was not worried about John, was he? It was fascinating to her that the guy could look so much like Elvis. Why Robert would be jealous of a mere boy on what should have been their wedding day was beyond her. As she thought about it, she got red in the face. *Really!*

Julie watched a myriad of expressions roll over her daughter's face and wondered what all was going through her head. Ashley was resilient, for sure, but this had been a tough, disappointing day and it still wasn't over. Perhaps there was some way to salvage it at the picnic tonight? Maybe it could be a romantic evening for the two even if they weren't married yet. *Hmm.* She'd have to think on that.

Pulling her tired body up, she found a side table with a washstand and placed the towels on it. She wasn't sure how this boarding house business worked. Maybe she had better look around to see if there was a privy out back and find out where she should wash up. Would they use the cold water in the pitcher on the stand or would someone supply them with warm water? What she wouldn't give for a restorative bath right now. She glanced at Ashley and found her eyes were shut. Poor dear, she needed some rest. Julie decided to scout the building and then come back for Ashley when it was time to go.

Chapter 20

With a furtive glance around to be sure no one watched, Annabeth shoved the last bite of apple pie into her mouth and chewed as fast as she could. She wiped up any excess filling with the fingertips of one hand while hiding her mouth behind the other. It was truly delicious. Forgetting herself for a moment, she sucked her fingers with a big smack to lick the last drop. She only sampled her own pie to be sure it tasted as good as it looked. It needed to be perfect if she were to win the heart of John Speer once and for all. He did love her pie, didn't he? Few young women had caught the interest of young Mr. Speer, and of those he favored, she fancied herself the front-runner.

"Annabeth Johnson," shrieked her mother, forgetting to whisper. "Put down that pie this minute. You have dripped filling all over the front of you."

Elizabeth Johnson, a large, mannish woman with little beady eyes, imagined herself the "Queen Bee" of Lawrence. She could out-bake, out-cook, and out-roast any other woman in the city. By sampling each and every dish she had ever created, she knew with great satisfaction that hers were always superior to everyone else's. Her expansive, solid figure was proof of that fact, not that anyone in town would argue the point. Undeniably, the best cook around, she was generous with her dishes, having fed half the town at one time or another.

Mrs. Johnson grabbed her daughter by the shoulders and proceeded to hastily dab at the cinnamon-laced blotch on her bodice with a handkerchief pulled from her apron pocket. "How can you ever expect to win a man when you slop yourself like a pig?"

Annabeth flinched. She hated her mother calling her a pig above all things because in her heart she suspected she was one . . . and feared it showed. After all, she was short rather than tall, and plump to boot. But Jimmy Cooper had whispered in her ear that she was "deliciously voluptuous" when he danced with her at Hannah Murphy's birthday party. It had made her shiver with excitement down to her toes and a couple of other places she hadn't expected.

Unfortunately, he had taken his devilish silver-tongue and moved on to Hannah herself. Those two were now engaged and would be married in less than a month. At first, she had been crushed, but then recently John Speer showed her much the same attention. He seemed to like her soft, fleshy body as much as he liked her pies.

"Do you want John, Jr. to find you like this?" her mother hissed in her ear.

"John likes me just the way I am," she retorted with a hint of bitterness that made her mother wince in return. It was enough to check Mrs. Johnson's tirade, causing her to only *humph* before shoving the soiled cloth back into her pocket.

With her black curls bouncing in time to her steps, Annabeth flounced away to meet Hannah and Louisa Schmidt. She hurried to cut them off before they reached the pie table to avoid dealing with her mother.

Annabeth did not hate her mother. After all, everyone said she would one day be an even better cook than her mama, and her mother agreed. Newly widowed, her mother told her all she wanted was for her daughter to be married and settled with a nice home of her own. That her mother had added, "Preferably before your figure explodes" sort of ruined the earlier message, but it was the curse of being a good cook. If she could land a good-looking buck like John Speer, her mama would rest easy. He was solid, intelligent and charming, and she thought he appreciated her for herself. Besides, she had not missed the way other young men around Lawrence ogled her full-figure. It wasn't just her baked goods they wanted to sample.

She greeted her friends with a roll of her eyes. They grinned in sympathy, having heard the ruckus her mother had kicked up only a moment ago.

"Is Jimmy here yet?" Hannah pulled her voluminous red curls out of her face to search for her fiancé. "I cannot wait to see him. It will be so lovely to be married and not kept apart."

"Quit rubbing it in," Louisa groaned. "It is not fair you have someone to love when we have no one."

"Yet!" Hannah pointed out.

Annabeth sighed in agreement and only halfway searched the park for John. He was usually late getting to affairs like this because he helped his father close up at the newspaper office. She would watch for him later. As she commented to Hannah on Alta Murtha's new pink gown, Jimmy Cooper swooped in and stole his bride-to-be with nary a hello or goodbye to the other two. Hannah flew off with her beloved without a backward glance. Feeling somewhat slighted, she and Louisa frowned at each other, then grimaced halfheartedly and started toward the food tables to ask if they needed help. She wondered if she might be able to snitch a second piece of pie without her mother knowing.

Seconds later, with Louisa at her elbow chattering on about Ella Sam's dress, Annabeth turned just in time to see *him*. With a huge smile on his face, John Speer headed straight to her. My, but he was handsome, she thought, her breath catching in her throat. Louisa spotted him, too, and with a conspiratorial grin, whispered, "Make him ask for your hand tonight, Beth." Before she could answer, Louisa shoved her in John's direction.

Her heart stuttered at the mere thought of being the fiancé of John Speer, Jr. It would be heaven. She straightened to her full height, thrust out her chest provocatively, and tried to give him her best seductive smile as he walked briskly toward her . . . and right on by.

All at once she realized he had not been looking at her at all, but someone behind her. She wheeled around and saw John approach a beautiful blonde girl she had never seen before. *Ugh.* And, he seemed to know her. Who was this woman with Mrs. Hoyt?

Upset, Annabeth reached out, grabbed Louisa's hand, and spun the girl around to face her, but words failed her. Not accustomed to sending vicious looks, she resorted to imagining her anger hot enough to scorch this blonde woman with a look. She would make her shrivel up faster than a water drop on a hot cast iron pan. Then she wobbled and didn't feel so good.

"Breathe!" Louisa commanded, slapping her on the back. "You are turning blue. Breathe!"

As commanded, she sucked in a shaky breath and regained her balance.

"No one else noticed what happened," Louisa lied. She patted her friend on the back, trying to reassure her John Speer had not just slighted her in front of everyone in the park. "I'm sure we were the only ones to see him behave so shamelessly."

As if on cue, Lucy Gates, the only other competition for John's affection, flitted up and cocked her head toward John. "Well, I guess your lock on that man's heart is faulty, right, Miss Pie-Face? Your famous apple pie has not done the trick despite you and your mama's blue ribbons."

Before Annabeth could collect her shattered self to make a response, Lucy sashayed off to her own mother's table and pitched in to help lay out the food.

"Why that shameless hussy! She needs to mind her own beeswax," Louisa seethed. "How dare she-"

"It's all right." Defeat colored Annabeth's voice. "She said nothing but the truth."

"Dearest Beth, I'm going to go find out who that woman is and why she is here. His interest in her may be completely innocent."

"Well, it doesn't look innocent to me. He is touching her and grinning while he does so."

"Yes, but notice how she is not returning his smiles with the same enthusiasm," Louisa observed. "She appears to be searching for someone who is not yet here. I will find out what I can. Don't do anything or go anywhere until I get back," she ordered and stalked off.

Annabeth felt more vulnerable at that moment than ever before. Her soul might as well have been ripped open and bared to all. Digging deeply for calm, she surreptitiously scanned the park to see who had witnessed her shame. That nasty Lucy Gates would enjoy spreading the story to anyone who would listen. As she turned, her gaze locked in on the activity of a group of new arrivals leaving their carriages.

Like a Greek god walking out of the mist, the most beautiful man she had ever slapped eyes on strode into the late afternoon sunshine. He simply stole her breath.

Her eyes drank him in and thoughts of John Speer disappeared faster than her mom's apple pie. This gorgeous specimen was taller than John, and built wider. She sighed. He was golden. His eyes, his hair. Golden. In the midst of scanning the park, his eyes found hers. He smiled. At her! Her heart fluttered. She smiled back.

He broke the connection a moment later and continued his search. His expression turned black, his brows furrowed and his lips flattened into a grim line. She followed his line of sight and was stunned to see it was aimed at John Speer and the mysterious blonde woman. Her mind raced as her eyes skipped from John to the woman and back again. Was this woman really his woman? Was John the cause of this dark look?

For once in her life, Annabeth Johnson knew exactly what to do. She needed no one--not her mother nor her friends--to tell her what to do or not to do. She just did what she wanted to do.

∞∞∞

A fresh-faced, black-haired girl with flashing violet eyes came charging Robert's way. He did not want to talk with anyone right now, let alone a pretty female. But judging from the spark in her eye, he did not see a way to thwart her. She marched right up to Robert, a step too close, and awkwardly thrust out her hand for him to take. He took it just as awkwardly and waited for her to speak.

"Welcome to Lawrence. I'm Annabeth Johnson and I think we might be of service to one another."

Robert had no idea what she was talking about until she directed his gaze to follow hers to the dessert area. There stood John Speer and Ashley, side by side. The bounder held Ashley's arm tucked within his as he busily whispered something in Ashley's ear that made her flush. Robert heated from the inside out like a coal sparked to life and suddenly he understood. His eyebrows shot up, and he looked questioningly at the woman for confirmation.

"Yes," she smiled with only her lips, her eyes narrowed and hard. "That is my fiancé-to-be over there behaving badly with someone I believe you might know?"

Robert returned her smile, his eyes trying to match the fire in hers, but only pain sounded in his voice. "Yes, she is my betrothed. We were supposed to marry today."

As his words registered, all the venom drained from the girl, and her eyes turned watery and grew as big as plums. "I-I'm so very sorry."

"As am I."

Before he could add anything else, the fiddlers stepped up on their rough wooden platform and kicked up a merry tune. Couples paired off and rushed to dance, their happy chatter and laughter making Robert and Annabeth feel even more forlorn.

Robert collected himself as the sweet-faced girl with the sad eyes stood in front of him, and called forth his best manners. "I am Robert Spycer. Would you care to dance with me, Miss Johnson?"

Annabeth's eyes grew wide and a smile broke evenly across her pink cheeks. "I would, Mr. Spycer. I believe I would."

As Robert took her hand and led her into the dancing, she

grinned at a big-eyed girl in an overly frilly skirt, who glared at them. That seemed to please his partner a great deal.

Robert, however, was not at all pleased. He had rushed out of the Speer home to say goodbye only to find the gig halfway down the road with John Speer's arm around Ashley. Her lilting laughter had floated across the meadow to assault his confidence. Then, he had arrived here in time to witness her cozily whispering with John like she had not a worry in the world. Did she not remember they were to have been married today?

His heart was somewhere down underneath his boots, being trod upon with every step of the dance. He was not sure why he had asked this girl to dance because dancing was the last thing on his mind, unless it was with Ashley. Furthermore, he knew not how they danced here, and he was afraid he was making a fool of himself. He grinned morosely at Annabeth who just smiled reassuringly at him and pretended that his stepping on her toes did not hurt at all. It might as well have been one of Josh's video games where he knew no rules and was not sure what to do next.

Fortunately, the mayor, Mr. Collamore, solved that problem by waving the dancing to a stop and calling everyone to attention for a prayer delivered by the Reverend Samuel Snyder. He introduced a lady who organized the dinner lines that had folks piling their tin plates high with all kinds of good food. Robert absently wondered if there were any chickens left in town because fried chicken was piled high on many huge platters. Hearty beef stews, corn on the cob, and green beans abounded. It was really a sumptuous town supper.

Billy and Josh found their way to the front of the line as only starving teenage boys can do without anyone else taking offense. Robert tried to work his way over to Ashley, but Annabeth held firmly onto his arm and chattered away. She pointed out the local celebrities like the banker, the owner of the hotel, and the blacksmith. He heard the names as she spouted them, but he did not connect with anything she said. His eyes were only on John Speer who kept grinning and speaking in Ashley's ear. She just laughed, rolled her eyes, and elbowed John with a familiarity that made him taste bile.

Perhaps sensing his eyes on her, Ashley turned and caught Robert staring at her. A smile lit up her face for a moment. Then she looked at his stark expression and at the lovely girl latched onto the side of him and frowned, raising a questioning eyebrow at him.

Robert noted the frown and tried to disengage from Annabeth in order to join her. Just then John spun Ashley around and introduced her to an older lady standing next to the drink table. Did John do that intentionally to avoid him? Before Robert could say anything to Annabeth, she had dragged him to the dessert table and was introducing him to her mother. It seemed he would not be joining up with Ashley anytime soon without calling entirely too much attention to himself.

He did his best to paste on a smile and meet Mrs. Johnson, fervently hoping that she would recognize his dilemma and help him escape her daughter. Alas, it was not to be. The sturdy woman viewed him through little round eyes that literally popped with pleasure as she sucked in the sight of him. He felt as trapped as a fly in a honey jar.

Mrs. Johnson shoved a piece of the most mouth-watering apple pie he had ever seen into his hands. Annabeth poked a bite of the flaky deliciousness into his mouth, and he decided hanging with the girl did afford one major perk.

Children and dogs ran wild, darting in and out of the clusters of adults that dotted the park at dusk. The evening was clear and a gentle breeze periodically shuddered through the thick leaves of the cottonwood trees to keep the heat from settling too closely about them.

Everyone from miles around had come for the evening's festivities. Robert listened to men talk of raids coming from over Missouri way and wondered if he should worry about that. A Mr. Dix assured him the rumor had "them bushwhackers" coming before the next full moon. Since the moon would be full tonight and the raiders had not come, they should be out-of-the-woods. Robert started to question the wisdom of that thinking when another gentleman interrupted and asked Mr. Dix about the weapons stored in the armory a few blocks away. Mr. Dix said they had practiced getting weapons out if under attack and could do it in record time once the enemy had been spotted. With no castle fortress to hold off an attack, Robert was about to ask if the city placed guards at night along the roads leading into town.

By then Annabeth was not suffering gladly the loss of Robert's attention. She pulled him away from the gentlemen and pushed him in the direction of the fiddles and dancing. Robert decided it was not his business, and since he did not think they would be staying here long he would leave those decisions to the town's men.

A laughing band of young teens darted by them, and Robert spied Josh running hand-in-hand with a flush-faced little redhead with dancing green eyes and an infectious giggle. The evening was turning out well for some folks.

As he did every few moments, he hunted for Ashley in the crowd. She was so beautiful and so full of life he had to admit he enjoyed watching her talk to people even though he would have preferred she be with him. Her eyes sparkled and the smile she shared with people was genuine, seeming to warm them in her aura. He could not love her more. Here they were time-crossed lovers, crossed one more time. Who could even imagine such a thing?

Unfortunately, this time when he spotted her, his hands clenched as that cad Speer bent over and gave her a kiss on her cheek. How dare he! Ashley jerked back like she'd been bitten and immediately sought Robert's eyes as if she had known precisely where he was, too, her face a picture of distress. He was set to tromp over and give that bounder a fist to jaw on, when Annabeth threw her arms around him and dragged him into the dancing. What could he do but go with her? Ashley's response was to look confused, perplexed, and bewildered by this person hanging all over her betrothed. Why was it so difficult to get together tonight?

∞∞∞

Julie stood on the sideline with Mrs. Hoyt, watching her children and Robert. She could tell this evening of a day-that-could-not-end-soon-enough was adding to the heartache Robert and Ashley were experiencing. What a non-wedding night they were having, she thought. Through no fault of their own, the two had been commandeered by a pair of locals Suzanna Richardson had informed her were an item themselves. What on earth was going on? She would not hesitate to interfere but was not sure what she could do other than demand that dance John Speer had promised her in the gig. A smile quirked her lips. If Ashley and Robert didn't get this figured out soon, that is exactly what she would do.

Meanwhile, Julie eased herself onto a nearby tree stump to take the load off her aching feet. She glanced at Ashley and marveled that the poor girl was even standing on her badly blistered feet. It was time now to keep an eye on Mrs. Hoyt in hopes of making an early escape back to the boarding house. She and the kids would find time tomorrow to regroup and figure out how to get safely back home. A gaping yawn sneaked up on her as she rubbed her tired brow. This time travel was no easy business.

Just then Josh and Billy whooped by, deep in a game of chase with the girls who had followed them all evening. She was glad she was not responsible for getting him home. He was wound to the max. She turned to watch them take off into the trees when she became aware of a body in front of her. Looking up into Mr. Speer's sparkling smile, she blinked almost blankly. He grinned and took her hand, helping her rise. "My friend here would like to meet you, Mrs. Duvall. May I introduce you to Mr.

D.C. Allison, the owner of Duncan and Allison right by my news-paper office downtown."

Julie peered into the stern face of a forty-something man sporting a thick, bushy brown beard and bushy eyebrows to match. He smiled rather stiffly, but Julie was quick to observe the man's eyes darken with interest as she said hello and smiled back at him.

"Ma'am, I would dearly like to dance with you, if you would be so kind?" Julie didn't think she had any choice because Mr. Allison had already taken her hand from Mr. Speer and was guiding her into the thick of the dancing.

She tried not to sigh or groan too loudly as her feet shuffled painfully to the music. Mr. Allison was having a good time and wasn't a bad dancer. At least he did not step on her feet to add to her misery. Her thoughts turned to how she could lose him if he got too amorous. He was pulling her a little too close for her comfort each time they came together in the dance. She wished she had not told Mr. Speer she was widowed when he had asked, so word had not spread. The song wound down none too soon. He swung her around just in time for her to see Mrs. Hoyt load the last of her things, climb up on her wagon, and head hell-bent for home.

She and Ashley would be walking back to the boarding house.

∞∞∞

John Speer whispered into Ashley's ear one time too many, finishing his endearment with a rakish swish of his tongue that made her ear crackle. Her hand came up to thwack him on the face, but he was too fast for her and caught her wrist, a wicked grin on his face.

"What do you think you are doing, John?"

"Why, I am only teasing you, pretty lady," he chuckled, his

brows innocently poised over his lop-sided Elvis sneer.

"Well, I'm done with your so-called teasing." Furious, she dried the inside of her ear with her fingertip. "My fiancé is dancing over there with someone else, and here I stand with you bent on giving my ear a tongue-washing."

John made no effort to hide his amusement at his own audacity. Ashley stomped her foot in exasperation and reach out to grab his ear. She gave it a satisfying twist.

"Enough!"

John yelped in pain, so she reluctantly let go before everyone in the park looked at them. "Who is that girl?" she managed to grind out through gritted teeth. "You must know since you are acquainted with everyone else here. And why is she still dancing with my fiancé?"

Rubbing his hand over his injured ear, John complained haughtily, "No need to get all high and mighty, Miss Ashley. The female in question is Miss Annabeth Johnson, the woman I intend to marry."

Ashley felt like her head might explode. "Then why on earth are you treating her as if she doesn't exist?" She thought about smacking him again. "You have spent the entire evening glued to my side, whispering stupidities in my ear for what reason?"

John's chin had tucked under, and he glared up at Ashley through those very blue eyes lined with thick, black lashes. "I wanted to make her jealous. She's too sure of me. Once we're hitched there's no goin' back, and it was fun to pretend to court you."

Ashley covered her hot face with both hands and sighed heavily. "You should be glad I am too tired to slap you, John Speer. Your ridiculous behavior has caused me no end of trouble tonight."

A firm hand grabbed her shoulder, and she peeked out to see her mother's kind eyes looking at her. "May I be of service here? You two could do with some time apart, I think." Julie winked at John. "And you, sir, promised me a dance, did you not?"

"Yes, Ma'am!" Happy to escape the wrath of Ashley, John could not take Julie's hand fast enough and tow her off to the dancing.

A still angry Ashley watched them go, grateful for her mother's timely intervention. She began searching the rest of the dancers for Robert and much to her chagrin could not find him. Was he angry with her? Why had he not come to dance with her? She had a feeling something was up, but had no idea what it might be. Becoming somewhat frantic, she walked around the mass of folks dancing their hearts out, to finally spot the young woman John had identified as Annabeth Johnson. After spending the whole evening on Robert's arm, the girl was standing alone, watching the dancing with a wistful look on her face.

Here goes nothing, she thought, as she marched over to Annabeth. She might as well introduce herself and hope she could keep this night from becoming any worse than it already was. When she slipped in beside the girl, she found her even shorter than she had seemed from across the park. She tapped on the girl's shoulder, which caused her head to whip around and send her black curls flying. Ashley stepped back as she beheld an astonishingly lovely face. Annabeth's big violet eyes were set in a sweet, heart-shaped face that stared back at Ashley as if hers was the face of Medusa.

"I'm not a monster, I promise," Ashley cautioned, sensing this girl was not the threat she had imagined only a moment ago. "I am just a little confused and thought you might help me sort out a few things."

The girl visibly relaxed as it registered that Ashley was not there to take her head off. She raised her eyebrows, tipped her head to the side, and gave Ashley a wistful, apologetic smile, "Hello, Miss Ashley."

"You know my name."

"Actually, I feel I know you quite well since Robert talked of nothing but you."

"Well, Annabeth, I apologize for not knowing all evening who you are." Those startling eyes showed honest surprise, forcing Ashley to tamp down her anger. "John confessed only a moment ago that you are the woman he is to marry, or I would not have tolerated his blatant flirting as long as I did."

The girl's eyes widened and her jaw dropped in sheer wonder. Thinking this young lady doubted her veracity Ashley felt she needed to defend herself. "Honestly, he was very entertaining and I knew he was playing or I would have stopped him much sooner."

"John Speer told you I was the woman he would marry?"

"Well, yes," Ashley answered, still not understanding the girl's astonishment. "You are planning to marry him, aren't you?"

Annabeth gaped at her for a moment and then burst out uncontrollably into giggles. Ashley thought perhaps the woman was a touch crazy, and she was unsure whether to be concerned or bemused by the outburst. "He said he was just trying to make you jealous." She hoped that information might calm the girl.

Finally, Annabeth got control of herself and the words started tumbling irrepressibly from her mouth. "Oh, Miss Ashley, that's the most wonderful thing I have ever heard. I have wanted him to ask me to marry him for months now, and I was hoping tonight he would do it, but when I saw him with you I thought it was all over, and he would never do it, but now you say he told you he wanted to make me jealous, and he means to marry me?"

Thankfully, Annabeth was forced to take a breath so Ashley was quick to jump in, "You mean to tell me he has never asked you to marry him?"

Her black hair bobbed as she nodded vigorously, her hands clasped to her bosom, still too breathless to answer.

"God's blood," Ashley cried, reverting momentarily to her Hertford days. "I can't believe his nerve. He said you were too sure of him and once you were married--hitched, I believe he

said--he'd never have another chance to flirt with anyone else. He thought he'd take advantage of the situation with me," she explained. "The arrogant fool!"

The girl's rosy-red lips sucked in a mouthful of air, "He said I was too sure of him?"

Ashley nodded disparagingly, annoyed to have been part of John's ruse.

"Amazing."

She was so smitten Ashley could not help but smile in spite of her ire. What a dramatic pair these two were--like old-time movie stars. Ashley burst out with a giggle herself. Elvis and who was that actress from the fifties with the violet eyes? She'd keep that observation to herself for now, but her mother would love it.

Looking up she realized Annabeth thought she was laughing at her and snapped out of her reverie. "I'm sorry, your fiancé is a handful, isn't he?" When all she got in response was a dreamy sigh, she figured it was time to get down to the real reason she was talking to the girl.

"Do you happen to know where Robert is?"

"Oh, dear," the girl gushed, "I am so sorry I have not thought a moment about you. Of course, you want to know where he is. I must admit to you I wanted to make John jealous, so I never let Robert get close to you all night." Her face puckered up and tears welled in her eyes. "He told me from the start you were his betrothed. You two would have been married today if not for the carriage accident, so it was most cruel of me to use him thusly."

"Well, you were not alone in that, so I guess I can't blame you. But, that's all water under the bridge." She paused, and calmed herself. "Do you know where Robert is now?"

"Forgive me!" the poor girl gasped. "I do not know why it has taken me so long to tell you. Your Robert has gone home with Mr. Speer and his son Rob." She continued knowledgeably, "Mr. Speer had to stop by the newspaper office to drop off Robbie. He is planning to spend the night there with my John so your men folk have a place to sleep at their house." She blushed, "I overheard him explain to Robert why he needed to leave."

"Did my brother Josh and Billy Speer go with them?" Ashley asked, scouting the park for the two.

"I think I heard tell they were going to stay a while longer with John and would walk home later." Annabeth hesitated when she recognized that information had once again been gleaned from eavesdropping. "Besides, it's not far."

Ashley sighed. There would be no more opportunity to patch it up with Robert tonight. She contemplated walking to the Speer's house herself, but gave up the notion. Her blistered feet would not be party to the long walk that would follow from the Speer's place back to Emily Hoyt's.

Hot tears flooded her eyes as she thought about how the day had gone from delicious excitement to frustrating disappointment. This should have been her wedding night, and here she and Robert were barely speaking to one another due to the machinations of another couple. It really was not at all fair.

Ashley became aware of a hand holding hers and looked up to find her mother steadily staring into her eyes, sending strength silently to her very soul. How did her mother always know the right thing to do? And at the right time, too?

Julie slipped an arm around Ashley's waist and whispered words of encouragement into her ear. Then she leaned back and gave a cheery hello to Annabeth, telling the girl how much she had enjoyed meeting her mother and exchanging recipes with her. The girl responded brightly, but was obviously still worried about upsetting Ashley. She excused herself as quickly as possible and headed to the dessert table and her own mother.

"Well, daughter, are you ready to walk back to Mrs. Hoyt's house?"

Ashley groaned her dismay. "You cannot be serious. The woman left us here?"

"Yes, ma'am, without a word of warning."

"My feet--"

As if rehearsed, a man stepped out of the shadows in

which he had been lurking and bowed his question. "May I give you charming ladies a ride to Mrs. Hoyt's? It seems she has left the park rather early."

Her mother's eyes widened in surprise, or was that alarm? Before her mother had time to gather her wits and perhaps refuse him, Ashley answered for her. "That would be most appreciated, Mr.--?"

"Allison," the man happily filled in.

"Thank you," Ashley beamed. Her mother did not argue, having been over-ruled by her feet.

"Fireworks will start soon. Are you sure you do not want to stay for them? Not many towns around here enjoy such a treat, you know," he boasted proudly, his bushy brows dancing a merry tune as he spoke.

Julie looked at Ashley for confirmation and both responded with a resounding, "No!" Julie turned a bright red so Ashley explained about her blistered feet and her desire to get to her room to take care of them. Mr. Allison was disappointed, but he handled it with grace. They said their goodbyes to Josh and Billy who serendipitously swooped by, and then Mr. Allison escorted them to his carriage and was the perfect gentleman helping them in.

Somehow Julie found herself in the middle of the long coachman's seat with Ashley on the far side. Somehow Mr. Allison found the need to steady her by putting his arm around her waist when they turned the nearest corner. Ashley snorted at that obvious move and tried to cover it by coughing. Was this standard dating procedure in Lawrence? She almost snorted again at the thought, but her mother's elbow in her ribs put a stop to it. Julie could only smile sweetly at Mr. Allison. Mercifully, the day-that-could-not-end-soon-enough was almost over.

Chapter 21

Crash!

John Speer, Sr. woke with a start. Sitting up he automatically reached for the thin wires of his glasses on the small table beside his bed and crammed them over his nose and ears. What had awakened him? He listened for a moment before a ruckus erupted near the barn. Then a loud moo sounded followed by breaking timber.

That damned animal is loose again. Why he still kept Romeo was a mystery. Wearily, he untangled himself from the bed covers, plopped his feet on the floor, and searched for a pair of pants. If he could not contain the beast any better than this, he would sell him and buy a calmer bull. This constant chasing after Romeo was becoming more intolerable by the day.

Making his way to the front porch he stood for a moment in the now silent predawn and cursed softly to himself. It was too quiet. The blasted bull had already made his escape. But in which direction? He peered down the road and found nothing to indicate Romeo had gone that way, but neither did he find any sign of him toward the river. *Drat.* Mr. Speer sighed heavily and shuffled into Billy's room to shake the boy awake.

∞∞∞∞

The fading moonlight cast eerie shadows on the surrounding landscape. Robert trudged along behind Billy and Josh as the three of them searched for Romeo. Josh and Robert had volunteered to go with Billy since his brothers were sleeping at the newspaper office and not available. Billy was sure the bull still had his heart set on the cornfield behind James Lane's house. That is where Romeo had gone to chase after some heifers a couple days ago. Since Romeo was, well, Romeo that was a good place to start. While the boys took off on foot headed west, Mr. Speer decided to ride east along the river, which was another favorite spot for the critter's adventures.

The roadway was empty as they passed Massachusetts, Kentucky and Tennessee Streets, and traveled over the foot-bridge that spanned the ravine leading to the western part of town. As they crossed Indiana, Billy pointed down the street to a brick house on a corner lot and identified it as the boarding house belonging to Mrs. Hoyt.

Robert's heart skipped a beat as he thought of Ashley still sound asleep in nothing but a thin night rail and had to stop himself from detouring to see her.

Correctly interpreting the look on Robert's face, Josh grinned and taunted in a singsong voice while daintily dancing down the road, "*Robert and Romeo, the love-sick duo. One looks blue while the other just moos!*" As if on cue, a familiar long, low moo answered his song.

In typical brotherly fashion, Billy guffawed loudly and took off for the cornfield to catch his critter. Josh, delighted with Romeo's excellent timing, made a dash after Billy, dodging Robert's attempt to grab him by a mere inch. The irritating pair, laughing and noisily tromping into the cornfield, disappeared down a row, leaving Robert's grimace to morph into a grin before he followed in their wake. The morning was clear and cool and it was hard not to let their infectious good spirits raise his own.

There would be time later to find Ashley and make amends for their lost evening. Once he held her in his arms again, all would be well. Warmth spread through him as he thought of the woman he loved. He grinned foolishly. His life had surely never been dull once she had entered it. How would he ever have imagined he could be in the middle of a place called Kansas in 1863 tracking down a lovelorn bull before daybreak?

Senator Lane's cornfield was a big one with its still-green corn towering over their heads. That prevented them from easily seeing Romeo, but they heard the beast calling forlornly to the females he pursued.

Ka-pow-wow-wow.

The sound echoed in the crisp morning air and all three froze. Romeo had no hesitation, however, and took off at top speed simultaneously with the shot. Robert and Josh sprang to life and zipped after him, but Billy wheeled and made his way to the edge of the cornfield, fear etched into his face.

"That sounds like a gunshot to me," Billy said aloud, even though the others probably couldn't hear him. "Why would anyone be shootin' anything in town right now? It ain't even light yet." He scanned the horizon trying to spot the source. Then, as if on some kind of signal, the air was rent by countless gunshots, making it seem as if an army had opened fire on the town.

"Bushwhackers!"

Billy whipped around and ran into the field yelling for Robert and Josh, coming up fast on them. They had somehow managed to grab Romeo and had the beast on a lead, dragging him along behind them.

Anxiety and fear mixed with excitement in Billy as his words spilled out, "Bushwhackers! Them bushwhackers have come! There must be hunnerds of 'em. Listen!"

Josh stood with his mouth ajar listening to the rapid gunfire. Robert thought instantly of Ashley and how he needed to find her and secret her away to a safe place. Just where that would be, he had no idea. Billy sprinted up the hill for a better view, leaving Robert and Josh impatiently waiting and trying to soothe a skittish Romeo. Billy rushed back towards them moments later with horror written on his face.

"Fire!" he hollered. He stumbled down the hill in his haste to reach them, sending an avalanche of rocks over their

feet. "Fires are ever'where, and I think our newspaper office is burnin'." He slammed into Josh, grabbed his arm and pulled him along. "Leave Romeo and come on. We got to git to town to see if my brothers need help."

Within seconds the smell of fire wafted in the breeze to confirm what Billy had said. It was a terrifying scene he described and the continual bursts of gunfire from all directions left no doubt what Billy said was true.

Robert's training as a warrior kicked in. He lifted Billy by the back of his shirt before he got away and swung him around. "Billy! You cannot go charging out there without any weapon and no plans or you will get yourself killed."

Billy stared dumbly at Robert for a moment before he cleared away his haze of anxiety and hatred long enough to understand what Robert had said. Finally, he nodded, "You are right. We should go by the armory first. By now it should be open, and we can arm ourselves before we go in the back way to the office."

"Better," Robert conceded, remembering what Mr. Dix had said about their weapons armory at the picnic. "Let us go there. We can plan our next move on the way."

"Romeo?" Josh questioned, still holding the lead on the animal.

"Bring him!" Robert commanded. "We will use him for cover or a diversion, if need be."

Billy gave no argument, already dashing off ahead of them in the direction of the ravine.

"You think Mom and Ashley are okay?" Josh's voice wavered as he pulled Romeo into a trot.

"For now," Robert responded through clenched teeth as he darted after Billy. "The action seems to be back toward the middle of town. We need to find Billy's brothers and then go to Mrs. Hoyt's as soon as we can."

They had barely stepped into the shadows of the ravine when several riders breezed by them. Fear made them freeze in their tracks. Even Romeo must have sensed things were not as they should be. With Robert holding the lead at his head, the bull stilled like a long-forgotten statue frozen in time. The men laughed and shouted as they fired shots into the air.

A rider pulled up beside them, and they thought for one terrible moment they had been seen. Instead, the man turned to whoop to the others behind him. "This way to the shenator's. I'ma gonna shoot that thievin' bastard right 'tween his eyesh. My Mary's gonna git her pi-aner back." It was all too clear from the man's slurred words that he was not only drunk, but was seeking retribution. *"Whoo-ee-e!"* he yipped and took off again, with the others on his heels.

Desperate now to make it to the armory, Billy motioned for Robert and Josh to follow him. They moved as quietly as three men and a bull could through the undergrowth, pausing only for the sound of horses coming their way. As they approached the turn off on 7th Street, they had to step out of the ravine and travel over a block to reach the armory without any foliage for cover. They scooted from shadow to shadow as fast as possible. The morning sun would be peeking through the trees shortly and their camouflage would disappear.

As they sneaked around the corner to the front doors of the armory, a lone rider burst around from the other side. They all thought they were done for, as there was no time to turn and run away. The rider wheeled the horse to a stop long enough for Billy to recognize the person mounted on the mare.

"S-Sallie? Sallie Young?" Billy stuttered. The rider leaned over her saddle and gaped at them through the morning haze. She was a young woman dressed in a split skirt and plain blouse with her dark hair in a single braid down her back. She handled her mount like she had been born on it.

"Billy Speer, what are you doing out here? Don't ya'll know that the order is to burn every house and kill every man? That's any male old enough to carry a gun. I heard that raider named Quantrill give the order himself right in front of the Eldridge hotel." Billy looked dumbstruck by this news. "Downtown is burning to the ground and he has loosed his men to do as he says. If they see you, they will kill you."

"My brothers?" Billy choked out.

Sallie shook her head sadly. "I do not know how they have fared, Billy. I am just tryin' to warn as many folks as I can before the raiders show up at their doors, but I fear I am too late. Fires and death are all around."

Robert moved to stand behind Billy and grasped his shoulders, fearing that Billy would crumple with the news.

"The women and young children have not been harmed, but men and boys are killed 'fore they can do anything to stop 'em. I heard tell there is a list they check in some cases, but in others they just shoot to kill."

Sallie raised an eyebrow questioningly at Josh, who was holding a very docile Romeo. Billy answered for him, "Romeo got out a couple hours ago, and we were chasing him down when the raid started."

She absently nodded her understanding and turned to Robert with a swivel of her head, "Is the armory open?"

Robert tried the doors, only to find them locked tight. He looked for another way in and found there was none.

"Thought so," Sallie sighed audibly. "Mr. Dix has the key and no one kin find him, so there's no tellin' when this place will git opened." She sagged like she might crater for a moment, but then abruptly sat up tall in the saddle. "Ah, well, you boys best take care. Stay covered and outta their way." With that Sallie kicked her mount and took off toward the ravine to continue her mission.

Robert was somewhat calmed with the news the raiders were not harming women and children. Still, every nerve in his body was ordering him to return to Emily Hoyt's place and Ashley. Billy interrupted his thoughts. "We got to find my brothers. Let's go!"

Robert looked to Josh for confirmation before both finally nodded in assent. This would not be easy. They were only a couple blocks from downtown when they saw fires burning brightly through the trees and over the prairie grasses in between. Billy assured them they would slip in through the back and not take to the main street at all, but Robert still felt his heart in his throat.

They stayed single file and in the shadows as much as possible. Billy dashed out in front to lead the way. Robert followed reluctantly behind him with Josh bringing up the rear. Dragging Romeo was getting more and more difficult as the bull became restless the closer they got to the smoke.

Josh had started to ask if they could tie up Romeo somewhere when raiders came flying out of the very alley Billy was ready to turn into. They nearly ran Billy into the ground. Thankful he was not right behind the boy, Robert immediately stepped back and hid with Josh behind a small horse shed, judging from the pungent aroma of manure.

Two raiders lost no time drawing a bead on the boy. One raider was astride a huge stallion that dwarfed Billy and proceeded to pin him neatly between the two men. Almost as huge as his horse, the man leaned over the beast, cocked his pistol in Billy's face and glared at him. Only his black eyes were visible above the bandana tied over his mouth and nose to keep out the smoke.

"What is your name, boy?" His deep voice rumbled out of his thick chest.

Billy stood slack-jawed until the second raider, a wiry, wild-eyed wisp of a man, poked him roughly in the chest with the end of his rifle. "Answer him, boy, or you die right here."

"John!" Billy blurted, "John Smith."

Josh and Robert nodded to each other in relief. Billy had remembered what Sallie told them about a list and changed his name. The nasty little man with the long gun looked disappointed as he examined his paper, while the bigger fellow kept his gun aimed at Billy's head.

"No John Smith on the list, Holt."

"Let him go then. He's just a runt anyway."

"He's not that little." The thin man raised his rifle to aim it at Billy's head. "Do we have to let him go?"

Josh could stand the stress no longer. He slapped Romeo on the rump, which sent the disturbed critter charging into the street with his lead trailing behind him.

Startled, the men's horses shied as Romeo canon-balled directly at them. While the raiders fought to keep their terrified animals under control, Billy took advantage of the moment to take off running after Romeo. "There he is! Romeo, come back!" Billy didn't look back. By the time the men got their horses calmed, Romeo and Billy were long gone. The men grumbled a bit but took off toward the armory, still grousing about that boy and his damned bull.

Not knowing which building housed the newspaper office, Josh and Robert slipped into what was left of the alley behind a big brick building. It was now clear of raiders, so they waited for Billy to return. A few very tense minutes passed until Billy slid in beside them, sans Romeo. He grinned and whispered, "Romeo is tearin' up Massachusetts St. causin' all kinds of havoc." His grin fell away. "Maybe he can keep someone else from bein' shot."

Robert clapped him on the back in silent agreement and they resumed their single file prowl toward the newspaper office.

Or where the newspaper office should have been.

Smoke was billowing out rooftops and filling the alleyway. Soon they had to duck down, breathing through their shirts pulled up over their faces to keep from coughing. The smoke was so thick Billy was forced to count the buildings as they passed them only to come up short before they reached his father's office. As if by some evil magic the buildings melted away, leaving them exposed to the world and facing a scene from hell. They stood behind the smoldering remains of a chimney, the only part left of the newspaper office, and squinted through the smoke at the horrific spectacle before them.

It was utter chaos.

Men on horseback fired indiscriminately at anything that moved and was male. Jayhawkers from Lawrence, in the name of abolition, had raided Bushwhacker plantations in Missouri in late March. Today Bushwhackers, who supported slavery, planned to even the score. It was open season on the residents of Lawrence who were defenseless with all their weapons securely stored in that armory no one could open. Raiders with torches set fire to whatever could burn. Smoke poured out of every window and crevice still standing on the street, while flames shot high into the sky along what was left of the rooflines. Silver candlesticks, paintings and other valuables littered the street, plunder waiting to be hauled off by the raiders when the time was right. Women screamed and threw themselves over the bodies of their men as they found them fallen in the street, their children crying and clinging to their mothers' skirts.

It was worse than horrific. There were no words for it.

Billy stood stupefyingly numb as he watched his town disintegrate into ash. Josh and Robert could only stare helplessly.

"It looks like all hell let loose, don't it?" a familiar voice growled right behind them. Three heads whipped around at the sound. Billy was the first to respond and tried not to whoop as he dived into the arms of his brother John, who caught him. "Glad to see you are not dead, little brother."

John turned with Josh and Robert to watch the pandemonium in the street. "Still enjoying your visit to our fine city?" He winced, and Billy realized John was hurt. Much of his shirt had been burned from his body and blisters were welling up on his back where the material seemed to have melded into the burn. "I'm fine, Billy. Just a little crispy around the edges," he joked, although his eyes clearly showed his pain.

"Where's Rob?" Billy held his breath as he waited for an answer.

"Don't know," John muttered through gritted teeth, gingerly trying to pull the blackened material away from his burns. "I have searched for him since this mess started. He took off at the first shots before I could even put my pants on, and I have not seen him since." He rolled his eyes at Billy. "I haven't found his body either, so I do not believe he is dead."

Billy sighed his relief and then explained their father had left before dawn to look for Romeo along the river east of town while they had headed west. "Good," John drawled, "perhaps trackin' that stupid critter will keep him out of all this."

Suddenly, Robert had had enough of the bedlam before him and took charge. They must get out of here and now. He could not wait another moment before finding Ashley. "Billy," he whispered. "Josh and I must find Ashley and their mother. Are you staying with your brother or are you coming with us?"

Before Billy could answer, John cut in, "I need to find Annabeth, so we will go with you."

"Annabeth Johnson?" Robert's jaw dropped.

Sheepishly, John grimaced, "Yes, I asked her to marry me last night before I left the picnic."

"What?" Billy cried. He caught himself a moment before he whopped his brother on his wounded shoulder.

A tense beat pulsed between the two men, Robert's eyes burning hotter than the fires around them.

"You kept me from my betrothed all evening when it was *Annabeth* you wished to marry?" John hung his head, knowing he was guilty, but said nothing more. Robert was swamped with way too many conflicting feelings. He was not sure if he wanted to shake the man's hand or take a flail to him. Since Ashley was no longer involved he might just punch him in the face, and then congratulate him on his betrothal to Annabeth. The need to sink his fist, first and foremost, into that smirking countenance was quickly winning out, however.

Noting the look on Robert's face, Josh grabbed his arm and headed him back out of the alley the same way they had come in.

"To the ravine and single file." Josh hoped to divert Robert's attention further before he punched John. "We've got enough going on without some stupid fight over girls."

"Yes, sir," snapped Billy, agreeing with Josh as he eyed the two men. "We've got a brother to find." Robert tried to contain his growl, shoved John in line behind Billy and brought up the rear, still clenching his teeth. They darted one at a time out of the alley and into the fray.

Chapter 22

Julie awoke sitting straight up in bed, drenched in sweat, without any idea why she was so disturbed. Her heart was pounding as she took in her surroundings in the still-darkened room, and yesterday's misadventures flooded into her over-taxed brain.

"No-o-o-o-o! Leave him alone!"

A woman's hysterical shriek echoed over the silence just before a gunshot cracked the air. Ashley dashed out of bed and to the window before Julie could recover from her shock.

"Get back, Ashley! Stay away from the window." Julie tripped over the bed covers as she tried to move her shell-shocked body to stop Ashley. "That was a *gunshot.*"

Suddenly, the once quiet morning exploded seemingly all around them as the sound of gunshots ricocheted across the landscape.

A now more cautious Ashley stood beside the window and peered out at the scene unfolding across the street. Julie took up a post on the opposite side of the window.

Three horseback riders were laughing and shooting at a disheveled man still half in his nightclothes who ran for his life from a fourth shooter on foot. The chase streaked around the yard, into the house and out the back while the shrieking woman tried valiantly to stop them.

Julie and Ashley screamed in unison as the man, now a bloody mess, was shot one last time and fell at the woman's feet. She threw herself over the man to protect him from further harm, sobbing loudly while the mounted raiders mocked her.

The shooter swaggered over to his victims and ceremoniously lifted the arm of the woman. He placed his pistol against the man's head and pulled the trigger.

The woman emitted a heart-rending, twisted sound of agony that Ashley hoped never to hear again. Ever. The murderer blew off the smoke from his gun to the guffaws of the men. To entertain his fellow raiders, he reached down and pulled off a ring from the woman's left hand, pocketing it in his vest. He swiftly remounted, and they all took off whooping down the street in search of more sport.

Julie's legs gave out from beneath her, and she sank to the floor in a puddle of nightgown, throwing her hands over her face. The moment the horrible man touched that woman's arm she knew what he would do. She had seen this played out before. Those errant fragments of history that had taunted her yesterday when they would not form a whole, dropped neatly into place in her addled, twenty-first century brain.

This is Quantrill's raid.

She had studied it in graduate school and seen it re-enacted in documentaries on the Civil War.

It was famous.

Her heart fluttered in distress as the rest of the information streamed back into her head, her eyes filling with tears. That would mean nearly two hundred men would die this day and there was *nothing anyone could do to stop the slaughter.*

"We've got to go help that poor lady." Ashley's voice broke. "There is no way her husband could have deserved that treatment." When her mother didn't answer, she forced herself to look away from the window and was alarmed to see her mom on the floor tucked into a ball and rocking back and forth. She was moaning softly.

"Mom! Are you all right?" Panic-stricken, Ashley swooped in to comfort her, anxiously pulling her mother's arms from her face to reveal the tears that flowed down her cheeks. "That was terrifying, I know, but we're safe. They've gone, Mom."

More gunshots rent the air and Ashley froze. "Are we

under attack?" She looked uncertainly at her mother's tortured face. "Who are those vicious people?" She cocked her head for a moment and then her eyes popped wide.

"Bushwhackers? Are they Bushwhackers, Mom?"

The sound of horses galloping in their direction penetrated their room and made Julie spring to life. She knocked Ashley off her feet as she jumped up from the floor, abruptly all business.

"We've got to warn Emily right now. These men won't hurt women and small children, but her son had better hide as fast as he can."

"What are you saying?"

Words tumbled out of Julie's mouth in a flurry as she pulled on the borrowed clothes she had worn to the picnic and shoved a shocked Ashley into hers.

"You know how this turns out?"

Julie closed her eyes to keep the world at bay for a moment and nodded. "It's a massacre, Ashley."

"Robert . . . and Josh!" Ashley's hands flew to her cheeks. "What will they do?"

"I don't know." Julie's heart felt like it had been wrung from her chest. "We can only do what we can, where we are."

Just then, loud pounding on the front door of the house startled them. Cries of "Open up!" reverberated through the house.

Julie ran out of the bedroom and down the stairs, grabbing Emily before she opened the front door. "Mrs. Hoyt, we'll hide your son. When you talk to these men, show them your strength. Don't back down, or they will burn your house."

Then she took a good look at the straight-laced, hard-nosed woman she whispered to as Emily all but rolled her eyes at Julie's superfluous suggestion. "Already hid the boy, and never fear, I'll not be losin' my home, Miz Duvall."

She pulled a shotgun from a nearby cupboard and expertly cocked it. Brazenly, she threw open the front door with a bang, and forced the knocker to step back. Emily marched onto the porch with a glint in her eye and faced down two riders near the steps and the man facing her who carried a torch.

One gaping bushwhacker still on horseback found his voice. "You got any men in there, lady?"

Without a quaver in her voice, Emily replied honestly, "Nary a one. My mister died seven years ago."

"This here's a boardin' house accordin' to yore sign. Who you got stayin' here?"

"Only a missus and her daughter," Emily answered in a matter-of-fact voice. As announced, Julie and Ashley bravely stepped into the doorway.

"I think she's *hidin'* someone in there," the craggy-faced man on the steps accused. "Let's jest torch the place and move on."

Emily calmly lifted her shotgun and aimed it at the man. "I don't think you want to do that, mister."

The two men still mounted guffawed, one spewing an ugly stream of chewing tobacco in the process. "Leave the little spit-fire be, Samuel. Ain't no men here. Least-ways none you want to git yer head blown off fer."

Defiantly, the man stepped onto the porch and jabbed his torch threateningly at the women. He then made his way back to his horse, swung himself up, and followed his partners at a gallop heading toward the big hill called Mount Oread.

Emily stepped forward and trained her shotgun at their heads as they rode out of sight.

Ashley and Julie had witnessed a very courageous woman in action. They were about to say so, when Emily turned and gripped the post at the top of the steps. The color had gone from her face and her eyes were pinched shut. Julie quickly moved to her and put an arm around her waist.

"This rifle ain't worked proper since my pap owned it 40 years ago," Emily whispered. "I jest keep it fer sentimental reasons."

Julie was awestruck by the enormous risk this brave woman had taken. "Let's get you inside, Mrs. Hoyt," she finally uttered. "Your gamble saved your house and your son."

Ashley turned to follow them, but stopped and sniffed. "Is that smoke?" Answering her own question as she searched the devastation across the street, she bellowed, "Those *bastards!* They set that poor woman's house on fire." Without another word to the two women, she sprinted up the stairs toward her room. Moments later, she flew downstairs with the blankets from their bed and raced across the street to start beating out the flames that threatened to engulf the house. The overwrought woman who lived there, somehow pulled herself from the body of her dead husband and stared silently at him. A moment later, she ripped off her petticoat and joined Ashley in an effort to save her home from destruction.

Chapter 23

Josh and his wingmen had just stepped onto Vermont Street when rowdy voices were heard up ahead. Without a word they all took cover and tried to see what was going on.

Seven men were lined up in the dusty street with raiders on horseback directing them to march. Remarkably compliant, the captured men did as they were told with their hands behind their heads. As the prisoners neared, Billy caught his breath and Robert realized the boy recognized the men. One of the marchers said something they struggled to make out. Then without warning, one of the raiders opened fire and began shooting the men in the back, mowing them down in order back to front.

Women watching from the porch of a nearby house screamed. Josh's eyes nearly popped from his head at the brazen brutality. John emitted a strangled cry, shoved Josh aside, and bolted out into the street to confront the raiders. Billy would have followed in his wake, but Robert snagged him by the collar at the last second and jerked him back. Then both Robert and Josh understood. *One of the seven men was Billy and John's brother Rob.*

What happened next, Robert thought, was like a gory scene from one of Josh's war video games come to life. John stood in the middle of the street waving his hands and bellowing in hopes of diverting the killers' attention from his brother who was seconds from being shot.

Rob threw up his palms and screeched, "No-o-o-o-o! Go back!" Having grabbed the attention of the shooters, John wheeled and tried to dive into the ditch beside him for cover.

The shooter paused to assess the diversion. For an instant it looked like John had succeeded in stopping the firing squad before they shot Rob and maybe lived to tell the tale.

But only for a moment.

As if by some demented choreography, the killers shot simultaneously, the tattoo of their shots sending John and Rob flying into the air in a deathly *pas de deux*. It ended only when the sickening thud of their bodies hit the ground.

Silence fell for a beat or two. Then it was broken by the shrieks and sobs from three women who rushed to the bodies of their fallen men, undoubtedly husbands, sons or neighbors.

At the moment, though, no one rushed to Rob's side as he lay dying on the ground. No one grieved over the fallen body of John, tossed like a forgotten trophy into the ditch. That was the worst kind of hell for Billy, who shook with rage and loss as he watched from the shadows. All Robert could do was hold the boy tightly with one hand stretched over his mouth to keep his cries from revealing their presence. If he let him go, the lad would likely hare off to his fallen brothers and meet the same fate.

Josh fell to his knees, wilting over his inability to do anything but get himself killed. Robert gritted his teeth as hot tears threatened to roll down his own cheeks over the unfairness of it all. How would he feel if one of those bodies lying out there were his brother Elric? Still, he would not allow Billy to sacrifice himself on the altar of his brothers' bodies.

Showing no mercy and with their work done, the raiders shouted their last insults at the wailing women and galloped past them on their way to find other men yet to be slain.

Robert could hold Billy no longer as the boy burst forth and flew to John's side to see if by some miracle he still lived. Josh followed him, uncertain as to what to do. Robert ran the distance to Rob's side only to realize that an entire side of the young man's head had been blown away. He gently tried to move Rob's head to spare Billy the sight of it, but realized there was no point to it. They needed to move the dead out of the roadway immediately or risk leaving the bodies subject to further atrocities if more raiders came their way.

He stared for a moment in sorrow at the bodies of the six men who had fallen along with Rob Speer. One woman, apparently aware of their vulnerability in the street, had already started pulling her husband's body toward the closest house. Robert jumped up and hurried to her side to help, only then recognizing her from the picnic.

The picnic that seemed a lifetime ago.

Looking down at the man she pulled, he saw that it was none other than Mr. Dix, the keeper of the armory key. Dressed haphazardly, he must have thrown on the nearest clothing when the shooting erupted.

Robert's hands shook as he searched the man's pockets, all the while explaining to the poor lady what he was doing. He thought it odd that Mrs. Dix neither helped nor answered, just continued her dogged mission to remove her husband from the street. It dawned on him she likely was in shock. He had seen that look before.

He found no key.

Bitterly disappointed there would be no weapons to fight these bloody raiders, he tried to reason with himself that it was probably too late to do much good anyway. The raiders would be gone soon. He set himself to the task of getting the ladies and their loved ones into the closest house. The need to find Ashley and her mother grew by the minute.

He whistled to Josh who had taken up an awkward stance beside Billy now hovering over the body of Rob. Seeing there was nothing more to do for John, Robert motioned to Josh that he needed help. Josh trotted to him, relieved to do something. One by one, they lifted the dead men and either dragged or carried them hastily into the house. The three distraught women, one quite elderly, rallied their strength to aid in the effort. In a short time the job was finished. John's body was the last to be brought in with the help of his little brother and laid out next to

Rob. It was almost too difficult to comprehend what this meant for the Speer family.

Robert looked at the jut of Billy's jaw. He was a tough lad, but what he had just witnessed would surely shake even the strongest Hertford warrior. These sticks that shot fire and took lives at a distance were more horrific than any weapon in his land. An arrow did not blow a hole in a person. It was suicide to meet one of these sticks unarmed. He only hoped Billy understood that.

What should he do with the boy now? Should he leave him alone to seek his father with the news of his brothers' deaths? Would Billy be smart and stay safe or would he get himself killed?

What he did know was that he and Josh were long past due to find Ashley and Julie. He could not justify waiting any longer to ensure their safety. Even though no woman had been shot to his knowledge, he knew not what horrors Ashley or her mother might be witnessing.

Robert did not have to make the call. The determination on Billy's face made him look more man than boy. "I must find my father. You need to find your womenfolk, and you know the location of the boarding house, so I will leave you now."

Before he took off, Josh grabbed him in a wordless bear hug. Robert squeezed the lad's shoulders and gruffly added, "Think before you act, Billy, and stay alive. Your parents have lost too many sons this day."

Billy's jaw jutted a bit more, but he managed a ragged nod before wheeling and taking off into the shrinking shadows of the now mid-morning sun. He headed back toward his family's home place, the bearer of the news no father wished to hear.

∞∞∞

Ashley sank with exhaustion onto the steps of the once-white frame house, Emily's singed and frayed blanket still in her sooty hands. She was sorry the borrowed clothes she wore were burned in places and full of holes. Different bands of raiders had streamed by on their path of destruction through town, setting fire to the house three times. She learned that the woman she helped was Mrs. Carpenter whose murdered husband was-- had been, she reminded herself--the new judge in town. Ashley feared Mrs. Carpenter's sanity was holding by the narrowest of threads. A baby started to cry in the midst of their struggle to put out the first fire. It was Ashley who tracked down and rescued the infant before the dear little thing inhaled too much smoke.

Throughout the morning Mrs. Carpenter slowly regained her tattered senses after the shocking murder of her husband. She now tenderly held their child in the shell of her badly burned house, crooning softly to the sweet baby. Ashley's heart bled for the little tyke who would never remember the father who had lost his life in such a wretched way.

She released a tired sigh, feeling herself deflate from what seemed like hours of frenzied work. Wiping an irritating cinder from her eye she thought about her own father. She missed him every day, but at least she enjoyed the memories of a happy childhood with him at her side. How many children would be left to miss their fathers after this dreadful day?

Rubbing her forehead to ease the persistent pain that throbbed there, she closed her eyes and tried to think of what to do next. Seconds later, she jumped in alarm as a soft hand patted her shoulder, but was relieved when her eyes darted up and discovered her mother's worried face.

"I'm okay, Mom," Ashley said, bringing her heart rate back under control. "Just bone-weary."

"Yeah, me, too." Julie sat down on the steps next to her bedraggled daughter. "Emily and I held off raiders so many times I lost count, but her house and her son are safe, so it was a victory." She looked sadly around at the fire-damaged house belonging to the Carpenters and let out a sigh to rival Ashley's.

"From what we can see from Emily's cupola, the raiders are gone now." She paused as she gathered her strength. "If the accounts I read of this raid are true, many of those boys and men we met last night at the picnic are now dead." She shuddered uncontrollably before she could finally spit out what she needed to say. "If you are up to it, Ashley, we should go to the center of town and offer our services. There is much to do before anyone can rest."

Ashley nodded, unable to speak as she thought about all the loved ones the town's folk must bury. It would need to be soon because unrefrigerated bodies would not keep for long. What a grizzly thought. She swallowed hard and tried to steel her nerves for what was to come.

"Have you heard from Robert or Josh?" Ashley held her breath, hoping for a positive response.

Julie studied her daughter's face for a moment. "No, I haven't," she sighed.

"Well, they'll just have to find us then, won't they?" She refused to think that something bad had happened to them. She could not contemplate what life without Robert would be like, not even for a moment, but her heart twisted involuntarily. Isn't that what had happened to her mother when her father disappeared? Suddenly, she couldn't breathe.

When Julie turned away and started down the walk, Ashley stood up to follow. Still struggling to get her breath, she was forced to grab the porch rail to steady herself. Woozy, she wasn't sure she had it in her to keep going, but somehow she'd have to dig down and find the strength. She had Robert and Josh to find. And besides, these good folks deserved her help.

She caught up with her mother and matched her steps, hooking arms so they could lean on each other. Together, they made their way toward Massachusetts Street.

Chapter 24

"Ashley!"

A woman's voice shrieked as Julie and Ashley rounded the corner of Massachusetts Street and took in the complete devastation of three blocks of downtown Lawrence.

"Ashley Duvall!"

Locating the source of the voice, Ashley recognized the cannonball of sooty muslin rushing them was none other than Annabeth Johnson. She skidded to a stop, grabbing Ashley's arm to keep from landing both of them on their backsides.

"I am so happy I found you. Have you seen John Speer? Might you know where he is?" Ashley opened her mouth to reply, but with a nod to Julie the girl kept going without so much as a breath. "He did it last night, Ashley. John asked me to marry him at the park after the fireworks and I told him *yes!* He walked me home to clear it with Mama, and we are to be married next month at the latest!" Here her eyes drooped, and she sucked in a big breath. "I have, however, not been able to find him, and since the newspaper office has burned, and he is nowhere to be found, I am sick with worry." Moment by moment, the girl rocketed between abject fear and extreme exhilaration, her emotions twisted into a knot.

"Have you seen him?" Her violet eyes searched theirs as if she could pluck out the response she wanted if she just tried hard enough.

Ashley truly wished she could answer in the affirmative, for the girl's sake. She tried to be positive. "Congratulations, Annabeth! I am very happy for you and John . . . but I don't know where he is." The girl looked at Julie for confirmation and her hopes were once again dashed when Julie shook her head. She turned away with tears springing to her eyes, ready to bolt off, but Ashley caught her arm.

"Wait! You haven't seen Robert and my brother Josh, have you?" Ashley's voice wavered in spite of her best efforts to sound confident. Like her friend, her whole future hung in the balance, too.

"I have not."

In motherly fashion, Julie gathered both girls into her arms. She hugged them in hopes everything would be all right, but they all knew it might not be right ever again.

Annabeth stepped back and suddenly the scene in its entirety rolled into view. No disaster movie ever prepared Ashley for the reality splayed in front of her. Bodies scattered the ground everywhere amidst the chaos of those still alive trying to put out the remaining fires and tend to the wounded. She mentally counted seventeen dead on the corner with five others stacked a few feet away. Never having seen a dead body, let alone these kinds of numbers, Ashley was overwhelmed. Horror kept her feet from moving and her mouth dumb. Julie was no better, her eyes like saucers.

Having had time to recover from her own shock at the sight, Annabeth tried to explain what was happening in the recovery response. Men who survived the attack by hiding in the ravine or cornfields around town were busy digging a huge trench for the burial of the many bodies before them. The Methodist church, nearby, was the designated temporary morgue, where the dead were placed for identification by loved ones before moving them to the burial site.

Ashley realized families had been torn apart in so many ways. Women and children were now homeless. The raiders had pulled whole families from their homes, killed the men, and burned their houses. All their possessions had gone up in smoke. They considered themselves lucky if they had more than the clothes, sometimes nightclothes, on their backs. Before the day was over, these poor souls would need to find a place to sleep. But now neighbors spilled out into the streets and helped their less fortunate neighbors. Food and drink arrived before long. Amazingly, the town was working harmoniously with grim determination in its efforts to take care of its own.

A unit of Union troops caused a stir by arriving in town mid-afternoon. Too late to protect the town from the raid, their new task was to assist in restoring order to the stricken city. Ashley stared in wonder at the uniforms she knew only from museums. Stone-faced and squinty-eyed men, dusty and tired-looking, still managed to efficiently help out where possible.

Still, there was no Robert or Josh among those on the streets of downtown. Every step Ashley took got heavier and heavier with the knowledge that the two might not ever arrive to find them. Not knowing where else to go, Ashley attached herself to Annabeth and the ladies serving food to the workers. She could make sandwiches and pass them out as well as anyone while keeping an eye on the street at all times, hoping for Robert and Josh to appear. Julie wandered off to find the first aid station, thinking they would be in need of volunteers.

As the day wore on, her friend's incessant chatter was about to drive Ashley's already frayed nerves over the edge. The girl confided at one point that nice Mr. Allison who had driven Ashley and her mother home after the picnic was a victim of the raid. Ashley decided she would spare her mother that information. It was as though the poor thing thought if she quit talking, reality would catch up and her world might end. Unfortunately, Ashley understood that questionable line of logic all too well. After watching Annabeth mindlessly shove an entire sandwich into her mouth in one bite, Ashley enjoyed the moment of ensuing silence long enough to decide she'd had enough. It was time to leave the food tables and go in search of her mother.

∞∞∞

"Doc!" Lt. Cavandish hollered from the doorway of the City Hotel. It was one of the few places virtually untouched by the raid. "The medical station is down the street in the butcher shop. Major Plumb wants you to help 'em out."

"*Butcher* shop it is, Lieutenant," he muttered, sending the man a quick salute. Fresh from skirmishes all over Missouri, he had seen the results of battles in Clear Creek, Garden Hollow, Pineville and Jack's Fork. The surgeons he had known through this war were four parts butcher and one part doctor. Not that evil dwelled in their hearts. These were good men. They just didn't know any better. He did his best to teach them simple techniques to save as many soldiers as he could from dying. Measles, chicken pox, typhus and pneumonia took their toll on enlisted men as much as infection from wounds. Exhausted after two years of bloody struggle, he wasn't sure how much more he would have to endure before he got to go home.

He was tired and filthy. Dust had sifted down to his bones during the long ride to Lawrence. Unfortunately, the devastation they found here meant it would be a long time before he saw relief from either. Judging from the looks of mainstreet, this little town was a disaster that promised more of the same he had just come from. No medical supplies, no skilled surgeons and lots of need.

He winced as he stepped on a rock that cut straight through one of the many holes in his worn-out boots. *God, I just want to go home and be with my family again.* There hadn't been a day when his wife and kids had not fill his mind. He took their love with him into battle and through every long, hard march. This last week they inhabited his thoughts even more than usual. Why? That made him somewhat uncomfortable. Were they in some sort of trouble? They were his responsibility, and he should be there to protect them. If something had happened to his family while that miserable witch had him stuck here, he'd have her head. Seriously, she had better hope he never got his hands on her or her long life would be history.

∞∞∞

Julie found the first aid station on Massachusetts Street in the shell of the butcher shop that was mostly still standing. She was not surprised to find people lined up on foot or towed by others for the services of the local doctor, who looked very frazzled. With no nurse in sight, Julie decided her best efforts would be spent in triage, separating out those in desperate need of a doctor from those whose injuries could wait. Many had severe burns from trying to put out fires, and it quickly became apparent there was little in the way of appropriate treatment available for them.

It was rough going for Julie as she repeatedly watched the doctor treat new patients without washing the blood from his hands or cleansing patient wounds in any way. Infection would be the end result of his doctoring. Something needed to be done to stop this. She flagged a woman outside the station and begged her to find a pot of hot water and some soap for their use. One would think she asked for the moon, Julie thought.

She found some relatively clean linens in a cupboard inside the store and offered the doctor several on which to wipe his hands. He gruffly refused, muttering something about having *no time for that nonsense.* To emphasize his point, he swiped his bloody fingers across the apron he wore tied around his middle, and doggedly moved on to the next patient.

By the time the woman returned with a cauldron of hot water and a healthy bar of homemade soap, Julie was at her wits' end. The need was far greater than the resources. She used the intervening time to tear the linens into strips for use in cleaning and bandaging. After that, she proceeded to set several women to the task of cleansing wounds before she sent them in to see the doctor. That helped some. The women tended to and bandaged as many as they could themselves, sending women, children and men on their way with family or friends. No hospital beds existed for even the worst cases.

She bent over a particularly nasty burn that had pieces of material melted into the skin on the forearm of a man she thought she remembered from the picnic. Someone moved to stand beside her and blocked her light, casting her work area in the dark. *How irritating.* She was about to ask this thoughtless person to move away when the shadow spoke to her in a soft baritone.

"If you soak that for about fifteen minutes in cow's milk, it will loosen the cloth and come off without taking more of his skin. Plus, the milk will help it heal."

Julie froze.

She knew the cadence and timbre of that voice. *She had married it twenty years ago.* Fearing that her weary mind was playing tricks on her ears, she wheeled around. But, no, *there he stood!*

Rick Duvall locked eyes with her and it was a toss up as to which of them was more astonished to see the other.

"Julie?" he breathed.

"Ri--, Ri--," Julie had not the strength to breathe, let alone to form sounds to say his name. If she glanced away would this vision of her husband, lost to her for two full years, disintegrate into the atmosphere like the remnants of smoke outside the shop?

Neither was sure how it happened, but they found each other's arms in an instant, squeezing each other so tightly neither could breathe. Once they parted in need of air, Julie's eyes drank in the sight of her husband, looking far removed from the man she thought she knew.

"You've a bushy beard," Julie squeaked, her fingertips searching through his beard in her need to stroke his face. She choked on her own tears. "I didn't think I'd ever see you again!" Her emotions banked for a moment, and then overflowed like a swollen river. "We thought you died."

"I know, honey. Of course you did." Rick smoothed her hair out of the way of her tears and stroked her back. "Courtesy of an old witch, I've been stuck in this war the whole time," Rick growled, bringing her in close for a kiss behind her ear. "Do you remember the old woman we saw in Lon--"

"Olde Gylda of Hampshire?" Julie supplied, taking her husband by surprise again as he reared back to search her face.

"Yes! What do you know about Gylda?"

"Ah, Rick, she's been hard at work with one of your children." Julie dried her eyes with a corner of her apron.

"Good God, she hasn't recruited one to work for her as a Guardian, has she?" His voice was so loud there was a good chance everyone inside and out on Massachusetts Street had heard him despite all the noise.

Julie sighed happily, "There is much I have to tell you, my dear."

"You mean like how you got here?" Rick shook his head, still shocked. He held Julie's hand like a lifeline.

Curious, but judgmental faces surrounded them and Julie realized their joy was out of place in the shop. "Let's go outside, Rick, where we can talk."

Chapter 25

Not sure where to find the medical station, Ashley was relieved to spot her mother stepping out of the meat market a mere thirty feet ahead. But then her mother tugged a bearded Union soldier out of the door behind her and fell into his arms right there in the middle of the street. Heedless of anyone else around, they kissed each other like long, lost lovers.

Wait, Ashley thought, like long, lost lovers? Her heart skipped a beat and then a second one as she took a hard look at the man her mother clutched like her life depended on it. He was the right height and his hair the right color, but surely not...?

The man broke the kiss and leaned back, bringing his face squarely into view. Ashley squealed like a pig poked with a stick and took off at a dead run, never stopping until she launched herself at her father. Fortunately, he heard the squeal in time to spot her and put his wife safely aside before catching his daughter.

Reunions of similar sorts had taken place all afternoon in the streets of Lawrence as family members happily or unhappily reunited. Their unfettered emotions gave no one but a moment's pause before going about their business.

Ashley could not believe she and her mom were tucked securely in her father's arms. Could this be true or had she finally lost it?

∞ ∞ ∞

Robert and Josh experienced nothing but frustration in their search for Ashley and Julie. They were trapped in the ravine for about twenty minutes while bands of raiders crossed the bridge heading back toward town. With any luck that meant the savages were leaving. By the time the two worked their way to the boarding house, they found no one there.

Across the street, a lady with a baby called to them by name and told them to go downtown. The way she sat on the steps of her burned house and rocked her baby made them wonder if she was quite all right. Yet there seemed to be nothing they could do for her, so they left her and took off across town. Smoke still billowed in the breeze that shimmered through a row of scorched cottonwood trees overhead.

They stopped to help some folks put out a fire and then recognized the place as the Dix house where they had left the bodies of the Speer brothers. Nothing remained but a burned-out shell. Sadly, even the bodies of Billy's brothers were now gone.

Josh left the scene with a nasty burn, thanks to falling debris that hit his arm. As they got closer to the center of town, he held his wounded arm gingerly, but shed not so much as a tear. It was not a day to worry over minor injuries.

"Mom will know what to do with it," he said, stiffly. "She always does."

They heard the activity of downtown Lawrence long before they saw it. Workers loaded wagons with bodies to be moved, and folks scavenged the skeletons of burned out buildings for anything of value that could be saved. The middle of the street held much of those salvaged goods, including loot the raiders did not take with them.

They spotted Mrs. Johnson dishing out food to workers from the back of a wagon and thought perhaps she might know the whereabouts of Ashley and Julie. Robert raised a hand to flag the lady's attention when Annabeth startled him by clutching his free arm with both hands.

"I am so relieved you and Josh are both safe," she gushed. "Ashley will be so happy you are found." Robert opened his mouth to question her further but then the girl dealt him a verbal punch to the gut. "I have searched everywhere for John Speer, but cannot find him. Have you seen him?"

Josh looked away, hoping desperately to escape the moment. Robert's eyes pinched shut and his brow furrowed. Could he rid himself of the memory of John's death so he might not have to answer?

It was not to be. The girl read their faces correctly and became hysterical in the span of a heartbeat.

"Do not say it! Do not say it!" Annabeth covered her ears and turned toward her mother. "He cannot be gone. We got engaged last night. Last night! It cannot be so."

Mrs. Johnson's moist, pudgy face squished as she tried to hold back her tears for her daughter's sake. In truth, Robert knew the dreams of both mother and daughter had been dashed. The two women clutched each other as if their very survival depended on the contact. The girl sobbed so hard Robert worried she might not be able to catch her breath again. What should he do? He turned to Josh for help, but the boy shrugged, equally clueless.

It was Emily Hoyt who came to the rescue. In her staunch, emotionless, yet oddly sympathetic way, she got the two women to sit down on the back of a wagon. She shoved a cup of water into Mrs. Johnson's hands, and as the woman sipped, her senses returned.

Mrs. Johnson found her words a moment later. "His . . . b-body?"

Robert looked first at her daughter and then resignedly locked eyes with Mrs. Johnson, silently begging her to ask no other questions. "Burned."

She sucked in a long breath and Robert feared she might

lose her composure again, but she did not. Annabeth was distraught. Her choking sobs were so gut wrenching he knew not if she understood what her mother had asked, let alone his response. Perhaps that was best. There would be time for details later.

Josh wandered a few feet away from the wagon and focused his attention anywhere else but on the painful scene behind him. Robert walked up beside him and noted the furrow of Josh's brow, his eyes glistening as they arrowed to a point further down the street. Puzzled, Robert followed his line of vision and was overjoyed to see ... Ashley!

She stood big as day in the middle of the street, hugged by a man in uniform who kissed her forehead like it was his right to do so. Oddly, the obvious comfort between them spoke of long familiarity. Who could this bearded fellow be?

Then Josh shot by him, running full out at Ashley, the man. . . and Julie? He had not noticed her at first. And what was Josh shouting?

"Dad? Da-a-a-d!"

∞∞∞

From out of nowhere Josh slammed into his father with a bear hug, knocking Ashley neatly into her mother with the force of the blow.

"I can't believe it! You're here! You're right in front of me!" He held his father in a death grip, repeating this litany for a full minute before he leaned back, and then frowned. "Where have you been, man?" He pulled in a breath, his eyes wide with awe, confusion and excitement, before blurting, "And that is one freakin' cool beard!" Grabbing a handful of the curly stuff, he gave it a tug to test if it were real. Josh's eyes shined impishly as he grinned slack-jawed into his dad's face.

Rick exploded with laughter at his son's rambling outburst and tried to reclaim his facial hair before it left the rest of his face for good. "Some things never change. You are as incorrigible as I remember." He stepped back for a moment and assessed Josh's growth. "About five inches maybe?"

"Six!" Josh puffed out his chest. "And almost twenty pounds."

What? Ashley took a hard look at Josh. He had grown half a foot. Ouch. How much would he change after she and Robert left him and went back to Hertford? She would think about that another day. Right now her whole family and Robert were within her reach.

Robert! Where is Robert?

Panic slid through her as she tore her eyes from Josh. Wheeling around, she realized for the first time Robert stood awkwardly behind her like he didn't belong in the family picture. Her heart squeezed at the lost expression on his face. Did he doubt for a moment her love for him? A whimper escaped her lips as she wasted no time in throwing her arms around his neck. Relief overwhelmed her as she clung to him. He belonged to her, and she would never let him go. Ever.

Robert is safe. Josh is here. My dad is here. Suddenly all was right with her world. Every pain of the last two years faded into oblivion. Robert wrapped his strong arms around her, pulled her snugly to him, and kissed her.

Ashley kissed him back with every ounce of passion she possessed. This was her man. The man she intended to share a life with, who would father her children, was now back in her arms. She had seen more dead bodies in the last few hours than she ever hoped to see for the rest of her life. All those hours of fearing the worst? Gone. Robert had survived. He was unhurt. He and Josh had made it through the nightmare of the raid.

A smile twitched up around Robert's handsome mouth as she kissed him. Neither cared if the entire world watched. Lost in the love they felt for each other, all the frustration, doubt, and hurt of the last twenty-four hours melted away in the heat of their embrace.

Sinking into the soft contours of her body, Robert's tongue slid into her mouth as he slipped a hand into her hair. He gripped the strands between his fingers as if they could tie her to him permanently. Ashley matched him stroke for stroke, one hand holding his neck, the other snaking through his sun-drenched hair as she pressed her breasts against his chest.

"Ah-hem!" a deep voice interrupted.

Oblivious to anything but each other, Ashley felt Robert's other hand drift down and cup her bottom, deliciously lifting her up and pressing her against him.

"AH-HEM!" The command in that voice was unmistakable this time. "That is quite enough, young man. Get your hands off my daughter!"

Ashley's head popped back, and she quickly freed herself from Robert's grasp as if she were back in seventh grade and caught smooching with Ryan on the front porch.

"Geez, Ash. Forget where you are much?" Josh sniggered, almost giddy with release after the struggles of the day. "Your face is the color of a slice of ripe watermelon." He turned a mock-serious expression at both of them and counseled, "You do remember that you aren't married yet, right?"

Ashley was mortified about completely forgetting herself in front of her father. The father she hadn't seen in two years. She tried to set herself to rights, tucking her hair behind her ears, smoothing down her dress and wiping her face with her hands. Dirty and in borrowed clothes that were burned and scorched half off her body, she guessed the effect was less than stellar on her dad.

∞∞∞

"Married?"

Rick shot a glance at Julie who raised her eyebrows and nodded. "To this *man?"* It was not an accident that his inflection hit the word *man*. Ashley was his little girl. This dude towered over them and was built like a pro wrestler. Yet, upon closer examination, Rick detected something unusual about him. He saw power and a kind of toughness that didn't come from playing sports, he didn't think. The man exhibited an unconscious swagger just standing beside Ashley. And what was she doing with a *man*, anyway? A *virile* man. That is, besides demonstrating a proficient knowledge of foreplay. If he had not stopped it, who knows where that exhibition would have ended.

His gaze turned from the man to Ashley and his heart skidded into his mouth and threatened to choke him. *What happened to my little girl?* This person was not a girl. She was a *woman*. A very *beautiful* woman, even slightly unkempt, which made her all the more lovely--like the heroine of a romance novel or some chick flick. She tucked her shoulder under the man's arm and stood there looking sweetly up at this guy like he hung the moon. *Didn't that used to be my job?*

He snapped to as he realized Julie was introducing him. This guy thrust out a hand at him and looked him straight in the eye with intensity. Apparently he had nothing to hide. He and Ashley were to be married? Should have already been married? *What?*

He clearly had some catching up to do. Being buried in gore up to his elbows for two years trying to save lives and limbs had in no way prepared him for the changes in his children. At eighteen, Ashley was ready to be married?

When he rolled his eyes at Julie with a mixture of horror and helplessness in them, she laughed at his fluster. "Yes, dear, it's a shock to the system, but when we have time, we have a lot more we need to tell you."

Just then, a voice as rough as an old crow's cackled at them, "Well, aren't ye all a pretty picture."

Rick's breath hitched upon hearing the old woman speak. He knew her voice well. As he turned to greet Olde Gylda, he noted Ashley and Robert weren't surprised to see her. Julie looked puzzled, like she couldn't quite place her. Only Josh was oblivious.

The old crone, dressed from head to toe in some kind of black widow's weeds, stared at them from a few feet away. Her ugly black bonnet made her head appear way too big for her skeletal frame.

She chortled again, "Nice to see ye, Duvall. Ye have used yer time wisely whilst in this land."

"Gylda," he breathed. Julie let out a gasp as she made the connection.

"It seems like years ago when we said goodbye at your place, Gylda. We've had such a dreadful time since you helped me go home." Ashley peeked up at Robert in time to see him nod in agreement. "Did you know Robert followed me?"

Now Rick was really confused. How did Ashley know Gylda? She couldn't possibly remember meeting her in London years ago, could she?

The old woman's face split open into a tooth-challenged grin. "But of course, my dear. Time-crossed love can never be stopped if one is as persistent as this one." Fondly, she turned her gap-toothed smile on Robert and gave him a wink. Robert blinked his relief.

"Whoa, you time traveled somewhere *else,* Ashley?" her father scowled. She flinched at his tone.

"Not by choice, Dad," she answered truthfully. "I was in England at one of Uncle Zeek's digs and had no idea I would be going anywhere unusual when it happened." She chewed her lower lip and chuckled, shaking her head. "I was a bit of a mess there and caused some trouble, but Cedric and Olde Gylda helped me get home."

"You are a Guardian? She's a Guardian?" Rick didn't seem to know whom to address, his head swiveling between Ashley and Olde Gylda as he tried to make sense of their words.

"She is, indeed, my boy," Gylda responded with obvious enthusiasm. "And a fine one she is at that."

Rick's attention landed on his son about the same time Josh asked, "Can I be a Guardian, too?"

"No!" Rick and Julie cried in one voice, a perfect example of brain sharing despite being apart for so long.

Olde Gylda simply laughed. "All in good time, my pet, all in good time.

Chapter 26

"I hate to break this up, you guys, but we are beginning to attract some attention I don't think we want." Ashley surreptitiously observed the folks around them. "Maybe we should find someplace more out of the way to talk."

They had all started to move out of the center of the street when Ashley noticed some commotion around the food wagon she had helped with. Looking a little closer, she spotted Mrs. Johnson hugging her daughter and whispering in her ear. What was this? Her heart plummeted as she thought of only one reason for their behavior. She grabbed Robert's arm, but addressed Josh as well as Robert, fear desperately edging her voice, "Do you know the whereabouts of the Speer brothers?" She prepared herself for the worst. *"Where are they?"*

Josh wordlessly searched his dad's face for help, his eyes betraying him. Robert sorrowfully held Ashley's eyes, finding no right words.

"No." Her voice faltered at the look in Robert's eye. "No-o-o-o, please don't tell me all of them are dead."

"In truth, Billy was fine the last time we saw him right before we went to find you and your mother." Robert sneaked a glance at Julie before continuing in a steady voice. "John and Rob are dead. We saw them get shot by the raiders."

Ashley and Julie gasped at the news, their eyes flew to Josh as they thought of what he had witnessed. "Yeah, and Robert held Billy back, or he'd be dead, too."

Ashley sank into Robert's arms, her legs threatening to buckle under her. "Annabeth will be destroyed by this. We've been searching all day among the dead, hoping against hope she wouldn't find John and I wouldn't find you guys. And now this . . ." Her voice faltered, and she couldn't continue so Robert just held her.

Julie reached out and grabbed Josh, pulling him so close to her he squirmed for a moment before his arms circled her, and he squeezed her equally hard. Ashley shuddered. What an awful thing to experience.

"I am so sorry you saw that, Josh. So sorry." Julie's breath hitched, and she held him out where she could look into his eyes. "But I am beyond thrilled and thankful the two of you survived the night unscathed but for a little dirt and a few cuts and scrapes."

"And a burn," Robert added, reaching out to pull up Josh's arm to display the injury. Josh took that moment to slide from his mother's grip, feeling the need to be strong for her.

"Let me see that." Josh did as his father asked and let him examine the wound. "It's bordering on a third degree burn, but we'll have a better idea when we clean it up. I'll dig out some salve that should heal it nicely."

"Are you planning to soak it in milk?" Julie winked at her husband, and Ashley suspected some private message had just been passed between them. Her dad laughed and his eyes roamed lovingly over his family, making Ashley's heart swell. She turned to catch Robert's eye to check out how he was managing the reunion with her dad, and *there was Gylda.* How could she forget the old witch? Why was she still here?

Rick followed Ashley's eyes and wheeled around, catching Julie off-balance and dragging her with him. Gylda's response was a throaty laugh that shrieked like rusty hinges on a weathered door.

"I wondered when ye would remember I was here," she grinned. The gaps between her teeth were so black they might have surrounded fine diamonds rather than stubs of age-yellowed teeth. Her ice blue eyes twinkled with the youth of a teenager, which was unnerving against the deep crinkling of her ancient, sagging skin.

She marched up to Josh and carefully took his injured arm in her crinkled hands. Without so much as looking at the injury, she held Josh's eyes as she asked, "Helping others, were ye?" Josh just nodded and smiled into those beguiling eyes. "Yer a good one, ye are," she proclaimed with satisfaction, passing her knobby fingers over his damaged skin as she let go of him.

Josh dropped his eyes to his arm and stammered, "Th-thank you!" Gylda had healed his arm while she talked to him. It was perfect again, much to Julie's wide-eyed surprise. Rick lifted an eyebrow and shrugged like it was nothing new.

Ashley and Robert had seen the old crone at work before, too. Not to be distracted by the old lady's theatrics, even though she had to admit she was impressed with her witchery, Ashley asked what they all wanted to know. "Gylda? Why are you here?"

Her dad was quick with a question of his own. "Am I finally going to go home?" His eyes flashed, daring Gylda to tell him otherwise.

"Ahhh," Gylda sighed, rubbing her chin with a withered hand as if trying to remember just why she was there. Then her face brightened and she waggled a knotted finger at Ashley. "'Tis ye I am here for, dearie, not yer father."

The fire in her dad's eyes burned so brightly she thought he might spontaneously combust. "I landed this time walk back in West Virginia on the Union side after the Battle of Rich Mountain in 1861. That was two years ago, Gylda. It's time I went home. Why can't I go back to Houston with my family? That's where you are sending Ashley, isn't it?"

Olde Gylda shook her head sadly at Rick, admonishing him without words to control himself. "I understand ye want to go home. Ye have been gone very long and slogged yer way through much, 'tis true. Ye have saved many lives." They all could hear what was coming before she said it. "Ye are still needed here, sir. Too many lives are at stake to let ye go home quite yet."

Her dad grabbed her mother's hand and held it to his lips

in a silent apology. Then he turned to Gylda and asked, "Where is Ashley going from here?"

Ashley thought that was a pretty good question, too. "We don't really know how we got here. Or why? We were running from Abasi's men and a Guardian stone appeared in the car. I read the inscription on it three times aloud and the whole car wound up here with all of us in it."

"You have a *car? Here?"* her dad asked, incredulous.

Ashley turned to him and tried to explain. "Yeah, we were being chased by Abasi's men in two big, black SUVs as we left the Vintage Rose Bazaar. We would have been caught if the car hadn't been sucked up into a vortex and taken here. And by the way, Mom's a wicked getaway driver."

"Julie! *You were driving?"* His mouth hung open as if he were Josh's age. Julie preened for a moment as the others praised her prowess behind the wheel. Still shocked, he mustered a couple more questions for them. "Who is Abasi? And what took you to the Vintage Rose Bazaar?"

"We were to have been married there," Robert interjected, rather forcefully.

"I don't like the sound of this at all. I need to go home now, Gylda. *Now.* I cannot let you send my family back to Houston without me to protect them. You know I can't," Rick snarled.

"I quite agree." The old crone's smile played wickedly at the corners of her mouth. When they all stopped and stared at her as one, she popped out her famous gap-toothed grin and explained, "No one is going to Houston quite yet." Rick and Julie cocked their heads in unison and waited for her to go on. "Yer wife and son may stay here with ye, Duvall, until 'tis safe for them to go home. But missy, here," she twirled to face Ashley, "and her husband will be traveling back to London with me." Her old face darkened into a scowl. "Trouble awaits there."

They all started talking at once until Rick managed to whistle for their attention. "One at a time," he ordered his family members. "Ashley, you first."

"Robert is not my husband yet and what trouble awaits

us there?" Breathlessly, she had run her thoughts together as if a nameless fear chased her.

The old lady giggled like a schoolgirl. "Ye will be wed before ye leave here so yer family is present." That caused everyone to talk at once again. She hushed them with a glower and a screech. "Ye must listen. Ye *must*." They quieted for her and she continued, "Abasi closed in on the Baron of Bedford who unwittingly followed these two. By now the wicked man likely has the bumbling fellow in his clutches. Modern day England does not agree with our medieval man, ye see."

"Who is this Bedford who time walked into modern London?" Rick glared, demanding an answer from Ashley. Before she could form one, his mind detoured when another thought clicked in as he stared at Robert. "Just where is it you come from, Robert?"

"I am the eldest son of the Earl of Hertford." Robert answered her father without hesitation. Ashley's heart fluttered when he stood tall and proudly looked every inch the aristocrat he was. "I met Lady Ashley when she came to Castle Hertford in August of the year 1363."

Rick clapped his mouth shut upon hearing the date and stared incredulously at Gylda. "*Lady* Ashley? Are you *insane*? You cannot let her marry a man from 1363 England."

"'Tis her destiny, Duvall. Just as yers is to advance medical needs here, hers is to help women discover their worth there."

Julie took her husband's hand and held it between her own, doing her best to calm him. Olde Gylda nodded her appreciation to Julie before turning again to Ashley.

"A friend of yer uncle's, a Dr. Wilson, has helped the baron stay alive, but he is sorely in need of ye to git him back home."

"Dr. Monica Wilson? The little birdlike lady?"

"One and the same, my dearie." Gylda smiled, stiffly. She obviously hated to be interrupted and gathered her voluminous gown around her, drawing herself up to her full not-very-tall height. "Although Zeek Duvall and I are aware of each other, I cannot work with him since he is not a Guardian, and I am allowed to work only through Guardians. So, ye see, if Abasi is to be stopped, ye are the one to do the job, Lady Ashley. I can only assist ye in getting back to London to help him. After that, ye must find your own way home to Hertford as planned."

"But what about Robert, Gylda? How does he get home to Hertford?" Ashley worried her lower lip over the answer.

The old crone crooked her eyebrow at Ashley and replied with a teasing chuckle, "Oh, me thinks he will follow in yer wake wherever ye be, child. Ye do not suppose he will let ye out o' his sight for long, do ye?"

In unison, Ashley and Robert sighed their relief. Perhaps they would return to Hertford safely yet. Then a giddy thought bubbled up to the surface. The birth of brain sharing emerged as they simultaneously said, *"When can we get married?"*

Startled, everyone laughed, but especially Ashley's parents as they recognized the bond, not unlike their own, that had developed already between Ashley and Robert.

"I think tomorrow would be soon enough, children, but ye will have to leave with me right after the ceremony as I cannot stay here."

∞∞∞

Julie watched a myriad of expressions flash across Ashley's face. Would her wedding to Robert take place this time or would some other obstacle stand in their way? Was it too much to hope for in their present circumstances that it would happen?

Her mind buzzing, Julie wondered how on earth they would pull off a ceremony under these bizarre conditions. How would they find a minister willing to marry a couple in the midst of burying 200 men? She had not even had time to think about the disconcerting fact that Gylda had said she and Josh would be staying for a time here in Lawrence. If she had to live among these folks for a while she would have to be careful in her handling of it. Julie looked up at her husband and found him smiling down at her like two years had never happened. *Unbelievable.*

Before she could contemplate how she might spirit away the bouquet for Ashley that she had left in the car, Josh surprised her by taking off at a run.

"Billy! Billy!"

Julie's heart clenched upon hearing the boy's name.

Billy Speer was charging on a beeline to meet Josh with his father slowly bringing up the rear. The only thing holding Mr. Speer together was pain, she thought. The man standing before them was nothing like the traditional, orderly, stable businessman of the day before. His hair drooped across his forehead, strands sweat-soaked and plastered there, as if they too, were too tired to move. His glasses, sitting askew on his nose, and his rumpled clothing told much of the heartbreak of this horrible day.

Billy was still running on adrenaline. He reached out to cuff Josh on the shoulder, failing to understand Josh's hand up in a high-five motion. The rest of them had to jog to catch up with Josh. They arrived in time to hear Billy regaling his friend with the tale of what had happened to him after he left Robert and Josh. Mr. Speer stood mutely behind his son, one hand firmly latched onto Billy's shoulder as if to prevent this son from being snatched away from him too.

From what Julie could make out, Billy had been cautiously wending his way home when he had to hide in the brush while a raider passed by. A spare rifle bounced off the back of the horse as the man jumped a small ravine. The rider never heard the gun drop, so Billy had hidden until it was clear to snatch what turned out to be a loaded weapon. Not ten minutes later, a lone rider, his saddle laden with pilfered goods, trotted by Billy's hiding place. Staying behind the man as closely as he could, Billy waited until the rider stopped and eyed a house for more plunder a short distance away. It was all the time Billy needed to find the scoundrel in the rifle sight and fire.

The man fell to the ground. Dead.

According to Mr. Speer, it was the only report thus far of a raider killed by a resident during the entire raid. Julie shook her head, marveling at Billy's grit. She had to hand it to the boy for avenging the deaths of his brothers when all the town's weapons had stayed locked away in the armory.

Julie knew it was retribution that gave Mr. Speer no joy.

Chapter 27

"Here . . . this is for you." Annabeth thrust a delicate cream-colored shawl into Ashley's hands. Little more than twenty-four hours had passed since the town had been turned upside down. Many facets of life in Lawrence would never be righted. The loss of Annabeth's fiancé was one of those, so Ashley had not expected to see her.

"Oh, my," Ashley breathed, running her hands over the soft fibers of an intricately knitted design. "It's truly lovely." She and Robert were excited to finally marry in an hour in the parlor at Emily's boarding house. The Reverend Cordley graciously agreed to perform the ceremony in between morning and afternoon services for those lost in the raid. Her very own father would actually give her away, something she thought could never happen only a short time ago.

She glanced up with a smile into the girl's glorious, violet eyes and was jolted by the pain that now inhabited them. Intuitively, Ashley realized the shawl had been meant for Annabeth's own wedding that would now not take place. She reached out and pulled the girl into her arms and hugged her tightly. Annabeth burst into tears and sobbed. Ashley could think of nothing to say that would possibly help, so she just held her friend until the distraught young woman got herself under control. When she raised her head, she confirmed Ashley's suspicions. "I made it last winter when I hoped John would ask me to be his wife."

"And he *did,*" Ashley reminded her, noting the dark circles under the girl's eyes. "You weren't wrong to think he wanted you." Her eyes drifted over Annabeth's shiny black hair, now pulled into a tight bun at the nape of her neck. She wore a plain black skirt and black blouse, the picture of a widow.

Watching Ashley's assessment, Annabeth responded, "I know we never married, but I feel I lost a husband, not an intended."

"Of course you do, but I cannot keep something as deeply personal as this. You must keep this lovely creation for yourself. Perhaps one day you will need it again." The girl's face puckered up and tears spilled forth.

Oops! See? She needed to keep her mouth shut. Wrong thing to say, but what should she say? She certainly didn't want to hurt her. Finally, she threw the shawl over her shoulder and grabbed both of her friend's hands and held them, securing the young woman's complete attention. "How about if I *borrow* the shawl today and then give it back to you for safe keeping. Would that be agreeable to you?"

Annabeth managed a bob of her head, and Ashley gave her a final hug before releasing her. Wistfully, the girl wished Ashley and Robert happy and went to find her mother. What a beautiful person to offer such a precious gift, Ashley thought.

Wedding plans were unfolding so fast she needed a moment to sit down and collect her whirling head before the ceremony began. It was not to be. The door opened to her room once again, and this time Mrs. Carpenter appeared with her baby in her arms. Sleep had bypassed her, judging from the puffy rings around her eyes, but she did not bear the kiss of death that marked her after the raid. Her wits were about her today. She would survive.

"Miss Duvall, I cannot thank you enough for all you did for me and little Abigail--." At this point she, like Annabeth before her, had tears streaming down her face and Ashley felt her own begin a similar trek.

It seemed to be a morning for unintended tears.

"Oh, no, I made you cry," Mrs. Carpenter wailed softly so as not to wake her baby. "I only thought to thank you for your kindness and wish you well on your wedding day. I heard that an accident before you arrived here kept you and your man from marrying as planned, so it is only fitting that you be married today. We never know what the day holds in store for us, do we?" She dried her eyes with a man's very damp handkerchief and shoved it back up the sleeve of her black gown.

Ashley breathed a sigh of relief that Mrs. Carpenter was not angry with her. She still worried the townsfolk would think them as insensitive as dirt clods for having a wedding today. Fearing anything she said would make the woman cry again, Ashley smiled sweetly and held her arms out to silently ask if she might hold the baby. Mrs. Carpenter carefully transferred the sleeping child from her arms to Ashley's with such tenderness it nearly broke her heart. The precious little babe enjoyed a sound snooze, oblivious to all the joys or woes of those around her.

"I have a small present for you," the young mother said. "I made it only last week, although it seems like a hundred years ago now." She smiled a wisp of a smile and handed Ashley a crisp, linen handkerchief, neatly folded and pressed.

Rocking the child in one hand and examining the hanky in the other, Ashley was delighted with the beautiful blue flowers embroidered around the edges. Ah, she thought with satisfaction, I have it all together now--something old, new, borrowed and blue. Her white dress, courtesy of Mrs. Hoyt, was nothing fancy and not new. Clean and without holes, it didn't smell of smoke, so it was a winner. She now wore a borrowed shawl and held a new, blue handkerchief, so she could always say she had followed her mother's superstitious recipe for a happy married life.

She wasn't one of those girls like Jazz who had planned every detail of her wedding by the time she turned twelve. Neither, however, had she imagined her wedding would be anything like the one in front of her now. At the last minute, the service was moved outside under a large elm tree in the front yard to accommodate the many people who came. Perhaps they needed to rejoice in something happy after the nightmare of the raid. Along with Annabeth and her mother, and Mrs. Carpenter and baby Abigail, several of the women Julie had worked with during the picnic arrived together. Robert also spotted some of the men he had talked with that were introduced to him by Mr. Dix. He was relieved to find not all of those he had met at the picnic had fallen prey to the raiders.

Even several of the men from her father's regiment came to meet Doc's family. The last to arrive, Mr. Speer and Billy appeared moments before the start of the ceremony. Josh grinned ear to ear when he saw his friend. By the time the service started late morning, some fifty people stretched out over the lawn, listening to the Rev. Cordley marry a couple few knew. How amazing! What was that old saying about the kindness of strangers?

Emily Hoyt thrust a small bouquet of garden blossoms tied with twine into her hands as the ceremony began. Ashley clutched the posy with white knuckles as she and her dad took their places at the back of the crowd. Unexpectedly, a man stepped forward and stood near the minister. To her amazement, he proceeded to play "Here Comes the Bride" on a wooden flute. Who arranged this? She didn't know, but her mother beamed at her, so she guessed it was not a complete surprise.

Copper hair coiled around the man's head like it was holding his face hostage. Dressed in a scruffy-looking plaid shirt and pants that had seen better days, he nervously played half a beat too fast with long, dirty fingers. A few notes sounded a bit suspect, but she couldn't complain. After all, she was walking to music down a makeshift aisle on her father's arm while her beloved medieval man waited for her beside the reverend.

Robert stood tall and strong above the throng, with his hair swept back from his brow and glowing like gold in the sunlight. His warm hazel eyes never left Ashley's for a moment. As Robert's best man, Josh proudly took his place next to him with only a hint of mischief in his eyes.

Her mother, acting as matron of honor, caught Ashley's eyes and held them for a moment, sending her love to Ashley more effectively than words ever could. But it was the look her mom sent to her husband that brought tears of joy to Ashley's eyes. Her father lived, and was here with her family on her wedding day.

What could be better than this? It was the perfect time-crossed wedding.

With no time to write vows, Ashley and Robert thought a long ceremony might not be appreciated anyway, so theirs lasted no more than ten minutes.

Too overcome by the importance of the moment to listen, she missed most of what the Rev. Cordley said. Instead, she peeped up through her lashes at the beautiful man beside her and wondered how she had been so lucky to have him love her. As if reading her mind, Robert met her gaze with soft eyes and smiled his lop-sided smile as he slipped his infamous signet ring onto her finger. She all but melted on the spot.

Josh and Billy exchanged ornery looks throughout the ceremony. When the reverend read the part about speaking up if anyone knew any reason why these two should not be joined in holy matrimony, they both started to snicker. Rick quelled those hi-jinks with a snap of his head, leaving the two guys grinning stupidly at each other and trying not to giggle. At last, the minister got to the only part Ashley and Robert wanted to hear.

"I now pronounce you man and wife. You may kiss the bride."

And boy did he.

Robert would like to have never let her go. After waiting far too long, traveling thousands of miles, not to mention hundreds of years, to get to this point, he now claimed her forever as his. As a matter of fact, a *whoop* from somewhere in the crowd went up after about a minute, reminding the happy couple they were not alone. The laughter and the chatter that followed were hearty, healthy and healing.

A wagon that looked suspiciously like the one belonging to Mr. Speer pulled up with enough refreshments for everyone. Pie and cake left over from the picnic festivities provided most of the sweet treats. Mrs. Johnson insisted that Ashley and Robert cut a slice of a freshly baked pie she had made just for them and serve each other bites as tradition dictated. There were sandwiches made from thick-crusted bread and cold chicken. Watered-down lemonade, served semi-warm, was the main beverage, if you didn't count the harder stuff that someone shared with the men folk. All in all, Ashley thought it was absolutely perfect.

As she and Robert signed the official marriage documents for Rev. Cordley, she felt a presence she was beginning to identify with ease. Sure enough, turning around she spied Olde Gylda sidling up to her dad. She immediately wanted to scream "No!" at the top of her lungs to the old woman. Frantically, she searched through the guests for her mother and Josh and found them talking with Mrs. Dix. In fact, Mrs. Dix hugged Josh like she had known him her whole life. What was all that about? Her mind skittered around itself trying to find a way to avoid what would certainly come next.

Too bad she couldn't stop time right here for at least a wedding night. But no, Olde Gylda itched to be on her way. She rapped on an empty pie tin and called for quiet in her scratchy-throated voice. "Thank ye all for coming to help these young folks celebrate their weddin' day. 'Twas right kind of ye," she said with a serious face, pausing to hold the eyes of each person present for just a moment. It occurred to Ashley the old crone was using her magic to relieve these well-wishers of some of the pain they suffered. The expressions on their faces lightened when her eyes passed by them. That made her smile, imagining fairy dust floating down over their shoulders.

"These newlyweds should have been in St. Louis today, so they must be headin' off now on their life's adventure together. Thus, they have a few words of farewell to say to ye before they go." Robert had no choice but to step forward and address those present. It was good he did so. She was too choked up to say anything because it meant her time with her family was at an end. Leaving for her was going to be as difficult as pulling a hundred-year-old oak out by the roots. Still, if Gylda said they needed to go, then they needed to go. It didn't make it any easier though.

"Friends, and I do mean friends, my wife and I will never forget your kindness this day." Robert searched for Rick and met his father-in-law's eye with a heart-felt gaze. "When we arrived we knew not that Ashley's father lived, having lost touch with him due to the war. Amidst great joy in finding him, we have witnessed great sorrow at the losses you have borne here in Lawrence. Your strength, courage, and determination to go forward are apparent in your being here with us today." Robert found Billy and Mr. Speer in the crowd and reached out to them with a fist over his heart. Mr. Speer bit his lip and removed his glasses to wipe them with his pocket cloth, clearly understanding Robert's silent message. Billy just nodded. "You have welcomed us to your town and made our wedding a remarkable occasion that we will hold dear in our hearts forever. Again, we say thank you to all of you."

Those gathered whooped their approval, and with the speech over, they slapped backs, hugged hard and promised each other better times ahead. In record time, the majority of guests faded from the premises, and it was time for the family goodbyes.

After all their struggles, how could she say good-bye to her family? She had not had enough time with her father who looked so thin and so much older than his years, and Josh was growing like a weed. He looked more like a man every time she saw him. *And her mother.* Her sweet, sweet mother was her rock and her advisor in all things. How could she say goodbye to her? They were all too dear. Too loved. Would she ever see them again?

She started to sob so hard she thought she might not ever breathe again until Olde Gylda came to her rescue with a gentle hand placed on her back. Instantly, her insides calmed, allowing Ashley to wipe the moisture from her face and take in a deep breath. Robert held her with an arm around her waist and such a forlorn face, that she promised to get herself under control.

Mo-o-o-o-o.

As if planned for comic relief, Romeo galloped down the hill and skidded to a stop beside Billy who was waiting impatiently for Josh to finish saying his goodbyes. Romeo, missing since the raid, still wore his halter. He had a rakish air about him, like he had enjoyed a romantic adventure or two while he'd been gone.

Ashley chuckled at the critter's antics in spite of herself, indelicately mopping her very wet nose and face with the backs of her hands. Soon everyone laughed at the silly animal that nudged Billy's pockets for a treat as if nothing were amiss. Some terrifying bull he was.

Somehow Romeo lightened the mood enough for Ashley to say her farewells to Emily Hoyt, Mr. Speer and Billy--three people she would always admire. They did not leave, however, so Ashley couldn't say aloud all she wanted to say to her family.

She reached out and ruffled Josh's hair, making him squirm away from her. "Hey, little bro', be good and stay safe."

The love in her eyes apparently knocked the smirk right off his face. Suddenly, much to her surprise, her rogue of a brother clenched her in an awkward hug.

"Missing ya' already, Ash," he whispered into her ear.

Next, her father scooped her up into his arms and hugged her close. "Daddy, I love you. Come see me, okay?"

Her dad winked at her in complete understanding and kissed her cheek with a big smack. "You can count on it, baby. I love you always." He squeezed her hard and reluctantly set her down in front of her mother.

Ah, this was the hardest part. Why was it always the toughest to say goodbye to her mother?

"Mom?" she squeaked out before her throat closed.

"Oh, baby girl," her mother crooned, fighting the tears that threatened to keep her words from flowing. "Getting you back has made it so much harder to let you go." She tenderly tucked a lock of hair behind Ashley's ear. "Life is so precious, sweetie. Love hard and be happy. Robert is a wonderful man to build a life with. I'll think of you both every day until we meet again."

Ashley all but dissolved with her mother's words. Though she tried to memorize every detail of the three beloved family members in front of her, they rapidly became nothing but a big blur blinding her sight.

Robert quietly said his own goodbyes right behind Ashley, with a bear hug for Josh, and a firm handshake for Rick. He placed a kiss on both of Julie's hands before pulling her into a heartfelt embrace, whispering in her ear, "Thank you, my lady, thank you."

Without further delay, Robert swept Ashley off her feet and loaded her into the rented gig that he would drive. She settled in beside Robert who held her steady with his arm around her waist in classic Lawrence style. Thinking back over the day, she was happy she had cornered her mom, dad and brother in Emily's house for a moment before the ceremony. She now carried a picture of the four of them that Robert had taken on her cell phone. A second photo taken with the timer set, allowed Robert to be in it too. The family unit was whole again. At least she had those pictures to carry with her to Hertford where she could look upon them when she needed to. It would likely be a long time before they would see one another.

Last night, Ashley's family had promised each other they would be together again through time travel, but none of them knew if they could really pull it off. Josh wanted to go with Ashley and Robert this time, but her dad had put the kibosh on that quickly. Ashley told herself if she and Robert could time travel, then the rest of her family could, too. It would happen. She was sure of it. *Really.*

Olde Gylda hitched a ride on the back of the buggy, and waved a goodbye that seemed to visibly lift the spirits of everyone left behind. Interesting, how all those unspoken words of solace found their way directly into each heart--no lips, teeth or breath needed.

Ashley waved until her family disappeared from sight. She turned to face the road before them, taking a cleansing breath. The aged beast pulling the creaky wagon kicked up enough dust to make her wish there were windshields on gigs. Ashley wondered what awaited them with Bedford once Gylda got them back to modern day.

Mostly, it was hard to believe she was married now, and off to London and beyond with her new husband. The future was unfolding right in front of her. Scary though it might be, it was exciting, too.

Robert's biggest question was of a different sort and weighed heavily on his mind. When would he get to hold his new wife in his arms and love every inch of her? They must rid themselves of a certain old crone before that could happen. But he was ready for married life. More than ready. *Now.*

Chapter 28

Ka-thunk.

Ashley crashed to the ground, landing hard upon her right hip. Or maybe Robert's leg? Groggily, she came to from out of the now-familiar haze of the Guardian stone whirlwind and searched anxiously for Robert.

Relief swamped her when she discovered she sat in Robert's lap. He had traveled in her wake without incident. Should she be concerned, however, that Olde Gylda did not come with them? She warned them that might be the case. Now what were they supposed to do here on their own?

Shortly after leaving Lawrence, they had changed out of their borrowed clothes and into the modern wedding clothes Josh had spirited from the Speer's house and tucked in the gig. That meant Ashley straddled Robert with her long white dress with the purple flowers splayed around them like a wreath. Robert held her close while sitting squarely in the dirt in his black pants and white shirt. They made a rather unseemly picture plunked down in the bushes. Ashley blushed at the thought of the activity anyone would suspect them of doing if they were seen.

She cautiously peeked through the thicket to see who might be looking in their direction and saw no one around at all. Weird. Birds fluttered about and chirped, but outside of the usual sounds of nature, there was nothing. Then she remembered the time difference. It must be very early in the day by London time. Had they missed nighttime altogether?

She glanced up at Robert and liked the gleam in his eye. From the smoldering look he sent her way as she wiggled on his lap trying to move her legs together, he would be most pleased if she stayed put. She grinned at him playfully, wiggled a bit more and made him groan. At that moment, dawn broke through into their nest and the sun framed Robert's golden hair like a halo. He was so beautiful he might have been an angel.

"Morning, husband," she beamed up at him, collecting her heady thoughts and leaning in for a kiss.

"Mynx," he growled. "You know what you do to me, wife." Before she could even so much as giggle, he pulled her into a possessive, spellbinding, glorious kiss. So much for angelic.

The sun was substantially higher in the sky by the time Robert gave Ashley a gentle push to her feet. He might be smiling at the moment, but he was still grumpy about not having a proper wedding night. Ashley's strappy sandals sank disconcertingly into the wet morning grass. *Ugh.*

Robert bounced to his feet and prowled around her like a big cat on a hunt in the jungle, his muscles rippling beneath his shirt. He pulled the branches of a tree back to take stock of their surroundings outside the little thicket.

"What?" His voice cracked, sounding most unlike the calm Robert she knew. Her heart stuttered for a moment and fear clutched at her core.

Is it Abasi?

He let the branch snap back with a thunk and grinned over his shoulder at her. "A statue stands right over there." He shrugged in confusion. "We seem to be by ourselves in the country, so where did that statue come from?"

Ashley breathed her relief and decided she better take a look for herself. Going the long way out and around the thicket, she came to a screeching stop. *"Whoa.* It can't be."

Right smack in front of her stood the Peter Pan statue where she had first encountered Olde Gylda when she met her as a little girl. Of course Gylda would put them down here. Her memories of the area returned in a rush. "This is Hyde Park and the water behind the statue is part of the Serpentine!" She turned to Robert and grinned up at him. "I know exactly where we are."

Relieved to not have to fight another battle, Ashley reached into her pocket and felt for her iPhone to see if it still held its charge. She relaxed as the bars lined up when she turned it on, and the icons popped in ready to go.

She felt ever so much better prepared for time travel this go round. Robert had attached a small bag to his belt before they traveled that held her solar phone charger and a few other small items she thought they would need. She was pleased she had loaded her smart phone while in Houston with all the books she knew she would like to reference at Hertford. Chief among them was a set of e-book encyclopedias, a Mayo Clinic family medical text, and a complete *How Things Work* manual.

To help them out while in London, her mother had given her all the cash she had in her wallet, along with her Visa card. Even though the money was U.S. dollars, they could exchange them, if necessary. Hopefully, they could pay their way in the city as long as they needed to.

Ashley wanted to talk to Uncle Zeek to find out what he knew before they attempted to locate the baron and Dr. Wilson. Perhaps he knew where to find them and it would save a lot of time, letting them all go back to Hertford quicker. Halfway through dialing Zeek's number, it flashed through her mind that perhaps she'd better not call him directly. Abasi, the wicked man, likely would pick up her phone number and be waiting for them at Zeek's when they got there. Undoubtedly, his place would be watched, too, so they would need to be careful how they approached. *Ugh.* This would not be easy.

Her uncle's flat was located a couple blocks north of the Marble Arch, so they started off in that direction. The noises of the city soon invaded the peace and quiet of the empty park, reminding them they were in the middle of a busy city. By the time they walked past the arch, people streamed in and out of the tube station like herds of cattle. A coffee shop on the corner with its delicious smells wafting out as they neared, all but invited them in. Ashley's stomach growled in response, so with an acknowledging smirk, Robert steered them into the busy place.

They stood in the long line waiting to check out with a couple of coffees and a pair of breakfast sandwiches in hand. Ashley noted that everyone seemed glued to a cell phone, just like in the States.

That's it! Why didn't she think of it sooner? If she texted from someone else's phone Abasi might not realize who it was from, and they wouldn't have to sneak into Zeek's place. She captured Robert's attention and tried to tell him with her eyes to play along. He cringed in confusion when she started talking loudly.

"I am going to be in so much trouble. Why did your car have to break down now? And how did it get so late? I'd better text my boss." Here she pulled out her phone and screeched, "My phone is dead. *Gah.*" She gave Robert a beseeching look. "Can I borrow yours?"

Robert stared at her like she'd lost her mind, but fumbled with a pocket as if searching for it.

"What?" she continued without so much as taking a breath. "No-o-o, you didn't forget your phone again, did you?" She whined, "He's gonna fire me for sure this time." She flapped her hands in the air and did her best impersonation of a silent Edvard Munch scream, before suddenly looking beseechingly at the person behind them in line.

"Could I perhaps pay you to use your phone for a moment to text my boss? You would likely keep me from the ranks of the unemployed if you would be so kind." Ashley gave the young woman, about her own age, an earnest smile. Then she realized the woman's eyes followed Robert's every move and had completely missed her rant. Everyone else, however, had begun to give her a wide berth. She wanted to crawl into a hole somewhere after that hideous acting performance and just stay there after embarrassing herself for nothing. Drooler girl flew in a different orbit at present. Robert's orbit.

Robert raised an eyebrow at Ashley, and to his credit, at last understood what she wanted him to do. He turned to the young woman and gave her his best, heart-stopping smile, throwing the full-wattage at her. She visibly melted and like warm honey, all but dripped down his leg. Ashley rolled her eyes, trying her best to stifle a full-fledged grin despite the fact she was a little ticked.

"Good morning," Robert crooned at the young woman. She all but buckled at the knees. "What is your name?"

"G-Ginger," the girl murmured after taking a moment to recover, still mesmerized by the beauty of the man before her. Of medium height and build with mahogany colored hair, she had cornflower blue eyes. She occupied herself by licking her bright red, plump and pouty lips and then chewing on them as she watched Robert intently.

"Ginger, would it be possible to borrow your phone for a moment?" He opened his mouth to cajole her further when the girl thrust her phone into his hands. In doing so she did not break eye contact for so much as a second.

Robert's lopsided grin held her attention as he thrust the phone into Ashley's hands. To give her time to text, he asked the girl about her plans for the day. *Whew.* At least she had some time. The girl would gladly listen to Robert all morning judging from the besotted expression on her face.

Faster than her nervous fingers wanted to move, Ashley texted Zeek's number and prayed that he would see it and know who it came from. "Back from visit. Missed U. Give us," she paused and backed up, deleting "us" and typed, "me a lift at Marble Arch Pret A Manger in 10? Thnx." She pressed the send button and held her breath. *Please be awake, Uncle Zeek. Please, please, please.* She held the phone against her chest willing it to ding a response.

As the line moved forward she dared keep it no longer, so she shoved the phone back at Robert just as it miraculously dinged. The screen showed the letter K and it made Ashley's face light up brighter than the morning sunshine streaming through the shop windows. Robert smiled at her and then graciously returned the phone to the girl in both hands outstretched as if it were his gift to her. The smitten Ginger reluctantly took it back knowing it meant the end of her conversation with Robert. Thankfully, they were next in line, and Ashley handed the Visa card to the cashier, holding her breath in hopes it would go through without a hitch.

It did.

Her stomach chose that moment to sing with such a loud gurgle the cute guy behind the cash register looked up. "Enjoy your meal," he said with a wink as his smiling eyes took a trip down to her belly and back up. She flushed beet red and hurried out the door, Robert following closely behind her.

"You'd better not be snickering, Mr. Spycer! By the way, I didn't know you could flirt like that."

"You have yet to discover many things about me, Mrs. Spycer," he smirked, waggling his eyebrows at her with desire shining in his gorgeous hazel eyes. Ashley didn't know words could make her feel quite like these did. It seemed her belly hungered in more ways than one.

By now, the streets teemed with people, red double-decker buses, bicycles and delivery trucks. It was almost impossible to watch in all directions at the same time, but Ashley guessed that Zeek would be coming from their side of the street. If he slowed down a bit as he passed by, they could slide into his vehicle undetected.

After a few tense minutes, Zeek's battered silver Jeep Wrangler pulled up beside them. Robert opened the back door with one hand, shoved Ashley in with the other, and glided in behind her. They sped off seconds later.

Ashley slid down in the seat and tugged on Robert's sleeve to pull him down, too. No sense making it easy for Abasi to catch them. They whisked around the corner and zoomed down Bond Street before anyone spoke.

Ashley took a deep breath, but Zeek beat her to it. "'Bout time you two showed up," he greeted them tersely, but with a hint of a grin perking up the corners of his mouth. Judging from his extreme case of bedhead and his prickly, gray-speckled jaw, her uncle had only rolled out of bed moments ago. Ashley shook her head and handed over her coffee. Zeek needed it more than she did.

Still slouching in the seat to the best of their ability, they drove around London while Ashley and Robert munched on their breakfast sandwiches and sipped from Robert's coffee. Meanwhile, Ashley filled her uncle in on everything that had happened since their departures from Houston. They almost hit a double-decker when Ashley let it slip without warning that her dad still lived.

"Oh-mah-god, Oh-mah-god, Oh-mah-god!" Zeek repeated the same incantation for several minutes while he processed the news. Ashley stifled a giggle. *Oh-mah-god?* When had her uncle taken to sounding like his students?

Stunned that his brother was safe and sound and reunited with his family, Zeek was shocked they were still in 1863 Lawrence, Kansas. His inner historian wanted to know all the details of Quantrill's Raid, and listened with his jaw in a permanently open position. *Gosh,* he looked like Josh. The resemblance made her happy.

Eventually Ashley suspected they were driving around in circles on their way seemingly to nowhere. *"Uh,* Uncle Zeek, where are we going?" she asked, looking at the center statue as they hit the same roundabout for a third time.

"Oh, sorry." Bemusement twitched at the corners of Zeek's mouth. "I guess I'm a little preoccupied with the news. It's not every day the brother you thought dead for two years comes back to life in another time period, ya' know."

"Yeah," Ashley smiled fondly at the memory. "You should have been there. Shocking doesn't begin to describe the jolt of seeing him again, and it makes me shiver thinking about it. My mom didn't let go of him for at least twenty-four hours."

"We are a pretty lucky family, aren't we?" Zeek turned off the roundabout and traveled north from the river. "I think it's time we found Monica and Damien, don't you?"

"Monica and Damien?" Ashley's jaw dropped open. "You are on a first name basis with the baron?"

"Uh-huh. He's a decent guy." Reading Ashley's scowl in his rear view mirror, he added, "I take it you don't like him?"

Robert snorted and couldn't contain himself any longer. "You would be right to say that. The baron tried to marry Ashley against her will, if you recall."

"Oh yeah, I guess there is that," he drawled, grinning at Ashley and then Robert in the mirror. "I don't think you have to worry about that anymore." What did he mean by that, Ashley wondered?

Zeek circled the British Museum while he gave them instructions. "Walk in through the front door, one at a time, and mix in with others entering. Then find Dr. Wilson who should be working the "Life and Death in Pompei and Herculaneum" exhibit in the Reading Room. She will take you where you need to go from there. I'll park and catch up to you as soon as I can."

As luck would have it, a tour bus unloading at the sidewalk on Montague St. provided the perfect cover for getting into the museum. Ashley and Robert fell in with the tour, spacing themselves between several visitors to avoid being side by side. Since they walked with the group, no one paid any attention to them.

Once in the door, Ashley went straight to the Reading Room entrance. There, she told the two guards inside the door that Dr. Monica Wilson expected her and a second guest who would be joining them soon. Zeek had assured her it was safe to ask a guard to find Dr. Wilson since they were not associated with Abasi, who was not a friend of the museum's administration. Ashley hoped by the time Dr. Wilson had been informed of her arrival, Robert would be standing by her side.

The younger of the guards was extra friendly and dutifully trotted off to find Dr. Wilson while Ashley stood and admired the domed ceiling of the Reading Room. Rumor had it that this glorious room would close along with this exhibit, so she drank in the sight. The cerulean sky peeked around the Oculus, blue and beautiful. What a gorgeous space.

Unexpectedly, an attractive older man approached her with a smile as she stood just inside the door. His dark hair was silver at the temples, and he wore a three-piece gray suit with a jaunty red bow tie. Black glasses in the latest style accented a very handsome face. Something struck a familiar chord about him, but Ashley could not remember meeting him with Uncle Zeek.

As he stepped lightly into the space next to her, he leaned in and whispered in her ear, "Hello, Lady Ashley, and so we meet again."

Ashley's head almost spun off her neck. She recognized the voice the moment he said her name. It belonged to Damien Lundeen, the Baron of Bedford.

Ashley's voice checked out like a library book from the old Reading Room, and she just stood there gaping at the man who was most entertained by her shock. Fortunately, Robert arrived and stood possessively by her a moment later. He, too, was taken aback when he recognized who stood next to her.

"Damien," Robert inspected his nemesis from top to bottom with one eyebrow trying its best to touch his hairline. "'Tis good to see you are well," he said, his dislike for the man all too obvious.

"And you, Lord Robert," Damien's tongue was as firmly between his teeth as Robert's. There really was no love lost between the two men, and Ashley was just happy they had not greeted each other with a fist to the face.

The crisp click of heels echoed on the floor a moment later, announcing the arrival of Dr. Wilson. The prim little lady wore a smile that did not reach her eyes until she glanced at the baron. One glimpse of him and the most beatific smile enveloped her otherwise sallow face, making her blush a lovely shade of pink. This smile lighted her from within, and suddenly Ashley knew exactly what had happened. Dr. Monica Wilson, the tiny little bird-like woman, had fallen in love with Damien

Lundeen, the infamous Baron of Bedford.

Ashley grinned wickedly at Robert whose eyes jumped from Damien to Dr. Wilson and back again, a little slower figuring out what was so obvious to her. He darted his eyes at Ashley for confirmation, and she nodded vigorously.

Oh. My.

With eyes on Damien, Dr. Wilson slid in beside him before turning her attention to Ashley and Robert. Clearly, they weren't among the baron's best friends, and Dr. Wilson obviously sided with the baron. Still, fate had them all in this together, so Monica must have decided to do whatever necessary to make matters work.

"Ashley. Robert," she snapped a nod in the direction of each. "You need to come with me." She smiled sweetly at Damien who gave her a head-swaggering smile that seemed to make her even more animated. "You, too, my dear," she said, crooking a finger at Damien.

They crossed the main floor of the Reading Room, and through the Pompei exhibit Ashley wished she had time to see. She wondered if perhaps one day she and Robert would travel there. If so, she hoped it would be well before Mount Vesuvius erupted. She had witnessed enough human carnage in Lawrence to last a lifetime.

Dr. Wilson led them into a room labeled Staff Only, and they found themselves in a small office stuffed with books, folders and journals. Perhaps the administrator's space, she wondered? Dr. Wilson reached behind the desk and pulled out a canvas gym bag and passed it to Ashley.

"You will find more comfortable clothes inside for each of you, courtesy of your uncle. He anticipated your need for some fresh garments and brought them in yesterday."

"Yes-s-s!" At last, she could change out of the long, travel-weary dress she had on. She pulled out some jeans, a t-shirt and sweatshirt for her and the same for Robert. Zeek had even put in boots for both of them and had remembered the appropriate sizes. *Go, Uncle Zeek.*

"We will leave you to dress in here in just a moment," Dr. Wilson informed them. "I am sorry you will have no privacy, but we do not want you roaming around the museum where Abasi's men might ID you."

"Oh, that's okay. We got married yesterday, so we don't really mind." She winked up at Robert and gave him a saucy eye-waggle. He grinned back, pulled her close and kissed the top of her head.

Dr. Wilson's eyes fell on Ashley's left hand and took note of the signet ring she wore there, nodding sagely. Damien started to say something, but Dr. Wilson shook her head, quieting him, and the two left them alone to change. Moments later, and feeling pretty good in their clean, comfortable clothes, they were ready to get on the road and head back home.

A sharp knock on the door made Ashley jump. Monica and Damien, now also dressed in casual clothes, entered without waiting for a response. Uncle Zeek followed them, and Ashley started to greet him, but stopped when a man slid into the room behind him.

A shudder passed through her as she recognized him.

Abasi.

Zeek looked sick. "Sorry," he muttered before glaring at the person who stood beside him. The unwelcome man's droopy-lidded eyes rapidly took in the scene in front of him. He gifted Dr. Wilson with an especially sensual smile before his eyes landed on Ashley, then flicked to Robert, and finally Damien.

"Ah, my fine friends. S-s-so happy to find all of you here in one place. S-s-so nice to see you again, Miss Duvall. I've missed you," Abasi hissed, reaching for Ashley's right hand to give it a kiss. She snatched it away and tucked it safely into the crook of Robert's arm. "But now you are found," he smirked. "And this-s-s must be . . .?"

"My husband, Robert." Ashley noted that Abasi eyed Robert's hands with interest. She had no doubt he was searching for the signet ring he suspected belonged to Robert. The man rolled his eyes from one to the other, questioningly. She and Robert responded by glaring at him straight in the eye. After a moment, he looked away.

Ashley held her left hand behind her back and carefully turned the face of the signet ring so that it sat enclosed in the palm of her hand. It would pass for a plain wedding band if Abasi saw it on her finger. She caught a movement out of the corner of her eye behind Abasi and saw Dr. Wilson doing something similar.

Wait. Did that mean she was wearing Damien's signet ring? Were they married, too? Looking at the fear on Monica's face as she stood facing Abasi's back, she would bet on it. Amazing! The Baron of Bedford has met his match. She couldn't wait to get back to Hertford and tell Elena.

And how was this little bird-woman daring enough to wear one of the very signet rings the museum believed stolen *while in the museum?* Her respect for this nervy lady doubled.

Abasi eyed Damien with suspicion. "And you are ...?"

"Damien Lundeen. I am a friend of Dr. Wilson's and I work here."

Great cover, Ashley thought. He did not add that he was the Baron of Bedford, so Abasi would not easily make the connection to the signet ring with a "B" on it. At least she didn't think so, but this was the wily antiquities dealer so one could never be sure.

Abasi examined each of them, noting the sweat dripping from Zeek's forehead and gave them a slow smile. "I believe it is time for you to meet some of my friends. They are outside waiting for you in two of my black SUVs that some of you are already familiar with." He swooped a hand at them to proceed out the door ahead of him. "Shall we go?"

Ashley's eyes flew to her uncle to see if they should do as Abasi said. That glance told her Zeek didn't know what to do any more than she did. She and Robert would just have to wing it. After she caught Robert's eye, he nodded minutely that he understood. Would Monica and Damien know to follow their lead? Should they try to get the attention of the guards? If they did so, would Abasi blow their cover and accuse them of taking the signet rings? How awkward would that be? They had better leave the museum before they tried to get away from the man.

They looked like quite a parade heading out of the little office. Exhibit visitors took note of them as if they were VIPs of some sort. One of Abasi's men appeared to lead the way, dressed in a black suit and tie like the men described by Jazz and Ryan. She noted two others, dressed the same, fell in beside them to ensure they made it outside to the waiting vehicles.

Once outside the front entrance of the museum, Ashley recognized the same model SUVs that had chased them so fiercely from the Vintage Rose Bazaar. Abasi must have a thing for big black cars, but then, they did look fierce.

As they started down the steps, the doors beside them blew open with a bang. A tour guide waving a little red flag burst forth to lead her troops onward to their waiting motor coach. "Hurry, everyone. Spit spot! We have to leave right now if we are to make our next stop on time." She motioned her large group along with a swish, swish of her hand and the tourists hurried toward their charter bus. Two teenagers broke into a high-spirited race to the coach door and were surprised to find Ashley and Robert running right behind them. A second later Monica and Damien took off at a dead run, leaving a furious Abasi standing on the steps with a surprised Uncle Zeek.

Having folded themselves into the middle of the group of tourists, Abasi and his men were powerless to reach them without causing a tremendous scene. To be sure he didn't chase after them, Zeek stepped in front of Abasi and picked a fight with him to distract the attention of onlookers from those fleeing.

"I ordered three *white* vehicles to pick up our people and you send two *black* ones? How are we supposed to recognize them, let alone put everyone in only two vehicles? We will be late for our next location." Zeek's words flowed viciously, "Who is your superior, sir? I want his name and number."

Abasi looked mad enough to smash precious antiquities

over Zeek's head. His men stood helplessly on the sidewalk as Ashley, Robert, Monica and Damien boarded the motor coach with the rest of the tour.

Working their way to the back of the bus to locate empty seats, Ashley prayed they wouldn't be discovered and thrown off before they left the museum. Would the guide identify them as interlopers and tell them to get off before the bus moved? She racked her brain trying to think of a reason she could give that they should stay on the bus if they got caught.

Unbelievably, the guide stood up in the front of the bus and said, "I counted you as you came out the doors, so we will be off straightaway. Our next stop is Stonehenge. We shall have about two hours there before returning to London by way of Salisbury where we shall stop for dinner." A plump blonde with frazzled hair, she plunked herself down in her seat and began imperiously giving directions to the driver.

Ashley and Monica stared wide-eyed at each other. Had they heard the woman correctly? They were on the way to Stonehenge? That was merely a few miles from Zeek's campsite and minutes from where Ashley needed to be to call the Guardian stone to take them home to Hertford.

Monica broke into an ear-to-ear grin. "Well done, Ashley. Robert. Did you know this bus was going to Stonehenge?"

"Uhm, no." Ashley upped her own smile to face splitting. "Just lucky."

"I am sure Abasi will not give up so quickly," Robert cautioned. "We will have to figure out how to avoid him once we get to Stonehenge. He will have men there to capture us as we leave this vehicle."

"Aye," Damien agreed. "We must think deviously."

"Are you saying you're good at that, sir?" Ashley challenged, still not sure if she liked this man.

Damien shot her a sly smile, "You have no idea, Lady Ashley. No idea at all. I protect with my life what is mine." That said, he picked up Monica's left hand to kiss it. There on her left ring finger sat the signet ring with a "B" that had caused them all a world of trouble.

"You *are* married!" Ashley had to work to bring down her shriek to a mere whisper.

"Aye," said the baron, looking tenderly into the loving eyes of Dr. Wilson. "That we are."

"And happily so," replied Monica, her voice soft as velvet.

Ashley caught her breath. "So you will be following Damien back to Hertford?"

"Yes." Her eyelids fluttered for a moment before they landed on Damien.

"Wow," Ashley responded with wonder. "Do you suppose all four of us can travel together?"

"We made it to Lawrence with four," Robert reminded her.

"Yeah, but we were in a car."

"True. We will have to figure it out when the time comes, sweeting."

"Maybe so," Ashley yawned, her exhaustion showing. *"Muhbee sho."*

Robert pulled her close and tucked her under his arm. My how she loved being his wife. She felt secure and loved.

"Perhaps, Damien, you might put that scheming mind of yours to work while we take a nap." Robert rested his head on Ashley's. "We have been awake for nearly two days as 'tis and could do with a rest before we get there and have to face Abasi's men."

Damien chuckled, "Ah, young ones, leave it to us wise older ones to plan the escape. Sweet dreams." He gave Monica a quick kiss on the cheek before they put their heads together over Monica's smart phone and began whispering.

Satisfied for the moment, Ashley and Robert closed their tired eyes. Ashley still questioned her sanity at leaving something as important as their safety in Damien's hands, but she could stay awake no longer. Robert was snoring softly when she gave it up and slept.

Chapter 29

Ashley woke up feeling thickheaded with her mouth so parched she envisioned her tongue a sandy rock in the midst of drought-stricken ground. Barely summoning enough saliva to speak, she rubbed open both eyes and found Robert through bleary orbs. "Are we at Stonehenge?"

Robert didn't look much better. His eyes were red-rimmed from not enough sleep, and he sported a nasty case of bed-head. Still, he was the best-looking thing Ashley had ever seen.

"Soon, sweeting," Robert crooned in her ear. "'Tis good to be going home, is it not?"

Slouched down in the privacy of their seats, they shut out the world for a few minutes, not ready to share themselves with the others.

"I can't wait," Ashley grinned, giving his hand a squeeze.

"Your journey home was not what you thought 'twould be, was it?"

"Hardly," Ashley snorted.

"I am happy I got to visit your home and meet your family, especially your father. 'Twas not what I expected, but now I understand many things about your life I could never have imagined otherwise."

"True. Being a Guardian of the Stones is not what I imagined, either, but I think I will like doing the work if you can travel with me." Ashley reached up to invite a kiss on her lips. Robert instantly obliged.

"I am good with that so long as we go back to Hertford when each job is done."

"Yeah, that's the main thing, right? *There's no place like home. There's no place like home.*" Robert didn't catch the reference. She smiled to herself, thinking she would one day tell him all about that old movie.

"Right now, we need to find out what Damien and Monica devised for us as an escape plan," Robert reminded her. That brought her back to reality with a thud.

"*Ugh.*" She sat up reluctantly, directing her attention to Damien and Monica. "Is Abasi following us?"

Robert's attention was on the baron whose eyes held steady on something behind the coach. Following his line of sight, Robert spotted a big, black SUV. Oh, yes, Abasi had found them.

"How long has that been behind us?" Robert asked in a low growl.

Monica replied with disgust playing about her mouth, "Oh, about an hour ago. One is in front, as well. It did not take him long to put a tail on us. Abasi does not appear to be in either one, however, so we may be spared that confrontation." She waved a hand at the SUV as if dismissing it from her thoughts as unimportant. "The man does seem to have men everywhere, does he not?"

Ashley nodded and rolled her eyes at Robert remembering the two SUVs that had chased them in Texas. Would they be able to shake Abasi's men again?

"We have not much time, so let us get the plan down before we have to leave this . . ." Damien struggled to find the right word, "conveyance."

"Coach or bus," Monica filled in.

"Right," he replied, smiling at her correction. "'Tis a lot to remember."

"For once we agree, Bedford," Robert chimed in. "Now what do we need to do?"

The four put their heads together there in the back of

the bus to work out the details. They finalized them just as the coach pulled into the Stonehenge visitor site and made its way to the tour parking lot. Their plan was simple, but Ashley thought it might work.

They hopped out of the coach and tried to get their bearings. Heavy, dark clouds oppressively covered the area, about as welcome as a wool blanket in August. From the motor coach lot, Ashley looked down the hill at the visitor center that stretched out before her. Visitors flowed in from the car parking lot off on the right. To the left, shuttles could be seen lined up like worker ants, crawling back and forth along the trail that delivered tourists to the site. Abasi's men parked in a pick up zone directly in front of the center. That meant the two couples would have no choice but to walk past the men whether into the center or straight to the site.

Phase One of the plan was to split up. Damien and Monica would head into the visitor center already swarming with people from all parts of the globe. Robert and Ashley would shuttle down the trail to the actual henge, maybe a mile away. That would make Abasi's men from the two SUVs have to split up, too, in order to have a tail on each couple. Divide and conquer.

Damien and Monica, dressed in casual khakis and white shirts, appeared to be an upscale couple on a day's adventure. They browsed the souvenir shop and lunched in the center, all the while pretending that Abasi's henchmen did not exist. After about thirty minutes, the men were completely bored. Exactly the reaction they wanted.

A second pair of men tailed Robert and Ashley to the official site. Clad in their dark suits with wrap-around sunglasses, the men wandered about the walkway never taking their eyes off their quarry.

Did Abasi think these guys weren't noticeable just hanging out, Ashley wondered? They certainly did not look like the usual tourists. Were they supposed to be intimidating? They might be sturdy and serious-looking, but Robert was bigger.

Heck, Damien would hold his own against them physically. Surely these hirelings would not use weapons on them with hundreds of tourists about. Abasi needed them alive and co-operating, so what were they to do? Threaten to smash their knuckles or something?

Robert had never seen Stonehenge before and Ashley enjoyed showing it to him, working to impress him with her knowledge of the World Heritage Site. He was aware of the place as a burial ground but no one at Hertford had given the place much thought. Mostly, he was amazed that modern day people cared about seeing old stones stacked oddly and scattered in disarray. Ashley explained that the mystery around the stones was the major draw. Robert nodded, but obviously was not impressed. Ashley couldn't help but smile at his disregard for the place. His attention was not on the site. The man just wanted to go home, and she couldn't blame him there.

Having studied the monument for the allotted thirty minutes, they were due to start back for the next phase of their escape plan. Ashley continued to watch for Abasi as cars streamed into the lot, but she never saw another one of his special SUVs. Where was the man? He had a beastly habit of popping up where and when you least wanted to see him.

As they disembarked from the open-sided shuttle that returned them to the visitor center, Robert was quick to spot Damien and Monica in the gift shop. Damien nodded to Robert, acknowledging their return, and approached an officer standing near the ticket office. Phase Two of their plan was in progress. This should be interesting, Ashley thought.

The officer walked with Damien and Monica toward the parking area, and Robert and Ashley could see a lot of gesticulating going on. As they got closer, they could hear the man.

"So what you are saying is the gentlemen in black over there next to the SUVs attempted to sell drugs to the teenagers on your tour?"

"That is right, officer," Monica confirmed in her most authoritative Dr. Wilson tone. "The children would not have said anything at all if we had not overheard them because they didn't want their parents to know they had been approached. You know how young people are. They do not want parental figures impeding their freedom." She smiled sagely up at the man who nodded in agreement.

"The men do look a bit out of place here," he mused, absently fingering his belted revolver.

"I might add one of our young men also reported a problem with one man in particular. He said the one there on the left reached behind the license plate of the other SUV and pulled out a baggie of white powder." Damien paused to gauge the officer's reaction. "He thought the substance might be cocaine, but he did not know for sure."

"Thank you both for reporting the incident to me. I will call for back up, and we will check it out." The man was visibly itching to move on to the confrontation he knew would follow. He turned as he stepped away and added, "I believe I would board your tour bus now so you do not become a target of these people."

"As you wish, officer." Monica worked to suppress a grin. "Thank you for your time."

Ashley and Robert waited until the first uniformed man was joined by a second, and then found Monica and Damien waiting for them at the coach park. As soon as the officers strode toward Abasi's men, now together and waiting beside their black cars, the couples boarded a coach.

The only catch was this bus was a different one parked next to their original and filled to near capacity with passengers waiting to leave. With coaches parked only inches apart, from a distance Abasi's men would not be able to see they had climbed into a second bus.

The tour guide belonging to the new bus, a paunchy man in his forties, was huddled with a guide from another bus, a pretty blonde half his age. The two were busy dissecting the companies they worked for and were oblivious to the four extra passengers sneaking onto the man's bus. Hopefully, with a little luck and the diversions they had set, Abasi's men would stay confused long enough for them to reach the site where Ashley could call for the Guardian stone.

Finding seats on the side nearest the visitor center, they ducked down to avoid being seen. The four watched with great satisfaction as the officers arrested the men for possession of the bag of white powder now in the hands of one of the officers. Abasi's men vehemently objected, but the security officers were having none of it.

"What's in the baggie?" Ashley whispered to Monica.

"Chalk from the ground. You know the chalky powder near the burial sites?" Ashley nodded. "We threw in some sugar substitute and mixed it up in a plastic bag from the luncheon sandwich we shared," she added smugly. "Damien planted the bait under the car while they waited for me to come out of the restroom. Ashley gave her a broad grin.

Abasi's men would be tied up for quite a while.

∞∞∞

Phase Three came not ten minutes later when the coach approached the second roundabout before turning onto the highway for the drive to Salisbury.

Damien and Robert stood up and hollered for the bus to stop. Flustered, the tour guide stared blankly at them and then panicked as he realized he had never seen them before.

Monica and Ashley joined their husbands and the four rushed to the front of the coach. Damien explained they were traveling together and accidentally boarded the wrong bus. Not happy with the extra duty, the driver reluctantly said he would turn around and return them to the parking area.

"Sir, we caused you the trouble with our own carelessness. It isn't far at all and it is not raining, at least not yet anyway," Robert smiled his most sincere smile. "We will call our guide and walk back to the visitor center." He turned next to the guide, who clearly was worried his job was on the line. "If our tour is ready to leave, they can pick us up on the way out since our bus is headed to Salisbury just like yours."

Anxious to be rid of them, the burly bus driver did not argue. Rather than wait for the lip-chewing guide to answer, he popped open the doors and raised his eyebrows at the foursome, indicating they should leave.

The tour guide shrugged and stepped out of the way.

Ashley pushed Robert's back to make him hurry to the exit. "Thanks!" she yelled over her shoulder as she bounced down the steps and onto the side of the road. A chorus of *thank you* followed, and they found themselves waving goodbye to those on the bus.

Yes. They started off into the open field hoping Abasi would not find them from the air. Seriously, the man was everywhere.

The coach had taken them to within two miles of the location where Ashley and Robert had been dropped by the Guardian stone not so very long ago. If they went cross-country instead of along the road, they would be there in just a few minutes.

Robert whipped out a cell phone from his pocket as they trudged along and pulled up a map of the area, so they could pinpoint the spot with ease.

Running along beside him, Ashley was incredulous. "Where did you get a phone?"

Robert tried to sound casual as he responded, but a grin broke out openly on his face after just a moment. "I was saving it as a surprise so I didn't give it to you earlier. Josh thought I should have my own phone and loaded it with games and 'cool guy stuff.' At least that is what he said when he gave it to me. He said you had already packed a solar powered charger?"

Ashley's jaw dropped. *"Wow,* Robert. He must really have bonded with you. I didn't think anything could come between Josh and his phone. And, yes, I have a solar charger this time. It's in the bag. No more worry over batteries running down."

Robert just grinned. "He said he wants his phone back the next time we visit your family, or when he comes to see us."

"I hope it works out that way," Ashley laughed, praying silently for that visit to be soon. "What a deal! I still can't believe he did that."

They scrambled over a stone fence and jogged as fast as they could across the wide-open terrain, Monica and Damien right behind them. The grasses were short and the earth hard, so they covered ground at a rapid pace. They raced across the Normanton Down Barrows according to the phone map, and past the dig site where Ashley had worked with Alex and Tiffany so long ago. A moment later, Robert recognized the big rock by the side of the dirt road that marked the place where Zeek had picked them up.

Grabbing Ashley by both arms, he swung her around in pure elation. "My love, we are here at last. We are going *home*."

She laughed in glee with her head thrown back like a figure skater spinning an inside spiral. "I can't wait to go home to the castle. I have so much to tell your sister."

"Ah, she can wait, wife," Robert answered, with a matching grin, pulling her back up for a kiss. "I have a few other plans for our arrival." His voice was soft and seductive in her ear.

"Save your celebration for later, my dears." Monica pulled Damien to a stop, so she could catch her breath. "We do not have the stone in hand yet." Damien rubbed her back as she recovered herself, bent over with her hands on her knees.

"Very true, Dr. Wilson, so let me take care of that right now." Caught up in the drama of the moment, she climbed on the rock, stood tall, and called to the heavens, not knowing what she was doing at all.

"Guardian stone, please appear,
Take all four of us from here.
Set us down near Hertford town,
Safe and sound where we'll be found."

She giggled at her pitiful attempt at casting a spell. At any rate, it was her best try. How was she to go about calling a stone? Olde Gylda had never told her what to do. She just said the stone would show itself when needed.

The wait seemed like an eternity. Ashley jumped down and trotted further away from the road. Where had she stood when she had been dumped out of the whirlwind? She spun around and around searching for the exact spot.

There! She saw it. The red feather she and Robert had played with while they waited for Zeek was lodged between two rocks. Ashley scampered over and pulled the fluff out, waving it victoriously at the other three.

Damien turned about the same shade of red, looking stricken. Finally, he spouted, "That's *my* feather. *Mine.* 'Twas pulled out of my hat by the wind that took you away, Lady Ashley."

Robert grabbed Ashley's hand and examined the plume she held. "God's blood, 'tis the same one. We wondered how it got here. How amazing." His eyes popped with excitement. "Ashley, call the stone again. I think we now are in the right place."

Ashley nodded and waved the feather about, repeating her awful verse. Still, nothing happened. Exasperated, she tipped her face to the sky and shrieked, *"Guardian stone, I command you to appear! This Guardian of the Stones needs you NOW!"*

Without warning, the sky darkened noticeably. Had the stone heard her? They looked breathlessly at one another.

A small dust devil rewarded her a moment later when it rose from under her feet and a stone surfaced beside her.

Ashley sucked in a breath that apparently swallowed her words, too. All she could do was snatch up the stone and hold it tightly, clutched to her chest, leaving the dust to settle over her feet.

Looking deep into Robert's smiling eyes for courage she held out the stone to read the inscription. It felt like the right stone, the same weight and size as the one she had unearthed by accident. The writing was the same: *Twll yn amser. A hole in time.*

Would it really put them down where they needed to go?

Ashley turned to Monica and Damien who were standing quietly, eyes huge, amazed the stone had actually appeared.

She cleared her throat and tried to swallow the lump lodged there. "We should hang on to one another to be sure we all get to the same place, don't you think?"

Everyone nodded and it was decided they should hook elbows in a tight circle with their backs to each other. Ashley held the stone in both hands. "Ready?" She read the words three times.

Twll yn amser.
Twll yn amser.
Twll yn amser.

No whirlwind appeared. They waited with bated breath. Nothing.

Then Damien heard it first. A buzzing noise seemed to be getting closer. Monica searched and found the sound was from an object heading straight at her. "Oh, no," she wailed. *"Damn him!"*

"What is it?" Adrenaline was pumping through Ashley on all cylinders now.

"What is *that?*" Robert's voice held part wonder and part worry as he spotted a mechanical bird-like creature flying toward them.

"It is a *drone,*" Monica answered with disgust.

"A drone?" Anxiety laced Ashley's voice as her eyes roamed the sky for the offending item. "Abasi has a drone?"

The ground started to shimmer, breaking into a dedicated shake a moment later.

"Ashley, he's trying to video our time travel. He's been flying drones over the camp since you left," Monica shouted, fear beginning to overwhelm her control. "It will prove what he has always suspected. He will blackmail us with the evidence should we reappear."

"And Zeek, too," Ashley screamed, the wind swirling around them with growing force. "But we can't stop the wind no-o-ow."

Everyone was talking but the wind hungrily gobbled up the sound so the rest of the conversation was lost.

The small white drone circled them and flew right at Robert's head. At the last second he let go of Ashley and Monica and impulsively jumped up and snagged a wing of the drone. He plucked it out of the sky as easily as an orange from a tree. Slamming the spy drone to the ground, he smashed it and ground its camera into the soil with his boot.

Take that, Abasi.

The drone lay broken to bits in the soil, like rotted bones at a burial site. That should make Ashley happy, he thought, rather pleased with himself. The thing was larger than Ashley's cell phone, but if it recorded pictures the same way, then this one would be recording secrets no longer.

Triumphantly, he turned back to the others and stepped into the swirl, but by now so much dust whirled he could not see them. He shrieked for Ashley, the sound swallowed up by the wind, but she did not answer.

Then, as suddenly as it came, the wind left, dying with the speed of a kite falling from the sky. Dust settled. The grasses were still, no longer rippling in the breeze. The sky looked the same as it had before.

Worst of all, Robert was alone in the field.

Ashley was gone.

Chapter 30

"Ouch!"

Ashley hit the ground with a solid thump. "We've got to stop meeting like this, Robert," she giggled. "I think my bum will be permanently bruised this time."

She sat up amidst a valley of yellow flowers that seemed very familiar. Where had she seen these before? She untangled herself from Monica and Damien. "Robert, do you have any idea where we are?"

Robert didn't answer. Beside her, she heard only Damien and Monica cooing to each other that they were okay.

Where is Robert?

Fear spiked through her making her shudder head to toe. Struggling to her feet, she spun around calling his name. Monica and Damien found their feet, too, and the three looked like spinning tops trying to find the missing Robert.

"D-did he . . .," she sucked in a steadying breath and tried again, "Did he not come with us?"

Her face betraying her, Monica tilted her eyes at Damien who shook his head. She put a hand on Ashley's shoulder and asked kindly, "Did you not feel him let go of you just before the wind took us?"

"No!" Ashley cried, horrified. *"He let go?"*

Monica nodded sympathetically.

"I was concentrating so hard on holding the stone . . ." She tried to remember the moment. "Are you sure he did?"

"I am sure, Ashley," Monica soothed. "He went after the drone to keep it from revealing our time travel." She paused and sent a rueful smile to Damien before focusing back on Ashley. "He smashed it to bits. That was the last thing I saw before the whirlwind took us away."

"He smashed it?" Ashley echoed, caught between dismay and pride. Had Robert grabbed the drone to keep Abasi from winning? If so, the antiquities dealer would lose his proof of time travel. Without video, he had nothing with which to blackmail any of them. Zeek would be safe, too. But then another thought struck her. Abasi would have Robert, but his signet ring resided on her finger. That made his connection to the ring impossible to prove, but would he know enough about modern times if the antiquities dealer grilled him closely? Robert had secured their safety at the price of his own.

Ashley sank to the ground, her head between her knees as her brain was pricked like an anxiety pincushion with one anxious thought after another boring in. How could she save him? Should she find the stone again and go back? Would he have left the area by now having been hauled off by Abasi and his men?

Hell and damnation. What was she to do?

She jumped to her feet, nearly passing out from the head rush, and screamed for the Guardian stone to appear.

It did not.

She tried again. And again. And again.

Nothing.

Why would the stone not come to her when she called? Her mind raced as she recalled that Robert had arrived after her by several minutes when he followed her to the Salisbury plains. Was he just late? Would he find the stone? It never stayed in her grip once they were within the whirlwind's power. Would it now be buried somewhere near Robert?

She let out a long moan that sounded like a dying wildcat as it bounced off the nearby hill. Her legs crumpled, and she found herself on the ground again, misery having overcome her.

Damien and Monica talked in quiet voices to her before pulling her to her feet and walking her between them. At first, she did not realize where they were taking her. Olde Gylda's crazy little cottage was only a short distance away. She had been so frantic looking for Robert that she had not even seen it.

Where else would Gylda drop them down, Ashley mused? Monica and Damien helped her plop on the stoop in front of the house where she sat like a deflated party balloon. It had all been too good, hadn't it? She should have known something would happen to keep them apart. Tears rolled down her cheeks, and she made no effort to wipe them away.

"My saddle is here right where I left it," Damien called to them with satisfaction from around the corner of the cottage. He came striding back with a big saddle in his hands and an even bigger smile for Monica.

"Stay here with Lady Ashley and I will go up on the hill and whistle for Titan. I think he will be close by. He never goes far when I leave him. We must depart now, so we can arrive at the inn in Ravensthorpe by dusk. We will return to my home on the morrow."

"*Our* home," Monica smiled back at him, her eyes twinkling with love as she corrected him.

"*Yes,*" Damien answered, with his familiar smirk in place. "*Our* home."

Well, at least someone is happy, Ashley thought, as Damien trotted off to find his stallion.

"I am not going anywhere," Ashley said firmly, her head still resting on her knees.

"But, my dear, it will be dark soon, and we cannot get inside Olde Gylda's house. Damien tried a few minutes ago. We should not spend the night in the open if we can find shelter."

This time Ashley raised her head and rolled it back to look squarely into Monica's face, "Then you and Damien need to go. I'm gonna stay here to wait for Robert ... or Olde Gylda ... or the stone. Whatever. I just know I need to stay here."

Monica started to argue the point, her face taking on that stubborn parental guise children so often see, when she was interrupted by Damien's shout from the hilltop. Her attention flipped back to the man she loved as if her head were on an invisible tether.

A glimmer of a smile passed over Ashley's face as she recognized that shared connection. Her amusement was swiftly squashed by the thought she and Robert may not experience that again if they could not find each other. What if he was lost in time? Had he only made it part of the way? To have come through so much only to be separated now was too cruel for words.

Mute, Ashley sat on the stoop, her eyes robotically following Damien as he jogged up the hillside in search of his horse. He returned with a victorious whoop a short time later leading his stallion and set about saddling the big animal. Titan dwarfed the tiny Monica who needed a boost and a lift from Damien to mount the beast. Finally, Ashley was aware of Damien shaking her shoulders, first gently and then a bit harder when her attention didn't surface. What was he saying? Oh, yeah, she had to tell him again.

"Damien, it's all right. I am staying here, and you and Monica are going. Don't worry, I will be fine."

Not comfortable at all with leaving Ashley alone at Gylda's, Damien decided he would just pick her up and put her on the saddle. Before he could hoist her into his arms, he was rewarded with a hard slap to the side of his head designed to leave his ear ringing.

"Get it through your thick head, Damien. I am not going anywhere without Robert." Ashley shoved him toward his horse. "*Go.* Ride to the inn before dark. When I find Robert, I will let you know."

Checking out the position of the sun, Damien could see the truth in her words. He looked helplessly at Monica.

"She has made her decision, my love. Ashley knows her own mind and we must respect that. Whatever happens, happens. This is her choice."

Damien listened and nodded.

Wow. When had her pig-headed baron started listening to a woman? Maybe his visit to the twenty-first century not only found him a wife but a new respect for women.

"She's right, Damien. Your light is fading. *Go.*"

"Goodbye, Ashley," Monica said with a face that read so much more. "Stay safe, dear girl."

Damien grimaced his concern to Ashley and shook his head in exasperation. He mounted Titan, pulled Monica tightly to him, and galloped off toward the village and its inn.

Ashley watched them ride over the hill, then dropped her head to between her knees and allowed herself to sob violently for all that was now lost to her.

Chapter 31

Robert was stunned.

He sat, a lonely soul, on a rocky knoll amidst the tall grasses in the wide-open spaces of Salisbury Plains. His mind kept replaying the last seconds of the whirlwind as he second-guessed his actions. He should not have stepped out to smash the drone. If they were leaving why did it matter? Abasi could not blackmail them if they were not there. Zeek would be fine. He was a man able to take care of himself. Robert let out a huge sigh. It was Ashley he had wanted to please. She was upset about the drone and his instinct to protect her won out. He smashed it for her, but it cost him Ashley.

Now what was he to do? Ashley had held the Guardian stone in her hands when the wind took them, so it would be back in 1363, right?

Wait. Did the stone ever leave its place of origin? He did not remember seeing the stone that took them to Kansas once they arrived there. Plus, he watched the stone bury itself in the ground when Ashley left from Gylda's. It did not go with her, or he and the baron would not have been able to follow her. He bounced to his feet with new vigor and began search-ing the area. The ground did not appear disturbed, and he saw no sign of the stone at all. He made concentric circles from the point where the wind took them and circled outward, carefully examining the ground, but to no avail. The stone was not to be so easily found.

Twilight was fast closing in and Robert sank to his knees in misery. He had expected Abasi and his men to show up at any moment, but so far, no one had appeared. Did he know Robert had destroyed the drone? Perhaps the man believed they were all gone, transported with no one remaining.

What should he do now?

He would have to find his way back to London and contact Zeek. Slowly, he got up and pulled out the phone Josh had given him, running his finger over the face of it. He should text Zeek and let him know of Ashley's return to Hertford. At least he hoped she was there. Damien and Monica would make sure she was returned to the castle safe and sound. Elena would be overjoyed to be reunited with her friend. But would his father let Ashley stay until he could find his way back to her? His heart plummeted at the thought. His father and Lady Margaret disliked Lady Ashley and would never allow her to remain, even if she showed them her ring and announced their marriage. They would not believe her and would insist it was evil magic that kept Robert away. Maybe Elric and Charissa would take her in. Yes, they would care for her. They loved her, too, did they not?

He found a photo of Ashley he had taken when she wasn't looking and gazed longingly at it. Smiling, he recalled how she had taken a picture of him on their way to Olde Gylda's before she was to time travel home. He had teased her about taking a bit of him back with her. Now he understood how she felt.

Strong fingers with razor-like nails gripped his shoulder, and he nearly jumped 650 years without a Guardian stone. He spun out from under the grip of the hand and landed in a warrior stance as he had been trained to do.

Sharp laughter peeled back the dark for a moment, and he found himself facing Olde Gylda.

"I do not think that phone is going to take me out, soldier," she cackled. "It does not look very battle worthy for hand-to-hand combat."

Robert glanced down and realized he was poised with Josh's cell phone pointing at Gylda as if it could stab her dead. Sheepishly, he raised his eyes at her as he relaxed his stance and stood tall, shoving the offending phone back in his pocket.

"Sorry, Gylda, but you scared years off my life just now."

That pleased the old woman even more, and her gap-toothed grin shone brightly in the rosy fingers of the setting sun.

"Did ye miss yer ride home, laddie?" she quizzed once her cackle died down.

"You might say that," Robert replied dryly. "I killed that drone thing following us and missed the whirlwind."

"Ahhh," she sighed. "Ye had to be the hero and save the day, eh?"

Robert groaned, "I just wanted to do it because it would please Ashley. She did not want her Uncle Zeek to be black-mailed by Abasi."

"And so ye did not make the wind in time, did ye?"

"No." Robert's arms hung limply by his sides. "No, I did not."

"Hmmm, I see," the old crone studied him for a moment, stroking her chin as she thought. "I happen to be going that way, now that our lost baron has been safely returned home. Ye would not want a lift, would ye?"

Robert's head shot up, and he peered closer at the witch. She was holding the Guardian stone.

"Yes. Yes, I would," he shouted, scooping up the old woman and swinging her around as if she were ten.

Gylda shrieked for him to put her down, but he knew from the sound of her voice she was delighted with his response. With a flourish he set her back on her feet a moment later and gave her a sound kiss on her wrinkly cheek, making her giggle like a girl.

"Well, young man, I shall take that as a yes," She straightened her gown and pulled down her sleeves, the light in her young eyes glowing. "I am not allowed to take ye with me." Gylda paused for effect. "But since ye stopped the drone from re-vealing our Guardian secrets, if ye watch me go and ye happens to spy where the stone lands, well. . . "

"Yes-s-s! I understand the rules. Like you explained back in Lawrence," he added. "Let us begin."

"Such a hurry, laddie, such a hurry ye be in," Gylda chortled.

Robert's face turned serious for a moment. "I have to know she is all right, Gylda. My father..."

"*Hmmm*, yes, I agree. Right ye are about yer father." She winked in acknowledgment. "See ye on t'other side."

Before he could say thank you, a whirlwind surrounded her, and she was gone. Robert tracked the stone's movement intently in the fading light and saw it bury itself only steps away. If he had not seen it with his own eyes, he would never have found it for the ground looked undisturbed.

Robert's pulse galloped at a runaway pace as he retrieved the stone, repeated the inscription three times, and let the swirling winds take him away.

∞ ∞ ∞

Robert found the love of his life curled into a tight ball, lying on her side on the ground outside Gylda's cottage. It was dusk and the dying sun made dewdrops sparkle on each blade of grass around her. Ashley's arms were wrapped around her body as if she intended to hold herself together by force of will. She looked exhausted and sad in her sleep.

Robert knelt beside her and smoothed the hair back from her face with tender fingers. He lifted her cold, wet form into his arms and hugged her to him so his body could warm her. She did not fully wake; instead, she snuggled her nose into the crook of his neck like a sleeping kitten as he carried her to the door. He raised his hand to knock, thinking Gylda might be inside, but the door swung open as if an invisible doorman had been waiting.

"Gylda?" Robert called, tentatively. "Gylda? Are you here?" No answer, but magically the room illuminated itself with a soft yellow glow emanating from a source he could not locate.

He remembered the three doors from before and started to walk to the one that held a bed, but apparently the witch's magic had something else in mind. The door at the far left opened on its own, and Robert strode to the entrance. What he found made his heart sing.

Before his eyes the dark room made a whooshing noise and a crackling fire combusted, dancing merrily in the fireplace to send the evening chill on its way. Dozens of candles dropped with a synchronized plop into place from the ceiling and gave the room a festive flare. Not to be left out, the floor invitingly unrolled a thick Persian carpet to adorn itself. Robert's heart raced with excitement as he looked to his right in time to catch the small wooden table burst forth with a tantalizing spread of meats and cheeses. A long-handled knife cut off a chunk of yellow cheese and then sliced a loaf of bread with deft, even strokes. One of several bottles of wine popped its own cork and poured itself into the two awaiting goblets. He groaned with pleasure at the magic and his stomach rumbled its approval.

A squeak from his left alerted him in time to step out of the way of an enormous canopied bed. It slid through the wall into the room as if on invisible runners. He rejoiced as the bed covers turned themselves down and the pillows bounced into place and plumped themselves. By now Robert was laughing aloud and thanking Gylda for her kindness.

With her eyes wide open and her body perfectly still, Ashley missed not a moment of the wonders before her. She thought for sure she was dreaming and feared that if she moved too much she would awaken and this magnificent moment would pass. Robert's laugh, however, sounded entirely too real to be in her imagination, so she pulled back to look in his face.

His eyes held such joy as they melded with hers. This was the moment they had dreamed of for so long. Unwilling to wait another second, Ashley reached up with both arms and pulled his head down, placing her mouth firmly over his.

Sparks may or may not have been visible to the human eye outside Gylda's place, but inside Ashley and Robert were onboard a lighted rocket. Clothes exploded from their heated bodies. Naked limbs entwined creating explosions of their own and food stayed untouched for hours. Somewhere up above, a cackle of pure delight reverberated around the cottage, eventually morphing into the magical, sensual strums of a harp. It was amazing. It was perfect.

It was a night to remember forever.

And they did.

Acknowledgements

Special thanks to Hope Mason, Laurie Sauerbry, Meredith Wise, and Jim May for once again coming to my aid with whatever I required of them, whenever I needed the help. Without your support I would still be struggling to finish this book. Thank you so much!

Thanks to the lovely Welsh folk singer Myron Lloyd for taking the time to meet with me after her performance at Ruthin Castle in Wales and confirm the Welsh translation of "Escape in Time" as "Dihangfa Mewn Amser." It was fun to talk with her and feel secure that I had the translation right.

Thanks to the Watkins Museum of History in Lawrence, Kansas, for an exhibit that walked me through Quantrill's raid from start to finish. It enabled me to recreate and blend the feel of the town and the real folks living there with my fictional characters.

Jane DeGray

Author Notes

What people or incidents in *Time-Crossed Wedding* were drawn from research regarding Quantrill's raid? Quite a few.

The Speer family published one of the three newspapers in Lawrence and had offices downtown. They did, in fact, lose two sons. The body of one of the brothers, who was sleeping at the newspaper office that night, was never found. When stopped by raiders, Billy did tell them his name was Smith in order to escape being killed. Quantrill had lived in Lawrence for a year and had a lengthy list of names as a result. The Speer men found out later all their names were on that list. The story of a raider dropping a gun that Billy picks up and uses against the man is also true. He was the only citizen to shoot a raider during the whole raid. He was fifteen.

Emily Hoyt was the owner of a boarding house in Lawrence. The house still stands today looking much as it did in 1863. Both Mr. Dix, the keeper of the armory key, and Mr. Allison, who drives Julie and Ashley home from the picnic, died in the actual raid. Locals reported that Sallie Young rode through the town to warn the residents, although there was some question initially as to which side she was on.

The location of Judge Carpenter's home was moved for my storyline so that it is across from Emily's house, but the account of his death is the same as told by eyewitnesses. Otherwise, the layout of 1863 Lawrence and the raid are as accurate as I could make them in a work of fiction.

Interesting facts about the raid:

Quantrill, 26 years old, led 400 men from slave-state Missouri across the border into slave-free Kansas without anyone stopping them. In the early hours of August 21, 1863, the raiders held Lawrence hostage for four hours of looting, burning and murdering that mercifully ended when lookouts on Mount Oread spotted the dust kicked up in the distance to the south that told them Union troops were on the way. They escaped with only one raider killed and no other notable casualties.

The 3,000 citizens of Lawrence suffered the deaths of 200 men and boys, leaving 85 widows to raise 250 fatherless children left homeless due to 185 houses burned to the ground. Some historians call it the greatest atrocity of the Civil War.

About The Author

Jane Degray

Jane DeGray, known to family and friends as Jane May, lives with her husband Jim and her cat Toby (her boys) in the little Texas town of Friendswood, tucked between Houston and Galveston. As a casting director for independent film (Lifetime's The Preacher's Daughter and The Preacher's Mistress), she decided to write a screenplay that somehow morphed into a novel. Now she spends her time writing novels, reading all she can, and traveling the world, always with the next story in mind.

Books By This Author

Time-Crossed Love: Guardians Of The Stones Time Travel, Book 1

Texas teen Ashley Duvall thrills to the romance of an archeology dig near Stonehenge when her Uncle Zeek offers her a spot in his university summer class. Her excitement fades as her big plans fail to pan out and it looks like it's going to be a long summer. That is, until Ashley uncovers an ancient stone that sweeps her away to 1363 England where romance and the friendships of a lifetime await her.

Medieval man, Lord Robert Spycer, warrior son and heir to the Earl of Hertford, is haunted by dreams of a mysterious woman. She is blonde, blue-eyed and beautiful but not his betrothed. Pining for a woman to love he intends to marry his childhood match. That is, until Ashley lands in his life and upsets everyone's best laid plans.

It's a midsummer night's designs gone astray that send mismatched couples scrambling for their true partners over the wishes of the powerful men who rule them. Will Ashley and Robert, with the help of a wizard, a witch and their friends, win the right to be together or will they be forced into loveless marriages. Will love or power win the day? Will Ashley stay forever or go back home? Will time bring them together or thrust them apart?

Dear Reader

Thank you so much for reading *Time-Crossed Wedding!* I hope you have enjoyed reading it as much as I enjoyed writing it. If you would be so kind, please consider writing a quick review wherever you purchased this book. Reviews help readers find books and help writers understand what you like to read.

If you missed *Time-Crossed Love, Guardians of the Stones, Book 1* that precedes this one, you can find it from my website at JaneDeGray.com. Please visit there for more pictures and accounts from *Time-Crossed Wedding.*

Also, please look for me on FaceBook, Twitter or Instagram as Jane Degray, Author and connect by liking or following the page. Thank you for your support! I look forward to hearing from you.

Happy reading!

All the best,
Jane DeGray

.

Made in the USA
Middletown, DE
28 August 2020